CHILDREN
OF THE
LIGHT

CHILDREN
OF THE
LIGHT

SUSAN B. WESTON

ST. MARTIN'S PRESS ○ NEW YORK

Library of Congress Cataloging in Publication Data
Weston, Susan B.
    Children of the light.
    I. Title.
PS3573.E9243C4   1985   813'.54   85-11812
ISBN 0-312-13236-0

First Edition

10 9 8 7 6 5 4 3 2 1

CHILDREN
OF THE
LIGHT

° ONE °

Bink-bink-bink, Jeremy battered an electronic apple, then skittered off sideways, *reedle-reedle-reedle.*

He was playing a computer game in which he was in charge of a little figure who dashed up and down, back and forth on a grid, stopping here and there to dig holes. The object of the game was to trap the apples that drifted along the grid, then batter them with the shovel. Jeremy could identify with the little figure, who was purposeful and noisy. *Reedle-reedle-reedle,* sideways; *diddle-diddle-diddle,* up a ladder; *boodle-boodle-boodle,* down. *Twap, twap, twap,* digging a hole. *Bink, bink, bink,* killing an apple. The better Jeremy got at the game, the more apples there were. They drifted silently and randomly up and down along the y axes, back and forth along the x axes. Random, they were unpredictable, and sometimes converged upon him. Touched by an apple, the figure disappeared with an electronic *zap.* Jeremy flinched each time he was vaporized.

After he had dispatched eight apples, the computer upped the ante and sent out butterflies. A butterfly could be trapped only by a hole that had another hole directly beneath it. Landing in a single hole, the butterfly rested for a moment, then fluttered out again, giving a sardonic titter as it emerged. Jeremy raced up and down the ladders, stopping here and there to dig holes. *Deedle-deedle-deedle, doodle-doodle-doodle, twap-twap-twap.* The grid was a seven-story house, the floors connected by ladders; it was his domain, which he must defend, as he defended himself, from the invaders.

Then he began to dig the holes in neat vertical lines so he could step into a hole and fall, silent for once, as if floating weightlessly down an elevator shaft of a seven-floor building. He touched the "escape" button, freezing the program: There he was, stalled, tacked up in a vertical corridor, an embattled stick figure.

This was not what he had intended to do with his spring vacation. He had not passed up a week in New York with his roommate, or a skiing trip in Colorado with Wendy, or a week in Honolulu with his parents and his brother, in order to sit mesmerized before a green monitor. He didn't know what epiphany was supposed to occur during a week's studied solitude, but it sure wasn't to find himself identifying with a stick figure suspended in a miniature elevator shaft.

He flicked the computer's toggle, changing the program, and sat strumming the attached piano keyboard, watching the bars of light on the monitor dance to his tune. He picked out simple melodies, then had the computer replay them more and more quickly, the bars of light jigging to a lunatic's version of "Row, Row, Row Your Boat." When the disk drive whirred, he imagined the minute circuitry within, the mystery of its bits and bytes and microprocessing parts that permitted his mother to compose her strange electronic music. His mother's music; the silicon chips: Odd, it was, odd and wonderful to harness an energy you understood nothing about.

His brother understood computers. But there was little poetry or music in Peter. Jeremy envied and disdained his older brother's fixity and steady purpose, the smallness of his dreams, the complacent salesman's tone of his declaration that geothermal energy would solve most of the world's future energy problems. Peter, the only practical and mechanical-minded member of the Towers family, was studying geothermal energy in Hawaii.

He could picture him—shorter and stockier than Jeremy, his hair bleached khaki by the constant sun—eating popovers in his parents' hotel and listening to but not assimilating his parents' conversation. Other people discussed their relatives, their health, their diets, their exercise programs; Jeremy's parents discussed the state of the world. Mr. Towers was a jovial naysayer. To whatever solution one proposed for a particular problem, Mr. Towers could list a network of objections or a catalogue of other equally pressing problems. "The deindustrialization of America, Third World nationalism, the fragmentation of the world into smaller and more and more fractious tribal regions . . ." As if he were fanning out cards from which his family could choose as they wished. Pick a problem, any problem. . . . "Acid rain, the greenhouse effect, the exhaustion of fossil fuels, the nuclear arms race . . ."

Jeremy's mother, by contrast, was always going to meetings or walking in marches. She joined peaceful demonstrations, signed petitions, and campaigned for the politicians she believed in. Jeremy had joined his mother in several demonstrations against the nuclear arms race. He marched and sat and sang, along with other students, young mothers, doctors, gray-haired women from the Women's International League for Peace, Republican account executives, and Democratic tool-and-die workers. A cross section of America, the newspapers said. Jeremy found the large demonstrations moving—inspiring, almost. This fusion of himself with others in a collective expression of a single purpose was like believing in God, like finding transcendence.

And on just those grounds, his father dismissed the activity. "You want oceanic, go to a cathedral," he'd mutter. The only way to slow the arms race—as far as *he* could see—would be to take the profit out of it, and demonstrations weren't pinching any pockets at the Pentagon.

And what would they discuss over popovers at the Halekulani Hotel on Waikiki Beach? Whatever dark and distressing thing it was would mock and be mocked by the scene. They'd be sitting in the cool stippled shadows, their arms on the brilliant white tablecloth, their faces raised to the turquoise curl of the waves and the talcum-soft sand glaring in the subtropical sun. His mother would insist that solutions were possible and political action imperative; his father would overwhelm them with the interconnected international enormity of the problems; then all three would rise from the table littered with popover crumbs and the bright-orange rinds of papaya, and head for the beach.

It was intolerable—this week, this spring, this year of Jeremy's life—intolerable: to know and not to act. To act with futility. To know, and futilely act, and spend a week in Hawaii . . . Not that he condemned his parents, or anyone else: only himself, for a massive failure of integrity.

Jeremy was taking a popular interdisciplinary course called War and Peace, in which they came at the topic anthropologically, historically, literarily, and politically. They studied wars between "primitive" tribes with exotic names, and wars between "civilized" tribes with familiar names. They learned the ways that technology had changed the conduct of war. The stirrup, for instance. The catapult. The crossbow. The gyroscope. The multiple independently targeted re-entry vehicle with the Anglo-Saxon–sounding acronym MIRV (which promptly became an in-group verb for a particular kind of sexual activity).

The students exercised an almost Jesuitical fervor over the dilemma posed by nuclear bombs, which had no military function except to prevent their own use. Nuclear deterrence was a system of mutual threats designed to prevent nuclear war. For the threat to be credible, the bombs had to be usable; but to safeguard the world, they couldn't be too usable. And—since the threat was to launch the bombs only in retaliation against the other side's prior attack—they really *had* to be targeted against civilian populations. Weapons poised against the other side's missile silos didn't make sense as weapons of retaliation; after all, if the other side did strike first, there wouldn't be many missiles in those silos. That was a boggle, that one: The logic of nuclear deterrence demanded the targeting of thousands of nuclear warheads against civilian populations.

The students struggled to square the doctrine of nuclear deterrence with centuries of inherited thought about ethical and moral behavior. They talked late into the night about just wars, and the just conduct of wars; about the use of force that was proportional (was it in proportion to annihilate Moscow if the Soviets made a conventional invasion of—well, say Berlin . . . ?) and discriminatory (you're really not supposed to kill innocent noncombatants). And did *threats* have to be proportional and discriminatory? Could they be if you were talking about nuclear bombs? And if somehow there were total nuclear disarmament, would that merely make the world safe for conventional war? Merely millions dead, then, instead of all?

For Jeremy it started as a fascinating intellectual problem that had little place in his emotional life. Did he think there'd be a nuclear war? Well, sure; in the same way he knew that eventually he would die, he knew that eventually there would be a nuclear war. Neither conviction much affected his hormones, or his energetic curiosity, or his exquisite sense of almost infinite personal possibility. And then one day—he was reading a newspaper article about the congressional battle over funding for ASATs, antisatellite missiles—it came over him with a physical shock that there really would be a nuclear war. How could he go surfing at Waikiki Beach when he knew that the world was going to end? On the other hand, why do anything else?

Welling up beneath responsible national debate was a flood of fantasy books and science-fiction stories set in post-holocaust landscapes. Now, this happened to suit Jeremy's taste in recreational literature: He actually liked reading about heroes who rode forth on genetic mutations of the horse to do battle with evil monsters called "leemutes" or "gamma gorts." But he was also capable of intuitive leaps, and he knew why these books were so popular. It was the domestication of a society's worst nightmare. Nuclear war as a return to frontier innocence, with an irradiated Huck Finn lighting out for the territories. Wipe the polluted, industrialized slate clean and start over, because it was unimaginable that there wouldn't be somebody to start over. As if, Jeremy thought, to that ultimate horror there might be an arcadian solution, a simplicity, a return to clear moral distinctions.

Jeremy wandered out into the backyard, where he noticed his mother's neglected vegetable garden. She had planted peas and lettuce, as she did every St. Patrick's Day. The garden was now clotted with weeds, as it always was when her enthusiasms turned to other things. The wind was from the south, carrying some pollution up from the city, and giving a dusky thickness to the sunshine. Juncos and sparrows chattered from the telephone wires and trees, swooping busily into the hedges; robins strutted fearlessly about the lawn. It was early spring: A green gauze lay over the ground and mantled some of the bushes, while most of the trees and hedges were bulging with russet nubs.

Jeremy squatted beside the first tiny tendriling pea plant and began to clear away weeds. Hunkered down, he weeded a circle the diameter of his arm span. *"Il faut cultiver notre jardin,"* Jeremy thought with a smile. Voltaire's advice, which on another occasion had made him rant about individual responsibility, today seemed sensible. He jogged back to the house for a jacket and a hoe, and spent the rest of the afternoon happily tilling and weeding.

A helicopter clattered closer and closer until, as it passed directly overhead, the sound of its rotors separated into distinct rhythmic thuds. It was probably monitoring traffic, watching the cars like molecules in the liquid stream of movement. Jeremy tried to see himself as he might look to the pilot: a tiny figure in one rectangle of the checkerboard plat of the suburb, each rectangle separated from the others by hedge or fence; each checkerboard connected to another, all of them intersected by highways and dotted with suburban shopping malls. Jeremy stared into the hazy sky. Somewhere above the helicopter, beyond his vision or the pilot's, great chunks of metal silently and gracefully orbited through space. Satellites beaming microwaves and television signals, transmitting phone calls and data about the weather and the movement of Soviet tanks.

Jeremy gawked up at the sky, struck with a painful sense of inappropriateness. The satellite circled the earth on which he was digging a tiny square with a hoe. What was he going to do with his life? What significant thing *could* a man do with his life? Here he was, seething with formless ambitions and hopes, a tiny ant on a vast mound he sometimes dreamed of rearranging, and sometimes of saving.

In the garage, Jeremy walked around his mother's car to hang up the hoe. The car was the family joke. It was so plastered with bumper stickers that it read like a scrapbook of his mother's political efforts. There were stickers for now-forgotten candidates in local and state elections—his mother's candidates seemed frequently to lose. "Preston's the best one." "Kuscinski cares." Above all there were bumper stickers for causes, many of them also lost. "Vote on November 3," said one. "Neutron Bombs: NO." "US Guns Kill US Nuns." "Nuclear Power for Peace." "Put the MX in Ronnie's Backyard." "One Nuclear Bomb Can Ruin Your Whole Day."

Jeremy gave the fender an affectionate thump and turned to go back to the house. As he turned, he struck his head on the aluminum canoe suspended by pulleys from the ceiling. He hadn't walked into the canoe since he was fifteen or so, and just becoming accustomed to his own height. Jeremy was now slightly taller than his father, who was one of those dark-haired, blue-eyed men who become more handsome with age. Jeremy had inherited his father's fine features and lean, agile build, and promised to be in his own time a startlingly handsome man. But first he'd have to outgrow the dazed, open-mouthed gawkiness that often made him look clumsy in spite of the easy physical grace with which he moved.

A childhood accident had left a small node of keloid tissue on the right corner of Jeremy's upper lip. This slight swelling gave an interesting irregularity to his face; it seemed to promise an angular Clark Gable smile, or a hint of leering sensuality. Unfortunately, Jeremy tended to worry the keloid by sucking it inside his lower lip. "Elephant lip," his brother used to call him.

He hit his head on the canoe with a dull metallic *clong,* and stood there with his mouth twisted up, flabbergasted that he had forgotten to duck his head, and then flooded with nostalgia for his early adolescence, when he went with his father on canoe trips. Day trips through urban back lots; week-long trips into the wilderness with huge packs. Cold rainy nights in the Quetico. The hum of mosquitoes and the rustle of corn on the Upper Iowa River. Times with no purpose but the rhythmic pull of the paddle through the water, no goal but a campsite at the end of the day.

It never occurred to Jeremy to leave his parents a note. What would it have said? "Gone canoeing. If I'm not back by the time you read this, call out the dogs"?

No, it just never occurred to him. He was preoccupied with disasters of a different magnitude, and didn't once imagine . . . well, all the things that nineteen-year-olds fail to imagine and that their parents so amply imagine for them. But his parents were in Honolulu until Sunday, and Jeremy had no one to answer to but himself.

Cottage Grove, the suburb where the Towerses lived, was one of dozens that had grown in an ever-widening crescent around the city. Toward the outer edge land use became complicated and odd:

Cattle grazed in pastures adjacent to field-long manufacturing complexes, and newer suburbs—those tracts of identical three-bedroom houses on tiny treeless lots—were crowded between spreading fields of corn or oats. Flowing through this complex landscape was a sluggish, polluted, and useless river. The Ashago came from the north, where the larger dairy and grain farms had retreated; it meandered through a forest preserve and the campus of a community college, behind fenced suburban yards, past the back lots of factories, and beneath highway overpasses, until it joined the larger water system southwest of the city.

This river was once a highway of clear water for Chippewa Indians and French voyageurs heading for the "horse portage." The accidents and whimsies that occurred to the French on their way down the Ashago found their way into the names they gave to the area—Presque Isle, Trempe l'Eau, Lac Vieux, Isle des Morts. By the twentieth century the names would have been as unrecognizable to the French as the land around the river. Presge. Trampalow. Lakeview. Idamore.

From Cottage Grove Jeremy could have gone southwest with the current. A day's canoe trip to the southwest was the Valparaiso Moraine. By water he could enter the huge tract owned by the Commonwealth Utilities Company, set off by cyclone fences and invisible from the main road. The nuclear power plant there, with its metallic forest of transformers, sat on disfigured land that looked like the dump of a mining operation. It was in fact the debris of a receding glacier that had formed the odd humps and hillocks.

On an earlier trip Jeremy and his brother had discovered that the litter of rounded rocks contained fossils. Most of the concretions had only the darkened circular depressions left by some sort of a jellyfish. Occasionally there were tiny skeletons or the veins of a plant. Jeremy liked most of all just to sit on top of one of the strange heaps, his hands on the dusty, sun-warmed rocks full of prehistoric marine life, and stare around him at the ancient waterway, the more ancient moraine, and the cylindrical white building of the nuclear power plant. Then he felt himself at the summit of a mystery, the conjunction of two almost unimaginable realms: the vastness of earth's time and change; the minuteness of particle physics.

But Jeremy decided against the Valparaiso Moraine. He disliked the long foul pull past the heavy industry stretching all the way up from Carbonville, and anyhow, he was fed up with being mystified. The whole point of the canoe trip was to do something merely physical and simple, like paddling upstream. So the trip that Jeremy planned consisted of a leisurely two-day jaunt: up the Ashago to Riverwoods for a night's camp at the forest preserve. Then south to the portage at Fennel Creek, and on to the Botanical Gardens at Idamore. Paddling back with the current, he'd be home from Idamore . . . oh, by midday tomorrow. For whom would he leave a note?

∘ TWO ∘

It certainly was no wilderness that Jeremy canoed through. But he hadn't set forth expecting to feel like a French voyageur on an expedition through uncharted land. For that you went way north, to the waters of northern Minnesota or the upper peninsula of Michigan, where you could dip your cup into the water and drink. Here you didn't even put your hands into it, dirty with God knew what filth. Jeremy didn't mind that, or the garbage strewn over the bank here and there, or the two grimy children staring at him through a wire fence from their backyard. What he enjoyed was the motive force of his own body—the strength of his shoulders and arms as he paddled the canoe through the water. And he liked being in an abandoned place; history had turned the houses toward the roads, making the river a special sort of wilderness, ignored, useless except as a dumping ground, and private.

The retaining wall gave way to a sloped bank of rushes where blackbirds were nesting. A male flew out from the rushes and sat boldly on the branch of a stunted tree. "Follow me," he sang again and again in his rusty liquid trill. Then his red shoulder patch flashed as he made feinting swoops around the intruder in the strange metal nest. Under the road bridges Jeremy sang and hallooed. The curved vaults created the same acoustical effect as a bathroom. His booming voice startled the swallows that roosted by the hundreds on the huge girders. In a tumult of flapping wings, they flew back and forth under the bridge as if trapped there, then broke out into the light.

The sky was increasingly overcast, but held its rain until well past midday. When it finally broke, Jeremy pulled the canoe out and prepared his lunch under a road bridge. He welcomed the rain: It would force him into the slow ritual pace of canoeing. Though he hadn't planned on a hot meal, he set up the tiny Primus and measured out a pot of water from the plastic jug. Rummaging through his pack, he found a packet of freeze-dried soup and emptied it into the pot. Then he settled down to wait for his meal.

Cars crossing the bridge above his head caused an echoing rumble around him. Sitting on the folded tarp with his back against a cement support slab, he appreciatively smelled the rain: rain on cement, rain on tarmacadam, rain bringing out the odor of the guano-covered walls and the metal of the river. It fell on either side of him, steady but not hard.

Good Lord, look where he was! He chuckled out loud at the picture of himself sitting perfectly contented in bird shit on the banks of a foul river on a chill rainy afternoon in early spring. Wendy would tell him he should have his head examined. Wendy, who was even crazier than he was. That reckless side of her character annoyed and excited him, charmed and appalled him. She'd probably risk pneumonia to swim in the river. Or stand up in the canoe. Or—what would she do? Jeremy looked around, trying to imagine what adventure Wendy would concoct in so unlikely a place.

Though he often played sensible scolding uncle to Wendy's

rashness, he couldn't deny that he enjoyed a vicarious thrill of reck-
lessness with her. So when he spotted the freckled mushrooms glistening in the rain, an odd smile came over his crooked mouth. He
left the shelter of the bridge to bend over the patch of mushrooms.
The rain pattered noisily on his vinyl slicker, which was bright
yellow and almost glowing in the dour noontime light. Today he
was his own light, his own adventurer. He ran his finger over the
slick fleshy dome of one speckled cap, broke it off, smelled it, nibbled it, then, with a carefree shrug at his sensible self, gathered a
handful of the sweet, musty mushrooms and threw them into the
pot of soup.

He ate this rehydrated concoction, spiced now with mushrooms
and daring, then sat back and sipped from a thermos of coffee.
When he was refreshed and rested, he set out again, watching the
leather of his boots darken with accumulated moisture, and grinning broadly as he paddled up the smelly river in the rain.

He paddled into a dense fog, wondering if he had passed
through the rain or if the rain itself had caused some rapid tem-
perature change that had created the fog. This was the sort of thing
Jeremy was apt to wonder about—is this the same thing in another
form, or a different thing, and how do they connect to each other
and to me? And this was the sort of thing that made him occasionally question his own competence to drive. "You'll daydream yourself right into a ditch someday, Jeremy Towers." On the Ashago
River, though, there were no rocks to run into, no road to lose, no
cars to collide with. Just this dense, slightly sulfurous-smelling fog.

The air was so thick and quiet that he becamed annoyed by the
rustle of his slicker, vinyl swishing against vinyl with every paddle
stroke. He removed it, throwing it across the center thwart, then
went on, taking care not to clang the paddle shaft against the metal
gunwale. The only sounds were the sounds of water—the soprano
gurgle of water dripping off the blade and the baritone slosh of
water slapping against the hollow bow stem. On either side of him
the banks dissolved in the mist. The murky river flowed out of a
soft white wall of fog that he approached and approached and
never entered.

Though he felt a little shiver of excitement, he never imagined getting lost. He planned to pull out when he ran through the low-hanging branches of the huge willows that grew near the bank at Riverwoods. So Jeremy paddled into the clear strip of water directly in front of him. The fog receded before his approach, beckoning and teasing him on and on. He lost track of space and time, and when he finally pulled out for sheer exhaustion, he had no idea how far he had gone. "Where the hell are those willows?" he complained, hauling the canoe into some shrubbery.

He climbed up the bank, peering around him into the fog. He walked backward and forward, puzzled—there were no trees at all. Could they have let the preserve go to the developers? Had he paddled past it? Was he in someone's suburban backyard? Where was he? Then Jeremy was seized with anxiety lest he should lose his way back to the river, back to the canoe. He kept the river to his left as he reconnoitered, plunging through the brush and watching for some substantial shape of house or tree to loom up before him in the fog.

The fog, the fear of becoming lost, the sound of his own labored breathing, the strange treelessness of the landscape—each thing escalated his anxiety until he was superstitious with fright. When he saw the sign of the animal shelter, he laughed with relief. It was a familiar landmark. As a child, Jeremy had asked to stop at the shelter each time the Towersers passed it driving north—to visit a dairy farm or pick apples or go into the north country. He liked to stroll back and forth past all the homeless, caged, and barking dogs, picking out the ones he'd adopt it he could: the shivering shy ones, the cheerful waggers anxious for affection, and all the puppies. The shelter must have been founded by someone as sentimental as Jeremy himself, for it was called Orphans of the Storm.

He walked through the white mist toward the kennel runs at the rear of the building. From moment to moment he expected to hear the racket of barking that his presence would cause. His boots crunched in the shifting gravel, then slopped through green mud. There were no dogs. Fog drifted through the sagging wire fences and along the empty cement runs.

At the squeal of a door on its hinges, Jeremy turned, eager to hear the story of the shelter's closing—due to lack of funding, no doubt—and eager, too, for company, for the exchange of banalities that would steady his overexcited imagination.

"Gwan," the man said in a husky, damaged voice.

"Hi," said Jeremy in a hearty conversational tone. "Just canoed up from Cottage Grove. I used to come up here all the time when I was a . . ." Jeremy's voice died in his throat. The man was testing the weight of a thick metal bar against his hand. But it was the man's face that made Jeremy gasp with horror. For the man *had* no face. His skull was enclosed by tissue-thin and featureless flesh. Tiny perforations of darkness marked the nasal and aural cavities; the mouth was a slot, a barely healed wound. Pulled taut across the bone, the skin had no folds, no soft protective flesh. Eyelids like reptilian shutters flicked over the eyes, which were disturbingly human, pale and full of hatred.

Jeremy bolted toward the river. He blundered through the underbrush and slid down the muddy bank, arriving at the canoe feet first on his back. He pushed off before he was properly balanced, and the canoe responded gaily to his hasty, shifting weight. Flailing, Jeremy fell against the thwart as the canoe swung broadside into the current. For one sickening moment he thought it was going to capsize. Then the canoe veered around and steadied, riding the slow current south. Jeremy steadied with it. He took his seat and ruddered with the paddle. Then he groaned with shame. "Oh, the poor guy, the poor guy." Jeremy couldn't imagine what accident—chemicals or fire?—could thus erase a face, but he could imagine the pain and humiliation, the self-horror and hatred the man must feel when people recoiled.

Jeremy wanted to go back and explain how the fog and the changed and empty place had worked on his imagination. Impossible, of course. What, tell him that if you'd encountered him at a bus stop on a busy street corner at noon, you wouldn't have shied like a hysterical horse? Might as well tell him he was like a nightmare. . . . And anyhow, he had that metal bar. He was ready to protect his isolation from the fascinated prying eyes of horrified strangers. Oh, and what an isolation it must be, Jeremy thought.

An abandoned animal shelter. Jeremy shook his head again and again, groaning out loud.

He pulled out several times, clambering up the bank and peering around, each time frowning with bewilderment. The fog was lifting, dispersed by a watery sun. Jeremy secured the canoe, tied his yellow slicker to a shrub as a marker, and set forth to find out where he was, and who the hell had chopped down all the trees. He would write to his senators. To the governor. To the Environmental Protection Agency. By God, to the president.

He traipsed through a lilliputian forest of mushrooms. They were everywhere on the spongy earth, and they came in every shape. Vertical stands of tiny luminously yellow mushrooms on thin stalks; ground-hugging saucers of scarlet flesh; clusters of black urns; glistening gelatinous wings like seaweed. Jeremy thought he recognized "artist's fungus." He'd once met an old man at a crafts fair who drew primitive pictures—flowers and sailing vessels were his two topics—on the soft white surfaces of the fungi, which dried quickly and varnished well, the old man said. On an ordinary day Jeremy would have been pleased to stop here, breaking off a section of the fungus and writing his name with a stick. Today he did it only to maintain his grip on the ordinary, which kept lurching, like the canoe broadside against the current, threatening to dash him into icy dark water.

Pocketing the inscribed fungus, Jeremy walked until he reached a street. The place looked like a rural slum. All along the street were dozens of rusted cars streaked with bird droppings and sunk on moldering tires. Grass and weeds grew up to the fenders and in lumpy hillocks over the disintegrating pavement of street and front walks. Scrawny chickens perched on several car hoods; others pecked and scratched along broken curbs.

He heard people singing in the distance, and proceeded stealthily toward them. At each intersection he saw a street like the one he was on. Irregularly spaced along the street were large brick houses with flaking mortar, rotted fascias, and peeling roofs. Between these were the foundations where other houses had been, rectangular pits of foul water. The exposed cement walls crumbled over half-submerged washing machines, driers, freezers, power tools, furnaces, and water heaters.

Some of the street signs remained. He was on Elm Street, passing Cherry. Orchard. Grove. But there were no trees. As he gazed up at the street signs, he noticed that there were no utility lines either. Though the metal street lights were intact, the familiar wooden poles were gone, and with them the electricity and phone lines. Jeremy was accustomed to walking under a complex embroidery of wires slung from pole to pole, connected to every house. The thick cables were so commonplace that they were invisible to him; absent, they became a shocking vacancy.

Block-long fields replaced once-suburban backyards. In one of these commons a group of people was working the soil and singing. Jeremy stood in the shadows at the side of a house some distance from the gathering and watched them—eight adults and five children—work in a haphazard cluster as they created the perfectly straight seeded rows. He cut around to the side of another house and stared in bewilderment at this band of raggedy scarecrows singing and hoeing.

As he struggled to account for these peculiar people and this ravaged place, he could think of no single explanation that covered the entire situation. He decided that they were inmates of a local mental hospital (what hospital?) that had recently released borderline patients in an effort to deal with soaring costs. And how had they come to be here? Well, because the residents of these once-fine brick houses with their curved driveways and attached garages had discovered that their homes were built on a toxic dump, and abandoned the area. With no publicity? Upper-class suburbanites, they had bought off the press. So the border-line lunatics were squatters on land so toxic that it no longer supported trees. . . . Here the web of his explanation stretched and broke, and he started with another premise. Ruthless land developers had leveled the area for extensive building, then their business failed in the housing crunch, so . . . No, that wouldn't do either.

One thing *was* clear: These people were in dire circumstances.

Whoever they were, they'd been left here to fend for themselves, and they weren't managing. As they turned at the end of a row, Jeremy could see that two of the women were pregnant and that one of the children had Down's syndrome, and another was in fact a small adult male. There were only two other men in the group, one of them an older man with some severe skin disease. All of them were gaunt and dirty.

The dark-haired pregnant woman wore a man's checked shirt over her blue jeans. Her hands were in constant motion, scratching her hair and neck, touching her groin, pressing her swollen belly. "Okay, okay," she said in a voice so stridently distinct that Jeremy shied back against the side of the house. She began to sing in a grudging way. "Ama-a-a-zing grace, amazing grace . . ."

"Sing, May," said the midget to a child bent earnestly over her hoe. Apparently she couldn't hoe and sing at the same time, for she straightened and dutifully sang, twisting her thin fingers around and around a lock of dirty brown hair. "I once was lost, but now am found," she piped. "Oh birds, come back to me. . . ."

Jeremy strained to hear the odd words. "Am-aaaaazing grace," boomed the midget heartily, swinging his lopped-off hoe. "Do not abandon us again, thou creatures of the air," went one stanza. And another: "Hide us in the shadow of your wings."

A sallow-faced young woman scratched and spat. "That's enough praying, Ben. Let's get to work now."

The fairer of the two pregnant women sank onto the porch steps with a sigh. The midget stroked her head. "Fog's lifted," he said, smoothing her tangled hair. "Birds are back. Sun's coming. Water's warming. Seeds'll grow. Baby'll be fine."

"All that, Ben?"

"All that, Maddy."

Jeremy watched the midget comfort the pregnant woman while the others conferred on tasks, pointing this way and that, nodding and smiling at each other. He hesitated at the side of the house, then turned away, heading back toward the river. Something here did not bear thinking about; he was going home now. Going home where he could arrange for help to be sent. Going back to the muddy river and riding its current south into the ordinary, into Cottage Grove, home.

° THREE °

The dirty turgid Ashago had become a clear burbling stream running through an unpeopled landscape. Along the bank, silhouetted against the late-afternoon sun, were the stark forms of dead trees. "Wait a minute, wait a minute," Jeremy kept saying, like a mantra by which he could transcend this nightmare and still the panic that shook him. But when he reached the Route 94 bridge where he'd put in, combers of panic were coursing through him, cresting and subsiding and cresting again, higher and higher as he walked the familiar streets of his hometown.

There was nothing to see here that he hadn't already seen in Idamore. Here were the same weather-beaten roads and buildings, the same ominous silence of an empty suburb. In contrast to the northern section of Idamore, here none of the houses had been torn down, and no one had collected the fallen trees for firewood. Draped with fungus, they lay across the roads, rotted in front yards, and leaned against houses. Red dust swirled and eddied along the empty streets.

Jeremy walked along Forrest Avenue to Milburn Street, the retail area a few blocks north of his house. The street was strewn with broken plate-glass windows, and the stores had been sacked. Amy's Boutique, Jenson's Five and Dime, Joy Cleaners. Some of the storefronts had been boarded up with rough sheets of plywood; much of the plywood had been torn down or burned out. At the empty showroom of Cottage Grove Cyclery, the heavy metal gate had been levered back and the plate glass shattered. The Long Ago antique store was bursting with debris—broken lamps, chairs with slashed upholstery, and china and bric-a-brac smashed under overturned furniture. "Wait a minute, wait . . ." Jeremy whispered.

He walked on: past the north branch of the Cottage Grove Library, the Parkview Restaurant, Today's New-Trition Health Food. The street was silent that should have been loud with cars, eager children, squeaking strollers, and pockets full of change, with ringing cash registers and swooshing doorways. The wind rattled loose metal signs and sighed through open doors. It was the only sound on the street, and it made Jeremy's flesh crawl.

At Merton's Drugs Jeremy cupped his hands around his eyes to peer through the undamaged but dirty glass into the interior. He surveyed the looted store, with its metal cabinets empty of everything but broken glass and some torn hot-water bottles. Against one wall was a display of pink cellophaned packages containing emery boards, hairpins, nail polish, and decorative rubber bands. A revolving rack still had some sunglasses on it, none undamaged. On the glass beside the door were the bright rectangles showing what charge cards were accepted at Merton's Drugs.

Out of the corner of his eye Jeremy saw something move, and he turned his head quickly. Yes, he was sure of it, there was someone moving around inside Today's New-Trition. "Hey," he yelled, running toward the store. "Hello." His voice echoed slightly between the buildings. He put his hand against the broken door and pushed, running into something wedged against it. "Hello?" he called. He remembered the faceless man at Orphans of the Storm, and warned himself not to flinch no matter what he saw. He leaned against the door, which abruptly fell off its hinges and landed with a soft thud, raising a cloud of chaffy foul-smelling dust. Jeremy flinched: Rats swarmed over the fallen door, cheeping angrily.

He backed away, retracing his steps. Now he saw rats everywhere at the periphery of his vision—scuttling like shadows across alleys, lurking like hunks of mud in doorways, darkening the aisles of the stores that he passed. He walked drunkenly, jerking his head left and right to catch sight of the rats, but seeing none. His breath came in short, terrified sobs as he turned off Milburn toward Gaffield, left on Gaffield to Haywood.

With a shock of recognition he saw his house. It had been painted colonial blue—a nice color, but not one his parents would have chosen—and the paint was badly peeled, the bare wood warping. The front door was locked, and when Jeremy went around to the side of the house, he saw the strange wallpaper, the unfamiliar furnishings. He was not just disappointed; he was furious. He began to kick and pound at the front door, then to batter with a thick branch at a window until it broke.

In a crescendo of rage, he assaulted the living room for its unfamiliarity, smashing a frail tea table against an offending mirror, gouging the floral wallpaper, overturning the sectional sofa. Clouds of dry dust rose around his violence as he broke, smashed, and hurled until there was nothing left in the room to destroy. Still holding the leg of a table, Jeremy walked into the kitchen. New stove, with an attached microwave oven. New cabinets. Only the refrigerator was the same. He saw the nick he had put in its corner with a metal airplane that he had once launched in the kitchen. As he walked slowly toward the refrigerator, the splintered end of the table leg slipped through his fingers. "Oh please," he whispered. He rested his forehead against the cool white surface. Refrigerator. Food. Nurture. Mother. "Oh please." But the appliance was lifeless; unpowered.

Jeremy walked stiffly up the stairs toward his bedroom. "This is just a dream," he assured himself. "I'm having some kind of hallucination. All I have to do is lie down in my own bed, and when I wake up . . ." But the bedroom he walked into was not his bedroom; it was a mausoleum. Sunlight through the broken window fell in patches over the moldering upholstered chair, the rotted carpet, the grisly bed. The room smelled of mildew and wet rot, but was otherwise peaceful and undisturbed. Old people, they must have been, for there was a cane propped on one side of the bed and a walker at the other side.

Jeremy had a sudden vision of Milburn Street, of people swarming as the rats had swarmed over the door, frantic and angry, bumping and jostling each other. People on the move, abandoning empty cars and stealing bicycles to go on, and going in circles as others bumped at their heels. Emptying the stores of every useful thing and destroying what was useless. And this couple—too old to run in circles, too frail to jostle and loot—they had retreated to this quiet bedroom, lain down facing each other, and peacefully died together. Jeremy hoped it was peaceful. It certainly had been a while ago.

How long ago? Were his parents dead, and had they died this way? And Peter? Jeremy wanted to say something for all of them. Like a prayer, a benediction. "Thou shalt rise up the foundations of many generations. . . ." What was that, where from . . . ? Isaiah by way of Eliot, Survey of Modern British Literature, Mon-Wed-Fri, 10:00 A.M. Professor Holliwell. Hopkins and the Heraclitan flux. Time and the river. The dirty turgid Ashago had become a clear burbling stream. . . .

Jeremy walked down the stairs and out the back door into the yard where he had spent so much of his childhood. "I wonder where we went," he said dully, hardly bothered by the strangeness of his question. "I wonder what became of us." He felt bereaved not only of his family, but of himself. No past, no future, no continuity, no connections. Jeremy lay down with his back pressed to the foundation of the house that was not his house, and then, as if he were emplacing a miniature tombstone, he took the artist's fungus from his pocket and set it above his head. He scooped dirt around his chest. He closed his eyes and poured handful after handful of the iron-rich dirt over his head. Night was coming on, and Jeremy Towers was dead.

He lay there forging blankness, denial, death.

His heart slowed to a steady, rhythmic thump. Just stop, he commanded it. Die.

He was severed from everything that made him Jeremy Towers: not just from his family, his friends, his pleasant memories, and his wavering expectations, but from the commonwealth of time and place to which he belonged, in which he knew himself. Jeremy Towers was dead.

o   o   o

It was one of young Laurel's jobs to learn the mushrooms, so she always went with Helena to gather them. Spring was the season of the morels, and morels were easy to spot: wrinkled dark thimbles on top of fat white stalks. They came in three crops. Early morels, black morels, and club-footed morels. "Very good, Laurel," said Helena, as the girl recited. "And what about these?"

Brown mushrooms, they were. They looked edible. Though Laurel stared at the fungi as if she were trying to remember, she was actually trying to read Helena, trying to sort through the hot waves of Helena's disapproval for the correct answer. Laurel wanted to please Helena, who got angry if Laurel guessed and impatient if Laurel said she didn't know. It was such a long dark cold time between gatherings. "They're honey mushrooms, Laney," Laurel declared, biting her bottom lip.

"You're sure?" said Helena. "You're sure they're not galerina?" Helena broke off a mushroom and handed it to Laurel. "Sure enough to eat one?"

Laurel would willingly have died before displeasing Helena, so she put the mushroom to her mouth to prove her certainty. "No," said Helena sharply. "It's a galerina, Laurel. And if you gave it to the others, it would make everyone sick. Not just you. Everyone else, too." Helena sighed. "Okay, let's go over it again. Try to listen, please. Honey mushrooms fruit in the autumn. Galerina fruits in spring *and* autumn, its spore deposit is rusty brown, and its stalk is much darker than . . . Never mind, Laurel. Please don't be upset. We'll study the honey mushrooms in the fall. What's the rule if you can't remember about a mushroom?"

"If you can't remember a mushroom, never, never, never eat it."

"Oh, look! Here's wild lettuce," exclaimed Helena, forgetting in her enthusiasm that she meant to be teaching mushrooms to Laurel. "I thought it wasn't coming anymore. I couldn't find any last year. Let me think, what was it that Simon called it? . . . Sass . . . no, saxifrage lettuce. Here, you pick the morels and I'll see if there's anything else . . ."

"Ooooh, Laney, I think I found the white ones, the killer ones, amarands, arma . . . what do you call 'em?"

"Amanitas," the woman said. "Not likely. They fruit in the fall."
"With the honey mushrooms?" the child called.
"Well . . . yes. Look over there, Laurel; there's a bunch of something."
The underbrush snapped and shushed around their movements. "Maybe Maddy will name the baby Morel. That'd be a nice name," said the girl, crashing through the underbrush toward the embankment.
"Just pray this one is healthy."
"Ooooh, Laney, there's a man there." Laurel might have been announcing another variety of mushrooms.
"Oh?" Helena turned to see the man paddling upstream toward them. He looked so pale and distraught that she thought for a moment he might be bringing disease. But this was an obviously healthy young man: tall and well fed, straight and manly, a little stupid-looking. "A Federal Man!" Helena decided, and felt her usual battery of emotions—jealous rage, humiliation at her appearance, disgust for an entire way of life, and hope for the future.

Jeremy returned to Idamore because he could not die, and alive, he could not be alone. There were people at Idamore. Two of them were right there on the bank: a honey-blond kid about twelve years old, and the sallow-faced woman about Jeremy's age who had scratched and spat.
He leaned down to lug the canoe up, then stood too quickly. He felt a moment's faintness, the spinning vacancy when blood rushes from the head, the tectonic slip of the earth beneath his feet. With the faintness came a moment of dissociation. Jeremy stood back from himself gawking up at the almond-eyed little girl and the dark-eyed young woman. So in the midst of nightmare, the dreamer stands on the ledge from which he has already fallen and, without waking, comforts himself: "This is just a dream." Jeremy watched himself clamber up the bank toward them. He saw himself as a visitor from another planet, a traveler from another time.

° FOUR °

"Did you bring salt?" the woman asked. She seemed neither surprised to see him nor interested in knowing him.

Jeremy had expected her to be frightened—startled, at least—as women will be of a strange man in an isolated place. He was the one startled, and dizzily tripping over a root. "Salt?" he said.

"What a population of freaks and idiots," the woman remarked to the girl, then stomped away to gather mushrooms and plants, apparently prepared to ignore him. He might have been an inept clerk in a supermarket. The girl stood her ground, staring up at Jeremy with a blank gaze.

"Well," said Jeremy, smiling and shrugging.

"How can you transport, using such a small boat?"

"It's twelve feet," he said, not tracking the conversation.

"You scheduled to be here? This is Idamore."

"Idamore. Yes, I know. What do you mean, transport?"

"Like salt and stuff. . . . You *are* a Federal Man, aren't you?"

"A Federal Man?" said Jeremy.

At this, the fierce young woman straightened up with a snort. Then she keeled over in a fit of laughter. She lay in the brush, rolling from side to side, shrieking and kicking. It was so infectious that Jeremy found himself grinning, though he half thought the woman was insane. When she scrambled to her feet and came toward him, still spluttering with laughter, Jeremy took an instinctive step away. She was grotesque: sallow and thin faced, with filthy tangled hair, and shapely white teeth dripping with blood.

She sucked at her teeth and spat. "It's not catching," she said gravely. "Honest. It's really not. This happens the end of every winter. Fresh vegetables, I think. . . ." She slid down the bank and

scooped water into her mouth. Then she peered into Jeremy's canoe. "No salt, huh?"

"Well, uh . . ."

Jeremy had not yet managed a coherent sentence, and the
woman's tone was becoming more and more the patient and patronizing voice one uses with morons. "My name's Helena. And
that is Laurel."

"Jeremy Towers," Jeremy said. He thrust his hand out and
tripped off the bank, falling at her feet.

"Jeremy falls," remarked Helena with a laugh. "What's in
there?" she said, pointing at the pack.

"Just some gear," Jeremy replied, slapping mud off his pants.
"Sleeping bag, food . . . Oh, and I do have . . ." He rooted through
the pack until he found the picnic-sized container of salt, which he
brought forth with a flourish. Helena looked blank. "Salt!" he said.

"That little . . . Hmph. Well, good for you." With a whimsical
smile, Helena remarked to Laurel, "Moses among the bullrushes,
huh?" Then she turned back to Jeremy. "What else you got?"

"Gee, not much," he said apologetically. He wondered how he
had blundered into this role of overgrown clumsy child. He ought
to have felt humiliated, but was actually comfortable—an emotional zero. He carried the pack up the bank and spread it open for
her inspection.

"What's this stuff?" Helena asked, shaking the packages of
freeze-dried foods and tossing them aside. She plunged her arm
into the pack, hauling out the clean towel, the folded clothes, and
the plastic bottle of campers' concentrated liquid soap. Three
oranges rolled across the green moss and settled, bright globes,
against a rotting tree stump covered with black fungi. Helena
looked at the oranges, she looked at Jeremy, and she looked at the
oranges. Her face went stiff with feigned indifference. "You
must've come a long way," she mused. She squatted, shamming
casualness by fiddling with the moss at her feet. "Farther than a
Federal Man, even. So you must be travel weary and anxious for a
place to sleep. We've got plenty of beds and no disease here. You're
welcome to stay. We'll trade you—uh—trade you a bed for those

. . . oranges, aren't they?" She sucked at her teeth and gave him a wary, sidelong glance.

Jeremy, who would gladly have given her anything but his canoe, at that moment would have given her even that. "Trade?" he repeated stupidly.

"This is Jeremy Echo," Helena said when she introduced him to the others.

Jeremy did little to correct their impression of him. He blundered among them like a sleepwalker, repeating their questions and answering them oddly, his conversation always a dazed half beat off. Handed a bowl, he bent over it eagerly, hungry and glad for a respite from their weird questions, their close looks. The group's sudden silence made him raise his head to find them exchanging puzzled glances. ("He doesn't look to *me* like he's starving," the strident dark pregnant one replied to some whispered comment from the quiet pale pregnant one.) He was, he realized, eating a portion meant for thirteen people.

He was grateful then for the crazy woman named Rose: Her agitation over the oranges briefly diverted the group's attention from him. Rose refused to touch her share of the oranges. "Hot, hot," she kept saying.

"They're not hot," the midget assured her. "They're sour and juicy and delicious. Eat, Rose."

Except for two of the women—dark Helena with the bleeding gums and this slender schizophrenic Rose—Jeremy couldn't even keep their names straight. Most of them seemed to come in neat pairs: two pregnant women; two preadolescent girls; two little boys (one of them was distinctively retarded). Even the trio of adults males caused difficulty, for their combined characteristics reminded Jeremy of Mickey Rooney. But the mute palsied man named Mick was neither short (Ben was the midget) nor ruddy (Dave was the one with the peeling skin).

"Well," said the midget at the conclusion of this uncomfortable snack or meal, "the oranges were wonderful. Now you get to choose your house, Jeremy Echo."

"Jeremy *Towers,*" he corrected somewhat delinquently.

The midget reared back to survey Jeremy's height. "Indeed he does, yes indeed," he said with a patronizing pat on Jeremy's arm. "Laney, help Jeremy Echo pick out an empty house. But don't take too long. Lots to do . . ."

"Wait a minute, wait a . . ." Jeremy didn't know how to put his questions: Where were all the others? What had happened here, and how long ago? What year was it? Was the world gone? "What happened . . . to the trees?" he finally burst out.

"You heard there were trees at Idamore?" the midget said with a pleased glance at Helena.

"Were . . . Trees. Yes!" Jeremy nodded vigorously, drunk with bewilderment.

"They're still very small," he apologized, "but Helena will show you."

The gaunt and dirty young woman extended her hand to Jeremy as to a lost child. Behind him Jeremy heard Ben clucking. "Dinosaurs also had small brains in their huge bodies. . . . You remember I told you about dinosaurs, May and Laurel? Birds may have descended from dinosaurs. . . ."

Helena took Jeremy through the village to a place Jeremy instantly recognized. The architecture of the cantilevered building with its four rectangular wings; the curved gravel pathways among miniature hills made of landfill. The series of three ponds fed by Fennel Creek. The last time Jeremy was here, there had been a county extension agent and experimental greenhouses, a Japanese garden, a Shakespeare garden, the Mrs. Elizabeth Hull Memorial Rose Garden, the spring tulip festival . . . "What . . . what . . ." Jeremy sputtered.

"Over here," Helena said, leading him to a nursery of trees. "We have apples and plums. These are beech. And this is elm." *Elem,* she pronounced it. "We found all sorts of seeds and things in there," she said, waving toward the administration building. "And this batch was all mixed up, so we don't know what they are. . . ."

"Maple," said Jeremy. "These are maple, and you've planted them too close . . . too close together." He couldn't control the trembling in his voice.

Helena gave him a sharp glance. "Is that what you're wandering around for, Jeremy Echo? You're looking for trees, poor soul? The Federal Man said that there are big trees in the north. When the birds came back, they brought the trees, and they're growing all *over* now, but there are *big* ones in the north."

"Oh God." Jeremy looked toward the bird-seeded saplings in the field, then at the neat row of saplings beside him. "Too close together. If they grow, they'll get huge. . . ."

"They'll grow," said Helena firmly. She tucked a hank of matted hair behind her ear.

"The birds," said Jeremy. "Why did the birds go away?"

"Dim, dim," Helena said to herself, looking at the ground and shaking her head. "You remember, Jeremy," she said in her false-patient voice. "The birds left after the time of the light."

"What light?"

Helena rolled her eyes. Then she rubbed her nose—less a scratch than a gesture of impatience. "You know. The light. People aren't supposed to just wander around, you know. We have our places to keep."

Jeremy shrugged with his hands. "*I* have no place," he replied.

"Things are really bad in the south, aren't they?" She paused only a moment for an answer, and when Jeremy frowned and looked away, she quickly continued. "Well, you're welcome at Ida-more. We don't turn people away from Idamore. Unless they're bringing disease," she added.

Jeremy interpreted this as a question and assured her that he was perfectly healthy. "Would you happen to know what year it is?" he asked, shrugging at the absurdity of his question: The woman would be convinced of his dim-witted madness.

"Year?" she said anxiously. "Time of year? Seed planting, can't you see that?" Helena was studying his face so closely that Jeremy stiffened and looked away. He was not ready to try to explain to her what he couldn't himself understand or accept.

"Have you hit your head?" she asked. "Sometimes when people hit their heads, they can't remember things. . . ."

"Oh, I remem—" His voice broke. If he said anything more, he'd be standing there sobbing and bellowing, and it was very important that he not break, not feel, not acknowledge. Miserable and dumb, he shook his head, and the two of them walked back through Idamore, where Helena pointed out the few houses that were already taken.

The house he chose was the one closest to the river and farthest from the others. For three days he isolated himself in that house on Elm Street, joining the others only when he was hungry. The rest of his time he spent searching for his exit. He paddled up and down the river, scanning the horizon for trees or polluted air or some tremor of change. When that didn't work, he tried walking. He walked the damaged tollway to the east of the Botanical Gardens, stepping over the boundary into Trampalow, then farther south, into Presge. He walked fast, covering acres of land, going nowhere. He half expected to encounter an invisible time shield, like a Plexiglas dome over him. A thing he could batter a hole in.

On the third day he retraced the path of his first canoe trip. He went back to the animal shelter at Riverwoods, thinking that the featureless man, alone and feisty and horribly damaged, might be guarding the entrance to Jeremy's nightmare. But Jeremy couldn't find him, and he wondered which chamber of time the man belonged to—or if he existed at all. In any case, the futile trip convinced Jeremy that physical travel was not going to get him home; he was hurling himself against the wrong boundaries.

On his way back, he noticed the metal boundary marker: Idamore, pop. 28,600. "Plenty of beds, and no disease," that had been Helena's promotion of Idamore. 28,600 beds, if you didn't count things like sofa beds, guest rooms, bunk beds, and the like. Plenty of beds to choose from. The present population was thirteen. Fourteen if Jeremy counted himself—which it never occurred to Jeremy to do. He was not one of them.

Dirty and louse-ridden, the people of Idamore slept and ate inside spacious houses that everywhere mocked the rudeness of their lives. Food was prepared in the kitchen, a useful place because of the drain in the sink, but then it had to be cooked in the living room in a fireplace that was not even designed to provide heat, much less an efficient stove. Water was stored outside in large tubs filled by buckets from the pond, then brought inside to be heated in the fireplace. It would have been like camping out—fetch the water, gather the fuel, make a fire, cook the food, heat the water to wash the dishes—except that all these activities took place in the context of a suburban neighborhood. It was as if a power failure had struck a community that went on living for years in the daily expectation that the power would resume tomorrow.

It wasn't long before Jeremy saw how one might persist in the patterns provided by the functionless houses, for on the evening of his third day in Idamore, Jeremy had diarrhea—whether from psychological distress or from the diet of wild mushroom soup and saxifrage lettuce he didn't bother to wonder. He made trip after trip to the river, carrying buckets of water to fill the tank of the toilet. His first maneuver was to methodically fill the tanks of all three toilets in his well-appointed house. But three toilets flushed once use as much water as one toilet flushed three times, he discovered, and was soon running back to the Ashago with his bucket. The next day Ben politely requested that Jeremy use the outhouse. "For the fields, you know."

For the fields. Jeremy remained in Idamore that day, his prison pacing checked by an uneasy stomach, and he saw for the first time that the others worked from morning to night. In the days that followed, he learned firsthand of the many chores. There were the latrines to be cleaned. The excrement had to be hauled by wheelbarrow to a pile some distance from their quarters. Urine was collected in tubs to use for tanning sheepskins. There were eggs to be gathered, seeds to be pounded, water to be fetched, and, once or twice a week, a chicken to be butchered and prepared. And there was the daily fuel crisis. "Pry the boards off this house?" Jeremy said on that first of his working days. "Take them right off the house?" he said, incredulously repeating the midget Ben's request. Yes, Ben said, yes, take them off and saw them up for firewood.

Jeremy worked like a healthy animal, stolid and openmouthed with amazement. "Take out the stairs?" he parroted back at big

blond Lily the next day. She was less patient than Ben and snapped
at him. Yes, yes, just hack them out. Split them. Carry them. Stack
them. He hacked, and split, and carried. He hauled and stacked,
sawed and pried. And he worked in the fields.

The fields. Those suburban backyards converted into commons
the length and width of a block. They had to be tilled and cultivated, the seeds guarded from the birds and the seedlings from the
ubiquitous insects. It was the children's job to pluck from the seedlings all sucking and chewing insects, and to watch for mites,
mildews, smuts, and rust. The job of watching over the two younger children fell randomly to nearby adults. The retarded boy,
Jules, kept them especially busy, for he was apt to eat the bugs he
picked off the plants or simply to wander away.

While they waited for the crops, their diet consisted of wild
plants and mushrooms, bony bluegills from the pond, crayfish,
stringy chicken, and flat dry pancaky things made of cattail flour
and pounded sedge seeds. Jeremy was always hungry and always
slightly disgusted. He hated the acid soapy taste of calamus, the
puttiness of the tubers, the mucilaginous gunk in the purslane. He
also hated to see the women browsing like ruminants over the
fields, eating as they foraged. Chickweeds and dandelions. Nettles.
Wild onion. Young shoots from cattails. He could not chew them
raw, the bitter, gritty weeds. And after hearing Helena's lecture on
hemlock, he thought them bitter, dirty, dangerous weeds.

Helena returned from foraging one day and sat with May and
Laurel to teach them the difference between "lace" and poison
hemlock. "Okay, now. You see how the stalk is hairy? And this
one is smooth? This is the only time of year you can gather lace
roots, when they look exactly like hemlock except for the hairy
stalks. How else can you tell the difference? Remember, May?"

May looked at Laurel, who wrinkled her nose. "Smell!" said
May.

Helena put the two roots behind her back and shuffled them.
"Which is hemlock? Which lace?" she said, extending the plants.

May and Laurel put their noses to the roots. Laurel rubbed the
leaves between her fingers and sniffed, first one hand, then the
other. "This is hemlock," she announced.

"Sure?" asked Helena.

"Sure," said Laurel. And she was.

Helena celebrated by stretching out in the field and happily laughing. "Oh, wonderful, wonderful. Be sure to wash your hands carefully now."

Jeremy was appalled to see the close resemblance between the two plants. One was a wild carrot, and he would have been sad to see it eliminated from their scanty diet just because it was practically indistinguishable from poison hemlock. How entirely his life depended on Helena's foraging skills! His total reliance on her, and on the community of the others' experience, made Jeremy persistently childlike, clumsy with bewilderment.

Occasionally before he went to sleep, he would sit on the edge of his bed and shake himself, rattling his head like a dog with fleas. "Jeremy Towers," he would say as he went to bed, "wake up, wake up."

He soon moved to Aspen Circle to be nearer the outhouse, the pond, and—he had to admit it—the others. For it was terribly dark at night. He had walked from room to room on the second floor of his Elm Street house, stumbling over what was left of the furniture, and looking out all the windows for light. There was none. No congenial rectangular glow from neighboring houses. No streetlights, no headlights. No luminous mauve-gray from the city to the south. He became reluctant to leave the others and walk past four blocks of empty houses in order to be alone in such darkness. He moved into the house next to the one Helena lived in with pale, pregnant Maddy, and he fetched his water where the others did, at the mouth of Fennel Creek.

He began to feel excluded from the community of adults, and made occasional forays into their conversations. One evening, for instance, Helena announced that Laurel could not manage the mushrooms.

"She must," said Ben.

"Well, she can't," Helena snapped.

"You must learn to be more patient, Laney," suggested Maddy, who was mild mannered and pale and hugely pregnant. "Perhaps it would help if you took May along."

"Ha!" said Pearl, who was also pregnant, but olive skinned where Maddy was pale, and hectic where Maddy was motionless.

"They do seem to learn better together. I'll try it." Helena brushed her hands against each other as if she'd just completed a chore.

"There just aren't enough of us," sighed Maddy.

"More coming all the time!" Ben boomed. His joviality was so forced that even Jeremy recognized the false note. Mystified, he glanced from Ben to Maddy, who managed a brave smile.

"Maybe *I* could learn the mushrooms," Jeremy ventured.

"I'm sure you could, Jermicho," said Pearl, "but that's not the point, is it, dear?"

"The point? No, I guess not." He left the group shaking his head.

What was the point? Not that they had dismissed him, or contracted his absurd name from Jeremy Echo to Jermicho, a pleasantly cooperative dim-witted set of shoulders. No, the point was that he had lived mindlessly, insensately among them for uncounted days, denying them in order to deny what was happening to him. He was neither here nor there, but suspended. Like an electronic stick figure, he thought with a shudder, frozen in a narrow vertical corridor of time.

◦ FIVE ◦

One day—it must have been sometime in early May—Jeremy discovered that he had lice. He scratched his neck and there they were. The hair on his skin rose up in protest, so he was sure they were crawling all over him. He stood in the field tearing off his clothes.

"Jermicho's having a fit," remarked one of the children. They were in his field picking bugs off the seedlings.

"I've got lice," he shouted, dancing to get out of his skin.
"Ben, Laney," Laurel screamed. "Jermicho's having a fit."
"I'm not having a fit, dammit," he yelled at Laurel. "I'm having a bath." He bundled up his clothes and strode off the field in his underwear. The children looked at each other and shrugged. Lily looked up from the board she was sawing. Helena and Dave with the peeling ruddy skin came to the edge of the adjacent field. Pale pregnant Maddy paused in the stirring of the tallow soap and watched Jeremy slam into his brick house. Moments later, when Jeremy came slamming out again, mute palsied Mick was also there, and Rose who heard voices, and the dark pregnant Pearl, and tiny Rachel, who made up in stamina what she lacked in strength.

Jeremy glared around at them. "There is no water in the goddamn taps," he raved. "There is no electricity in the wires. There is no gasoline in the cars. There are no trees on Orchard Street, and there are goddamn *sheep* grazing on the Elizabeth Hull Memorial Rose Garden. Who took my soap?"

"I'll get it, Jeremy," said Maddy quietly. She hoisted her pregnant bulk over her spindly legs and fetched the soap. The plastic bottle she handed him was still full, the jade liquid glinting clear and gemlike in the sun. Jeremy nodded curtly and trotted toward the Ashago River to bathe.

He plunged, snorting and gasping, into the icy river, then stood on the edge vigorously scrubbing himself from head to toe. Ah, the rich lather, the sweet piny smell of it! Not like the soap made of sheep fat and wood ashes, which got nothing clean and left grease on your hands. But maybe lye from wood ashes would work better on lice? Jeremy paused to read the plastic bottle, which was crowded with information. Highly concentrated, use sparingly, it said, but didn't list the ingredients. Concentrated what? Or was all soap made of lye? "Excellent for cooking and eating utensils, yet mild enough for a baby's skin . . ." Jeremy winced: Maddy had been saving the soap for the baby she carried so heavily.

At the bottom of the bottle was the advice, "Help prevent pollution—avoid use in lakes and streams. Mountain Enterprises, Inc. Mercer, Missouri." Jeremy looked at the scummy foam flecking over the stones at his feet. The river caught at it and caught at it, dispersing it in a film over the surface, stretching it on the current until it broke and was gone. Flowing south on the sparkling water. South. To Mercer, Missouri, he thought. Were there mountains in Missouri?

He put his head into the stream and raked his fingers through his hair to expose the lice to the numbing water. He slammed his head into the water again and again, as if he could kill them by knocking himself unconscious. "Die, you fuckers," he snarled.

He stripped off his filthy underwear and washed it, then found a piece of rough stone to rub over his lathered skin. "Aaaah," he murmured gratefully. "Aaaahhh." Immediately he wanted more: wanted hot water cascading over him from a shower head. Wanted steam condensing on a mirror. Wanted a thick soft towel. Wanted clean clothes. Aching with want, he was. To walk into Merton's Pharmacy and be given whatever it was that killed lice. "Charge it, please." Yes, and to drive the car to a Jack-in-the-Box and bellow his order into the intercom set into the ridiculous clown's head. "Hamburger, french fries, and a Coke." Lots of salt on the fries. Also a bowl of sugar. Jeremy wiped his mouth. Yes, and to sit in front of the late show making fun of the ads for cars and Kotex and floor wax, just sit there and call out for pizza with pepperoni sausage. Chinese food to go, lots of soy sauce.

He tried to lapse into his unconscious state again, to pretend that he was roughing it, just like in the north country. Hot water and clean laundry on the other side, as soon as he chose to come out of the wilderness. Jeremy looked south along the river. But he *wasn't* very far from home. Maybe a day's walk. Just minutes by car. How far *was* he? Would he get back?

When he turned, he saw Ben sitting on the bank above him. The sun shone through the branches of the shrubs, creating a lattice of shadows like prison stripes on Ben's clothes. "Feeling better now, Jermicho?"

Jeremy looked away, ashamed not of his nakedness but of his attitude. He had taken Maddy's soap. He wanted to go home. If given the opportunity, he would have walked through time's door and slammed it behind him without a backward glance at Ida-more's people. Jeremy gazed down the river, blinking rapidly, fighting tears. "Oh, Ben, I feel guilty as hell. . . ."

"Ah. You shed blood? Is that what you're running from?"

Jeremy gave Ben a startled glance. "No, I meant about the soap. Look at that." He tossed the plastic bottle up the bank. "'Mild enough for a baby's skin,' it says. Oh God." Jeremy tromped back and forth along the river, swinging his arms and stomping to warm himself. "Biodegradable. Hypoallergenic. Organic. Organic, ha! *Maddy's* soap is organic. I'd like to tell those folks in Mercer, Missouri, about organic."

"Do you read, Jermicho?" asked Ben, staring down at the bottle.

"Anything in front of me," bantered Jeremy, shuddering as he stepped into his cold wet shorts. "Cereal boxes, soap bottles, other people's mail . . ." He stopped then, and turned slowly. "*Read,* Ben?"

"We have many books, but few words," said Ben, apparently making a joke. "It is a very hard thing to teach, this reading. And it requires practice. Time. We have so little time, Jeremy."

Reading—it had not been on his list of wants. A bowl of sugar, heavily salted french fries, *and* an electric light to read by at the end of a hard day? It was entirely too much to ask. Jeremy hoisted himself up the bank and stretched out on the warm moss.

"You look like a very healthy male, Jermicho. Healthier even than the Federal Men—"

"Ben, who are these Federal Men?"

"The Federal Men are— Well, you'll meet ours. He comes twice a year—soon after the birds and then again before first snow. He's late this year," said Ben with a little frown that deepened the permanent line between his brows.

"He comes to . . . Did the birds once . . . When . . ." All the questions that Jeremy had suppressed were now competing to be asked first. "What," he said determinedly. "Ben, what happened?"

"To the birds? We don't know. They went away, and then they came back."

"And the trees?"

"They died."

"What do you mean, they died?" Jeremy objected. "How could they die? All the trees just *died*? That's absurd. . . ."

"Were there trees where you came from, Jeremy?"

"Yes, but they're gone now." Somehow he had gotten them off on the wrong track; he was asking the wrong questions, and then stupidly objecting to the answers.

"And electricity?" Ben went on.

Jeremy nodded absently, then sat up. "Ah. That's it. Ben, tell me about the time of the light. What's that?"

"You have been with us all these meals without making some electricity for us, Jeremy? How is that possible?"

"Making some! . . . *I* don't know how to . . . Just like that, make electricity!" He scrambled to his feet and glared down at Ben. "What do you think it is, magic? I just waggle my fingers and *zap!* power?"

Ben glared back at him, then his face softened to a look of awe. "Where do you come from, Jeremy, that you don't have a Federal Man or know about the time of the light?"

"Cottage Grove," said Jeremy grimly.

"Cott—Oh, you mean you came through there on your way. . . . No, what I . . . Ah, Jeremy, always we're talking like this." Ben intersected his arms to indicate their frequent misunderstandings. "No, what I meant was, perhaps you could take us to your place— no? Why so quickly no?"

Jeremy finally stopped shaking his head and sat cross-legged in front of Ben. "Let's straighten this out. You tell me about the time of the light, then I'll tell you about where I came from. Okay?"

"Okay," said Ben. He scratched his temple. He rubbed his chin. He fluttered. "But I don't understand how you can *not* know that."

"Well, I don't. But if everybody else knows it, it shouldn't be too hard to tell me, should it?" he asked somewhat testily.

"In the time of the light there were birds and trees and great cities. There was light everywhere, and at all times. The sun was gentle, and the power was great." Ben was talking in the rhythmic affectless tone of a person reciting something he doesn't understand. "There was a power that drove the cars, and every person had a car that drove. Power came through the wires and kept things cold and made things hot. There were pictures and words in the wires—"

"Stop, stop. I know about *that,* you don't have to tell me about that—"

"Well, I thought you must know about it," Ben said with a relieved smile.

"And what I want to know is," Jeremy went on, "what happened? Why did the lights go off? Why did the . . ." He hesitated, afraid to put any specific question for fear of losing the larger topic. "What happened to the power?"

Ben looked uneasy. "Too much power," he said, avoiding Jeremy's eyes. "The power stretched out along the skies and hammered the floor of the earth, so the sky became dark and the floor of the earth tattered." Jeremy rested his chin on his knees and looked at the river, so he could separate Ben's sonorous voice from his awkwardly tiny body. It was a pulpit voice, a mountain voice, a voice to believe in.

"The city rolled back its gates and melted into the earth, and all the citizens of the city melted into the earth, and from the streets of the city came no voice of gladness and no voice of pain. Then came the days of the invisible ash that had no heat but burned. The water was fouled and the plants parched and the flesh of men and animals seared. The long cool flames of the ash blasted the seeds and disfigured all things of beauty and grace, so that the trees clapped their hands in horror and shrank into the ground, the birds pulled away from the earth, disappearing into the sky. There were no moving shadows on the face of the land until the swarm of raiders came to plunder the bodies that lay like dung in the fields and on the cemented places. The moving shadows brought disease. Those who were not for the fire went to the fire's ash, and those who were not for the ash fell to the famine and disease."

When Ben was silent, Jeremy remained with his arms wrapped around his legs and his knees drawn up under his chin. "You don't really know what happened," he had started to say several times.

Jeremy wanted history, not myth. Dates, duration, megatonnage, extent of damage, and the name of the first offender. And knowing that, what would he know that Ben didn't know? He would know whom to blame. He needed to know whom to blame. But each time he started to interrupt, he was arrested by Ben's voice. Ben invoked no wrathful god or ungodly enemy. If there was a god in Ben's account, it was the power itself, a source of life as well as of destruction.

Jeremy listened to the sigh of the wind through the tall grass and the purl of the water over the stones. Finally he raised his head. "Why in the world would you want to re-create the power that could do that, Ben?"

The veil of fine wrinkles over Ben's face shifted as he grimaced with impatience. "Enough, Jermicho. Tell me about the place you have left."

Now it was Jeremy's turn to hesitate and scratch. How to explain what he didn't himself understand, to put it in a way that Ben might grasp? "Ben," Jeremy said slowly, "I was born during the time of plenty. I—"

Ben gasped. "The invisible ash could make you . . . ?"

"Just wait a minute, will you? I don't even know how long ago that was, from this time. . . . I don't know how old that would make me. You've lost track of time, and I'm lost *in* it. See, Ben, somehow I stepped outside my own time." He glanced at Ben and laughed uneasily at the look of incredulous bewilderment on the man's wrinkled face. "Nutsy Moran, huh? But I'm serious. I took a canoe trip from Cottage Grove one fine—well, no, one rainy morning in April, and paddled right into the future. And I guess I've been trying to paddle back ever since, which is why I've been so . . . absent." He tapped his head with a tentative smile.

"You paddled into the future?" said Ben.

"My future. Your present. Now."

"You come from the time of plenty, from the past." Ben looked impressed. "I didn't know that they could do that."

"Oh, they couldn't—we can't . . ." Jeremy got tangled up trying to belong to two places at once. "You must understand how absolutely incredible this is. Incredible. I'm sure I'm having a bad dream." He was a twentieth-century man, he believed in explanations psychological or physical. He looked helplessly up at the sky as if there might be some neglected principle of physics written there.

But to Ben, time traveling was less astonishing than the fact that Jeremy could come from the time of plenty without knowing how to make electricity. "You can look among the books," he said. "A man who reads cannot be entirely stupid, can he?" He labored to his feet and began to walk away. Then he turned, looked up at Jeremy, and clasped his hands, smiling with excitement.

Jeremy groaned. "I don't think you understand—"

"I understand only that we must have power. We have burned the fences. The furniture. The big poles. We burn the houses. When there is nothing left, we will burn the books. And then . . ." Ben stopped, averting his head.

"But there are hundreds of houses around us. And the trees are growing. Electricity isn't going to—"

"We must restore the power," Ben said angrily. He stopped and tugged at Jeremy's sleeve to make him bend closer. "You can see we haven't stabilized."

"Stabilized?" It seemed an odd word for Ben to use.

"Jeremy," Ben said in a fierce whisper. He actually glanced around to make sure that no one could overhear them, and Jeremy bent over him like a conspirator. "Jeremy, we are still dying!"

Jeremy knelt on the buckled road to grasp the shoulders of the valiant little man who had just confessed his most terrible secret. Ben, who kept them enduring and coping, who spoke with pride of Idamore's trees and Idamore's future, Ben did not believe that they would survive.

○ SIX ○

Jeremy, reading by the light of a fireplace and two candles, had spread before him Volume I, A–Byz, of the encyclopedia, open at "battery," and Volume VI, L–Met, open at "manganese dioxide." (A battery creates electrical energy from chemical energy. By staging a chemical reaction. Between two metals bathed in an acidic or alkaline solution. You have to use the right metals, of course. Pure zinc, for instance. Powdered manganese dioxide with granulated carbon. It probably doesn't matter if you don't know the chemical equations; can you find the metals?)

Also Volume II, C–Eye, open at "Edison, Thomas Alva." This volume also contained "electricity," "electric motor," "electric power," and "electrochemical reactions," but Jeremy was backing into the nineteenth century.

He was comfortable enough in the nineteenth century. The few science courses he'd taken had consisted largely of classroom re-enactments of the experiments by great nineteenth-century inventors. Michael Faraday and his rotating magnet, the joke about Volta's piles, and so on. Up to, well, say, Max Planck, though that was probably stretching it. Planck could relate the frequency of radiation to the quantum of energy possessed by that radiation, but Jeremy couldn't, and didn't care to.

Under "electromagnetism": "If the moving wire is forced to slide between two stationary contact wires parallel to v, then there will be a potential difference $V = El = vBl$ between the two wires. This difference can act as the electromagnetic force in a circuit connected between the terminal points." (A party of mountaineers started at the 4190-meter level and climbed to the top of Mont Blanc. It took them ten hours to reach the summit and return to their starting position, counting a one-hour rest at the top. If the party ascended at an average rate of 120 meters per hour and descended at an average of twice that rate, how many were in the party?)

Oh, the principles and problems were clear enough. Problem one: generate electricity. Problem two: transmit it. The principles: convert chemical or mechanical energy into electrical energy. Besides batteries, there are generators that convert mechanical energy into electrical energy. You need (1) a prime mover, a source of energy to (2) revolve a turbine, which in turn (3) rotates a wire loop around a magnet. How do you get a turbine whirling? Burn fossil fuels to create heated gases or steam. Scratch that—no fuel. Or use the heat generated by fission of nuclear fuels in a reactor. Forget that. Use flowing or falling water.

By dawn Jeremy had reached the end of the alphabet. Util–Zwingli. He had moved from the great inventions of the nineteenth century to those of the ancient world. Sixty-five B.C. King Mithradates has water mill.

Two thousand years to arrive at this? Jeremy Echo will resurrect from the wreckage around him the miracles of twentieth-century technology with a water wheel. In the dimness of early dawn Jeremy prowled the rooms of a late twentieth-century house, chuckling at its machines. His house had four radios, two televisions, a stereo, a home computer center, and a slide projector. Disposal, dishwasher, toaster, toaster-oven, and microwave. Electric pencil sharpener, jetstream tooth cleaner, vacuum, hair drier . . . Everywhere in the house, machines. He could feel them throbbing with potential, aching to convert electrical energy back into mechanical energy. The agitator of the washing machine, the drum of the drier. Fan belts and electric heating coils. The compressors that squeeze refrigerant liquids in the air conditioner and the refrigerator. He stood in the damp basement marveling at the house itself, with all its concealed wires for receiving alternating current, its underground and between-walls pipes for the flow and discharge of water. Ducts and flues and conduits of the essential: Heat. Light. Water.

He knew people who could do it. Their neighbor, Norm Peiffer, for instance, who came home from his high position at Federal Bank and worked around his house, rewiring, replacing pipes, repairing television sets, installing appliances. Norm Peiffer knew how things worked. Or that electrical engineer on Forrest Street. The mechanic at the Central Street gas station. Why, his own brother, Peter, the boy you'd most like to have along on a shipwreck, was better equipped than Jeremy for this . . . what was it? An adventure? A dream? A rescue mission?

Put his brother Peter in Jeremy's shoes, and maybe you *would* have an adventure. Like *Mysterious Island*. Silly story, a boy's fantasy. Men—only men—shipwrecked on an island, with one among them capable of doing anything, from making gunpowder to generating electricity. You don't ask how he hooked up the wires or made a vacuum bulb. You trust him: He has all of nineteenth-century science in his brain, a benevolent island at his fingertips, and plenty of time. Time, training, and tools. The quantum leaps of possibility springboarding off the continuity of learning. How many years did Luigi Galvani spend over twitching frogs' legs before he realized that he'd discovered not the mystery of life but the principle of the electrochemical cell? How many hours a day did Edison spend in his well-equipped lab?

"Why don't you wait until winter?" Helena had suggested to the two of them. "Jeremy is a good worker."

"Wait!" Ben had said, because he believed they were running out of time.

"Until winter!" Jeremy had said, because he didn't believe he would be with them through the winter.

Time: duration, interval, rate. Lifetime, having the time of your life. Time geologic and time cultural. "Back in the time of light," he had begun, feeling that he was relating some outlandish story in which all he could talk about was food.

"But tell us about the *power*," Ben had kept interrupting.

"Tell us about how babies were born and kept," said Maddy.

"Tell us how you spent your *time,* Jermicho," said Helena.

How had he spent his time? He remembered being terribly

busy, always pressed for time. If he spent the winter with them, how old would he be when he got back to Cottage Grove? Was he missing his final exams? Did it matter?

Jeremy stretched now to ease the ache in his back. Up all night delving the incomprehensible by poor light, and heavy physical work ahead. He wished there were coffee to brew. He plodded into the bathroom, turned on the tap, and cupped his hands under the faucet. In that expectant position he remained for a long moment, feeling the surprise physically—as if he'd tried to descend a step that wasn't there. Only his hands wilted, falling palms up against the dry porcelain. Frequently now he committed the gestures of old habits: waking in the night, he switched on the lights; in the morning, he glanced at the clock; thirsty, he went to the kitchen tap for a glass of water. Jeremy straightened slowly and looked in the mirror. Another habitual gesture: mirror gazing goes with washing, with shaving, with combing shampooed hair. He hadn't looked in a mirror for . . . for days. (He didn't know how long. Should he start making marks on the wall?) The man he saw in the mirror looked like a savage. Jeremy pressed his gums to see if they would bleed. A healthy savage.

He fetched some clothes from the closet, promising himself that today he would remember to look for a house that had once belonged to a bigger man. This man's clothes were a size too small for Jeremy. That was all Jeremy knew about him—that he wore size 9½ shoes and 14½–33 shirts. All his papers and much of his furniture had long since gone for firewood. And if Jeremy failed to make electricity, the house itself would be taken apart: first the moldings and the doors, then the stairs, the floors, the fascia. Dismantled thus, the mortar would quickly deteriorate, and you could get the studs between the walls. Unless the carpenter ants got them first. There were an awful lot of bugs to compete with, Jeremy thought, unconsciously scratching.

He had to go through the books—all the books that Ben had saved, all the houses that had books—hunting for the ones that he needed. Something like *Basic House Wiring,* which Jeremy had found frustratingly useful because it stopped short at the "service entrance," the special door by which the servant power entered the house. He wouldn't mind going through the books, for he was a browsing, meditative sort of person. But with the best will and all the time in the world, he wasn't sure he could turn himself into an engineer. Oh, he might contrive a current flowing through wires between a magnet, but electricity for cooking? For winter heating?

He stood on the back porch, his nostrils flaring at the rich smells of the moist dawn air. The birds were beginning their first tentative cheeps against the silence, and the sky was swelling with the pink glow of imminent sunrise. Uninterrupted by tall trees, the sky seemed vast, extending limitlessly, dwarfing the low, flat earth. Jeremy put his hands into his pockets and looked up at the stately procession of clouds.

"You sent the wrong guy, you idiot." His voice was mild, almost jovial: He didn't believe in God. Or at least not in a domesticated personal God whom you could address, who helped you win basketball games or get into the college of your choice. God was Jeremy's metaphor for the inexplicable. Beyond the dictates of every physical law, Jeremy was here, and "here" was not a place but a time. And he was the wrong man for the job. "I think you meant my brother, Peter Towers," he said to the empty sky.

He took a bucket and padded toward the tubs of water at the back of the house where Helena and Maddy lived. The tubs were utility sinks removed from basements and put outside to catch rainwater and provide a convenient place to empty buckets from the pond. Jeremy stopped suddenly, looking from the tubs to the roof. Suppose you put the tubs on the roof? he thought. Easy enough with a pully. And hooked them into one big central pipe? He smiled and broke into a song he'd often sung at the Unitarian Church. "Blackbird has spoken, like the first bird," he warbled happily as he approached the house. "Praise for the morning . . ."

Maddy was sitting on the metal porch swing, rocking lightly back and forth. "Well, you're up before the birds, Jermicho," she said with a listless wave.

"You too, Maddy. Feeling okay?"

Maddy nodded with her taut, brave smile. Jeremy moved the

screen door that was placed over the tubs to keep out dirt and insects. He dipped his bucket and squatted by it to drink thirstily from his cupped hands, then sluice water over his face and neck. He wiped his hands on his shirt and smiled at Maddy.

"Could you bring me some water, Jeremy?" Maddy asked apologetically.

"The moon, Maddy." His extravagance was meant to check her tendency to apologize for asking the smallest favors. He took the steps two at a time to get a plastic glass from the kitchen, then vaulted off the porch to the ground. Returning more slowly with the full glass, he looked anxiously at her pale face. It was veiled with perspiration. Off he flew again, fetching a towel to wet with the cool water. As he sat beside her, he stopped bustling. The still atmosphere around the pregnant woman enveloped him. Gently he wiped her face, then held the cool cloth to her forehead. She murmured gratefully and let her head fall against his shoulder. "What else can I do? Is there anything I can get you?"

"Mmm-nnn." Her stillness was like an injunction: Be calm, be strong. He held her, rocking the swing smoothly.

"Ah!" said Maddy. She took Jeremy's hand and placed it on her belly. Surprised by the feel of it, he spread his fingers. Somehow he'd thought it was soft, like fat, this swelling. It was as rigid and smooth as old tire rubber. Undulating against it, pushing and bumping beneath Jeremy's hand, the baby swam and kicked. With his fingers spread and listening, Jeremy watched the sun rise.

"Well, sun's up," Maddy said after a while. She stirred, but he held her.

"A little while yet," he protested. He was half asleep over her and reluctant to move. "No one's up yet." He took a mental survey of the sleepers in the houses around them. Big blond matronly Lily and tiny fierce Rachel were in the adjacent house with crazy Rose and the two boys, Jules and August. Upstairs was Helena. Helena, with her bleeding gums and her richly inflected voice, smooth as amber. Across the field was tiny gnarled Ben, who had somehow been delegated leader. Mute Mick with his trembling head and his palsied liver-spotted hands. Dave with the raw patches where the skin came off his face . . . "Maddy," said Jeremy, suddenly wakeful with curiosity. "Who's the baby's father?"

"Jermicho, sometimes you're so strange," Maddy said with a reedy chuckle.

"No, really, who is?"

"Why, the Federal Man, of course. Who else?"

"Oh," he said blankly. "Pearl's too?" Against his arm her head moved. Pearl's too. A shudder passed wriggling through his shoulders. He pressed his cheek sadly against Maddy's tangled sour hair. "Oh, Maddy," he whispered sadly. "Oh, Maddy."

∘ SEVEN ∘

Helena stood at the far edge of the pond with her hands on her hips. She was reluctant to step into the numbing water, and lingered, staring over the dark surface rilled here and there by the breeze and by the skimmers darting on their little outrigger legs. This was the hard time, she thought—not winter, when you thought you were going to die, but spring, when you hoped you were going to live. She had dug roots when the ground was frozen and the wind flayed her fingers. Why should it be so hard today, with the sun warm on her back, to wade into the black water and squish around for lily roots? Because the birds were flying and the land was greening like a promise of plenty. It was hard to wait any longer.

Not far from Helena, Rose rooted on her hands and knees, babbling to herself as she pulled up chickweed and clover and comfrey. Someone would have to sort what she gathered, Helena knew, for Rose was not reliable when her voices distracted her. She could bring baskets of dogbane, talking in an odd voice about bones or stones or the man with the green breath.

Rose had had no voices, not even her own, when she first came to Idamore. The Federal Man had brought her from Oakton. He was the sad one who rescued even broken people. Before Rose, he had brought Mick from . . . oh, where was it? She mustn't forget anything. She must remember everything she heard and saw. . . . Of course, Cottage Grove. "Last survivor," the Federal Man had said each time. He had thrown his schedule off by weeks, keeping Mick in isolation down in Township to make sure Mick's palsy wasn't a disease he'd bring into Idamore. Yes, he was a nice one, a maker and keeper of people. He brought Mick, and he made Laurel; he brought Rose, and he made May. Rose and Helena were about the same age when Rose arrived, but the baby May had talked before Rose did. Rose was silent until her first blood. Then there were ten voices where none had been.

Ben used to spend hours with Rose. "Tell me what the voices say, Rose." Patient, hopeful Ben. He had thought her voices were like the invisible voices in the air, wanting only wires. That if he fine-tuned her, she'd open her mouth and out would come clear directions about the power. Helena had never doubted Ben until that time, and then the doubt had come like a wall collapsing over her: If Ben was looking for guidance from that tortured, broken girl, then Ben didn't know how to bring back the light or the time of plenty. Ben didn't know anything at all, and Simon was gone! Helena had become hostile and defiant, and it was many seasons before she recognized the skill with which Ben had converted her long defiance into useful labor. He had placed Simon's responsibilities on her shoulders, and she had never even felt the weight. And then, just as she did feel it, the weight shifted and she saw how much of it Ben bore. Now she and Ben were a team, perfectly matched and balanced, tone for tone, skill for skill, sometimes hauling against each other, but rarely in opposite directions.

Behind her Rose was arguing. "Oh, I couldn't do that. Build a whole house of bones? Pluck the teeth. Root the hair. . . ."

Ben would have knelt by the woman and held her face in his small gnarled hands. "Look at me, Rose," Ben would have said. But cold water also worked. Helena splashed at her, shouting.

"Rose! Pay attention." Rose looked up, smiling vaguely and extending a bunch of clover to Helena. "Fine," Helena said. "Keep at it."
    With one convulsive shiver Helena waded into the water. She
kept her mind on the warm spot on top of her head as she wriggled
in the mud, feeling with her toes for the tubers. She watched Jeremy
Echo and Ben walking around with the big brown book, stopping to
look at it, Jeremy shaking his head each time Ben nodded. Ben was
as small as a midday shadow cast by the big man. For two days now
they had been arguing, and Helena could see they were still at it.
Jeremy stopped and bent at the waist to speak, angrily scissoring his
arms. Ben pointed at the river, then at a house. Suddenly Jeremy
seized Ben under the arms and held him up, shaking him. Helena
watched, grinning. She had often wanted to do that, she realized. To
bring Ben up to eye level and give him a good shake.
    Ben needed to be forced to listen to what Jeremy was saying; so
far he had heard only what he wanted to hear. What he chose to
hear coincided with the Federal Man's picture of what they must
do: restore the power and restore the ancient division of labor. The
Federal Man made it sound like a delicate puzzle that would fit
together all at once. "After we stabilize each sector," he promised.
"Till then, you must wait." Each year there was a different excuse
for the delay. "Trouble with the communications system," he said,
or "Breakdown in the transport sector." "Well, Carbonville's out
again. Epidemic. We'll start 'er up again in the spring. You must
wait. You must be patient."
    They had waited, they had been patient. They watched him
carry off portions of the food they had worked so hard to raise,
because Idamore must do its part. If Idamore did its part, soon all
the pieces of the puzzle would come together. *Click,* there would be
coal from Carbonville, salt from Freehold across the great lake.
They could picture that exchange; and from there Ben transported
them to a vision of Idamore with lights burning in every house, its
buildings bursting with food and fodder for the animals, and the
two factories down there on the edge of town manufacturing something to send to the south and across the great lake. They believed
in that vision of Idamore. "The glory of the light shone on a great

city. That time is coming again." Not that they could picture themselves in it—it was too vague, too removed from the Idamore they worked—but it was what they were waiting for.

Even when she had doubted Ben and distrusted the Federal Man, Helena had believed in Ben's vision. She didn't anymore. Jeremy had unwittingly demonstrated its impossibility with his ignorance and his misunderstandings. "The south" to Jeremy did not mean Carbonville, but a winterless place where sugar and cotton and oranges grew. Electric power used to come from the south— her south, around Carbonville—where they split little rocks. Particles, Jeremy called them, but he didn't know how to split them in that special way. Well, he did not know how to do any of the things Ben presumed everyone could do in the time of plenty. Everything Jeremy said indicated a vast complicated web—thousands of people and huge amounts of space— in which everyone worked at a task essential to others, who couldn't do that task but performed others. The words in the wires came from studios, transmitted by people who knew how to do that. Some people worked metal and sent it to other people who made parts, which were sent to other people who made cars and planes and machines. Food, too, was treated like parts, grown here and there in batches, and taken to other places by people who could fly airplanes or drive trucks, which were built and repaired by other kinds of people and fueled by oil that was pumped from the ground by still other kinds of people. Well, it would be a cold day in hell before Idamore was a spoke in that wheel; by the time they had enough people, no one would know how to perform the tasks.

But Ben was determined not to hear what Helena heard. Last night, when Jeremy demonstrated the generation of electricity, Ben did not see what Helena saw. Jeremy had taken apart a house machine and removed a magnet, which he mounted on a bar with a crank handle. He coiled some wire and stuck it around the magnet, and attached the ends of the wire to a flashlight bulb. "Okay," he said with that look—scary, the angry stubbornness of that look—"okay, all you have to do is turn the handle fast enough to . . ." He cranked the handle, and the bulb lit up. "Ahhh," went the deep awed murmur around the room. Mick made queer sounds in his throat—"Uh, uh, uh"—and when Helena looked at him there were tears streaming down his cheeks, which he wiped clumsily with his shaking hand. Helena put her arm around his shoulder and said he should have first turn at cranking. Everyone had a turn, grinning because the faster they turned, the brighter the bulb. Oh, it was wonderful, God, it was wonderful, cranking away there, making light! They jostled each other to have a turn, joking to see who could turn the hardest for the longest time. "My God," said Ben, "is it so simple?"

"It's that simple," said Jeremy grimly. "We just generated enough electricity to light a flashlight. If we all crank all night, maybe we can get the refrigerator cold. But I doubt it."

Ben saw only the simplicity of the procedure. Helena understood that Jeremy had meant to demonstrate something else—not just the principle, but the scale of the undertaking. "Couldn't you just . . ." and "All you have to do is . . ." Ben kept saying, and Jeremy would groan and extend his arms to show how much more was necessary.

Helena found the tubers and pried them up with her toes. Now she had to bend into the water to retrieve them. She shrank from it only for a moment, trying to extend her arm without getting her breasts wet, then yielded to it, plunging in to her shoulders. Behind her Rose said, "Use the lungs for bellows, the stomachs for bags. Twine the veins and weave the hair."

"I'll weave *your* hair, Rose, if you pick any dogbane today," commented Helena.

Then she saw Jules and August coming from the direction of the river. Bellowing in his cow voice, Jules was dragging the younger boy by the hand. August walked with his head thrown awkwardly back and his mouth open, tripping and stumbling in Jules' firm grasp. No one said out loud what they were all beginning to suspect: that Rachel's son August was like Pearl's son—retarded. Helena waited for a moment to see what adult was behind them, then frowned. They had been down at the river alone, then, or Ben was so busy arguing with Jeremy Echo about the stupid power that he'd forgotten to watch them. . . . She waded out of the water, dripping and martyred, to fetch the two children. "Come play over here," she said impatiently. "And don't move."

"Are there clams?" asked Jeremy Echo as he came to the pond. With a comical screech, Helena lobbed a tuber at him. It hit his chest, spattering mud over his shirt. He turned the root with his foot, then shrugged. "You look like you're digging for clams. Shall I help?"

"Well, yes, you might help. You like baths," she teased. She unbuttoned her shirt, which was heavy and cold with water, and when she looked up, he was hurrying across the field. Helena shook her head at his retreating back. Not retarded, as she had first thought, but certainly strange. Had he forgotten his offer as soon as he said it? With a memory like that, it was a wonder that he could complete chores. With a memory like that, you'd forget what you were doing before you started it.

Well, but he must have a memory, or he wouldn't be able to read. She and Ben worked at reading during the winter, so she knew how hard it was, what a special kind of memory it required. Laurel had that kind of memory, Helena knew, for the girl grasped the strings of black letters more quickly than she did. Helena herself was better at it than Ben, who seemed to remember things that went through his ears rather than through his eyes.

Ben remembered what he heard. That was because of Paul, whom Helena thought of as "Father," though he was Ben and Simon's father. One of Helena's earliest memories was of Paul reading to the boys while they worked a field. Somehow Helena thought she remembered riding everywhere with Paul in his wheelchair, but probably only because she had been told that she spent her infancy on his lap. He followed the round of the children's labors with a book, reading, incessantly reading out loud to them. Even after he was too weak for the wheelchair, he had a bed improvised in the field so he could remind them of the urgency of his mission. "Say it, Ben. 'The Lord is my shepherd, I shall not want.' You must remember the octet *exactly*, Simon! Say it again." His voice getting weaker, and his body against Helena's getting bonier and developing a strange smell, he had kept himself alive long past the time he might comfortably have died. Helena had taken her first steps beside his field bed, pulling herself up by the bars as another child might once have used the edge of a playpen. She remembered the bars of that bed. And the smell of his body. The sound of his voice. And most of all she remembered Simon coming over to them and touching the down on Helena's head, but looking only at his father. "Rest now, Father. Rest now. It's not that important." Paul said it was as important as food. But he argued only once that children should be permitted time away from the fields. Just before he died, he made a mysterious remark: "Allison was right." Apparently it didn't matter who was right; children had to work in the fields or starve.

Helena could read the children's books that she had collected from the various houses. She and Laurel learned together, piecing the puzzles from simple picture books. A, apple. B, butterfly. But there were too many strange animals and queer shapes and peculiar machines. She reached a point at which she stuck, past which she could not go, and at which Ben fussed and dithered. Ben's method was painstaking and hopeless: They took the first section of Genesis, which Ben knew by heart, and compared the printed words to the ones that Ben said out loud. "'In the beginning God created the heaven and the earth,'" Ben said, and Helena read, "'In the beginning' . . . this next word is not 'God,' Ben. The next word is 'of.'"

"It can't be," said Ben.

And Helena would struggle on, trying to read the word "God" into the word "of," knowing it was wrong and feeling somewhat as Laurel must feel when faced with a mushroom. They had not understood what they were doing wrong until Jeremy read the Bible they were using. "'In the beginning of creation, when God made heaven and earth,'" he read, "'the earth was without form and void, with darkness over the face of the—'"

"No," said Ben.

"What do you mean, no?" said Jeremy. "You want me to read this or not?"

"It's not the way I know it," said Ben, looking defensively at Helena.

"You must've learned a different translation, that's all," Jeremy said, and he read on, so easily, so quickly. "'Let there be lights in the vault of heaven to separate day from night, and let them serve as signs—'"

"'And for seasons, and for days, and for years,'" sighed Ben.

"Close," said Jeremy with a smile.

Now Ben had Jeremy half hysterical looking through books all night. "Find the Bible I know," Ben had asked him. "What book is this? Read this to us. Look up electricity. Look up leavening agents. Look up salt. Do you know a writer named Shakespeare, who wrote sonnets? Read a sonnet."

Helena puzzled over Jeremy Echo as she grasped the lily roots between her toes, crooked them up to her hand, and tossed them to the edge of the pond. Perhaps Jeremy had compartments, as Rose did. Rose had different voices, and he had different kinds of re-membering. He could remember words read, but not words said, maybe? How else to explain a man who offered to help you dig tubers and then walked away? Who repeated everything you said to him as if he were turning it over before taking it into his head?

Each time Helena stood, the cold water streamed down her chest, and the sun was warm on her shoulders. She squinted into the bright sky. Getting time to be wearing hats? Not yet. The tubers were still soft with starch, and the first crop was only to her ankle. Oh, but everything was going well—the days were warm, with just enough rain, some of the trees were almost as tall as she was, and Laurel was learning the mushrooms.

Helena waded out of the water and gathered the tubers into her basket. She took off her jeans, wrung them out, and spread them out on the grass. Then she spread out her shirt and lay down. Jules and August were still there, plucking and patting the grass; Rose was gathering comfrey as she muttered to herself; everything was going so well. "I am a plant," Helena said to herself, "absorbing sun. I will grow and live a long time. A very long time."

Overhead a flock of martins bobbed on the buoyant air, catching insects as they flew, calling "Tee-hee, tee-tee." Ah, Helena thought, but sometimes I wish I was a bird instead. A martin with a pointed tail like the tail of the peculiar and wonderful black jacket that hung in a closet of her house. "Martin," she said out loud, smiling. That's what they would call Maddy's baby. Not April or May or August, giving the child a month name assigned by the Federal Man, to whom time was so important. Not Rose or Lily or Laurel, though those were fine, rooted names. But Martin. And maybe he'd grow up to be free. A winged creature. And they'd call Pearl's baby . . . hmmm. "Grackle," she said. The word sounded like her laugh, which started in her throat. "Grackle, cackle, caw," went the laugh, moving down to her chest, then into her belly. And she lay there on her back, whooping and stomping her foot against the stubbly grass.

Something soft fell on her, and she let out a shriek as she clawed it off. "Sorry I startled you," said Jeremy, once again walking away. "I brought you a dry shirt. Put it on. I need your advice."

"I thought you put on a thinking *hat*," she said.

"Huh?"

"Is this a *thinking* shirt?"

"I'm in no mood for jokes, Laney."

They were obviously having one of their misunderstandings, so Helena fell silent, buttoning the large shirt stiff with soap and fresh air. "I have on the shirt," she said, but Jeremy continued to pace around the edge of the pond with his hands in his pockets.

"I need to know what's important," he said as he paced past her. "I don't know what's important anymore."

"Are you talking to me or to yourself?" she asked, getting up to pace beside him.

"Do you know how long it will take me to build a dam? And that's just the necessary first step, a purely physical labor. Then there's a wheel. Where do I get a wheel, and how do I mount it? And supposing I get a wheel and do mount it, how do I build a generator big enough to supply electricity for thirteen people—"

"Fourteen," she said.

"—and for what, exactly? That's the question. What exactly is this for?"

"You can't do it, can you?"

"Oh, well, I probably could if I had enough time. I'd need to find the right books, and I'd need to wander all the hell over the place looking for a wheel and a generator. There's no mechanic on the corner to give me advice, so it'd be a lot of trial and error. And a *lot* of time." He flopped down on his belly, fingering weeds and poking in the dirt. "Sometimes when I'm with Ben, I get to believing that if I generate electricity, we'll have everything else—processed cheese and refined bread, for God's sake. And then I stop and think, what *is* it for? To run a washing machine, when we have no running water and the soap we have would clog the machine? To light electric bulbs when we're too tired to read at night? So Lily can run a vacuum in a house that she shares with chickens? You understand, Laney?" He nibbled at a piece of clover, then pulled up a handful of chickweed and ate it.

"I think so," she said slowly, looking at the way the dark hair lay smooth across the muscled flesh of his forearm. Almost she reached out to stroke the hair and touch the arm, and then stammered in confusion. "I—uh—yes ... Oh dear, oh my." Suddenly she wanted to go away from him. He was a big male, taller and fuller than the Federal Man. More addlepated, but younger, stronger. Maler. Not to be treated like a woman, with the exchange of soft, long touches. "You ever make a baby, Jermicho?" Helena asked, standing over his prone body.

Jeremy sighed wearily. "No, I've never made a baby. Come on, Laney, pay attention. I need someone sensible to bounce ideas off. Listen, I thought we'd make a list of the things we need."

Helena felt almost comfortable again: He was not like the Federal Man; he was like Ben. She sat cross-legged beside him and looked at the stubby pencil and folded paper he pulled from his pocket. "*Ba*—what does it say?"

"*Basic House Wiring.* I tore out the front page. Well, other people have torn out pages from better books than this ..." he began defensively, then laughed. "Better in this case means more useless, I'm beginning to think. Guess what's first on my list."

"Salt?"

He shook his head. "No, no, I'm making a list of things we can do for ourselves; I don't know any way we can manufacture salt—

"Oh, I know. A bath."

"Right. Hot running water. I had flush toilets listed, but I decided that the composting is probably pretty important. What do you think?"

It took Helena a while to warm to this interesting game. She kept suggesting things they couldn't make—animals to help in the field, sugarcane so they'd have something sweet. "Well, what *can* we make, Jermicho?"

"Talking to you, I realize there's not much we can make that's really crucial. But I think I can rig a wheel to pump water, and we could refit the houses with some solar collectors for heat. That would take the pressure off the wood supply some. And maybe we could find some old Franklin stoves—something besides the fireplaces for heating and cooking. Or even—I read about some guy who outfitted a cabin with two oil drums. The fire burned inside one, and he rigged a—you know, just a flat piece of metal over it for cooking?—and then he routed the hot smoke into a second drum, which helped heat the room. Hell, if we think about this right, there's a lot we could do." Jeremy paused, studying the houses and the fields. "Helena, I can't understand why you haven't done more. How come Ben's got this all-or-nothing idea about the power?"

"Bo-bo-bo-bo," moaned Jules, his flat moon face held up to the sun, his body rocking slightly to some interior music. August was staggering around, falling and getting up again, paddling the air. Helena studied August as she considered Jeremy's question. "What you're saying is against the law," she finally replied. "You're telling us to . . . um, recede?"

"Recede!"

"No, secede. That's it. Local isolationism, the Federal Man calls it. Jeopardize the collective effort with local isolationism."

"Oh, Christ."

"Secede and go off on our own, so that we'd have nothing to look forward to? Nothing but what we could do for ourselves?"

"Show me what the Federal Man has done, Helena. Show me."

"What do you know about it, Jeremy? How long have you been here? What do you know about our dreams? Oh, I'm not saying you're wrong. It's a matter of degree. One winter—it was three, maybe four winters ago—the Federal Man took the usual amount of food and lambs, but we'd had a bad season. Oh, God, it really was bad," Helena said, clenching her fists at the memory of it. "And, oh, I . . ." Jeremy heard the effort with which she controlled her voice, and his heart went out to her, for he'd never heard her complain or cry. He took her fist between his hands and stroked the rough skin. "No, not that part," she said, thrusting the memory off and taking back her hand. "I told Ben we should hide some of the food and a few of the lambs. I said it was a question of survival, not isolationism. Ben and I quarreled all through that spring."

"Who won?"

"I did," she said with a queer crooked smile.

"So he takes food from you."

"Only for the winter. For the others . . ."

"For the collective effort," said Jeremy bitterly.

"Ben said I was withholding just because I was angry at the Federal Man. He said it was just because my first baby was stillborn. But Maddy lost hers that winter, too. And all of us almost starved. . . ."

"How old are you, Laney?" Jeremy asked. He had taken her for eighteen, maybe twenty; awfully young to have carried a child as long as three—maybe four—winters ago. Immediately he wanted to bite his tongue, for this was the one question he had finally learned not to ask. Questions about time made them vague and embarrassed or irritable. But apparently Helena hadn't even heard him; she had curled up, hugging her legs against her chest, so taut that Jeremy hesitated to comfort her for fear she'd fly apart. "Really bad, huh?" he said, because that was the worst he'd ever heard from her.

"I don't blame them. I don't blame them. We were starving. But surely it was reason enough to keep some food for ourselves. To have lambs to eat, you understand? To have corn to keep the chickens alive, so we'd have eggs. Well, we eat the young and unborn. We eat eggs, we eat baby sheep. Well, we do, so how can I blame them? We were starving. We lost three that winter, plus the two babies." She looked at him, her brown eyes wide and dry and fierce. "We ate them, Jeremy. We ate them all. That's how I won my argument with Ben. Because we became savages while we were waiting for the Federal Man to resurrect the light."

Jeremy closed his eyes and put his forehead against the ground.

"You are . . . disgusted? I disgust you? I was sick that winter, Jeremy, I didn't even know—"

"Oh, Helena, no. I'm . . . sad." They would have to do, the simple words, the words Helena used—bad, sad, glad. A girl fourteen—maybe fifteen—bears a child gladly in a bad time, then finds that she has been sustained by her child. Who was he, indeed, to judge their dream of the future, that myth of the past? Without dreams, would they have a reason to live, a way of surviving the crimes they committed against themselves in order to live? It felt to Jeremy as if he, the dreamer, had been dreamed up, summoned from the time of plenty, the time of light. He might be their ancestor—if he returned to Cottage Grove and lived a normal life. And he had come to them with nothing to offer, no wisdom, no aid. "I will never have children," Jeremy said suddenly, pounding his fist against the ground.

"Ah well, it doesn't matter, Jermicho. Who'd want to be a Federal Man, anyhow?"

Jeremy turned on his side to question her, but he was too tired to pursue another one of the strange side roads they meandered in their cross-purposed conversations.

"Do you think August is acting more strangely than usual?" Helena asked. She shouted for the boy to come back, for he was headed—falling and getting up, falling and getting up—back toward the river. "Oh, damn," Helena muttered, standing up. "Lil-eee," she yelled, making Jeremy wince. "Turn August around, will you?"

"My God, I should never have lain down. I'm exhausted."

She wiggled a muddy foot against his ribs. "Up. Work for your dinner."

"Ruthless," he complained as he got to his feet.

Helena picked up the basket of tubers, said something admonitory to Rose, and walked beside Jeremy toward the houses. "He doesn't know any of what I told you, you know," she said, pointing at the sky. "When he comes, I wouldn't want you to somehow say anything—"

"What?! Does he fly?" exclaimed Jeremy, gaping up at the sky. Nothing about the Federal Man seemed impossible or even unlikely anymore. This added a new dimension to the protean figure who had taken shape in Jeremy's mind. Now Jeremy imagined him landing delicately, toe first, his blue cape fluttering behind his powerful broad shoulders, lantern-jawed and benign as George Washington, his brow dark and evil, and his hand like Napoleon's tucked inside his shirt.

"In a—" Helena twirled her finger, and her laugh began to percolate. *Nngghh-nngghh. Ruck-ruck-ruck.* Jeremy's mouth quivered just to listen to her. Melting amber? Nothing so lovely. She doubled over, slapping her thigh and pointing at him. "Does he fly?" she whooped. Jeremy tucked his hands under his armpits and flapped around, squawking and yucking.

All over the village they heard Helena and Jeremy laughing. Lily pressed her hand against August's sweating forehead and looked up smiling. Pearl was between labor contractions, and she turned her head against the pillow, smiling. Rachel and Maddy smiled at each other across Pearl's bed. Mick looked up from his hoe, the tremor in his head stilled for a moment as he listened. "Uh-uh-uh," he said in his cracked whisper to Ben. Ben rested his chin on the sawed-off handle of his hoe.

"I know," he said, smiling at Mick. "That's Helena's gift, and she doesn't even know what she gives."

◦ EIGHT ◦

Jeremy ignored the noisy scuffle behind him as he squatted beside August, who lay on Lily's lap. Drenched with sweat and tears and saliva, the child was distilling himself at every pore. His eyes were unfocused, the pupils constricted. Helena was screaming at the older boy, shaking him by the shoulders. Jules was passive in Helena's grasp, his head rolling and snapping to her vicious jerks. "What did he eat? What did he eat?" she kept yelling at Jules.

"Stop it," cried Ben, tearing at Helena's hands and scratching her arms. "Stop it, you impatient, worthless girl, stop."

Jeremy frowned at Lily. "I'm taking him to the hos—" As he spoke, Jeremy completed a little gyre: He rose full of purpose, acting on his first instinct—to get help for this medical emergency; he wheeled around as he fathomed the depth of their isolation—no car, no phone, no hospital, no help anywhere; then sank back to his squatting position beside August. "Did you make him vomit?" he asked Lily.

"No. I wasn't sure to do that, or to give him some milk."

"Do we have any milk?"

"No," she said with downcast eyes.

"So. There we are." Lily nodded, and Jeremy took August under his arm. "Sorry, old man," said Jeremy, as he slid his fingers down the slippery soft passage of August's throat. August gagged and gagged until Jeremy himself was ready to be sick; then, with a last protesting cough, he spewed forth the half-digested mushrooms.

"Better do it again," said Helena.

"*You* do it again," he snapped at her. "Get him a drink of water so he has something to bring up." He went over to Jules to examine his oriental but blue eyes, his round face with the idiotic, oddly sweet expression. "You didn't eat any of the mushrooms, did you? Smart kid," said Jeremy, rumpling his hair.

"Buh-buh-buh-buh," said Jules, rocking sadly from foot to foot.

"I think Augie'll be okay," Jeremy called to Rachel, who was holding on to the porch railing with both hands and staring white-faced at her son. She turned toward Jeremy, her tiny sharp face framed by a dark nimbus of wildly curling hair. Through narrowed eyes she looked at him, a glance that turned Jeremy into an astonished stone. Then, almost in slow motion, as if she were miming some important message, she lifted her hands from the porch railing and shrugged.

Jeremy continued to stare at her even after she released him and turned her eyes to the others. "What?" he murmured. He looked from Rachel to August and back again. "What?" Rachel went back into the house, leaving Jeremy staring at the place where she had been.

Helena was scolding as she helped August drink the water. "I should have noticed, Lily. I mean, I *did* notice. Oh, Lily, I *did* notice. . . . Whoopsee-do, good boy, Augie. Ahhh, you'll feel better soon." Jeremy listened to her resinous voice through the sound of August's retching. Lily said something in an undertone, and Helena said, "Yes, exactly. That was exactly what I was thinking. A kid eats some poison mushrooms and you decide that he's retarded. Oh boy."

"How old is August?" asked Jeremy.

"Aw, Jermicho . . ." began Lily in a whine.

"Oh. I mean . . . Laney, was he born that winter you just told me about?"

"Yes. He's three. Or is it four now? We should keep track," she remarked to Lily.

Lily shrugged. "Call this year one?"

"Well, we could. Why not?" said Helena with a sad laugh. "You look terrible, Jermicho. I don't think you can go without sleep."

He was once again staring at the porch, trying to reckon the meaning of Rachel's look, Rachel's shrug. What had it been like, that winter? What had it been like to bear a child that survived when the others died? To have dined on horror for the sake of a child that might be retarded . . . an extra mouth to feed, a useless member of a crippled community, a son. The love she bore this child must be as complex and cruel as diamonds. The porch swam before his eyes.

"Jeremy," said Helena, hearing his stifled anguished sounds. "Oh, Jeremy, don't. Augie's all right. Everything's all right. Oh," she said, wringing her hands as Jeremy staggered to the porch and rested his head against the railing. "Oh, Lily."

"He's just overtired," said Lily. "Come here, pet, come sit with Lily for a little rest." She led Jeremy onto the porch steps and sat rocking on her haunches, cooing and patting and smoothing. He rested against the big-boned woman, sobbing with helplessness and pain and exhaustion. "A miracle a day, that's Jeremy Echo," cooed Lily. "He makes light, he saves lives. Now he gets to rest. There, there, pet, it's all right." A little later she led him to the couch in Rachel's living room, where he fell immediately and deeply asleep and dreamed that he was sailing a tiny boat with a bright-red sail on a horizonless lake glittering with sunlight.

He was awakened by Helena's low voice. "Baby's coming," she said, shaking him. "Wake up, Jermicho. Baby's coming." The sun had set, so he had no idea what time of day it was. On the hearth were two cups with sputtering tallow candles that gave the room a soft glow and a musky smell.

"Baby?" he said groggily. He sat up, rubbing the small of his back where a broken spring had impaled him. "Baby?" he said more sharply. "Oh, I can't . . . No, I can't help with that."

"Hurry," Helena whispered, already starting back to the bedroom. "I let you sleep to the last minute."

Jeremy went out the front door to urinate on the street—nothing edible grew on the street—and when he came back, it was all over. Pearl had delivered a big healthy baby girl. The entire population of Idamore had been gathered in that bedroom, and it now swirled around the living room, quietly celebrating. "Phoebe," Helena was saying in a combative but jovial way to Ben.

"Well, okay, if Pearl likes it. Phoebe." Ben grinned. "Phoebe, the flycatcher. That's wonderful, Laney."

"Tell Maddy to get off her feet. Look at Maddy's ankles," said Lily, popping into the living room and then out again.

Maddy's face was flushed with pleasure, her smile more relaxed and genuine than Jeremy had ever seen. She sank awkwardly onto the couch and put her swollen feet on the chair that Rachel brought. "Why, Jeremy," Maddy said, looking at him with surprise. "You missed it!"

"I had to pee," he said with a sheepish smile.

Maddy giggled. "You'll have lots of time to do that when it's my turn. I'm not so fast as Pearl."

"Tea, Jermicho?" said Rachel. She held a battered metal tray with seven chipped cups on it, and kept her head bent over it.

"Thank you, Rachel," he said in a formal way. He stared at the dark swirl of hair, willing her to raise her head, but she bent even further to extend the tray to Maddy. She had broken him today— he had snapped as cleanly as brittle board across the sharp knee of her shrug, and he wanted to be acknowledged. She moved past him, servile and bent. "Yecch, I hate this tea," Jeremy said. Then Rachel paused, shook back her hair, and looked at him. It was a complicated gaze, defiant, embarrassed, grateful, apologetic, friendly.

"August is better."

"I'm glad, Rachel," said Jeremy. He felt as if they had just solemnly shaken hands.

Lily entered the room with the baby in her arms. "What gift shall we give this child?" she asked in a ceremonial voice, her long, loose face creased with joy.

"We give this child her name," said Ben, standing next to Lily, his head even with her elbow. "We call her Phoebe."

"We give her a name with wings," said Helena. Then, casting a quick grin at Jeremy, she added, "So she may fly without metal."

"Uh, uh, uh," whispered Mick, fluttering his hands around his throat.

"I don't understand, Mickey," said Ben.

"We give her a name with song," interpreted Lily, her eyes glistening.

"A wonderful gift," said Ben, nodding.

"Oh, yes," said Helena, giving Mick a hug and continuing across the room to Jeremy as if she were going to hug him, too. She stopped short in front of him. "You asked me what was important? *This* is important."

Jeremy nodded. He was deeply moved, and did not want to break the spell of the moment with one of their crooked discrepant conversations. Helena's dark eyes flashed in the erratic glow of the candles, and the thin planes of her face were softened by shadows. For a moment he pictured her half naked, lean as a boy, the nipples of her small breasts crinkled with cold. He saw her lying in the tall grass laughing her wonderful shrieking laugh. He tried to turn away, as he had turned away in the field, frowning at himself, but he could not take his eyes off her.

As Helena stared back at him, a puzzled frown flitted across her face and she backed away from him. "I have to . . . um, help. . . ." She hurried across the room, fluttered around Rose for a moment, then settled on the floor beside Rachel. The two women whispered together, and Rachel stroked Helena's arm, nodding.

Jeremy watched them with a thrill of sexual horror. "Oh, I get it," he murmured. "Oh, pretty." But he was the one made ugly: rawboned and crude and full of ungainly yearning. He gulped his tea and shuddered. "Give Pearl my congratulations," he said to Maddy as he headed for the back door.

That night Jeremy decided that he would not winter with them if he could possibly help it, and the next day he went about restoring Idamore to the twentieth century with the furious stubbornness of a man working for his freedom. He had the vague notion that if he performed a certain number of tasks, he would be released from this enchantment. Three tasks, it should be—like in a fairy tale. Each task more impossible than the last.

First, he was going to construct a solar water heater. Step by step. He would install it on the roof; the utility tubs could collect rainwater that would flow through the collector and down through the pipes. He could do this. He ran up and down basement steps and in and out of garages, collecting his materials: storm windows for the glazing, fiberglass insulation, corrugated aluminum sheets, copper tubing. He needed some black paint to make the metal absorb solar radiation, and he was a little worried about finding it. But he couldn't keep bouncing from one project to another, rebounding off one difficulty onto another; he had to take hold of a single project and see it through.

When a house was dismantled, nothing was thrown out (well, how could it be, after all, when there was no garbage collection, Jeremy thought bitterly). There were ducts, pipes, and flues. Odds and ends of hardware. Sheets of corrugated aluminum and molded fiberglass. Rolls of insulation, yards of wire. Huge attic fans. And a lot of storm windows. Jeremy could build solar greenhouses and solar space heaters. Solar ovens and solar stills. If he ran out of storm windows here, he could walk three blocks south and take apart unused houses. How many dwelling units in a town of 28,600? Multiplied by, oh, say an average of sixteen windows per house . . . "People who live in glass houses," he thought, "would never throw stones."

The problem was water. He kept coming back to the river: a waterwheel to pump water through his solar collectors. Power to pump heated water from storage tanks through ducts that would warm a house. "Never mind, never mind," Jeremy scolded himself. "Just get on with it. Step by step."

He measured and sketched, carried and stacked and arranged, and then surveyed the area for a likely house. None of Idamore's houses resembled the energy-efficient houses featured in the Sunday magazine articles, but Jeremy did see several that might be remodeled. He was particularly taken with the pitch of the roof on a lanky ranch house. Its northern wall was too high and exposed, but he might mound earth against it. And maybe he could rebuild the southern exposure with more glass and some big black drums to hold the heat. . . . When Jeremy finally conferred with Ben, Ben stared at him. "You mean you're building *yourself* a house for the winter?"

"Oh fuck off." Jeremy stalked away, ignoring the puzzled expression on Ben's face. Here he was blundering his way toward a jerry-rigged solar house, and Ben still wanted a metropolitan power plant!

Jeremy felt lonely, disgruntled, and misunderstood. He found himself avoiding Helena and snapping at Ben's every word. He was annoyed with all of them—simpleminded, nonverbal, unimaginative people. Furthermore, he needed to make a scavenging expedition to find some black paint. To set forth, traveling back toward the rats and skeletons for a can of black paint, seemed to Jeremy a grievous injustice. He prowled around Rachel's kitchen looking for some food to take with him. "Rachel," he called from the porch. She was in the compost area, shoveling shit. "Aren't there any of those biscuits left from breakfast?"

"Maddy's feeding the chickens," she called back.

"Maddy," Jeremy yelled, "where are you? Stop what you're doing."

"Over here," came her thin voice.

"Save me some— For God's sake, Maddy, go sit down," Jeremy said. "Look at your ankles." The chickens flapped and pecked and bickered in a circle around her ankles, which swelled over the unlaced wingtip shoes.

"It's such a busy time to be laid up with a baby. . . . You wanted a biscuit?" She held out the last morsel of the dry cake.

He looked at it distastefully, then tucked it into his shirt pocket. "I'm going down to Township to look for some black paint. That's where I'll be—if anybody asks."

"You're very cranky, Jermicho. You shouldn't let Ben . . ." Maddy, who lived listlessly among them with her attention focused inward and her skin turning transparent, collected herself for a brief flash outward. "Ben says our dreams for us, but he does not govern them."

"Thanks, Maddy. I needed that. Come sit down now."

She took a step, then looked down at her feet. Water was streaming down her legs and puddling at her feet. Jeremy thought she had lost control of her bladder, and flushed with embarrassment for her. "It's all right, Maddy," he said, as the water poured out of her.

"It's not all right," she said. "Dry labor is not all right."

"Oh, that was . . . Uh-oh." Jeremy scooped her up and carried her, shouting for Lily as he passed the field. She was farther away, in the far field where they were starting the corn, and the calls for her went like a bucket brigade of voices. On the steps Jeremy staggered slightly under Maddy's weight and entered the house, blinking in the dimness. Maddy leaned her head against his shoulder and gave a small angry sob. He hurried to put her down in the first bedroom. "I'd better get a fire started. Hot water . . ."

"Easy, Jermicho. There's lots of time. Start the fire, then go on to Township." Maddy's hazel eyes were almost yellow in the oblique light of the bedroom, and her face was paler than the soiled pillow beneath her head.

"Okay, okay," he panted, anxious to find Lily and to get the fire started. He had no intention of going to Township; he had barely heard what she said. "Lil-eee," he bellowed as he ran for firewood. She was ambling toward the house. "Hurry," he yelled, running back in the house. The slowness of the fire infuriated him. He ran for water, slopping a trail to the fireplace in his haste.

"You put water on for the tea! Good for you, Jermicho," said Lily.

"Tea?"

"Helena's special tea."

"But don't you need to boil . . . ? Clean the instruments . . . ?"

Lily frowned. "We put nothing inside her. The inside of the body is clean. I cannot boil my hands," she said, examining them sadly, caked with the dirt of the field. "We wash our hands carefully, and we wash her very carefully, and we—"

"But that bed is filthy!"

"The cloth we spread under her has been boiled, dried in the sun, and kept carefully in a cabinet closed to mice." Her eyes challenged him to do better. When he looked away, she added, "The more we do, the more the sickness comes . . ."

"I see. So—there's nothing more that I can do?"

"Just perhaps what you were doing before."

Jeremy worked in a frenzy. He worked fast and hard, as if his own hard labor would lighten and speed Maddy's. Laurel was underfoot, having somehow chosen this very house as the place where she must dry her vegetables. She lugged the crude wire trays up into the attic—more a crawl space than an attic—and sat up there arranging the vegetables. It must have been 110 degrees beneath the roof. Later, to Jeremy's infinite annoyance, she loitered at the foot of the ladder, poked around in the tool chest, and walked around the stacks of storm windows. When she fiddled with the pulley he'd devised to lift the utility tubs to the roof, he barked at her. Her face fell into its usual grave blankness. "Don't you have things you're supposed to be doing?" he asked.

"Supposed to do the soap ashes. Then the firewood. Carry water for dinner. Clean the chicken-floor . . ."

"Well, then."

"Well, I was just wondering . . . why are you building a *solar* water heater when we have the other kind?"

"The others run on gas or electricity, and we don't have gas or electricity."

"But we *will?*"

Jeremy hesitated a moment, then wagged his head. "No. I don't think we will. No more big power, no more time of the light." He hesitated again, studying her face for the effect of his words. Was he shattering her world by denying her a future modeled on the past? Or was he delivering her from a hopeless expectant passivity? He could read nothing from her expression. "We'll try to use the sun and the river, we'll make power in little ways. This, here, for instance, will work by trapping the heat of the sun behind the glass. . . ." Jeremy kept working and he kept talking. Hammering and glazing, he told her about time, geological pressures, the conversion of organic matter to coal and oil. He told her about their dependence on the sun.

He glanced at Laurel, who was attentive but noncommittal. "Laurel, we have always lived in a time of light. We live in a time of light now," he said, pointing to the sun. "What Ben means is that special time, that very brief time, when people knew how to use all the power that was around them. But that didn't mean they were exempt from—" Jeremy struggled to find the right words. "Even with all that knowledge, they were still dependent on the sun. They lived in the same kind of light we do. Understand?"

Laurel nodded expressionlessly and tagged along when he went to find a water heater to use for a storage tank inside the attic.

"Can it be *any* water heater?" she asked. He supposed it could, and she tugged at his sleeve with a shyly eager look coming over her face. "This one, please," she said, leading him to an open foundation. The black water looked deep enough to be up to his knees, and Jeremy looked dubiously from the basement hole to Laurel's anxious face. "I really just wanted you to read the big word on it," she quickly explained. "See the big word on it?"

Jeremy bent over the jagged remnant of wall. "'Glasslined,' you mean?"

"Oh! A glasslined gas water heater. Glasslined. Just two little words put together. I'm so dumb. . . ."

"It's hard to read, the way they've got it printed." He lowered himself into the water and waded toward the tank. Interrupted, the water released its cargo of foul gases around Jeremy's legs. "Phew. Smell the swamp gas! Holy cow! Must be an open sewer pipe under here. . . ." He struggled with the aged pipe connections, applying the wrench, whacking to loosen them, then trying again.

Laurel dangled her legs over the basement wall, working her heel into the crumbling mortar and watching Jeremy's every move. "*Swamp* gas?" she said.

"Yeah. It's a by-product of decomposition or something like that. Anaerobic digestion, that's it. Anaerobic means without air. Certain kinds of bacteria only live without air—like under this water— and they're busy breaking down sewage, I guess it is. . . ."

"Swamp *gas?*" Laurel repeated insistently.

"Oh, but not the kind of gas you can use for heating. . . ." Jeremy's attention suddenly contracted, focusing on the girl seated above him. Whatever it was that usually dulled and flattened her face was gone now, supplanted by curiosity. She was a bright monochrome of honey-colored hair and eyes and skin, a kind of harvest shade, as if she had gathered and gentled a season's sun within herself. He stared at her, feeling the brightness suffuse him. "Methane!" he exclaimed. "Methane. Laurel, you're a genius. Methane!" He sloshed excitedly around in the foul water.

By the time Rachel called him, Jeremy had fashioned a bizarre unit for collecting methane gas, using sawhorses and pipes and an inner tube from a truck tire. If it worked, the tire would expand, and then he could test the gas; if the gas burned, he'd figure a more efficient way to collect it. Laurel had long since returned to her many chores, and it was almost twilight when Rachel called. He looked up, suddenly mindful of Maddy. "Is it time?" he asked.

"Time for dinner."

Jeremy slumped with disappointment, and followed her into the house where the others were sitting on the floor around the fireplace. When Lily came in, she nodded at Rachel, who got up and left. "How's it going?" Jeremy asked. "How's Maddy?"

"Be a while yet," said Lily laconically.

Jeremy ate quickly and ravenously, anxious to get back to work. Mutton stew with mushrooms, wild carrots, and some tuber that tonight tasted to Jeremy like potatoes. It was full of herbs that almost masked the lack of salt. "Delicious," he muttered with his mouth full. Still eating, he began to talk about the difference between aerobic and anaerobic digestion. "We've got to close up the latrine," he said.

Ben paused with his fork halfway to his mouth. "Close up the . . . ?"

"And start gathering the chicken manure to put in. Close it up and let it brew. . . . I know they were doing stuff like this in India—producing methane gas for fuel. I've got to find some undamaged books to check out—"

"I've never heard of such a thing!" Ben protested loudly.

There was a sudden buzz of voices. What would they do for fertilizer, old Dave wanted to know. And surely it was unhealthy to use sewage for fuel, objected Lily. "I told you not to push him so hard," Helena complained to Ben; she obviously thought Jeremy had gone around the bend.

"This is America!" said Ben. "This is America, not India. I've never heard of such a thing. . . ." Laurel tried to make herself heard, saying over and over again how bad it smelled, how it smelled just like the swampy pond past Fennel Creek, just that awful.

Undaunted, Jeremy talked through the general commotion, explaining to no one that anaerobic digestion produced both fertilizer and gas; that the high temperatures killed harmful bacteria. . . . He stood up and took a second helping from the large pot by the fireplace. Helena started to say something in a sharp voice that was interrupted by Lily, who remarked, "Well, another day without rain. We may have to water the fields."

Dave groaned, and a thoughtful silence fell over the group. Jeremy ate faster. A waterwheel for irrigation. A waterwheel for pumping. He shoveled the last spoonful of stew into his mouth. "I'm gonna go build a dam," he said, scrambling to his feet.

"In the dark?" sneered Helena, but Jeremy was already gone.

It was not quite dark, and the air at the riverbank was thick with tiny mosquitoes. Jeremy walked along the bank, looking for a place where the river narrowed. He was walking north, following a hunch. Probably more a memory than a hunch, for twice now he had gone as far north as Riverwoods. Jeremy hadn't walked twenty-five yards before he found the place. He could hear it— water rushing through a constricted place. Several hard pulls it had been to get the canoe through it, he remembered now. Jeremy looked back toward the houses and detected the gentle downward slope of the land. This was the spot. Here, or nowhere.

Jeremy sat in the dusk, slapping the mosquitoes that gathered around his head. He imagined the rig, conjured it there on its scrap-metal mount, an overshot wheel built of two large circles— tabletops? industrial spools?—with boards put in at angles to act as scooping buckets. He had to narrow the river some more to increase its velocity, and then, without diminishing the velocity, he had to raise the water into a sluice flowing onto the top of the wheel. He could see it. Wheels, gears, belts, and bearings. A simple miracle. A beginning. There were so many simple miraculous things to begin.

° NINE °

When he joined the others, Jeremy brought two books: *The Collected Shakespeare* and *Basic House Wiring*. In the back pages of the wiring book he sketched waterwheels. Side views and front views, aerial views and cross sections. His vision by the river was dissolving in the minutiae of design problems: Should the wheel be wide or narrow? At what angle should the scoops be installed? (How do you trap methane, and how do you pipe it? Can it be used in a gas-burning stove?) He sighed and handed the book to Ben. "Something like this. But just for pumping water, you understand? If I can find a pump. If I can . . ." He broke off and pressed a finger against the corner of his eye to still a muscle spasm.

Helena and Mick each leaned over Ben to peer at the sketches. "Uhhhh," said Mick, a long and excited sigh. He touched the crude sketch, his trembling finger descending slowly and with terrible imprecision until it landed on the circle that was Jeremy's axle. Then he looked up and rapidly twirled his hands around each other. "Uhh?"

"You've got it," agreed Jeremy. "A waterwheel." He looked at Mick, curious about the older man's sudden fits of excitement. Then he turned to Ben. "How 'bout a sonnet, Ben?" He'd brought the Shakespeare with Ben in mind: a gift, a peace offering. In his frenetic state Jeremy desperately needed some peace.

He adjusted two cookie sheets to magnify the flickering light from the fireplace and candles, then settled cross-legged with the volume of Shakespeare. As he flipped the thin leaves of the book, he saw that someone had written all over the pages. Up and down the narrow margins, across the tops and bottoms, and in the spaces between the poems or scenes. For a moment Jeremy was as shocked as the book's original owner would have been. Robert McNulty, who had left his name in his books—*ex libris* stickers—must have been a methodical and orderly man. He would have hated to see his library, for the front and back pages had been torn out of most of the books, and now, look, someone had written all over the Shakespeare. Jeremy's next reaction was urgent curiosity; he wanted to be left alone to read that journal.

Nevertheless he proceeded to read to Ben. He would read a sonnet out loud, pause to decipher the strange and often illegible comments along the margins, then read out loud again. It didn't take him long to hit upon the sonnet that Ben remembered hearing in his childhood; that old warhorse, it was: "Shall I compare thee to a summer's day?"

Ben liked the poems that depended on the existence of an audience to verify them. "So long as men can breathe, or eyes can see, so long lives this, and this gives life to thee" pleased Ben mightily, for he felt that as he listened (and by listening soon memorized), he was fulfilling Shakespeare's promise to his love. For his part, Jeremy was so caught up in the problems of material existence that he read with a new attention, noting with a kind of awe how few of the details of physical life were revealed. The fuss about time and mortality went on no matter how the sewage was disposed of and the water delivered.

The person who had written in the margins of the book had a different reaction: *Knowing about evolution and genetics and all that is no advantage, for I cannot think as they did that God will start the world over again, with a new Adam and a new Eve, a new audience for the same old Shakespeare who prevails no matter what. This belief in some kind of immortality—through God, through print, through generation—is strained these days, and only the Bible thumpers find comfort. Oh, but this is a flimsy ark. . . .*

Here, though there was no space and the handwriting remained close and crabbed, there was a curious break in the line of thought *Tom is clearly going mad. He has taken to sifting earth through his fingers and talking about the . . .* Jeremy shifted the book, squinting, then ran his finger along the scribbled line, trying to establish a context for the indecipherable word. . . . *the microbes. The earth is teeming with microbes. Tom tries to manufacture antibiotics by growing molds. These dishes of his get bigger and bigger, he sprinkles earth on them, he rubs the green mold on his suppurating leg and the red mold on Ed's cancer. The air is teeming with microbes. The water. He holds discourse with the invisible powers in earth, air, and water. Poor Tom, whom the foul fiend hath led through fire and through flame . . . Poor Tom's a-cold.* What followed was so obviously unrelated that Jeremy began to see the diary as a complex puzzle created by the writer's mental associations.

"Poor Tom's a-cold," what play was that from? Jeremy had read that play. Sitting between Joe Harkness and Wendy Trumbull . . . In his mind's eye, Jeremy saw the blue ink of the syllabus, the blond veneer of the desk arm, and Wendy's beautiful clear sturdy nails tapping at the indicated examination date. "He gives hard exams," she had whispered to Jeremy and Joe. Pretty blond Wendy, who had cried in his room one night because she was so afraid of "getting involved." *She* knew exactly what she was going to do with her life, and it meant no marriage and no kids for—oh, ten years at least. They had laughed later that a young man should comfort a young woman by assuring her that he had no intentions of getting involved; wasn't the world getting more and more peculiar, they had laughed. Pretty blond reckless Wendy Trumbull: Jeremy *had* become involved, though he didn't say as much to Wendy. He was monogamous by temperament, and content to be with her on the terms she set. Maybe she was saving his seat, his empty seat with the desk arm folded down to the floor.

King Lear, of course. Jeremy flipped the pages, ignoring Ben's objections. "I haven't got that other one yet," Ben protested.

"Just a sec . . ." Jeremy mumbled, and then looked up with a triumphant smile. "I found it. Listen, this handwritten stuff was written after . . . after the time of the light. Listen to this, Ben. This is about a doctor who came here . . . here to Idamore."

"A doctor?" said Helena.

"He *wrote?* In the book?" breathed Ben.

"Just listen. *Poor naked wretch, he cannot stand it that he is powerless. For us death has one face. For Tom it is the spider's eye, a thousand orbs, each with a name—cholera, typhoid, cancer, septicemia, pneumonia. He can diagnose, but not cure. He reinvents his power by becoming a pharmacist of molds—"*

"The spider's eye, the spider's eye," said Rose. "The spider's eye. The spider's eye. The spider's eye . . ."

"Rose!" yelled Helena, as Ben went over to the writhing figure.

"Please go on, Jeremy," said Rachel, listening from the doorway.

Jeremy held his fingers against the tic in his eye. "Okay, let's see. *What can he teach the children, when he has no lab, no plasma, no chemicals, no X-ray machines, no anesthetic. Oh, Lord, let me become a list maker of nots. No hospital, no pharmaceutical companies, no sutures, no bandages. And yet Tom was a high-priority citizen. Isn't that funny? Funny, how they planned everything and foresaw nothing. Because he is utterly helpless, and it is Helena who keeps us alive. What computer—"*

"That's where *my* name comes from," said Helena.

"Hush . . ."

"*What computer would have chosen her? A pretty little thing, vibrant and slightly bored housewife who had taken up edible wild foods as a hobby. The Euell Gibbons of the cocktail circuit. Helena Adelstein, second wife of Dr. Thomas Adelstein, internist. What computer would have chosen her?"*

"I *told* you," said Rachel to Helena, who pinched her mouth tight and thin, and looked down at her hands clasped around her ankles. "Didn't we tell her, Ben?"

Ben was holding Rose and nodding sadly. "What did you tell her?" asked Jeremy, suddenly conscious that there was much to misunderstand here, that he should give a running commentary. What would he explicate? The connections made by the journalist between the mad physician Tom Adelstein and the Elizabethan play *King Lear*? The role of the computer? A society in which it was possible for a young woman to be a bored member of a cocktail circuit? "What did you tell her?" he asked again, angrily.

"That men took more than one wife," said Rachel.

"Esau took his *wives* of the daughters of Canaan," said Ben solemnly.

"Oh, for Pete's sake," said Jeremy, slapping the book closed.

They didn't deserve to be read to. Silly, petty people, he would never understand them. Maddy split the quiet air with another long scream that descended in register from a high shriek to a low, tired moan. "Is it almost over? Does she have long . . . ?"

"Pretty long yet," Rachel replied.

Jeremy leaned against the brick hearth and opened the book again. He had more in common with the margin scribbler than he did with the people around him. The scribbler was, in any case, Jeremy's only link. He alone might explain what had happened, how they had gotten here. The trouble was, Jeremy didn't quite like the scribbler, and resented the time and effort required to read his handwriting and follow his mental associations. Entry after entry promised a message and delivered none. *It has come to me at last,* said one. *Probably too late, for I am dying.* "I alone am left to tell the . . . blub." *Ha-ha, all of M.D. in a sentence fragment. . . .*

What was it you wanted to know? another entry asked, making Jeremy oddly uncomfortable. *Closer yet approach me. . . . You know what happened to the Whitman, don't you? I burned it. Elizabeth's mother once suggested I must value property more than books, or I'd burn the furniture first. And do you know what I said? That we had no right, that they'd never forgive us for burning the furniture. They could replace the books more easily than their houses, and so on and so on. And do you know why I was raving like that? Because I believed they were coming back. They'd reclaim their house and file for damages. Sue! Yes, and on Monday the banks would open. Train service would resume on Wednesday. Full employment by late Friday afternoon. Ah, the restful memoirs of an agitated broken iconoclast (ha—get it? Do I irritate you? I irritate myself).*

Yes, he *was* irritating. But tonight Jeremy had time, and the effort of attending to the journal took his mind off the distressing sounds from the other room. He discovered that if he followed the writer long enough, he could glean bits of history from the wanderings.

Disasters I now remember fondly, said a note. *1) The housing shortage caused by random population movements. 2) The imposition of martial law. 3) Labor conscription and food incentives. There is much to be said for outlines: conciseness, and lack of emotional overtone; not getting stuck. If you write 1, you tend to go on to 2. Otherwise you might get stuck at 1. Random migrations. You know, like the cab driver and his family. The professor of English and his family. The account executive and his family. All. Looking. For. Food. Remember that? The Chicano was hands down the best provider. We were utterly routed. Poor Father, with his checkbook, his three charge cards, and his civility. He was so worried about the demise of higher education that he forgot to watch for the demise of civility. A kind of literacy of life-style. Don't wipe your ass with the hand you eat with. Don't let the menstrual blood drip down your leg. . . .*

Here Jeremy paused with a frown. It had never occurred to him that the writer might be a woman. Now the possibility became one more irritating mystery to solve, one more clue in a maze of pointless clues leading nowhere.

Father was never concerned with that part of life, the private civilization of personal behavior that depends on eight kinds of toilet bowl cleaner and the deodorizing of human secretions. One might adapt to a long slow slide into prehistory—or no, call it posthistory, a time after written records have crumbled and the record keepers fallen—one might adapt to that, but to lose overnight both the Brandenburg Concertos and toilet paper leaves you hard put to make rational decisions.

Oh, poor capitalism. Only capitalism could create eight kinds of toilet bowl cleaner; surely no other system can afford so spendthrift a marketing device? . . .

The next entry was in another ink. Jeremy sighed. Why couldn't s/he have kept the diary entries in chronological order, like any ordinary person? He flipped the thin pages, noting the different pens, the deteriorating script. The various ballpoint pens were succeeded by a damaged primitive nib dipped into a homemade ink that ran and blotted.

Like a furious fuzzy blue aureole around the strict rectangular blocks of *Hamlet* was another long entry on the housing shortage, the random hysterical travel of people in flight from a radioactive peril they couldn't see. Along the bottom margin was the primitive scrawl of the older person: *Tom's daughter has delivered a healthy baby boy! Generation! Perhaps the tide is turning? That was unfair, what I said before about Sam. He was a good man in evil circumstances.*

Jeremy would have thought, since he'd been lucky enough to stumble on this book, that he'd be eager to assemble the facts and derive a history of the war. But what history there was was delivered in a querulous ironic voice that irritated him and told him little that he hadn't already imagined. He began to skip the early small-scripted entries, watching for the later ones in thin, runny ink. He didn't know what he was looking for until he found this entry:

Sam Waters says things like "The Tide Is Turning" and "Victory Is in Sight." All in capital letters, don't you know. Samuel Waters from Federal Recovery and Reclamation Center Proclaims Turning Tide. His job is not to help us recover, but to make sure the Federal Government recovers.

I suppose bureaucrats are an unextinguishable species, like rats. We have at present two. For a while I thought McGiverty was getting promotions, but now I see that his changing titles—from local to county to area supervisor—have less to do with his competence than with the shrinking population he supervises. We've seen this at Idamore, of course, yet we have maintained our belief that there are other places better off than we are. Sam has used and manipulated this peculiar optimism, which in fact feels like galloping apathetic self-pity. He fosters our belief that we are a "local disaster" and that he represents the first of the "outside disaster relief measures." Now that I've stopped working in the fields and have time to think about things, I can't for the life of me think why the Federal Government has taken this line. Are they denying the reality, or somehow lopsidedly trying to deal with it? We drift passively, seeing only to our immediate personal survival, waiting for help from elsewhere. "Elsewhere" has come to mean Sam . . . Sam, Sam, the Federal Man, I call him, to tease him. Now when McGiverty comes along in his jeep, the children call him the Federal Man. Our unelected officials, our assigned bureaucrats, are becoming nameless. (Come to think of it, so are we. Allison Pachek once was I. But when was the last time I introduced myself to a stranger? Old Ally is sufficient around here.) Our heritage, like our population, dies by inches.

This young McGiverty's like a sailor, Sam tells me: a girl in every port. I do think, however, that Tom's daughter is too young for this; is it just that, or do I resent the unabashed cock-of-the-walk way McGiverty has, as if every female between puberty and menopause were somehow his domain? Peter's son, Paul—spare me, Lord, from another generation of Bible thumpers!—trembles with rage when he sees McGiverty rattling up in his jeep. It won't be long, I think, before McGiverty has some sexual competition in our biological community of Idamore. Go, Paul! Oh, listen to me. The longer I take at my dying, the more I become a low-down, querulous, and queer old woman. . . .

Yes, this was what Jeremy wanted. Not a history of the explosive demise of *his* world, but a map marking the route from that vast wreckage to this constricted world. This room. These passive patient people listening to the periodic wail of an anemic woman in unassisted childbirth. Waiting for Sam, Sam the Federal Man. A Mother Goose character invented by a wiseacre old woman.

The fire had burned low, leaving Jeremy in a diminished circle of light that threatened to go out altogether. The people around him were dense blots of shifting darkness in the dark room. He closed the book carefully and gave in to the pull of the floor, sliding down the length of his arm until his head was resting.

Jeremy slept fitfully, jerking awake to the terrible sounds of Maddy's labor. He would note the degree of darkness outside the house and the disposition of sleeping bodies around him. "Is it much longer?" he would ask if anyone was awake, then doze again because it was "pretty long yet." At dawn he got up and picked his way over the other sleepers, tiptoeing down the hall toward the silent bedroom. Lily was snoring lightly in the big chair next to Maddy's bed. Maddy was obviously dead, her face gray and still and bloodless.

He must have made some sound, for Lily wakened with a little snort and Maddy's eyelashes fluttered. Jeremy breathed a sigh of relief, and rested the palm of his hand against Maddy's clammy cheek. "I've been climbing a big hill," Maddy said thickly. "There is a wonderful light at the top. . . . Jeremy, tell Ben about the light."

Jeremy looked at Lily, who shook her head that she didn't understand, either. "I'll tell him, Maddy," he said, then turned to Lily and quietly asked, "How long, Lily?"

She walked out into the hall with him, and gulped air as if the bedroom had air enough only for Maddy. "It's too long now. It's way too long."

Late that morning Laurel yelled from the porch, "Baby's coming." Rachel called to Helena, who called to Ben, who called to Jeremy. "Baby's coming." Thank heaven, they said, straightening their clothes as they trooped in, thank heaven it would soon be over. But this delivery was not like Pearl's, and the children were told to wait outside. Dave soon left to watch over the children, and then Rose was sent from the room for babbling. Jeremy stood by the head of Maddy's bed, hoping to be sent out, too, and unable to think of an excuse to leave.

"Push, Maddy," shouted Lily. "I see the feet. Push."

But Maddy was beyond effort. At some signal from Lily, Rachel and Helena took her under the armpits, supporting her weight.

Good God! Jeremy thought. Why were they hauling this helpless suffering woman upright?

"Couldn't you hold her up, Jermicho? Could you . . . help?" Rachel said. "Please . . . help."

Jeremy hesitated until Lily shouted, "Get under her and lift." Then it was his strength hoisting Maddy into a squatting position, holding her virtually suspended on her helpless legs above the bed. Maybe the baby would fall out, he thought. "Push, Maddy, push!" Lily shouted. Mick and Ben got under Maddy's thighs, while Lily yelled encouragement.

There was no sound from Maddy. The five people supporting her body held their breath and grunted, all trying to push the baby out of Maddy's womb. "Let her down. Quick, let her down," Lily said to the trio at Maddy's head. "Ben, shove that back in there," she snapped.

"Oh, God," murmured Ben, holding a cloth against something

between Maddy's legs. "Okay, keep pulling, Lily." Mick looked away, making sobbing grunts.

"Oh please, oh please, oh please," Helena was whispering, holding tight to one of Maddy's hands. Jeremy found himself shivering uncontrollably, and grunting like Mick. Then Lily put her bloodied hands over her face and threw back her head. She made no sound, but her mouth was stretched taut and open, a horrifying silent scream of protest. Jeremy looked at the grisly object of Maddy's long labor, and quickly turned away. It was alive, but it couldn't live many moments more.

"It's a boy," said Ben quietly. "It's a boy, Maddy."

Maddy lay limp and still against the pillow. Helena looked at the hand she was holding, and with exaggerated care put it down on the bed. Spattered from shoulder to wrist with Maddy's blood, Ben leaned over the bed. "Maddy, darling, we know it's a long weary way, but think of the milk you can give to the children. Think of the milk."

"Let her go, Ben," said Lily.

"Stay with us, Maddy," begged Ben.

"In the time of the light," said Helena quietly to Jeremy, "did you know how to let people die? Teach that to Ben."

"We do not want her to die," Ben said in a childlike way. He clenched his teeth, shuddered, and then he gave in, wilting. The bed seemed a mountain he had to scale in order to kiss Maddy on the forehead. "Maddy, darling, it's been a long weary way, hasn't it? Rest, now. No one ever worked harder to bear us sons."

° TEN °

Jeremy and Mick had just passed under the crumbling bridge at the southern boundary of Idamore when they heard the helicopter. "Oh look, oh, let's go back!" Jeremy flung himself around in the sensitive canoe, which tipped and teetered. In the bow, Mick grabbed onto the gunwales as if he could hold the boat steady.

"Huh-nuh, huh-nuh," said Mick, aspirating with vehemence and paddling so hard that the canoe surged through the water.

"What the hell . . . ?" said Jeremy, not for the first time. No one knew what had gotten into Mick. He had been dogging Jeremy's footsteps since the night of Maddy's labor, and when Jeremy announced that he was going downstream to look for black paint, Mick bolted from the field, croaking and tugging Jeremy's sleeve, thumping himself on the chest and pointing south. It was soon apparent that he wasn't along just to keep Jeremy company. When they came to Reese Street, where Jeremy had planned to stop, Mick held his paddle like a battering ram, indicating that they must continue south. "Kuh . . . Kuh . . ." Mick had croaked, touching his throat in despair. And Jeremy had quickly yielded out of pity.

"He'll still be there when we get back?" Jeremy asked now.

When Mick shook his head, his filthy iron-gray hair clung to his shirt, moving at a different tempo from his head, dragging in reluctant curved hanks along his neck. He turned cautiously in his seat and began a grunting, gesturing explanation. He pointed to the south, swept his arm in a long northerly arc that concluded not at Idamore, but somewhere to the east. Pointing to the east, he raised one finger, two fingers, then repeated the broad sweeping gesture, this time pointing toward Idamore.

"What? Do it again. . . . He comes from the south . . . flies north . . . and then *east*?" Mick wagged happily, making Jeremy feel as if he were being unusually adept at an urgent game of charades. One finger, two fingers. "He brings back another person?" No, no, no. "He . . . he . . . there's a woman having a baby over there. . . ." Definitely not. "One, two . . . buckle my shoe. Forget it, Mick."

Mick turned, insistently paddling. "The Federal Man *is* coming to Idamore, isn't he, Mick?" When Mick nodded, Jeremy was content to go on. Imagine missing him—Santa Claus, Rasputin, the father of the future generations of Idamore.

Unbidden came the image of the deformed male infant between

Maddy's legs, and Jeremy tried to push it back into the dark corner of his mind.

It had taken the birth of that baby, and Ben's parting words to Maddy, to make Jeremy see what would have been immediately obvious to an older man. The sudden apprehension left Jeremy sick and speechless. He could build a hundred water mills, a thousand generating plants, restore the power tenfold, and Ben's hope for the future would still elude them. Because if they couldn't bear healthy male infants, there *was* no future. Technology had been able to do many things, but it had never permitted man to escape the simple fact of his animal life. The people of Idamore faced biological extinction.

Jeremy found that he couldn't think about this except with scientific detachment, an anthropologist's observation: The people of Idamore faced biological extinction. A deformed baby lying in a pool of blood between the lifeless legs of a woman he knew. Maddy dead. It could have been Helena. Dark Rachel. Mad Rose.

Always when you imagine disaster, somebody's left afterward. To record, to witness, to testify. To begin again. They clatter noisily onto the stage, bright armies of the future. They're always there, and always male. The physically stronger sex of the species, born blissfully ignorant of his fragility, unhumbled by the precariousness of male fetal development. "Call me Ishmaela. I alone am left to tell the . . . blub." Ha-ha, Allison. Ha, ha, ha.

When the canoe passed under the Route 94 overpass, Jeremy held his breath, half expecting some change of air, some compression or touch of cobwebs to indicate reentry. Surely now he would be returned; he had seen what he was meant to see. Jeremy concluded that if he had no purpose here, then his purpose must remain back in Cottage Grove.

Nothing happened. Nothing at all. And in that instant of acute anticipation, he imagined himself restored to his own time: a crank on the corner preaching the end of the world. "Repent, repent." A social embarrassment, a family tragedy. Jeremy Towers giving his life to an obsession. Bad as joining the Hare Krishnas, or becoming a macrobiotic occultist. Might as well drown as return to tell the

tale no one wanted to hear. Might as well stay in Idamore . . . where he'd spend the rest of his life waiting to step
through an invisible veil from one chamber of time into another?
Like a man poised forever on a high diving board, neither here nor
there? "That's where I put in," he said, his voice cracking dan-
gerously.

Mick turned in his seat. "Kuh . . ." he said again sadly.

"Cottage Grove?" said Jeremy.

When Mick nodded vigorously, Jeremy stared at him. "You
know Cottage Grove?" Mick thumped his chest, pointed toward
the southwest, and thumped again. "No kidding," said Jeremy.
"Well, I'll be damned." The two men grinned foolishly at each
other. "There's a big hardware store over there a couple of miles,"
Jeremy said, pointing east. Mick gestured emphatically to the
southwest. "Is there a hardware store down there? We've *got* to
find some black paint."

They paddled until Mick raised his hand, then walked the crumbly
highway toward the hardware store, which Mick assured him with
repeated gestures was on this road. The store, tucked off on a side
street, stood almost unchanged, as quiet as if it were a Sunday
afternoon. "Oh, hell," said Jeremy, staring helplessly through the
dirty window. Mick touched his arm, then opened the unlocked
door.

As he walked up and down the emptied aisles, Jeremy was
struck by the antagonism of everything that was still available to
them. There were fans and compressors, mowers and pumps, beau-
tifully wrought machines, all requiring electricity or gas. It reminded Jeremy of a picture he'd once seen: an African family
bathing in a mudhole against the backdrop of a modern city.
Sugar-white skyscrapers, blue sky, muddy water. There was no
romance to that poverty; those starving dirty people wanted to live
inside that fortress of wealth. Jeremy had felt that their simplest
gestures of survival must have been mocked and thwarted by the
presence of those tall white buildings. So it was now; they were
hedged in by the achievements of the past. How could you invent

the wheel if you lived next to an international airport? How arrive at the iron age by way of the space age?

At an empty pegboard that proclaimed the best hand tools for the home gardener, Jeremy smiled thinly: It had come to the point where gardening was a hobby, foraging a weekend diversion, survival in the wilderness a summer vacation. When people said "wilderness" they meant big trees and white water; they meant the past, when the earth was still there to be conquered. Bare-handed. With ham radios in case of accident or illness. The confidence of outside help.

Though there was little that was useful, they did find some paint in the back of the store. Walking out the unlocked back door, Jeremy asked, "How come this area wasn't so looted . . . so picked over as the north part of Cottage Grove?" The answer to Jeremy's question was a charming pantomime of walking fingers—ten, then five, then fists; fists knocked together and a gesture toward the sky—at which Jeremy smiled. He shook his head. "Never mind," he said when Mick started over again. "Just one more mystery. I'm learning to live with them."

They left the hardware store pushing a shopping cart full of black paint, mineral spirits, and assorted paintbrushes. "You know what we need?" Jeremy said cheerfully. He felt quite companionable with Mick now, no longer bothered by the odd one-sided conversations he conducted. "We need to trade in the *Collected Shakespeare* for one live Elizabethan millwright. 'Cause there *is* a middle ground. There is," he said, nodding at Mick, "a place between subsistence and luxury. Before the time of plenty—hell, before the Industrial Revolution—there were thousands of years of middle ground. We just have to stop letting all this"—he waved his arm at the street, making Mick peer around—"trap us. We'll use what's useful, and rethink the rest."

They clattered down the street, the noisy wheels of the cart whacking against the rough pavement. Jeremy slackened his pace because Mick was breathing so loudly, but Mick strode ahead of him. "I was born in St. Francis Hospital, just around that corner. . . ." Jeremy started to say, and then came to a halt. "Mick, let's stop at the hospital. Maybe there'd be some antiseptic. Some bandages . . ."

Mick looked frightened and shook his head in a way scarcely distinguishable from the palsy that kept it in continual motion. "What's the hurry, man?" said Jeremy, losing patience with him. "We're near a hospital, we should see if there's anything useful." Mick stood there shaking, his trembling hand extended. "Well, wait here, then," said Jeremy, and turned on his heel. "Cough medicine. Nose drops. Throat lozenges. Who knows?" he muttered to himself as he walked the length of Linden Avenue. "I wonder what's the shelf life of penicillin." He heard Mick coming more slowly behind him.

The sign on the door should have stopped him, but it didn't. It was a hand-lettered sign. "This hospital does not have the facilities to care for any more people. Please seek medical help at Idamore or Oakton." Someone had used a thick black Magic Marker to draw a line through some of the words, so that the sign said simply, "This hospital does not care any more."

Mick waited several yards from the entrance. He neither sat nor paced; he stood motionless but trembling like an aspen on the wide walkway. Jeremy Echo was inside the hospital for a considerable time, and when he came out, he pushed the door as if he were moving a boulder. He trudged toward Mick carrying a large white box and a small brown bottle. "I found some syrup of ipecac," Jeremy said dully. "And some Kotex. I guess nobody was coming in for poisoning or maternity. . . ."

Suddenly Mick was holding him. Jeremy wasn't sure whether he had stepped into Mick's arms or if Mick had come to him. Jeremy felt the knobbed trembling hand stroking his back, heard the damaged larynx tying to comfort, smelled the stink of Mick's sweat and filthy clothes, and he clung to the man because he was alive, because they were both alive. Gone, useless, all the ceremonies of polite distance maintained by men in Jeremy's time, for whom holding was either an expression of power or a confession of weakness. Jeremy held Mick because he was there, and alive, and because only in this way could they talk about what Jeremy had seen. "Oh Mick," said Jeremy, looking over the man's head toward the hospital door, "I just hate rats."

∘ ELEVEN ∘

The Federal Man sounded like a horde of insects coming toward Idamore, so that Helena first raised her head in alarm. Alarm quickly gave way to suspicion, for the helicopter described a wider-than-usual arc, swinging northeast along the tollway and continuing north past Idamore. Was he snooping, she wondered as she watched the helicopter circle Riverwoods; somewhere up there was Edgar tending the hidden sheep. Ben had been right about the effects of withholding: Once you began to hide things, you had things to hide. So here she was, suspicious and wary, sure that he was snooping, this man who meant everything to them.

Helena had thought Jeremy was a Federal Man on that first day she ever saw him. Another Federal Man! she had thought with both dismay and hope; but no, it was only Jeremy Echo, come bumbling out of the south, out of the time of plenty, with news of all the things he couldn't do, of all the things he'd never seen. "I've never seen a baby born. I've never seen anybody die," he said outside Maddy's room. How, how, how was that possible? What sort of world had he come from? She resented his ignorance, and she resented his dumb pain, for hadn't she known Maddy longer, been through births and deaths, privations and lovemaking with Maddy? Jeremy's grief made Helena feel dull and thick-skinned and unfeeling.

Now he was gone, just as the Federal Man arrived. Their paths must have crossed, Jeremy's sleek metal canoe gliding silently south on the water while the Federal Man beat the air, *chub-chub-chub-chub,* coming north. Helena felt a superstitious quiver of dread. Perhaps she would never see Jeremy Echo again. Only the Federal Man came and went; it was his place to have no place.

Then, with one of those leaps of logic the heart makes to avoid pain, Helena decided it would be better if Jeremy *didn't* come back: He didn't belong here; he was not good for them.

It was bad enough that he filled Laurel's head with all that non-sense about the sun, and Laurel doing none of her work but fol-lowing Jeremy around, interrupting him, taking him from his tasks. "What is this word, Jermicho?" ("Whirlpool") and "What is this word, Jermicho?" ("Kitchen-Aid") and "What is this word, Jermicho?" ("Bolton Heating and Plumbing Company"). Finding plastered all over town words that no one else even noticed any-more. "Why didn't they label them right, Jermicho? Why didn't they say 'washing machine' and 'dishwasher' and 'furnace'?" "Why . . ." and "why . . ." and "why . . ." until Helena thought she was going to have to throttle Laurel.

Bad enough Laurel. But then Rose, too. Well, Rose wasn't such a good worker, so it probably didn't matter, but it was curious. After Jeremy left, with Mick shuffle-running after him, Rose threw a fit. A new kind of fit. First she was doing her stone thing, but she couldn't seem to get it just right. Twitch, fidget, and kick. She was lying there and no one was paying much attention to her; there was too much to do and it had been too much interrupted lately. Then Rose was screaming, an eerie, night-sounding shriek that for a moment paralyzed everyone. She held her hands up to her panic-stricken face and shrieked again. "Oh my, oh my," dithered Ben helplessly, "what is the matter with her? What is the matter, Rose?" Had she seen maggots in the fat flesh of her palm? Was there pus pouring out her nose? No. Rose was crying, and scream-ing that the rock was melting! melting! melting!

"Fruit-loop," Helena had declared, but she hadn't said it right. When Jeremy called Rose fruit-loop, the name sounded fond and funny. For an instant Helena felt almost as crazy as Rose was; she wanted to jump up and down shouting, "Fruit-loop." Go berserk.

Maddy was dead. Rose was crying. And everybody was going nuts. Including Mick. Mick was so busy watching Jermicho that he wasn't doing his work, either. "Mick, you're walking in the seed furrows," Helena would snap at him. "Mick, you're smushing my row. Watch what you're doing. . . ." But he could not, would not watch anything but Jeremy.

Ever since the night Jeremy read from the book with the matching words—day-May, dimm'd-untrimm'd, see-thee, (oh, lovely, they were; better even than Ben's)—ever since that night, Mick had been distracted. By something Jermicho read? Something he said? Or was it that Mick, too, had been captured by the light on Jeremy's face? It was just the rectangles of reflective metal that Jeremy had propped around the two candles. That's all it was. But when he looked up, Jeremy's blue eyes had turned the deep ambiguous color of martins' wings.

Jeremy was not teaching them to fly; he was chipping the earth away under their feet. Everything he said undermined them. It would be best if he were lost.

Watching the helicopter hover over the parking lot of the Botanical Gardens, Helena exclaimed, "Oh, why can't we just live out our lives and be done with it?" She meant her own life: She did not want to die in childbirth as Maddy had; she did not want to give her life to the future.

"Laney, Laney, Laney . . ." Lily said, like a mother out of patience with a wayward child.

Lily had straightened to wave at the helicopter, and continued to stand, rubbing her lower back, staring at the now-silent helicopter. "Hank's older than *I* am," she commented almost dreamily. She went off to collect the sheep that the Federal Man had come for. He'd take them to Freehold and be back in Idamore, with salt, in two days.

Lily exchanged a sad, cordial hug with Hank and helped him unload the helicopter while she gave him news of Idamore: They had one healthy girl infant; Helena had miscarried early in the winter; Maddy was dead. Hank paused in the noisy business of rolling the

metal drum of coal off the helicopter, as if to give Maddy a moment of reverent silence. "Aw, quiet Maddy," he said. "Too bad."
He off-loaded the seeds and the tank of fish to stock their pond,
apologizing that he was so late, so behind schedule. "Those are not
what you'd call young sheep, Lil," he complained.

"Neither are you," she retorted, "and half the fish in that tank
are so old they're dead."

Hank grunted. Then he stood in the doorway of the helicopter
to have a brief look around Idamore before he set off again. It was
an administrative rather than a proprietal glance, and fond.
"What's all that junk?"

Lily followed Hank's gaze, and saw the litter of Jeremy Echo's
many uncompleted projects. Mounted on three open basements
were inner tubes on sawhorses, looking like gigantic insects that
had extended their narrow copper-tubing tongues to drink from
the foul water. An old water heater lay on its side inside a half-
completed solar box, and around it were pipes, another tank, and a
pile of lumber. An umbrella-shaped device made of aluminum
sheets was going to be a solar oven. Lily giggled because it did look
like a mess of junk, and there was more that Hank couldn't see—a
·house with a hole in its roof, old oil drums Jeremy had laboriously
divided, then welded together again backward. "A windmill for
pumping water," he had said, and even he looked dubious about
that one. Jeremy himself was off looking for black paint to finish
his several solar projects; he was not here to meet Hank or to
defend his loony projects.

"We're—uh—experimenting. . . ." Lily herself was amazed by
this moment of absolute disloyalty to Hank; was Jeremy Echo one
of Helena's hidden lambs to be withheld from the Federal Man?
"We'll tell you all about it when you come back," she quickly
added. "It's a long story."

"Is it, Lil?" said Hank. He seemed distracted, heavy-footed with
some other purpose. "I've got news, too. Which I'll give you when
I come back." He nodded, more to himself than her, then took her
in his arms: old Lil. She'd been here since he first became a Federal
Man; they'd been through a lot of times together. "Idamore is a
kind of paradise, you know that?"

"Things are bad in the south?"

"Pretty bad, yeah. See you in a couple of days."

She cocked her head at him. "Hello, good-bye," she said, walking backward away from the dangerous flying machine.

Hank was behind schedule, slightly feverish, and reluctant to give the news he was supposed to deliver along with the exchange goods at each stop. It was not good news, and it wouldn't hurt to postpone his announcement to Idamore until his return trip. He clattered into the empty air, heading east on the last leg of his last trip.

Idamore became a small green clearing, distinguished from others by virtue of its ponds. He could see the river and its tributaries, meandering through the gridwork towns. Railway lines, highways, the jogs in the roads where one town met another. If he looked south, he could see the epicenters, with their weird geometry of intersecting circles made interesting—or visible, even—by triangular stands of buildings that stood on the tangents. Huge circular carpets of trash enclosed in other circles of vertical char, like iron filings blazed out from some invisible magnet; and between the circles those peculiar pockets of undamaged buildings. But he didn't look south, he'd already been over the south; he looked east: toward the blue flash of the great lake.

"Experimenting?" he said, as if only here, alone in the familiar noisiness of his helicopter, could he think about what Lily had meant. It wasn't like Idamore to experiment. He was annoyed, because he was trying to decide whether to retire to Idamore or to Freehold, and he didn't want new information cluttering up his decision. Different as they were from each other, he was fond of both places—their rootedness, their continuity, their isolation from the horrors of the south. Until recently Hank had thought the differences between them were due to their histories. Freehold had been founded by a mad engineer who systematically destroyed or removed every piece of machinery in the area; Idamore had been founded by a Baptist preacher who had no argument with the machines because he thought destruction was the work of God.

He saw now that everything was more complicated than he'd once thought; he resented the additional complication of Idamore

"Things are bad in the south?"

"Pretty bad, yeah. See you in a couple of days."

She cocked her head at him. "Hello, good-bye," she said, walking backward away from the dangerous flying machine.

Hank was behind schedule, slightly feverish, and reluctant to give the news he was supposed to deliver along with the exchange goods at each stop. It was not good news, and it wouldn't hurt to postpone his announcement to Idamore until his return trip. He clattered into the empty air, heading east on the last leg of his last trip.

Idamore became a small green clearing, distinguished from others by virtue of its ponds. He could see the river and its tributaries, meandering through the gridwork towns. Railway lines, highways, the jogs in the roads where one town met another. If he looked south, he could see the epicenters, with their weird geometry of intersecting circles made interesting—or visible, even—by triangular stands of buildings that stood on the tangents. Huge circular carpets of trash enclosed in other circles of vertical char, like iron filings blazed out from some invisible magnet; and between the circles those peculiar pockets of undamaged buildings. But he didn't look south, he'd already been over the south; he looked east: toward the blue flash of the great lake.

"Experimenting?" he said, as if only here, alone in the familiar noisiness of his helicopter, could he think about what Lily had meant. It wasn't like Idamore to experiment. He was annoyed, because he was trying to decide whether to retire to Idamore or to Freehold, and he didn't want new information cluttering up his decision. Different as they were from each other, he was fond of both places—their rootedness, their continuity, their isolation from the horrors of the south. Until recently Hank had thought the differences between them were due to their histories. Freehold had been founded by a mad engineer who systematically destroyed or removed every piece of machinery in the area; Idamore had been founded by a Baptist preacher who had no argument with the machines because he thought destruction was the work of God.

He saw now that everything was more complicated than he'd once thought; he resented the additional complication of Idamore "experimenting." He wanted to choose between the placid, sociable people of Idamore and the fierce, private people of Freehold. He needed to decide where he was going to spend the rest of his life, grounded.

He knew—he finally knew—that the clarity he felt up here was only the clarity of height, of speed, of noisy power. "The big picture," Mr. Passmore called it. "The overview," he called it. The underview was that it would take the folks down there in that little bit of a clearing a half day to walk from Idamore to the western shore of the great lake, and what they would see on the way would be nothing Mr. Passmore would include in his overview report. Hank thought all those reports and reports-on-reports were very silly, with their little tags: HB 123. EO 459. HQ-2, FEM-3, Report #871.

Mister Passmore. Of the Federal Emergency Management Agency. When he had occasion to meet a FEMA rep, Passmore said that it was not the Senate but the reps who did the important work—in tones that suggested quite the opposite was true. Hank didn't mind the tone: Mr. Passmore made policy, and that *was* important work. But without Hank Mr. Passmore was a eunuch, a muttering old man in a deep bunker dictating policy statements to no one and for no one. *With* Hank he sat at the center of a gorgeous web. That's what Hank had always felt when he was flying: that he carried the system of federal government over the land; that he connected everything with the light-catching, fragile threads of order and policy. He was the link between the government and the people, the representative of each to the other.

When Hank reported the withholding of stores in Kendallville and Idamore, the policy report came back, recommending toleration for displays of community initiative. Which was fine while Hank was at HQ 2 or in the air. But when he landed, he felt the disruptive clunk of both the helicopter and his own clarity: How many hidden sheep represented a display of initiative, and how many more a rebellion?

He knew there was no "community initiative" in Idamore; Helena had won an argument with Ben. The Idamore group functioned in a kind of emotional draft that blew them gently from one activity or position to another. Only in Kendallville could you see anything like a uniform community will. In Kendallville, where the people watched the limestone bluffs inch upward from the earth like bones breaking through the skin, they hated Hank with the sullen, underhanded hostility of an impotent people. And they hated each other. They withheld not only from him and the collective effort, but from each other. Community initiative? Or collective suicide?

The point was, there were people down there. It wasn't Idamore or Kendallville or Freehold, but people. The Senate loved the people—loved them fiercely—but as "the people of Idamore," "the people of Kendallville," and so on. Not individuals, but collections, explained with this or that theory. Which held up as long as Hank was at HQ 2 or in the air. That was part of the reason he didn't report the people who here and there had chosen to live alone. They utterly escaped theory. He'd spot them quite by accident, and thenceforth look for them eagerly, incredulously. Like the old woman who used to live alone at the northern tree line and said no, she didn't need his help; no, she didn't want to be a part of the nation; no, she didn't want a town to go to, thank you and goodbye. He always looked especially for her, using her to excuse the fuel he wasted in these flights over the north.

The fact was, he just loved to fly over the trees.

As the Senate's explanations of people had failed him, Hank had come up with his own theories. His favorite was his tree theory. He'd decided that the places at the northernmost stretch of his sector were faring better than the southern places because they were closer to the big trees. He treasured this idea too much to tell anyone: He didn't want to give anyone an opportunity to show him that it was as silly as his other theories. He couldn't have offered reasons for his certainty that there was goodness there, among the trees. He just felt it. Like an ecstasy, it was, to fly over them, and to walk under them, peace. Only north of the tree line did he feel a continuity between up and down, height-clarity and ground-sense. When he landed to walk among the big trees, with their special shadows dappling the rich leaf mold underfoot, he never felt the terrible disruption of the theoretical overview that occurred when he stepped from the helicopter into a group of people.

Hank's inchoate tree theory included the taste of an apple. Also the time he'd seen a wild animal walk into a clearing. A thing so delicate-boned and watchful, so liquid-eyed and vulnerable, that Hank's heart had stopped. What kind of an animal was that? he wondered. A cross between a cow and a sheep, with a grace that neither had. What kind of a thing was that, to hurt his heart? He had lived his life at a distance, so that women who looked like that animal wouldn't disrupt the implementation of policy. Hank was not a bright man, so he included in his tree theory that glimpse of a wild animal, which had revealed to him for a moment a whole world hidden inside himself.

Even so, he had never doubted his program, his work. He always did what he was told, he reported on what he did, and sometimes, on the basis of his input, policies were adjusted and theories reformulated. The basic theory remained the same. Forthright, it was, simple, courageous, and right. With the cooperation of the people (of Idamore, of Kendallville, and so on) the Senate would continue to do what it had always done: regulate industry, supply necessities, manage exchange, control distribution. (Hank loved the manly vigor of the linking words: regulate, manage, secure, provide, facilitate, direct.) To that end, and in this period of limited resources, the Senate had decreed recovery of the national structure to be of overriding importance.

Same speech every year, sector in, sector out. The justification for everything. "Well, look," Passmore explained to the three apprentice administrators, "where would the limited petroleum do the most good in the long run? Should we give it to people to heat their houses, or use it to rebuild industry? What are we going to rebuild? Industry or social services? And how do we get people to work in the industrial camps if we have no incentives? Which would benefit everybody the most in the long run? *In the long run.*"

On his first training run with his predecessor, when Hank was talking enthusiastically about the recovery of the industrial sector,

Lew had quietly asked him which one should be first. "Huh?" Hank said.

"Well, pick one to work on first. Let's say the drug industry. Or is there another one more important?"

"Okay, let's say the drug industry," conceded Hank, who thought it was a good thing Lew was retiring.

"Okay, so start it. What would you do first?"

"Huh?" said Hank.

"You see my point," said Lew.

"Not at all."

"South of Idamore Gardens"—he called the place where the people lived Idamore Gardens to distinguish it from unpopulated Idamore Town—"there's some industry waiting for us. There is, for instance, a tool-and-die factory of some kind. I poked around in there. They make 'Body by Fischer.'"

"'Body by Fischer'?" Hank echoed.

"So I thought, great. Idamore can make bodies. Car bodies, I guessed, though the plant seemed kind of small for cars, and cars seemed like an item we didn't just entirely need right now. But no matter—I thought 'Body by Fischer' would make Idamore a real useful part of the national recovery program. You know what I'm saying?"

Hank had shifted uncomfortably. He knew Lew was setting him up for something; getting ready to poke holes in one of Hank's theories, or worse yet, undermine the policy of the federal government. "Yeah."

"So this factory down there on the southeast border of Idamore township makes 'Body by Fischer.' What they are is little metal plates"—Lew held up two fingers to indicate the size of them—"that go inside a car door. Ever seen those?"

"Nope."

"Yeah, well, it's a little metal plate, says 'Body by Fischer.' Fischer makes the body, see, but this little plant in Idamore makes the plate that says 'Body by Fischer.' You see what I mean?"

"Yeah."

No.

Today, Hank wished he knew where his predecessor had retired to. Hank wanted to find him—though he was surely dead now; he must be over fifty—and have him repeat what he'd first told Hank. "Say again. I didn't quite catch it that first time." Lewison-Clark was his name—his section had named him after one of the early explorers—and though people afterward called him only "Lew," he'd always introduced himself with special care as "Lewison-Clark." He did everything with special care, which made him—to the underview, anyhow—a better FEMA rep than Hank. Hank would never have bothered taking that trembly old mute to Idamore, and he told Lew as much. "That's the Senate's overview," Lew had replied, "but think, man, think. Population means people, and people come along one by one. Population assistance means helping one person, not just groups of people."

Hank had dismissed this as Lew's twisted version of the Senate's policy. He had dismissed most of what Lew said. If he had listened, he couldn't have stayed with FEMA, and if he hadn't become a FEMA rep, where would he end up? At Carbonville, dispatching his civic duty underground? He hadn't believed what Lew had told him about the men of Carbonville, either. "We called it a strike in the report," Lew said, "but it was actually an uprising. Or call it a week of diseased bloodlust. I dunno." Hank still didn't believe that the kind of people he saw at Carbonville could have done the kinds of things Lew said. Or that anybody could do those things. Rape dead women, then hack them up for snacks, when women were sacred for their fertility? Nah, he didn't believe it.

Lew said he'd picked up Idamore's Rose, a little bit of a girl then, in Oakton after the strike, and Hank always wished Rose weren't so crazy, so he could ask her if what Lew said was true. Did they really do that to Oakton, Rose? Nah. He knew they didn't. There was disease and starvation; no one would massacre whole towns. Oh, he'd seen violence, of course. In Kendallville, where people hated each other, and the hatred erupted into bloody arguments; and in Freehold, where they hated strangers and trained the girls from childhood to a disciplined military kind of violence. But surely no one would kill whole towns. . . .

Hank sighed. He had a headache, he felt feverish, he felt totally misguided. All because Mr. Passmore had asked him, "You think we're making a mistake?" He asked Hank, who had never been asked before. Hank was floored. "Well, it's *your* sector," said Passmore. "We're planning to close it, and you should have some input."

The effect of Passmore's question was seismic, passing over Hank like the two stages of a tidal wave. First, Hank felt himself sucked clean, empty of all thought, reaction, or purpose. Then the wave gathered, a torrent of opinions rushing into the vacuous harbor of his mind. Every image of doubt—from the fragile wild creature in the stippled shadow of the woods to the blank- and dirty-faced zombies of the Carbonville mines—came to him as proof. Yes, he thought they were making a mistake; he wished that Passmore hadn't asked him. Because if they were making a mistake now, it seemed equally possible that they'd been making mistakes for a long, long time. It came to him with a conviction as unshakable as his tree theory that there was something circular about the Senate's policy. Its sole aim was to restore itself so that it could once again manage the collective security of the people. There was something wrong in there, wasn't there?

"Damn, damn, damn," said Hank, rapping his fist lightly against the control panel. Here he was, flying around his sector at the end of truly loyal civic service, having a crisis of faith. Here he was, bringing an important message from the federal government, and he, the administrator of Sector Two's population-assistance and federal-recovery program, didn't believe in the Federal Government.

"Maybe I'll just take old Lil up to the north trees. Maybe just the two of us. She'll make me a cup of tea for my headache, and we'll eat apples all winter long." And the helicopter? There wasn't really anyone to come for it.

Hank bit his lip. There wasn't anyone to come for the helicopter. Wasn't that incredible? That they'd been wrong all that time, and he just now knew it for sure?

∘ TWELVE ∘

When Jeremy and Mick were still gone the next day, Helena gave them up for dead or lost. She was so convinced of this, and so prepared to live with it, that when she saw Mick shambling from the river with two large cans of black paint, she looked at him in disbelief. Then she threw down her hoe and ran hullooing past Mick to the river. At the empty canoe—empty of Jeremy, full of cans and brushes—she put her hand over her heart, letting it heal. She had known worse pain, worse disappointment, worse loss; she had known worse; she could live through this. Mechanically, she began to unload the canoe.

"Oh?" said Ben, coming to help carry. "Where's Jermicho?"

"I guess he's gone," said Helena, because she had known all along that he wouldn't come back.

Mick shambled back for another load. "Jermicho's gone?" Ben asked him. Mick nodded south along the river, then pantomimed pulling a rope over his shoulder. With a stifled cry Helena flung down the paintbrushes and set off along the bank, tripping through the underbrush in her haste. Ben and Mick looked thoughtfully at each other. "I think Helena would like to elect Jermicho the Federal Man," Ben said with a smile.

Mick grunted and put his hands over his crotch, gesturing crudely.

"Apparently not," Ben replied. "At least he told Helena that he couldn't. I once tried to ask him, but it seems to be a thing he doesn't talk about. Sad, isn't it?" Ben held a paintbrush in each small hand. "They *were* making babies in test tubes, you know. There must have been a reason for that. . . ."

Helena saw the barge in the river before she saw Jeremy on the bank. It looked hastily built and cumbersome, a raft riding on oil drums that slogged against the current. On the raft was a piece of machinery that looked like part of the Federal Man's helicopter, a huge white cone with three blades. Harnessed like a towpath mule and leaning hard against the weight, Jeremy was hauling this contraption up the river.

She would go to help him in just a moment. Just a moment she needed, to look at him and to once more put a healing hand over her heart. She was accustomed to pain; this joy was undoing her. As he labored nearer, she could hear him talking to himself, muttering phrases between panted breaths. "The barge she sat in. Like a burnish'd throne. Burn'd on the water. Geez, in one ear and out the other. Can't remember a thing. Age cannot wither her, nor custom stale . . . Something, something. Oh boy. The barge she sat in. Hullo, I see legs." He looked up at her, his blue eyes shining in his dirty sweat-streaked face. "Helena," he said happily, "am I almost . . . ?" Then he straightened, staggering a little as the barge pulled in the current. "What's the matter? My God, what's happened?" He had never seen her cry.

"Welcome home," she sobbed. "Welcome home."

"Helena," he scolded gently. He would have liked to let go of the barge and put his arms around her; he would have liked that, to cross the safety zone she kept between them like a skittish untamed animal. "You thought I wasn't coming back?"

She wiped her eyes with the heel of her hand, sniffed noisily, and then stepped into the ropes beside him. "Don't you even want to know. What it is you're pulling?" he asked, panting.

"What am I pulling?" she asked, bending with him against the ropes. She felt that she could move the earth, haul impossible weights for endless hours.

"A windmill." She could hear in his voice that this was important, and glanced back at the barge. "It was in Cottage Grove. In a garage. Just sitting there. I could never make one. Like this. A Cleopatra of windmills. Thank God for the. Alternate energy people."

"I can tell you just spent two days with Mickey."

"How can you tell that?" he asked curiously.

"'Cause you're talking so much."

He lowered his chin and chuckled. It was true; he wanted to tell her everything at once. He wanted especially to tell her what wonderful conversations he and Mick had had. One outside the hospital. Another in the doorway of the garage, where Mick stood twirling his hands, and Jeremy danced around him like a wild Indian, hollering and leaping with delight. "There was electricity down here?" Jeremy had said incredulously, and Mick had taught him how useless it could be by scooping a handful of soil and letting it run through his fingers. "But things *are* growing in Idamore," Jeremy had objected. Mick had nodded contentedly, pointing with his chin at the windmill and patting the soil. Idamore with both food and power. A vision of paradise.

Jeremy and Helena hauled together in silence. "If it's going to be a world of women," Jeremy commented after a while, "they'd better get some bigger shoulders." Helena responded by leaning further forward and pulling harder.

A *world* of women? Jeremy reflected. What could he know of the world? He knew only Idamore's women, governed by a midget male and an absentee federal official. "I saw the helicopter," Jeremy said. "Will he be here soon?"

Helena stopped abruptly, causing a momentary tangle of ropes that almost tripped Jeremy. "When we get to Idamore, you should go on to Riverwoods. Edgar's up there somewhere with the sheep. He has food. Shelter. You go on to Riverwoods."

"Edgar? Edgar! I thought that man was a dream. . . ." Jeremy shucked off the ropes and tied them to some bushes, muttering. "Can't talk hauling a damn windmill up a damn river. . . ." He tested the weight of the barge against the fragility of the bushes before he let go of the ropes. He turned toward her, walking unsteadily. "Whew, I'm floating. When you were a kid, did you ever push your arms as hard as you could against the doorjambs for sixty seconds, so they'd float when you stopped pushing?"

Helena knit her eyebrows. "The doorjambs?"

"No, the—" He chuckled. "I'm glad to *be* home. Tell me about Edgar. The man with no face?"

"You've *seen* him?"

"On my way from Cottage Grove the first time. He threatened me with a crowbar."

Helena gasped. "Edgar threatened you? Oh, Jermicho, he must've thought you were a Federal Man. He'd never hurt anyone, you know. He was just protecting the sheep. I told you about the sheep."

"Ah. So Edgar and the sheep come back to Idamore after the Federal Man leaves?" Helena nodded. "And you want me to hide up there until the Federal Man leaves?" Helena nodded again, and Jeremy sat down on the bank. "Mick explains things with his hands. You've got a voice. A really very beautiful voice. Please use it."

"You are . . . you are so big. He will think that you are strong. He will think . . ." Up and down went Helena's beautiful voice, cracked now, sharp as glass. "And he will take you . . . to work . . . at Carbonville. I . . ." She bit her lower lip, frowning with confusion. "I know it is wrong, but I do not want you to go."

She reminded him of Ben saying "We do not want her to die." The candid statement of the heart's wish in the face of incontrovertible odds. "Must I go if he wants me to go?"

"Oh, of course."

The Federal Man as fate. Or a figure out of the Old West. So tall he blocked out the sun, which glinted against his low-slung revolvers. Low-angle camera view: The Federal Man as phallic figure. "Helena, if you think I'm going to miss seeing this person," he said with a quirky grin, "if you think I'm going to skulk around with a bunch of sheep up in Riverwoods while the Federal Man is here, you're crazy." He was chastened by her look of distress. "Is he a giant? Does he have guns? Special . . . powers?"

"He is in charge of this sector."

Jeremy made a rude noise and leaned back on his elbows. "I'm gonna punch him in the nose."

"What?" she said in alarm. "What are you— Jeremy, you mustn't. Oh, please."

"Why must you take everything so literally? Can't you see that I'm not the fighting type? I haven't been in a fight since junior high school. But hiding . . . Laney, keeping things from him by deception is just a . . ." He was about to say "coward's way," but that sounded too harsh. "Just a devious way of saying no. I will not go to Carbonville if I can possibly help it, but I will not hide."

If he would not hide, perhaps she could hide him? Helena toyed briefly with the idea of asserting Jeremy's feeblemindedness. "See, he's of no use at all," she'd say to the Federal Man. "Oh, he's quite useless." Helena looked over at Jeremy. The whole fearful length of him was sprawled in an attitude of relaxed indifference that conveyed to Helena coiled energy, potential power. His feet were planted wide apart. The position of his arms strained the shirt across his chest, so there were little triangles of exposed skin between the buttons. Why must he sit there looking like that? His shirt was going to fly apart! Why couldn't he shrink, wilt, wither, shamble?

"I didn't mean hide," she said finally. "Just leave for a while. Just leave. Please leave!" And the words felt so wrong, so contrary, that Helena once again burst into tears.

"Laney . . ." Jeremy said softly. He worked his tongue around his lower teeth, then abruptly got to his feet. "There are lots of people to feed around here. We'd better get to work." But he said something more complicated with his eyes: that he would not hide or be hidden; that she need not be so frightened; that he would not leave Idamore. . . . Did he say that with his eyes? Or was that what she put there? And what had he done to her that her way had become as looped and oddly woven as a cloth full of hidden threads? Secrets, and lies, and deviousness.

Mick insisted, in his speechless way, on helping Jeremy install the windmill, and the two of them worked on it all the next day, oblivious to the turmoil around them. Back and forth past them went a battery of busy women, while Jeremy labored to interpret Mick's instructions. "This flange here? No? Oh, the screw. I see." Jeremy suggested that they put the windmill on a building with a flat roof, but Mick shook his head and pointed to a knoll beyond the administration building. "So far?" asked Jeremy. But Mick was insistent, and Jeremy yielded to him again and again.

It was Mick who selected the metal tower and Jeremy who loosed and hauled it. "You don't need me, you need a mule," Jeremy complained. He dug holes while Mick arranged pulleys to hoist the tower. When they rested, Jeremy reread sections of *Basic House Wiring*. "This'll be direct current, Mick-o. We'll need an inverter. Would you know an inverter if you saw one? Hmm, me neither. Well, we'll experiment on an empty house. If it blows, it blows," Jeremy said with a jaunty smile. Mick frowned and tapped the housing of the windmill. "Oh, we could burn out the generator. . . . Hmmm." Jeremy studied the book.

Helena and Lily trooped by carrying firewood toward the river. Then came Rachel and Rose with large tubs, followed by Laurel with her hands full of clothes and towels. "Jermicho," said Laurel, "why does the—"

"Not just now, Laurel," said Pearl.

Jeremy exchanged quick shrugs with Laurel and waved to Ben, who rattled a bucket in greeting.

When the tower was standing, Jeremy shaded his eyes to look at its pinnacle. "My God, Mick, how will we get this monster to the top of the tower? Geez, we'll never . . ." Mick rotated his hands. "The windmill?" No. "The helicopter!" Jeremy exclaimed. "We'll lift it with the helicopter!" Yes, yes, Mick indicated, clapping Jeremy's back.

Ben returned from the river and stopped to admire their tower. Mick squatted and ran his hand with slow pride over the curved housing of the windmill. "Soon we'll compete in power with . . ." Ben paused, searching for the right name. "Nigara?"

"Niagara," Jeremy growled. "Niagara Falls. Which is bigger than all of Idamore put together. Ben, I wish you'd listen to me—"

"Not now, not now—firewood, bathwater, chickens . . ." Off he hurried, his short legs swiveling in jerky curves that took him sideways before they took him forward.

Mick gave Jeremy a wry smile. "Yeah," sighed Jeremy. "Oh well." With that, he looped some wires over his shoulder and climbed the tower.

"Uhhh."

"Yeah, I'll be careful, Mick."

Thirty-five feet above Idamore Jeremy admired the pattern and texture of the place he lived in. The dark geometry of roofs, hard and flat and standing in rows along the shifting dense blocks of deep-green corn and buff-colored wheat. The untilled fields looked softer, plusher. The tall grasses were interspersed with flowers— spiky, lacy, clustered, and petaled; blue, yellow, purple, and white—all modeled by light to an Impressionistie blur. When he looked toward the river, he saw the women bathing. The long white curve of Helena's back as she bent over the tubs, her hair half in the water, her elbows raised. The crescents of Rachel's breasts and belly and buttocks. Jeremy framed the women between the diagonal lines of the riverbanks; complicated the frame with the line of the horizon and the vertical line of the house on the left. Women bathing . . . how beautiful they were.

Rose was upsetting Jeremy's structure. In ceaseless motion she moved at the center of his picture. She curved over to touch her foot and then ran her hands slowly the length of her body. Then she raised her arms over her head and bent over to touch the other leg. As she ran her fingers through the triangle of her pubic hair, Jeremy found himself sucking on his scarred upper lip. With a small groan, he pressed himself against the metal strut of the tower. Below him Mick whacked a wrench against the base, and the sound came to Jeremy as a vibration.

At the clang, the women looked up and saw Jeremy clinging to the airy triangles of the metal structure. "Yo, Jermicho!" shouted Lily with a friendly wave.

Helena stared at him for a moment, then turned her back. She crossed her arms over her breasts, shivering. What she felt was not cold, but naked. She had never felt naked before. Cold, yes, and needing warmth. But not naked and needing cover. She snatched up the white dress and pulled it over her head, her rough fingers catching on the slithery-smooth fabric. "Oh, I hate these dresses!"

Jeremy had begun a cautious descent of the tower when Rose resumed her song. "I know the man with the suns in his hand," Rose chanted, running her soap-slicked hands up and down her body, "and the man with the green breath knows me. . . ."

"Wait for the Federal Man, Rose," said Rachel. "He loves the way you dance."

"I'm dancing for the sun!" shouted Rose. She clambered up the bank and headed for the tower. "Dance for the sun," she said, doing her slow-motion masturbatory dance at the base of the tower.

"Don't dance for Jeremy." Lily laughed. "Dance for the Federal Man."

Helena jammed her feet into her shoes and flew toward the naked woman. "Don't," she yelled in a piercing voice. "You'll make him fall." It was the terrible look on Jeremy's face—white, taut, frightened—that reminded her of Simon. When she had been about May's age, Helena had watched Simon fall off a roof. In the time of his falling, she kept expecting Simon to twist around and fly. Simon the builder, Simon the forager, Simon the winged guide. Simon, so different from his brother Ben. "We only fly in our dreams," he had said to her afterward. "And we must dream of flight in flocks." Simon's version of what Jeremy sneeringly called the cooperative effort. She had thought she was meant for Simon, but he never fathered anything. Nor had his broken leg healed properly; when he left for Carbonville, he limped away.

"Don't fall," she prayed to Jeremy. Then she prayed that he would fall. "Break, limp. Stay with us. Don't fall." In her shrieking confusion, it was she herself who fell, stumbling over her unlaced shoes and going down heavily. She scrambled to her feet and immediately fell again; the twisted ankle would not carry her. "Stop," she screamed.

Into the center of this commotion came Ben. His silent disapproving glare had the effect of a camera, catching everyone in a frozen gesture. Then Helena fell to her hands, Jeremy came down from the tower, and Rose curled up on the ground, a rigid fetus. "Look what you've done to Rose," Ben said, though he must have known no one was to blame for anything that Rose did. Sometimes she lay like that for days at a time, refusing food and soiling her clothes. They'd had to carry her—rigid as stone—into a house to get her out of the rain.

"Not their fault," said Lily, and stooped to examine Helena's ankle.

There was another long painful silence; they all gazed at Ben, waiting for him to restore order. "We are . . . we must . . ." He gave a distracted pull on his earlobe. "What's happening to us?" he murmured. "I don't know. . . ."

Lily said quietly, "Sometimes a person has a feeling different from others'. It gets weary, you know, Ben, always being 'we.'" She paused, waiting for Ben, and when he said nothing, she began barking orders. "Mick, go get that stretcher we made, find Dave, and have him help you carry Rose into the house. Jermicho, help me get Helena to her room. Rachel, Ben . . ." She made everyone scurry when she added, "Hurry, now. The Federal Man could be here any time."

Helena pivoted on her bottom. "I can crawl. . . ."

"Good. Crawl. I've had enough of your nonsense today. And this of all days!" She walked away. "Jeremy," she called over her shoulder, "carry the tubs from the river, will you?"

Jeremy stood rocking slightly back and forth on his heels, watching Helena crawl through the tall grass. She looked ridiculous, wearing sneakers and a glistening white slip that twitched over her shifting buttocks. The sharp bones of her shoulders jutted like wings, now one, now the other, as she landed on each hand. Jeremy laughed, a short uncertain whinny. "I could easily carry you."

She stopped, letting her head hang down between her arms. "I haven't been carried since the winter I fell into the pond." She meant to convey pride, but what Jeremy heard was nostalgia and longing. He hesitated beside her: Unless she cooperated, he could get a purchase on her only by slinging her up like a sack. He wanted to carry her in his arms, he wanted to cherish her, he wanted to feel the weight of her legs. . . . Jeremy found that he was trembling with desire, and he put his hand on her firm, round haunch.

Almost sullenly, Helena turned and extended her arms. At first she tried to hold herself away from him, but his arms tightened around her, and she yielded against him. He walked through the bright field of wild flowers and tall grasses. "Rose was like a wild animal," he said into Helena's damp hair. "Like a cat in heat. We are not animals."

But Jeremy was rapidly losing this argument with himself. Perhaps he chose to lose it, for it was not absolutely necessary that he dwell on the day's images. He might have forced himself to think of something other than the bright curves of Rachel's breast and belly as she washed herself; other than the dark hair that ran down the inside of Helena's thighs; other than—oh, above all—other than slender Rose with her eyes fixed on his while she stroked herself and stroked herself until Jeremy thought he was going to die. Like pornography in the startled broad daylight, leaving him helpless with unfocused generalized lust. The images played and replayed in his mind with the inexorable drive of a wet dream which he was going to have. Must have. Would have.

He stopped in the tall grass. His breath came in short rasping sobs. "We are not animals," he said hoarsely. He imagined himself, savage and swift as a wild animal in the bright field. "Forgive me," he said as he toppled her over. "Forgive me," he said, yanking and pulling at clothes. But his fumbling frantic fingers were too slow for his mind. Grunting helplessly, he ejaculated, wetting the lacy hem of her nylon slip.

Helena sat up. "Did you just . . . was that . . . are you . . . ?" she gabbled.

"Oh God, I'm sorry, I'm so sorry," he said, apologizing again for a violation he had committed only in his mind. He knelt in the grass, adjusting his clothes and looking guiltily around for witnesses.

"But why did you lie to me? Wait, oh, you're just sterile, is that it? And I thought you meant—"

"What are you talking about?"

"You told me you couldn't have babies, and I thought you meant—"

"I never said any such—"

"You certainly did. Right over there, by the pond. I told you about the winter we lost our babies, and you said—"

"I said I *wouldn't* have them. Not couldn't. Wouldn't."

"Wouldn't?" she repeated after him, as if it were a foreign word. *"Choose* not to have . . ." She stared at him for a moment, then looked down at her slip. "So you do it this way?"

"Laney, we're having a big misunderstanding here—"

Her lip curled with disgust. "You cannot stay with us in Idamore." She stood up, winced, hopped. Romantic that he was, he expected that she would lean on him, fall into his arms. She spat at his extended hand, then fell to her knees, crawling through the high grass to her porch of her house.

She negotiated the steps on her bottom. "When the Federal Man comes, you'll go with him. . . ." Helena pulled herself up by the back of a chair, which she then used as a crutch to hobble through the door.

"Helena," he called, then mounted the steps and followed her into the house. "Helena, I am from the time of plenty. Don't you know that there were plenty of children, too? So many children that people tried to choose when to have them, and how many to have. You have been thinking about me as if I were born in your time. And I . . . I have been judging things as if they were happening in mine." Jeremy threw himself into the easy chair, which collapsed under him. He looked up, hoping to hear her laugh.

The angry scraping of the chair stopped, and she stood there, her knuckles white against the backrest, like a ferocious hostess offering him a seat. "You have been with us all these nights without making babies? Jeremy, how is that possible?"

"Jesus, that's just what Ben said about the power."

"But *this,* this you can do?"

"Well, I've never come at it from quite that direction, but I don't see why not." He shrugged uncomfortably.

"Now?"

"Well . . . okay. No!" he exclaimed as she lay down on the couch with her slip bunched around her waist. "No, don't just . . . not like that."

"You need me to dance for you?"

"Dance . . . ? Oh God." He was stabbed by the sudden picture of Helena's time with the Federal Man. And Rachel's time. And

Pearl's. Maddy's . . . This making of babies was a very practical business, much more demeaning than the animal life that Jeremy's inflamed imagination had tried so hard to repudiate. He adjusted the slip over her hips, his chapped hands catching and scraping on the slithery cool fabric. "I need," he said very carefully, "to dance for you."

Helena started angrily. "You must not. Never, never . . ."

Jeremy bent over her for a moment, like a Muslim at prayer. "How can I explain . . . ?" he began. "What do you call what you do with the Federal Man?"

"Making babies."

"And what do you call what you do with Rachel?"

"Oh, that—that is making love." Helena blushed.

"So, Laney, I want to do both. Combine them, hey?"

The blush deepened. "Just the two of us?! Here? Now?"

Jeremy couldn't help grinning at her: Which of them was the innocent of Idamore? "Anywhere you say. Anytime you choose."

"Oh boy." Helena put her hands over her face. Then she whispered into her fingers. "Now."

◦ THIRTEEN ◦

Jeremy woke a few hours later in an empty bed. Roused by a familiar sound becoming unfamiliarly loud, he woke thinking he was in his dorm room and a helicopter was landing on the roof. . . . The roar of the rotors brought Jeremy to his feet with a surge of adrenaline. "Here we go," he thought.

Blocking the door to the porch was Helena's crutch-chair with a small bowl of wild berries on its seat. She had left him a gift where he couldn't miss it. He was seized with a fierce pride when he thought of Helena crawling along the riverbank foraging on her sturdy hands and knees—for him! for him! His earthbound Eve, who smelled of mushrooms and moss: He had changed everything for her now.

He popped a handful of berries into his mouth and stood on the porch. His nerves jangled at the congress of sensations: The sweet taste of the berries became sharply sour in the back of his throat; the tiny seeds rasped between his teeth; the approaching helicopter battered his ears; the draft of the rotors bent the corn as if a shadow animal were passing through the field.

"Here we go," he thought again. Jeremy was prepared to stand up against great odds for his own freedom, such as it was here in Idamore, and for Helena's. He was prepared to match wits and maybe even physical strength with a superior man. He was prepared to meet a villain or a god. . . . He was prepared for a good deal, but not for the middle-aged man who stumbled to the door of the helicopter and looked down, gesturing wildly for everyone to stay back.

"That's not him," Jeremy said out loud. "That can't be him."

Jeremy tried to muster a laugh. The trapped thing in his throat must be a laugh. What could be funnier than this balding, bony—why, he looked like a starved Oklahoman ranch hand—exacting such solicitude, such respect? Jeremy wanted Helena on the porch with him, so they could roll on the floor with laughter. "Does he fly?" —Yes. In a helicopter. "Does he have special . . . powers?" —Yes. Those we wish he had. "Does he govern the future?" —Yes. From a dirty mattress. Jeremy wanted Helena to come back on the porch. "Come teach me your laugh again, Laney," he whispered, for the thing in his throat was terrible.

But he didn't see her there among the others, all their chins tilted, their mouths gaping. Something wrong, something wrong . . . Jeremy stepped off the porch and scanned the row of houses, checking all the porches. He gazed past the helicopter toward the ponds, looking for her white-clad figure among the reeds and grasses, and then let his eyes run in and out of furrows, up and down streets, until he was looking toward the river, squinting against the late-afternoon sun. Her arrival would be slowed by her ankle, he assured himself, but his heart raced with the premonition of some disaster.

He began to run toward the river, paused, then backtracked toward the ponds. Skittery and uncertain, he once more scanned the fields, the porches, the horizon behind the helicopter. "Where's . . . ?" Jeremy started to call, and then the Federal Man, the bearer of Idamore's future and Idamore's salt, the absentee official and mythic seed bearer, fell out of his helicopter. Rubbery-boned and limp, he fell to the earth. A long stunned moment later, the small crowd reacted as if he had exploded and sent them reeling outward with a blast of searing air. He was just an ordinary man, and what he had brought them this trip was disease.

Ben summoned everyone together on the knoll where the windmill tower was being installed. "We must consider what to do," Ben said.

Jeremy immediately balked: "You're having a *meeting*?" he yelled. "The Federal Man is lying unconscious beside his helicopter, Helena is missing, and you're having a fucking *meeting*?"

Ben dismissed him with a glance and turned to the others. "We heard what he said. 'This sector is closed.' We must consider carefully what to do. . . ."

"This *sector* . . . ?" grumbled Jeremy, then stopped interrupting because Ben was speaking in his pulpit voice. This was the talk that Jeremy was later to call Ben's "Sermon on the Knoll":

"We are not the children of Israel, for Israel was blessed. God promised to multiply Israel's seed as the stars of the heaven and as the sand upon the seashore. We are the children of America, and because we are not blessed, we do today what we have always done: We run from the man bringing disease. Because we have no blessing from God, we can have no responsibility to a man bringing disease. Our responsibility is only to ourselves, to survive and reproduce, to become one of the nations which walk in the city of the light.

"We stand by the river in Idamore, by the roads and houses in Idamore, and we know of the greatness of the light, of the cities by the thousands that had the river of the water of life running through them. The cities of light had no need of the sun or of the moon to shine upon them, for they shone with their own light. The nations of them which were saved walked in the light of the cities, beside the pure waters, and into those cities nothing unclean did enter, nothing accursed or foul.

"We do not permit people with disease.

"We are not the children of Israel. We live more like bees. No single one of us counts; the hive counts. We forage and labor and cherish one another to continue the hive. If one of us dies, we nudge the body out as carelessly as we can. There can be no mourning except for the hive itself, and in that case there will be no mourners. Idamore is a hive; the hive is in a sector; the sector was once a city of light. The many hives of America are all connected, just like Idamore, by these rivers, these roads, these wires, these Federal Men. America was one vast city of light. It is written that every accursed thing disappeared; nothing unclean did enter. We do not permit disease.

"However. If this sector is closed, we no longer . . . exist. Yet here we are, breathing beneath the sun. We are a hive without a sector. We must decide what this means. . . ."

Ben stumbled now, repeating himself, though it was perfectly clear to all of them what this meant: the end of the line. Pearl's baby Phoebe was the last of the clan of Idamore. "Do we wish to live as long as we can, or may we now act as we would wish to? For ourselves. For one's self . . ." Deprived of his vision, Ben's rich tenor had begun to thin out; now his voice shrank to suit him: He was a midget standing on a knoll, and addressing the group in a high strained voice. He didn't know how to say "I wish, I want," for he had no desire or identity separate from the group's.

As Ben visibly shrank, Jeremy felt settle over him a weight so intolerable that he sat down. It was not enough to build a windmill or capture bio-gas. It was not enough to teach Laurel to read and reason. It was not enough to show Ben that he had telescoped thousands of years of history into a single glorious moment, a mythic Eden of postindustrial America described in phrases from the ancient Book of Revelations. Nothing would suffice but Jeremy himself. Jeremy, who had always been the "I" at the center of his large universe, looked up at Ben, who knew only the "we" of his tiny community. It was a moment of intersection, more fateful than the one Helena had dreaded when she had heard the helicopter bearing the Federal Man. "Ben," Jeremy called in a tone of dreadful calm. "Ben, I can be a Federal Man."

Ben's voice seemed to have completely deserted him. His jaw worked soundlessly. It was Mick who posed the question by putting his hands over his crotch and gesturing. "Uhhh?"

Jeremy flushed with humiliation. Seated on the grass, he had to look up at the circle of intent amazed faces. The one face he would have gladly seen was absent, and he found that he could not look directly at Pearl or Rachel. He flashed a headline for Idamore's nonexistent newspaper: "Young Stud Imported from Chicago Zoo." "Why me?" he thought bitterly. There must have been thousands of red-blooded American males who would welcome the job. Rise to the occasion, as it were. He himself had too much imagination, and the task before him made him feel anything but ruggedly masculine. "Yes," he answered, fixing his eyes on the ground.

"Jeremy!" said Ben, his tone divided between accusation and delight.

Lily sobbed. "Oh, I'm sorry, I'm sorry, but I've been exposed to him. I can't stay here with you, and I can't just leave him lying there."

"Oh, we can't just leave him. . . ." As much as Lily wanted to help Hank, Jeremy wanted to talk to him. To question him: How many others were there, and where? Why were they closing this sector, and who were "they"? Where were they based? Did they pay him to do this job? And what exactly did he do? Jeremy stood up, and looked from Ben to Lily. "Couldn't we separate into two groups for a while? The breeders," he said with grim humor, "and the . . ." His voice trailed off. Dispensable? Lily, who nursed and midwived and plowed with the strength of a man? Ben, who spoke their dreams for them and hoed his furrow with a sawed-off tool? Mickey, whose memory and native talents were constructing for them a workable windmill? "Or . . . I don't know. Is that what we should do?"

Simultaneously Lily said, "Yes," and Ben said, "Oh no!" Mick was shaking his head and pointing at the windmill still lying under a sheet of black plastic in the field. Dave removed the soft battered hat from his head and ran his hand through his hair, which was coming out in patches. "I could do it alone. Don't figure I've got much time left anyhow. . . ."

Jeremy looked at Dave, and saw for the first time that the man was dying. "Each person must do what he or she thinks best," declared Jeremy. When Lily moved past Ben and stood next to Dave, the group began to divide, leaving Ben at the apex of a triangular space. "But once you've been exposed to . . . to Hank, you're quarantined from our group. Which includes the kids, of course, and Rose. And . . . where *is* Helena?" The triangle briefly closed while they conferred on the details of the quarantine; then the group dispersed.

Jeremy went in search of Helena, with the women and children trailing behind him. Laurel thought Helena had gone to the meadow, Rachel thought she was at home resting her ankle, and Pearl was certain that she had gone to the river for berries. These conflicting accounts of Helena's whereabouts further roused Jeremy's anxiety. He could imagine her bustling from chore to chore, using a chair as a crutch, or determinedly crawling from the meadow to the river; but surely only an accident would prevent her from coming back to greet the Federal Man—who was only "Hank" now that he was sick in a nonsector. "How far could she get on that ankle?"

Walking in the opposite direction, Lily and Dave approached the helicopter. "It'll be like having a vacation, won't it?" Lily remarked.

"Dying?"

"No, you old fool, not working the fields."

"We'll probably have a guaranteed field," Dave replied.

"Quarantined, he called it. I guess we'd better, if we want to eat."

Only Ben and Mick were left at the knoll. Ben watched the group separate into its component parts. He had watched them separate before, each person to an assigned task. Dig, forage, chop. Shovel, compost, haul. But today he was a witness to dismemberment. Pulled in two directions at once, he was paralyzed and frightened. "Each person must decide . . ." Jeremy had said; but Ben had never chosen anything for himself alone: Always, always he had thought of Idamore, of the city of light. "This sector is closed." But they were going on anyway. They were going on. No more civilization. No more light. Just raw life.

Ben watched the eager twosome hurrying toward death and the reluctant group assuming the burden of life. Jeremy was walking backward in order to speak to Rachel. "There will be NO DANCING!" Ben heard him bellow.

"I *do* like that boy," Ben remarked to Mick. Then, with a little backward wave, he walked toward the helicopter.

With his palms on the sun-warmed metal of the generator, Mick watched through a haze of tears as Ben walked toward the diseased Federal Man. He wanted to cry out, "Stay with us, Ben." But Mick was a mute, and knew no gestures to argue for life. Except the one he made by remaining where he was.

In Cottage Grove he had learned that survival was what you snatched, hoarded, withheld from your neighbor. As a boy he had survived malnutrition and neglect—he was thought retarded—and then he had survived the last epidemic. Cottage Grove was a collection of rough shards each saying "I." Forty-two I's, thirty I's, twenty-one, seventeen, nine, four. And then one. He inherited the dry reluctant fields of his neighbors, the dismantled windmill, the houses full of bones.

When he found himself alone there, he felt neither abandoned nor guilty to be the last survivor. He didn't even feel touched by magic or saved for some divine future purpose. He had no reason to live, but he had never had a reason, so he was as unfamiliar with despair as he was with hope. He felt just as he always had: irrelevant. Overlooked.

Mick had one talent, and it too was irrelevant, overlooked. His useless, trembling hands steadied on metal and sang with the mystery of machines. He had been tolerated by Cottage Grove's mechanics, three generations of frail birdlike women who did what they knew how to do and were revered for their ancient knowledge—though everyone saw that the machines could not feed them or warm them or cure them of disease. What he learned from the gradual extinction of Cottage Grove was later confirmed in the perilous vitality of Idamore: that there was a sacred, secret life hidden not in machines, but in seeds. Man seed, wheat seed, hen seed, corn seed. Kernel and sperm, germ and egg. And that he was excluded from that moist dark world of planted seeds. He was a useless, sterile mute.

When Lewison-Clark found Mick upriver from the undug graveyard of Cottage Grove, he flew him north to a place where people said "we" and meant everyone. Though Mick was useless, he was fed. Though he could not speak, he was spoken to. For a long time Mick wished that Lewison-Clark had deposited him somewhere else, someplace where people understood that survival came before charity. Not that Mick now counted his own survival as important. No, it was that he was sure that *they* wouldn't survive, these reckless, inefficient people, and oh! they looked in his eyes when they spoke to him. They nudged him in the ribs when they laughed. They took his hand in the circles of reverence. Could he let them create holes in his heart, which would become one vast swallowing hole when they all died? As die they must, for they turned no one away, and shared everything.

"What shall we do first, Mick? Irrigate or fish?" they asked him. "What do *you* think, Mick?" they said. So he had to learn to answer. With his hands, with his head, pointing and making faces. Relying on their patience. "You mean . . . ? No? Ah! You mean . . . Oh, *good* idea."

Oh!

Season by season he came to feel cherished, this useless, sterile old mute. Again and again he offered up his life in exchange for theirs. When he fasted through the days of famine in exchange for Helena's recovery, he was making no compact with the invisible gods of life; he was keeping his food for Helena. Her cheeks were still round with childhood as she sipped the broth and thanked him for bringing it. He, the only one who couldn't tell her what it was that nourished her. When he tended Ben and Helena and Lily through the spring of the dysentery epidemic, he was not superstitiously risking his life that they would live; he was protecting Rachel and Pearl from exposure to the infection. Each episode that didn't kill him left him a little more glad to be alive. He still retained the one thing he could give them.

Then Jeremy came. Jeremy Echo came and ranted at Ben, waving books in the air and saying, "No, no power, impossible." It wasn't long before Mick began to understand what Ben meant by the "power." Ben meant machines. Ben meant generators and pumps. Ben meant electricity. Mick knew as well as Jeremy how little life machines conferred, but he also knew that Idamore was blessed, and could turn the cursed machines of Cottage Grove into benign auxiliary presences. If they wanted machines, then Mick was no longer irrelevant. He had a use, a life's function. He would be Idamore's mechanic.

But to let Ben and Dave and Lily go to one side while he went to the other? To choose life? To have a reason to avoid death . . . ? With his palms on the warm housing of the useless old generator, he knelt, a useless old mute, and all the holes in his heart opened wide to sing with sorrow and pride. He had chosen now. He had chosen, and he wouldn't fail them.

∘ FOURTEEN ∘

As soon as Jeremy discovered that his canoe was missing, he felt certain that Helena had gone to Riverwoods. Where else would she go? To Carbonville, for God's sake? How stupid did she think he was? he muttered angrily to himself. What was she thinking of, to crawl to the river and take off in his canoe? By then it was too late for him to start for Riverwoods, and Rachel and Pearl were busy hauling water to heat his bath. The Federal Man always had a bath.

Laurel giggled at him. "Jermicho's a Federal Man!"

"Just for us. Just for Idamore," he said, wondering how much of all this Laurel actually understood.

"You'll be Federal Man for me, too, won't you? After my first blood? It won't be long. Look, I'm getting breasts." Like a much younger child gravely showing off a scrape or bruise, Laurel pulled up her T-shirt to show Jeremy the slight roundings on her chest.

"Buds," said Jeremy, smiling at the flat, childish nipples. He looked over at Pearl, who had opened her blouse to suckle Phoebe at one milk-swollen, blue-veined breast. As if by magic, the other nipple sprang with huge beads of milk, which dripped steadily into the cup Pearl held beneath that breast. Jeremy felt comfortable with Laurel's adolescence and Pearl's abundant breasts, and smiled to remember how discomfited he had been that day when Helena had casually unbuttoned and removed her sodden shirt. Slowly, his fine civilized embarrassments were leaving him; he could get used to anything. He would get used to this, too—this stud service. Maybe one day it would seem as natural to him as Pearl's breasts did now. Maybe one day he'd stop making a romance out of sexuality. . . . Jeremy shifted unhappily in his chair.

"Laurel shouldn't get pregnant for a couple of years after her first period, you know. The babies of young teenagers aren't always strong, and it might damage Laurel herself." When Pearl and Rachel exchanged a significant look, Jeremy leaned forward in his chair. "You know that, don't you?"

"Damage how?" asked Laurel.

"Well, you're growing, aren't you, and the baby would take a lot of your growing energy away from you," Jeremy replied.

Rachel put another log on the fire, adjusted the bucket of water over it, then stepped away from the hearth. She wiped the sweat off her face with the edge of her shirt. "Laurel, honey, go get one more bucket of water, will you, please? Look how big Jermicho is for so little water! And on your way back, tell May to bring the boys in for dinner." Rachel waited until Laurel was out the door, then turned. "Is that why Laney loses all her babies? Because she had the first one too soon?"

"Loses . . . ?"

"Little boys," Pearl chimed in. She put the cup down on the armrest and held her fingers apart to indicate the size of the lost fetuses. *"Lots* of blood."

With a groan, Jeremy slid down his chair until he was half lying on his back. "I don't think I can do this."

"We'll help you, Jermicho," said Pearl.

"I don't want—"

"And anyhow, it's just me now," said Rachel, stooping by his chair. "Rose is a stone right now, Pearl's too soon with Phoebe, and Helena's gone. I'm sure she ran away because she hates to be with the Federal Man. She just hates it, and it's so useless after all. I don't hate it as much as she does, and I can carry a baby to the birthtime. I've given birth to three besides Augie, and they were all healthy for several seasons. . . . So it's just me, and I really don't mind."

"You don't mind . . ." he repeated absentmindedly. "So we'll just leave her up there?"

"What's the harm, Jeremy?" asked Pearl in her aggressive way. "If they close this sector, we can do anything we want. It doesn't matter anymore. Leave her alone."

He didn't know why Helena had run away, but her reasons had to be more complicated than Rachel and Pearl supposed. He had, after all, been with her only a few hours before, and he knew that she didn't "just hate it." He was groping for a good reason to fetch her home when he said, "Just suppose that *I* can give Helena healthy babies that she can carry to term—to the birthtime. If that's even a remote possibility, should she come back?"

Rachel was blinking at him, her mouth half open.

"Absolutely," said Pearl with strident authority.

Rachel's nails dug into Jeremy's arm. "What do you mean, 'suppose'?"

"It could be Hank making the bad babies, that's all I'm saying. It *could* be. It could also be anemia, malnutrition, vitamin deficiency, genetic damage . . . Christ, what do I know?" He scratched savagely at his beard, which irritated his skin when he sweat. "But it's possible that it's Hank's problem. And if it is, then *I* could make—"

Jeremy was interrupted by the children clattering into the room. Laurel and May came in complaining of the overheated room and of each other. "May wouldn't help carry."

"Laurel spilled water all over the book she stole."

"Didn't."

"Did, did."

"Didn't. Ben *said* I could have it."

August came straight to Rachel and wrapped his arms around her legs. Last came Jules, who tripped over the threshold and entered the room at a falling gallop, as if he were racing to get to Pearl before he went down. Reaching her, he fell against the chair, knocking the cup of milk to the floor. "Muh-muh-muh-muh," he bellowed.

Rachel's hands were like talons on Jeremy's bare skin. "Sons, Jeremy?"

"I'm not making any promises, Rachel. Just babies," he reminded her later, when they were upstairs. As soon as he spoke, he found himself clinically wondering about his sperm count. This was his third time today: once that afternoon, like Onan in the field; once with Helena; and now inside this dry vessel waiting only to be filled. Rachel recoiled from his touch and insisted impatiently that he get on with it and be done. She was as unresponsive at the end as she was at the beginning. Jeremy had a vivid image of numerous faceless and naked women passing on a conveyor belt beneath him. Like a piece of machinery, he was raised up and down, up and down, a huge mechanical nozzle depositing cookie batter.

He didn't protest when she left him to go to Pearl. He lay alone in the dark room with his arm thrown over his eyes. Tomorrow morning he was going to get Helena. If she had become suddenly afraid of another pregnancy—and well she might be, after watching Maddy die in labor—he'd tell her he didn't care about that.

There was Rachel to get pregnant. There was even Rose. Pearl, soon enough. After that, Laurel. He didn't need to get Helena pregnant; he just needed her.

The next morning in a shouted conversation from field to porch, Jeremy told Lily he was going to look for Helena. He learned that Hank was still unconscious; he had a high fever and he was covered with a fine red rash. It could be anything, Jeremy thought, from measles to typhus to some new or ancient disease. It could be viral or bacterial; waterborne, airborne, or—his skin prickled at the thought—insect borne. Lice, fleas, flies, mosquitoes—they had them all. No quarantine would stop a louse.

Lily was in oddly high spirits, as if glad to be doing battle with the unknown for Hank's life. "Bring back the sheep," she shouted gaily. "Bring back Edgar." But Ben, sitting on the porch swing, was as listless as Lily was animated. "Ben should have stayed with us," Jeremy thought.

Jeremy stopped in Rachel's kitchen to get some biscuits for the long walk, then remembered the bowl of berries he'd left in Helena's doorway.

When he picked up the bowl, Helena's note flew off the chair, yawing in the sudden draft. He read it, frowning and smiling at once. It was a dedication page torn from a book: "To Bea and Warren with gratitude and love," it said in an elegant linotype face. Beneath were the vast, tortured letters of an illiterate sounding out words. Surely she had meant to say something else, something more than the crude phonetic spellings would permit.

i hv qWr tu ƙvƙwbz BHwz
gbBi

He got the "gbBi" without effort—good-bye, g'bye—but that other one had him stumped. "I have gone to Riverwoods backwhiz. Bookwise. Backwards." When he guffawed at the possibilities, it was as if Helena had launched his journey toward her with laughter. A good sign, he was sure. A good sign.

He walked for hours in the steadily increasing heat, then for hours more crisscrossed Riverwoods in search of her. He rehearsed what he would say and imagined how she would respond. Every minute he expected to see her in the next clearing or just past the next street; with each disappointment he harbored ever more fantastic visions of their happy reunion. He finally found her sitting on a low hillside surrounded by some forty yellowish sheep. "Hello," she said, then returned her gaze to the sheep.

Vexed and hurt by the placid calm of her greeting, he armored himself in an offhanded manner. Pulling the note from his pocket, he asked—as if he had just walked all the way from Idamore only to ask—"What's this 'backwhiz'?"

"Because." She was wearing a battered straw hat that shadowed her face in intricate, shifting diamonds that prevented Jeremy from quite catching her expressions.

"Oh. I have gone to Riverwoods because. I see." He bit his lower lip. He hadn't walked all this way to be caustic and petty; he had come to bring her home. But he was thwarted by the emotional blankness of this woman who seemed very little like the Helena he had known yesterday. "How's your ankle?" he asked.

"Getting better."

"I like your crutch." Beside her in the grass was a crutch contrived from the back and legs of a dining-room chair.

"Your canoe's over by the animal shelter."

He had been dismissed. "Yeah, I know. I saw it," he said dully. "I didn't come up to get the canoe. I came up to . . . Listen, Laney, you've got to come home. You won't have to be with Hank, and we . . . you and I . . . we can play it any way you want. We don't have to make babies if you don't want. We don't even have to make love. . . . Please come home," he said hoarsely.

"Hank came?"

Jeremy was confounded. "Hey, I'm saying I love you, I need you. Is there anybody at home to hear?" He reached over and removed her hat. She flinched from his hand. "Yeah, Hank came. He's sick."

"Oh?" She leaned forward, keeping her head bent. "How sick?"

"Very sick, I think."

"Ah," she said, almost as if she had known all along.

"You'll come home?"

"I can't, Jeremy."

"But why, for heaven's sake? Tell me why and maybe I can live with it."

"You won't. You'll just argue. . . ." She played with the brim of her hat, bending the unraveled pieces of straw until they broke off in her fingers. "I am very selfish, Jeremy. You know that. I'm a selfish, impatient, worthless person. Not like Lily. I think Lily feels about Hank the same way that I feel about you. But she has never complained, she has never run away. Hank comes and goes, and she says hello and good-bye. Yesterday, when I thought you were gone forever, I was fine. But then you came back, and . . ." Without raising her head, she patted her chest. "Here, you know. Where you say welcome or good-bye." Her voice was flat and steady. "I can't say good-bye to you many more times."

"But I'm not going anywhere!"

For an instant she raised her head with an accusing look that said, "I told you that you'd argue." Then the dull mask dropped again. "You'll be a Federal Man now, Jeremy. Even if Hank wasn't sick, you'd have to be. If he's sick, well, more than ever . . . You can't choose otherwise."

"I can. I do. I won't. I . . ." Jeremy stopped, aghast.

"Yesterday I lay beside you while you slept, and I planned all the lies I would tell. Lie and lie and lie, so I could keep you with me. The lies got thicker and sourer, and pretty soon I realized that I'd have to go on making babies with Hank—that would be part of the lie, of course. And that made me feel all . . . hot. You know, ashamed? Because after yesterday, I don't think I could—" She stopped, cleared her throat, and gazed at the sheep with a strange fixed smile.

"But—"

"Wait. Let me finish."

"Sorry." Jeremy lay back in the rough grass and worried his upper lip.

"Anyhow," she continued in the dead voice that troubled Jeremy almost more than anything she was saying, "I got to thinking how it would go on and on, and how the lying would feel worse, and the shame would grow like Maddy's baby inside me. I have loved other people besides you, and never felt like this. This is something else, and it's wrong. You are not a sheep that I am keeping from the others, Jeremy. You're a healthy man."

"So you're— You finished? Okay . . . so you're too selfish to be like Lily, but not selfish enough to keep me all to yourself. Is that about it?"

"How tidy," she said cuttingly.

"I could commute," he suggested.

"Commute what?"

"*Commute.* Go back and forth between here and Idamore. Be what I ought to be in Idamore, and come up here to be what I want to be with you. . . . I need you, Helena. I can't do it without you."

"Why can't you leave me alone? I am peaceful now—"

"This isn't peaceful, Helena. This is dead."

"I'd rather be dead than live the way you're talking about. Hello, good-bye, hello, good-bye. I am not Lily, I can't, I can't, I can't, I can't. . . ." She put her hand over her mouth, then sank her teeth into her index finger.

Jeremy watched with alarm; he saw now the cost of her icy calm, and the turbulence it covered. He felt by contrast almost facile and unfeeling. "Stop it!" He grabbed her wrists and shook her. "I'll stay here with you. Just the two of us, and some sheep. . . . I'll take most of the herd back to Idamore, and then I'll come back. It'll be the new frontier."

He had struck a chord: He could see it in the look that passed over her face like a bright breeze. When she picked up the crutch, Jeremy thought she intended to stand, and he prepared to stand with her. So she caught him off-balance and flabbergasted by the swipe of the wood against his shoulder. The crutch broke, and one beveled chair leg sailed into the air. "Holy shit," he yelled, grabbing what was left of it.

"You're more selfish than I am," she snarled, trying to wrestle the crutch from him.

He abruptly let go of his end. Helena tumbled backward, but Jeremy ignored her. He was gazing east, toward the town of Riverwoods, visible from the hillside as an odd stand of roofs in a vast prairie of tall grass. "There is no frontier," he murmured; he meant that there could be no frontier where there were no populated settlements. As horrifying as it was to walk through the empty streets of Cottage Grove or Idamore or Riverwoods, Jeremy hadn't yet managed to shake off the conviction that this was a kind of island shipwreck: He still took for granted the existence of large numbers of people somewhere across the ocean of this eerie solitude. Beyond him there was still the steady hum of traffic on the eight-lane by-pass around Milwaukee; the endless clack of metal wheels on Chicago's network of railway lines; the continual billow of yellow smoke from a thousand industrial smokestacks in Gary; the sizzle of molten metal in a Detroit plant . . . Cincinnati. Cleveland. Columbus . . . "We have closed this sector." "Unbelievable," Jeremy whispered.

Helena put her hand on his forearm, stroking the dark hair that curled so winningly on his tanned skin. "I'm sorry, Jermicho. It's hard being a man, isn't it? Was it easier in the time of the light?"

"Are you kidding?" he said harshly. "People had choices. Most people had so many choices they were miserable trying to make up their minds. And we spent a lot of time thinking about what it was that motivated people—were their choices determined by their natures or by the way they'd been brought up? The more random or pathological, the more determined we thought the choice was. As if only perfection were freely chosen—funny, huh? Some historian with all the facts about what happened could show precisely why it happened, and why it *had* to happen. Everybody knew it was going to happen. It had to—eventually. We lived with that. The FUTURE DEATH. It even became part of the scenario of determined choices. Oh, it accounted for everything, from the high divorce rate to the apathy of my generation. It was even the—" He stopped, aware that he had been shouting. "Ha! Listen to me," he said.

"I am listening to you, Jermicho, but I don't understand."

He stooped beside her and took her hands. "You haven't thought this through, Helena. You can't stay up here. It has nothing to do with us—this isn't the time for a grand passion that pits love against honor. There just aren't enough people to cast as survivors when the principles are dead. . . ."

"Principles? Jeremy, what are you talking about?"

"It was once possible—there used to be so many people that one person could choose for himself how to live and even whether to live. We can't do that. I can't choose to stay here with you. You can't choose to stay up here alone and die—"

"Die?! I'm not going to—"

"You're damn right you're not. You're coming home, and you're going to have a baby. It's settled." He glared down at her, expecting an argument. She was stubbornly silent and expressionless. "Where's Edgar?" he finally asked. "We'll all go back together."

"You're really taking the sheep back?" she stared at him, her eyes going narrow with hatred. "You're a Federal Man now, aren't you? You're a Federal Man."

"What the hell . . . ?" He looked helplessly at her. "I'm damned if I do and damned if I don't, Helena. I almost rape you, and then it turns out that's what I *should* have done. I have absolutely the best time I've ever had with a woman, and you run away. I become a Federal Man, and then you look at me like I'm the serpent in the garden. What the hell? I'm going back. I'm taking the sheep and Edgar, if he wants to come. You do what you want. But I can't understand why you'd choose nothing when we could have something. It's less than you *should* have, but more than you'd ever expected, I think."

He stared at the crown of her motionless bent head, his throat tight with anger and pity: so much less than he had thought to expect; so much more than she had ever known. She loved him, but her heart was schooled in death and deprivation—stillbirths and miscarriages; starvation and disease; the specter of annihilation. Imagine the pain of that heart pumping red flowers of love.

Jeremy stood over her, feeling the sturdy rhythmic thump of his own heart, which was so slow to understand. "I'll leave the canoe for you," he said. He put his hand on her head for a moment, then went to find Edgar.

◦ FIFTEEN ◦

"Jerenee Echo, fruh the tine of the light," said Edgar, immediately conveying such warmth and sympathy with his husky lilting voice that Jeremy was ashamed of his own roiling stomach and shifty eyes. The man stood with a lamb in his arms, and on his skull-like head was a cloth hat that looked like a medical student's idea of a joke. Between the lashless eyelids were blue eyes, and Jeremy tried to smile into the humanity he found there.

"We've met before," Jeremy said, finally fixing his eyes on the lamb in Edgar's oddly glazed but strong arms.

Edgar nodded: Helena had told him everything. "Sad Helena," he called her. His voice was astounding: husky, as if the larynx were damaged; yet full, almost oracular, as if it issued from a cavern through the tiny slot of his mouth; and highly inflected to compensate for the many consonants he couldn't sound. "Sad Helena says there are many things you haven't seen. No death, no birth . . ." (pronounced "earth," so Jeremy at first misunderstood him). "Maybe you've never seen the lambs, either, heh? Or known a shepherd who looks like a dead man? I do not see myself until I see you." There was a strange ticking in his throat.

Jeremy blushed. "I'm sorry. It's true. I've never seen . . . When I first saw you, I didn't even know I was lost. . . . You thought I was a Federal Man, didn't you? And now I *am*. . . ." Jeremy's incoherent apology became an obsessive explanation. He found himself telling Edgar everything—every uncertainty and disappointment and panic and pain. He'd stop, apologize—"I don't know why I'm telling you all this"—then babble on. It was as if Edgar had opened one of Jeremy's veins, and there was nothing Jeremy could do to stanch the flow of words. Soon he had a lamb in his lap—"an or-han," said Edgar—and Jeremy was gabbling into the soft wool of the spindly little animal.

"Becoming a Federal Man's like becoming my own worst enemy, somehow. Because . . . because everything I heard made me expect something special. Someone worth hating and battling. Not just an ordinary man—"

"Like you—"

"Yes. Weak. Sick."

"You are strong and healthy."

"But does this make me a friend or an enemy, Edgar?"

"The shepherd of a large flock may look like the enemy to the sheep in the far pasture when he takes from them to give to the sheep in the near pasture, but the shepherd does what he has to do."

"Well, there'll be no more of *that*. It's only us now." Jeremy scrubbed his arm over his sweaty face. "Before Hank collapsed, he said this sector was closed. Good thing, too. I don't know how to fly a helicopter. . . . Oh damn, damn," he remarked, suddenly thinking of the windmill that was to have been emplaced by means of the helicopter.

"This sector is closed?" Edgar hissed. His tongue was bright red against the white parchment of his disfigured mouth. "You told Helena?"

"Yes. Or, no. I forgot. I don't see what difference it makes, really—a little salt and a lot of symbol, as far as I can see."

Edgar ticked again. "The shepherd looks over the sickly sheep in the far pasture, cuts them from the flock, and abandons them. They will be dead by the end of the winter. We were once a nation, heh, Jerenee? The nation of the saved who walked the streets of the city of light knowing nothing of birth or death."

Jeremy sighed fretfully, but didn't reply. He watched Helena hobbling toward them, bent low over her broken crutch. She could have been an old woman or a cripple. "This sector is closed," he shouted to her, making the lamb start and struggle in his arms. "Hank says this sector is closed. So I'm not a *Federal* Man, Laney! I'm just a . . . I'm just a local bank."

Helena stopped, then hobbled faster, then stopped again. "This sector is closed? They've closed this sector?" She slouched crookedly over the crutch to gaze toward Idamore. Her face was a dark rainbow of shifting emotions under the prevailing look of bewildered astonishment. She looked from Jeremy to Edgar. "They've given up on us?"

"But look what we've got," Edgar rasped. "Look what we've got, sitting there with a lamb on his lap."

With a cry—half whoop, half protesting scream—Helena tossed the crutch into the air. Was she going to dance? Pronounce the miracle of her cure? Jeremy watched Helena, who watched the crutch until it fell to the ground with a thud. Then she scratched and spat. "Well, let's *go.*"

It was a bizarre and solemn trio that made its way along the toll-way toward Idamore. At the front of the agitated herd walked Edgar, carrying his "or-han" and speaking to the sheep in his cavernous and calming voice. The slick hairless flesh of his arms gleamed like rose quartz in the sun, and his head, deeply shadowed by his hat, was more than ever a death's head. Behind the flock was Jeremy, trundling Helena in a wheelbarrow. Trying to distribute her weight evenly over the single wheel, Helena sat with her calves resting on the corners of the barrow. Her extended feet and the rim of her straw hat quaked and jounced to the uncushioned shock of the rough road. Perhaps she should have insisted on returning in the canoe, instead of yielding so easily to Jeremy's foolish notion that the three of them should stay together.

Along the road were the sharp declivities and rises of manmade hills and valleys; stands of gigantic utility poles with thick sagging cables; and, on the frontage roads, a predictable assortment of motels and restaurants, car dealerships and small shopping centers. The sky was low and white, hazy with sun. Nothing moved except the road ahead of them, which shimmered lazily in the distracting heat. Helena once gasped and leaned forward, thinking that she saw a moving vehicle; it was an abandoned car quivering in the dark metallic sheet of the mirage. The patch of oscillating wetness stayed so precisely ahead of them that it felt as if they, too, were motionless, plodding noisily forward and going nowhere.

After Helena asked him to read a weathered bumper sticker that said, "Escape to Wisconsin," Jeremy began to look more closely at the abandoned cars baking on the road. He read the rear windows naming colleges, and the announcements of people who braked for animals, or wanted you to honk for Jesus, or wondered if you'd hugged your kid today. And there were jokes: "Be Kind to Animals. Kiss a Hockey Player." Jeremy felt a wave of homesickness for these shared complexities, and then he shivered, in spite of the heat, to think of the countless cars abandoned on the endless network of roads taking people nowhere. For the fact was, these cars were empty. No one had died in these cars. They had driven as far as they could—some of them from Pennsylvania, Kentucky, and Ohio—and then they had gotten out and walked. Where? Turned away at hospital doors they would have been sorry to enter, for bodies had apparently been stacked in the corridors; starving, and few of them with the skills of the hunter, forager, or thief. It meant that many people had died slowly. He hoped his parents had died before they had to die this way.

"Which way is that?"

"What?" Jeremy wondered if he had missed part of a conversation. It was hard to hear her, for she sat with her back to him, very still and straight.

"Wisconsin."

"Why, Helena!" said Jeremy. He stopped the wheelbarrow to give her a brief civics and geography lesson. But what he really wanted to teach her was that sense of implacable selfhood that came to every child who ever placed himself first in the hierarchy of address:

Jeremy Towers
412 Gaffield Street
Cottage Grove
Illinois
U.S.A.
North America
Planet Earth
Solar System
Universe

Not merely a citizen of his boundaried street and of the boundless universe, but himself the end result of history, which had conspired to found and populate the world's places so that destiny might arrive at his particular country, his town, his street. Yes, the prize inside the thousand nesting boxes of history: the child of twentieth-century Western civilization.

But Helena, who had no last name and lived outside history, was also a child of that civilization, and she interrupted his lecture on the divisions and compartments of America. "I thought it was a message for *us*. How sad!"

"Anyhow, that's not a message. It's just promotional stuff. Wisconsin used to advertise itself as a nice place to escape from the big city. Half of Illinois spent its Saturdays on this tollway. Can you imagine, Laney, so many cars that they were backed up from one tollgate to another?"

"How many people would that be?"

"God, I don't know. . . ."

"Half of Illinois?"

"Oh, no. I was exaggerating."

"Escape from the big city? What would they want to escape, Jermicho?"

"Urban crime, air pollution, noise and bustle . . . nothing, really. People just like a change of scenery   "

Helena listened to his voice, which, though it was not particularly deep, was resonant and pleasant and came to her clearly over the racket of the wheel and the bleat of the sheep. The world he came from was both more and less complicated than she had thought, and she was not sure she would have liked it. One idea of a place stacked inside a larger idea of a place, like living in a world of imaginary bowls or spoons. And all those people. Choosing, constantly choosing. Urban, suburban, rural. Choosing their work, their places of residence, their spouses. And, according to Jeremy, wondering if they had really chosen; rearranging their lives in order to choose again. Helena thought she would have been a terrible person in such a world, wanting to sample all there was and making herself sick on novelty and selfishness.

All her life she had rebelled against Ben's vision and Simon's work and the Federal Men's efforts to restore the cooperative unity. Now that they were all learning from Jeremy that there had never been a unity, and the order had not been cooperative, but pell-mell, she should feel pleased. Now that the unconscious wish of a lifetime had come true—they lived in a closed sector—she should feel free. What more could she want? Idamore was alone, and had the only two things it needed. Jeremy was Idamore's. Just as the sheep were Idamore's. But she couldn't shake off the plodding weariness of this return to Idamore. The sense that she was doing the right thing, but doing it joylessly, merely yielding. What did she want? She wanted Jeremy. But not as the prized possession of Idamore, more important even than sheep. She wanted something simpler than that.

She wanted to feel that they had chosen each other.

She shifted carefully in her metal bowl. She was tired from holding herself so still, and hot, dripping with sweat that didn't cool her. She could also feel the almost uncomfortable tug, the slow downward dissolving of her womb preparing to empty itself. She was not pregnant. Maybe she wouldn't get pregnant anymore; maybe she had lost her last child; maybe she had no business keeping Jeremy at all. "Oh," she exclaimed with a little cry, and swiveled around to speak to him.

The shift of her weight over the wheel was so abrupt that the barrow tipped, dumping her onto the road. Jeremy rushed to help her. "Are you all right?" She nodded carelessly, pulling herself to her feet on his arm. Her buttocks were sore more from the ride than the fall. "We must all be more careful," he lectured. "We can't afford to get sick or hurt. Very careful. We have this huge responsibility. . . ." Watching the worry darken his face, she waited for the moment when he would suck the small lump on his upper lip into his mouth. His beard had grown in dark and soft. It made more of his chin and a nest around his broad mouth. He frowned at her. "What are you doing to your mouth?"

Caught imitating his gesture, Helena looked away.

"Elephant lip," he said.

"Fruit-loop," she replied, and shut her eyes tight against the sudden tears. She rested her cheek against his sodden shirt for a moment, and Jeremy leaned down and kissed her searchingly on the mouth.

The blood rushed into her face. She was still confused by Jeremy as both lover and baby maker, and as uncertain of her own responses as she was of his motives. "This isn't a good time for me, Jermicho," she whispered.

"What? Good grief! Certainly not!" He held himself stiffly, a picture of wounded dignity. "Be a while yet before I rut on a road." When he began to sing, Helena watched him with an unhappy smile on her face. It was a silly song, practically the same line over and over again. "Why don't we do it in the road? Why don't we do it in the road?" He hit a high note and his voice broke. He shrugged irritably.

"I know one." Helena began to sing: "Onward, Christian sooooouls, marching as to ward. . . ."

"With the cross of Jesus going on before," came Jeremy's tenor. A Unitarian atheist readily makes a joke of "Onward, Christian Soldiers," and as he sang, he pumped his arms and strutted in place. Helena soon stopped singing in order to hear Jeremy's version of the song. "Soldiers," it was. "War," he sang, grinning.

"Stop!" she said, putting her hands over her ears. "I don't like it anymore."

"Oh, Laney, I didn't mean to . . . I was just trying to make you laugh. I miss your laugh. Ahhh, God . . ."

They went on again, for uncounted miles, unclocked hours, until Helena pointed to an open field where they might stop. Helena crawled around looking for forage. Where she could find moist edible weeds, berries, and mushrooms, Jeremy still saw only a barren wilderness of tall grasses. "Disgusting-looking things," he said of the warty mushrooms, which he ate gratefully. He lay in the sun, shielding his face with his arm.

Edgar broke into a nearby house, then another, until he found a hat, which he dropped on Jeremy's stomach. "Cover your head from the sun, boy, or you'll look like Dave. Or me." He ticked quietly as he disappeared among the sheep.

Jeremy ran the palm of his hand over the sweat on his face, and licked his hand; he collected the sweat inside his shirt and again licked his hand. Then he noticed what he was doing. "I'm starving," he complained from under his hat. "Colonel Sanders," he moaned, but he couldn't amuse himself: He thought he might literally be starving. He was doing continual heavy physical work on a diet of grass and fungus. Between the rim of his hat and the bridge of his nose, he could see the sheep shifting around Edgar. What the hell was he doing, crawling around between their feet? Jeremy's mouth sprang with saliva at the sudden thought of what Edgar might be doing. He got to his knees. "Edgar?" he begged. "Edgar, is there milk?"

"Hold on, Jermicho. Sheep grudge their milk."

"Sheeb grudge their milg?" Jeremy repeated, giggling. He felt light-headed and heavy limbed. He lay down again and felt his forehead. "Oh, please, don't let me get sick."

Jeremy gulped eagerly from the tin cup that Edgar handed him. He paused, offended by the taste of the thick, oddly sweet liquid, then drank again. Only then did he look into the cup. He put his hand over his mouth and raised his head slowly to stare in disbelief at Edgar. Then he walked a short distance away and leaned on his thighs, willing himself to vomit. He huffed and gagged, but his satisfied stomach wouldn't turn. His throat closed against him, and his mouth, wet and wide, commanded, "More. More." Making a guttural sound in the back of his throat, Jeremy staggered back, picked up the cup, and drank again. Between swallows, he lowed like an animal, baring his teeth in a grotesque grin of disgust.

"Oh boy, *now* what?" said Helena.

"Jeremy doesn't like the bloody milk," said Edgar.

"Blooby milg," mimicked Jeremy. He touched nervous fingers to his face, and found his mouth again. "Blooby milg," he said through his fingers, and curled up on the ground.

Helena cradled his head on her lap, pressing her hands against his temples as if he might have a headache. "Careful," she warned. "Careful."

Jeremy breathed deeply and exhaled, a long shuddering sigh. Helena felt his warm, moist breath through the cloth on her thigh. She thought that there could be nothing more important than that, that breathing, that life. She didn't like to see him so distraught. "They shall hunger no more," she began in a chanting voice. "Edgar, what's that bit about the lamb?"

"'They shall hunger no more, neither thirst any more. . . . For the Lamb shall feed them, and shall lead them unto living fountains,'" rasped Edgar. "We can live on the blood of the lamb without killing the animal. Unless we do it too much," he added.

"Yagghhh!" Jeremy roared. "Listen to this, old Allison Pachek, listen, old bones, and laugh. *Ba-room,* the great symbol explodes and creates a population of literalists. Somebody reads the Book of Revelation and says, 'Ah-ha, the living fountain. Excellent idea.' Yaggh-aah!"

"He's feeling better," Helena remarked to Edgar.

"He was probably just hungry," Edgar said.

"That's what he was," agreed Jeremy. "His body wins every argument he has with it. . . ." He was disgusted with himself—because he had just consumed a cupful of warm blood and milk, because he had carried on about it, and because he felt so much better as a result of it. Jeremy pressed his head against Helena's thigh as if he could assimilate from her the wisdom of the animal body, the dignity of literalness. He inhaled the dark, ripe-fruit smell of her body. When she moved, he pressed his head against her lap, but she pushed him off and struggled up on the crutch.

"I want to get more of those berries to take back—"

"Good grief, Helena, what did you sit in?"

"Blood." She brushed her hand across the back of her pants. She was wet and sticky, and would be much wetter before she reached Idamore, where there were reliably clean rags. "My blood," she added, mistaking Jeremy's heightened color for puzzled amazement. Poor Jeremy was so easily confused; he'd think she'd sat on her cup.

She looked at him for a moment, trying to picture herself purposely sitting on a tiny tin cup. Her eyes widened in a startled way, and then she broke, like shattered ice, into a thousand sharp pieces of shining laughter. Edgar stood there ticking merrily, and Jeremy, who hadn't a clue about the joke, laughed just to hear what he'd despaired of hearing again. Even after she went off foraging, her raucous chortle rose up from the tall grass like the sudden argument of birds. *Rrragh-oo-hee-hee. Ya-ha.*

Jeremy, musing lazily in the sun, grinned each time Helena laughed. He studied her from under the brim of his hat. Helena, a lamb of life, a living fountain; Helena, the seasonal forager with her pants stained dark rust by the flux of time. Abruptly sitting up, he stared at the menstrual blood on Helena's clothes.

A few minutes later he ran into the house that Edgar had opened and ransacked its shelves. Moving quickly through the house in search of an oversize picture book, he saw and ignored the grinning corruption in the upstairs bed. When he found what he wanted—an enormous book of glossy photographs of Yorkshire, England—he scrabbled in the fireplace for a cinder.

"Hey!" he shouted, running toward Helena. "We'll make a calendar." He made a mark on the top left corner of the first gleaming blank verso, and held it open toward her. "One!" he said, biting his lip with excitement. "Like this, see? Day one."

"But the Federal Men are in charge of time."

"No, darlin'. *You're* in charge of time."

◦ SIXTEEN ◦

Helena's calendar became quite elaborate, recording the fullness of the moon, then the onset of Rachel's blood, then of Rose's.

Each morning she marked the day, then gazed at the adjacent picture, with its foregrounded field of heather falling sharply into a valley of trees. Those curved hills of purple heather, those steep river ravines, those meandering stone fences: Everything arrived at trees. Trees clear to the hazy horizon. She liked to imagine that one day Idamore would look like Yorkshire. Each morning she then stepped onto the porch and looked through the fine mist of small insects, across the flat, regular fields and the straight rows of houses, to the irregular and sloped hillocks and ponds of the Botanical Gardens. Idamore's trees were growing.

Idamore's people lived in an atmosphere charged with contradictory expectations. Waiting for conception, for new life, they were also waiting for death, wondering if the disease would cross the invisible boundary of their quarantine. Hot as it was, they were apt to clump together, working and eating side by side, rather than coolly separate. They labored the length of each long day, gathering food for immediate use as well as for the coming winter. They tended the fields, the sheep, the chickens, the latrine; they dried more vegetables than they ate, and ceaselessly carried things.

Jeremy had too many projects, each competing with another in importance, canceling themselves and canceling Jeremy's resolve. Though he was full of ingenuity and enterprise, everything that he built leaked or backed up or stalled. He could point to pictures and sketchy designs in the books that he'd found, and insist to his doubting audience that it could be done, it had been done, it was very sensible, really. "All we have to do . . ." he'd say, uncon-

sciously echoing Ben; when he planned it, it always sounded simple. All we have to do is build the latrine over a closed tank, like
this old water heater; all we have to do is install a water tank
beneath a roof, so it'll gravity feed into these pipes; all we have to
do is put these inside-out oil drums on a high bank so the wind'll
turn 'em and then hook them up to a pump. . . . He could visu-
alize the entire thing—a methane generator, for instance—but he
couldn't seem to master the small mysteries of crankcasings, eccen-
tric drives, or ball bearings. It drove him wild to spend an hour
with Mick, tinkering with one pipe connection, when the women
were toiling away at the many really essential labors.

Pottering at his projects, Jeremy took to singing "Joshua Fit de
Battle of Jericho," remembering that as a child he'd once asked
how it was that Joshua "fit" a battle. "Fought," his mother had
said, explaining that it was a song in southern black dialect. Now,
Jeremy felt, his original misunderstanding was appropriate, if taken
ironically: He was unfit. Rose seemed to agree with the sentiment,
for she too began to hum the tune, pointing first at him and then at
herself. "Jericho. Jessico."

"What're you trying to tell me, Rose?" he would say tolerantly.
"You think I'm crazy, is that it?"

Helena often got up in the middle of the night and padded
down the stairs. When Jeremy proposed chamber pots, Helena replied that it was easier to carry it down the stairs "this way," she
said—patting her lower belly with a smile. He had only to imagine
the scene in wintertime to be convinced that nothing could be more
important than making an indoor privy for each house. Then he
saw the women carry laundry, menstrual rags, and dirty diapers to
the river to be rinsed, to a pot over a fire to be washed, to another
pot to be rinsed; and the sheer weight of the enterprise—the fuel
carried for fire, the tremendous amounts of water, the water-heavy
clothes to be hung—made him think that nothing could be more
important than giving them running water and electricity. Then
some comment garbling history with the Book of Revelation would
convince him that nothing, nothing at all, could be more important
than reading.

So he sat in the evenings between the two exhausted girls, Laurel and May, and read to them until both had fallen asleep. Mother Goose. E. B. White. Kipling. Helena was somewhat upset by the fantastic stories. "If the elephant's nose didn't get stretched that way, then why tell the story?" she complained. "Why confuse us?" She was still troubled by that bumper sticker "Escape to Wisconsin," which was not a message or a command, but a kind of shared secret of no significance at all. "How will we *know?*" she demanded rather shrilly. She was furious to find that being able to read didn't mean that she would read appropriately. She had no context for understanding. She was still excluded from the past.

Jeremy, too, was chastened. He had assumed that if he taught them to read, they could make their way through the books, accurately distinguishing fact from fiction, cherishing Shakespeare for his imagery and the Time-Life Books for its comprehensible science. He had thought he could, single-handedly, salvage Western civilization in and for Idamore. But this tiny handful of people might *be* Western civilization. A community that had steadily contracted to this fragile nucleus, that might now be poised on the brink of renewal or of extinction. "There can be no mourning except for the hive itself," Ben had said. "And in that case there will be no mourners."

Hank's death didn't upset Jeremy so much as it thwarted him. He had counted on talking to the one man who might place Idamore in some larger context. Old Allison Pachek had a larger context, too, of course, but the conversation was one-sided: Jeremy couldn't alter the flow of her thoughts with a pointed question, or interrupt her except by closing the book. Which he often did, as much out of irritation as physical exhaustion. Perhaps he wouldn't have been so profoundly annoyed if he hadn't been reading at the end of the day—tired and squinting in the poorly reflected light; perhaps in another time and place he would have had larger reserves of pity to tap for this woman who held her anguish at arm's length with irony and wordplay.

Even now, I sidle around the words, one entry said. *Even now, alone. Am I alone, or are you there?* "Closer yet I approach you" . . . *you.* ("Oh, stuff it, Ally!" Jeremy growled.) *You. I am talking to myself unless you make your presence felt. Which means that it is not I, but you (you who?) who (what, an owl? Oh, let the birds return!) must play the poet reaching through time.*

This is useless drivel. ("Damn right.") *If you are there, then there's a future. If you are not there, then I'm talking to myself. In either case, I am useless. I am therefore free. I can say the words.*

She didn't say them. Or at least not on that page. And Jeremy, mistaking her intent, sat on the floor enunciating for her benefit every anatomical and dirty word he could think of. "Just say it, and quit wasting my time."

Hank's death gave him the impetus he needed to return to the journals. The crabbed, almost illegible script made it impossible to skim, so he'd use the first few sentences of a section as the litmus test of its relevance. *The housing shortage. Always I'm back to the housing shortage. . . .*

"God, you are, you are! Leave off . . ." he muttered, turning the thin page. But on the next page there was an interesting entry—in different ink, a later comment on the earlier one—so Jeremy went back and read again:

The housing shortage. Always I'm back to the housing shortage.

How many of us in that house, holding our elbows in from each other's differences and each other's stinks. Well, that didn't last very long after all. One looks back fondly on what seemed at the time worst-case scenarios. As they say in the military. We withstood a lot because it was temporary. We were right—it was temporary—but not in the way we thought. Remember the time the electricity came on? The electromagnetic pulse had damaged so much of the electric equipment—capacitors, transistors, computers—and what we needed was an encouraging chat from the Oval Office. A familiar face, an authoritative voice. "This is what we're doing for you, folks. My fellow Americans," and so on, but no, we were utterly isolated, community from community, and community from nation. We needed to know what exactly had happened, and what exactly would happen, and who was doing what for whom.

We had no news and knew nothing, so things like the resumption of electrical power were comforting. Things that we'd never considered before were now implied in the successful flick of a light switch. When a light went on, there were competent people at work somewhere. There was fuel to be burned, and people to burn it properly. There was some kind of central power plant. There was hierarchy, there was order. Two months of light, as I recall, was what we actually had. Even after the lights went out again, we waited, fully confident. "Temporary disruption of power."

Crammed along the edge of the thin paper, and in places crosshatching the entry that Jeremy had been reading, was this afterthought:

Temporary—that was our downfall, right there. I have blamed the bureaucrats for this. One wants to assign blame so one doesn't feel guilty. True? We have lived from day to day, snatching survival from the air and water and ground, feeling guilty even to be alive. This is guilt enough, and crippling. Add to it this belief in a "temporary disruption of power" and stir; simmer over low heat, and when thoroughly charred, consume ashes. I mean: We have lived a generation waiting for the lights to go on, the banks to open, the trains to take commuters to their full employment. I mean: While we have been waiting for the schools to open, we have taught the children only to know edible mushrooms and weeds because that is their daily bread. I mean: We have taught them to live one life in the constant expectation of another. I mean: We have utterly failed them; we are guilty. . . .

By this time the primitive scrawl was unrelated to the entry it surrounded, and Jeremy tore himself away from the one in order to dive into the other. Back and forth, in and out of sequence he read, and the effect was of some odd antiphonal fugue, thought and afterthought, comment and correction.

. . . my own version of peace on earth. Peace on earth and goodwill to McGiverty. No. I'll never forgive him. Imagine, arriving with a microscope to do sperm counts. Just . . . oh God, and the boys were so proud! Then, to convince Liz and Burt and the shy gentle Lily Dwight that their sons were being "honored"! As if Lily gave a damn about her son's virility. Though apparently she did. Apparently she felt some pride

that he'd become a "man" now; I suppose she had to find something to justify a mother's brave farewell as the boy went off with McGiverty to . . . Oh, God, the whole thing's so unspeakable.

Edward, for once, was on my side. Though he was the one being practical and arguing that McGiverty was leaving us pretty short-handed. I was the one taking a moral stand. If an old harridan shriek-ing obscenities from the porch can be seen as standing on the high moral ground.

Edward and I have grown old battling each other for the children's minds, perhaps succeeding only in canceling each other out and leaving the children to a peril we—Edward and I! Linked in my mind? The foolish bastard!—we never imagined. He saw the . . . well, our experi-ence, call it, as a chapter from one of the brimstone prophets. God's punishment of the wicked. And now a new home and a new earth, all the kiddies prattling the memorized bits and pieces of the King James before they gather round me in the dark room for a story from the Book of Evolutions. Once upon a time great dinosaurs roamed the earth, and once upon a time after that, a vast meteor collided with the planet, raising so much dust that the climate changed and all the dinosaurs died. See, it has happened before, it can happen again. Here we are, the last of the dinosaurs, and we don't even know what little mammals of the future secretly suck dry our eggs. . . .

. . . Well, my little mammals, perhaps I've had the final word, after all. What was I thinking of, what was my plan? To use his Bible thumping against him? Or was it some prettier motive? Let's say I wanted to make sure they were pacifists, these little mammals of the future, so I used the tools that Edward bequeathed me. His Bible. But only the tiniest shards of his Bible. Carefully annotated and edited. None of the bloody, war-minded Psalms. No Abraham willing to sacri-fice his son.

Once I started down that road, I was even tempted to leave out Jesus: I was a little worried about what he was beating those plowshares <u>from,</u> you see. I didn't want pacifists by conviction, but by exclusion: able to imagine nothing else. The Law Concerning Bloodshed have I selected as our text, brethren and children. Oh yes. Again and again; memorize it. Take it to heart. . . .

... *I was thinking recently of the many ways that we have failed the children; this failure must be the first, the greatest, the source. The Victorian equivalent of sex. I'm not sure I understand our secretiveness—our shame—before the children, but it is true; we do not say what happened. Are we ashamed because we feel responsible—or helpless? The history we've taught them is ancient, the Bible we read them is censored; the explanations we give them are oblique, and quickly become nostalgic description of what used to be and will be again. And now that Edward is dead, I'm the only one left; it is no longer "we" but "I"—and I am sick with remorse. Please, Edward's God, give me time to correct the evil I have done. For I am dying, and I don't even know how old I am. Please, Edward's God, let me rise up from this foul bed and say aloud the words I write. Those were bombs. That was war.*

"Once upon a time, there was a woman named Allison Pachek": This was what had happened. As best they could determine. As accurately as they could tell. Having only old Ally's queer rambling word for it. "Those were bombs. That was war."

When Jeremy first read from the journal, Edgar cowered with his hands over his head. He said later that he thought the earth would open and swallow them up. The sky would darken, thunder clap, and lightning strike them dead. For those were forbidden, shameful words. He remembered hushed conversations he was not meant to overhear, a bedridden child who should have died in the house fire that left him hideously disfigured. Those were words left so conscientiously unspoken that their shame was almost obliterated for Helena, who felt only a thrill of dread at their power. "Bombs?" she whispered. "War?"

"You mean *that* was the time of light?" exclaimed May, disappointed.

"It was not as Ben said?" asked Pearl.

"Oh, it must have been exactly as Ben says," Jeremy replied. "Just that terrible—"

"But we thought it was a nuclear exchange."

"It *was*, dammit, it was. Nuclear bombs. Nuclear war." It was Jeremy's turn to shudder. He was as guilty as they were of giving mythic properties to the "power." The myth of men with the power of gods; the reality of men with the power of gods. "I am become Death, the shatterer of worlds."

"What you haven't understood," he said almost angrily, "is that there were *people* in charge of the power. People created it, used it, destroyed with it. . . ." Again and again Jeremy tried to explain the centralization of power—both kinds, he realized, both energy and government—necessary to a huge population with high expectations. "People wanted roads and water and central heating, they wanted electricity and garbage collection and sewage disposal, but they didn't want to do it all themselves. 'Cause if you make your own electricity, there isn't much time left to do other stuff, see?" (Yes, they knew about that: Didn't they encourage Jeremy to leave off the essential chores to work on his projects?) "So they gave money to the government and to the utility companies, they paid to have other people do it for them. . . ."

He showed them that the power was merely the work of ingenious men. But as their attitudes changed, so did his, leaving him befuddled and hesitant. It wasn't just that the incredible ingenuity had ultimately destroyed itself—that was obvious enough. It was that their ingenuity had made a myth of things they'd originally valued: personal freedom, mobility, individual choice. Yes, freedom, but circumscribed, and blind to its own shallow limits. As if in its hunger for power, the whole system had secretly cannibalized itself, leaving behind a brittle empty skin of apparent freedom, apparent choice. Oh, but God, hadn't it been wonderful? Privileged. The exercise of a thousand trivial freedoms. The golden cities of the light, the silver suburbs . . .

Jeremy's reading of Allison Pachek's journal inspired reminiscences of other, more recent times. "Could that Paul be *our* Paul?" Rachel exclaimed. Or Edgar: "The jeep-driving Federal Man! I remember about him. . . . When I was little, there were a lot, a lot more people here." *(". . . a lod, a lod, nore beeble . . .")*

"How big was the—" Jeremy paused to correct his question. "Did anyone ever name the different places in this sector?"

Each of them had hoarded a separate piece of the Federal Men's tales. "There was a dry place—all dust blowing in the air—"

"—called Reserve—"

"—that had fuel."

"The place of white bluffs and steep pastures—"

"They had cows—"

"The cow we got from them died—"

"Kendallville!"

"That's right. There was Freehold, of course—"

"Oh yes, and Alligator—"

"Some of the people there had very dark skin, and they wanted a dark-skinned Federal Man—"

"—And a place where everyone lived in the mud and ate crabs—"

"—called—"

"—Creole."

Jeremy listened attentively to this collaborative account of the Federal Men's travels, though he knew almost instantly that he wasn't going to recognize any of the place names: the small towns of America, the odd places on the map where people happened to survive a little longer. Only "Creole" provided a clue, and Jeremy shook his head in wonderment. The territory was larger than he had suspected, and the time since the bombs was shorter. Meshing details from Allison Pachek's journal with what he learned from the group, Jeremy now figured that his dark resinous-voiced Helena might be no less than Helena Adelstein's granddaughter. Great-granddaughter at the most.

The generations were brief, the mortality high. After they stopped dying from the bombs, they died of other, older things: the various red-rash fevers, sore throat closing up the air passages, the muck that settled in the lungs during the winter. Childbirth and childbed fever. The accidents that happen to people who heat their houses with wood; untreated infections; poisonous food . . . He began to understand how people schooled every day for some twenty years of their lives might not have had time in a day or time in a life to teach their children to read. He had once thought it should have been the last thing they'd relinquish; he saw now it could be the first, and he forgave them.

"Creole was closed down," Pearl said in conclusion.

"Mmmm. Is Idamore closed down, if the sector is closed?" Jeremy asked.

"I suppose."

"So there could be people still there, still living on their Creole crabs?"

Pearl looked at him dubiously.

"Well, there *could* be, couldn't there?" said Helena.

"Without exchange of good?" asked Rachel.

"Goods," Jeremy corrected mindlessly. "Exchange of goods."

"It could be done," said Edgar. "We will do it."

"We will," said Jeremy with a pleased smile. "Oh, we will." It was enough to keep him going with a kind of dumb persistence and even, occasionally, joy.

∘ SEVENTEEN ∘

When Hank died, Helena left the event unmarked on her calendar. The function of the calendar was to trace patterns and cycles: theirs and the moon's and the disease's. His death put Hank outside all cycles.

Only the moon showed a pattern: seven days from full to half, seven days from half to new. The morning after the new moon, Helena began a different calendar. She didn't like measuring time against herself. She was erratic, wavering, selfish, and apt to die. The moon was ancient and regular. Carefully she made a dark circle and beneath it indicated the eighteenth day of her cycle, the fourteenth of Rachel's, and the seventh of Rose's. She imagined the three of them dancing beneath the moon, waxing and waning; Jeremy was the sun, permanent and bright.

Sadly, Helena held the calender out for Jeremy to examine. "It's probably time for you to be with Rachel," she told him. She couldn't understand why two people she loved didn't love each other.

Jeremy did his gorilla act, slumping forward to let his arms hang loosely, beetling his brow, and jutting his lower jaw. Pummeling his chest, he yodeled. Then he made a disgusted gesture, giving up all attempts at humor. "It's hard for Rachel, too," he said, as much to himself as to Helena. "You, on the other hand, are a born heterosexual. Thank God." He rumpled her hair. "See you later."

In the midst of Rachel's fertile time, Helena recorded the beginning of Dave's illness. If she had been keeping clock time, she could almost have recorded the hour of his illness, for she wasn't far from him when it began.

She was looking for berries beside the pond when Dave came to fetch water. As she greeted him, she walked farther away, hating the violent politeness imposed on them by distance. Watching the weariness with which he lifted the full buckets, she pressed her hands against her sides. "Didn't we leave enough water this morning?" she asked.

"Lily's boiling everything," Dave called back. "Means a lot of water and a lot of wood." He turned, rubbery legged with the weight of the buckets, and tottered away. When he fell, he tried to avoid upsetting the buckets. Helena never forgot that—the heroism of that effort to set the buckets down as he fell.

Dave pressed his head against the parched tumultuous ground, and saw the dry soil dark with spilled water. A waste, to haul a heavy thing so far, then spill it. Raking his chin along the ground, he turned his head to look at the dirt on his other side. He might at least have fallen in the corn, where the water would have done some good.

He closed his fingers in the damp soil. "I have loved this land," he thought, though the land he loved was bucking under him like an untamed creature, huge backed and wild. "I never cared so much about the light, but I have loved the land." He looked up at Helena. "Irrigate," he shouted. The ground lunged up at him as he struggled to his feet. "Remember to—"

Helena watched him thrash and flail. He gathered himself under his spine, which curved up with reaching, but his helpless, liquid limbs refused to follow. He might have been a man in water, or a fish out of it, a bluegill battering its tail and jerking in the dust. Helena ran a crazy circle around him, coming closer and closer.

Dave lay still and spoke to her. "Love-a-God, Laney, get away from me now."

He couldn't tell how long it was before Lily came through the fields and sat beside him, the dry grass crackling beneath her. It might have been the length of heartbeats or the time between meals. "Well, Dave," she said as she put a wet cloth over his forehead.

"Yes, Lily."

They were silent for a few minutes, listening to the scrape of insects and the rustle of wind over dry grasses. There was a sudden percussion of metal: Helena and Rachel were hauling the ducts they used to irrigate the fields. Half a day's work it would be to lay them end to end from the crops to the river, elevating them on progressively taller sawhorses. The irrigation itself meant pouring bucket after bucket of water into the pipe. It was heavy, tedious work, to stand in the river all day, dipping and lifting the bucket up to the person on the bank, who then poured it into the mouth of the duct. Dipping and lifting, pouring and passing, dipping and lifting. Dave was sorry he couldn't help. He stared up at the cloudless sky, and saw that it would not rain soon.

"I'll get you a drink of water," said Lily, "then we'll get you back to the house."

He sipped at the water she brought him, then fell back. "I'd like to just stay here, Lily."

"Hard on the others," she commented, though it would be just as hard on her, to leave him dying in a dry field.

"I'll be quick about it," he promised.

"It's very hot out here, Dave—"

"Please, Lily."

She got to her feet. "I'll be back and forth. If you change your mind, Ben and I can get you back. Just shout. . . ."

He nodded at her. She was a large dark comforting shape backed by the vast light of the day. "Throw a bucket of water over me, will you, old girl?"

The others watched, troubled and amazed, as Lily went tirelessly to and fro. She built a lean-to over Dave to protect him from the sun, and regularly threw a bucket of water over him as if she had gone mad. She also built fires, carried heavy buckets, and bent over a steaming cauldron in the afternoon sun to stir boiling clothes.

The next morning the body lying in the field was lifeless. Solemnly but with no ceremony, Rachel, Edgar, and Jeremy dug his grave, then left so that Ben and Lily could bury him. From the porch they watched Lily and Ben wrestle the dead body onto a tarpaulin and slide it along the ground until they reached the grave hole. They saw the maternal gesture Lily made, putting her arm around Ben's shoulder as the two walked back to their house. And they saw Lily's brief sympathetic look toward them, the silent group on the porch. She knew as well as anyone what a cruel middle ground they had chosen to stand on: Either the contaminated dying bees should be pushed from the hive, where they could enact their private destinies, forgotten by the others; or they should be kept and included, their fortunes the hive's.

"Twenty days from Hank's arrival to today," said Helena. "We'll wait another twenty, and that's it. . . ." She was announcing a closure to this period of anxiety and separation. She reminded herself that they had lived through worse times than this. The bad winter, for instance. Or the spring of the dysentery epidemic. The summer of the army worms. Oh, those were much worse, for just think: only one dead so far. (Helena, unlike Lily, did not count Hank as a member of any community of the heart.)

No one asked out loud the obvious questions: Suppose those two get sick? Who will care for them? Suppose both of them die? Who will bury the the last one? When Helena grabbed his hand with the convulsive grasp of someone in pain, Jeremy knew that the answers were as obvious as the questions. Another house containing the unburied dead—what did it matter, except to the people who once called the bones by name and now shunned the house? What did it matter, as long as there were people left to feel the anguish of their choice?

But it did matter. Jeremy felt that it mattered more than anything else. He was impaled by the sharpness of its suddenly mattering. For he wanted to go on believing that each life was important. Not just biological life—the continuation of the species—but its individual expression: in Helena's laughter, in Ben's special pulpit voice, in Laurel's eager honey-colored eyes, in Mick's storytelling hands. . . . In all of them. And in himself. Most of all in himself. For the first time, it occurred to Jeremy that he, too, could die.

∘ EIGHTEEN ∘

From the porch Rose watched the big man in the strange masked outfit: He was digging. Why was he dressed like that? Why was he digging? Oh, she remembered why he was digging. He was planting people. Rose thought this planting of people was foolish. They never grew again.

Who was being planted today? Maddy-mother-stone? Maddy was a round mother-stone with a pit inside her. Pit-baby. Fruit of stone. Was it Maddy, or was it a different time now? (Not the mother-other-time: not enough bodies for that. The mother-time was back when her name was Jess, Jessie, Jessica.) Rose was her real name now. Rose, the Federal Man had called her, so she wouldn't have to be planted anymore.

Jessie, Jessica, those were her names before, but she could forget about those other girls. They were dead. When her mother died, Jessica died, and she had no more name until she became a bleeding Rose.

Jessie had a memory though. Such a memory. Always bothering Rose. Pester, pester, fester-mind.

That man standing there with his feet in the earth, with his hands in the earth, he was not planting Maddy. He was planting Lily. He was planting Ben. If you wanted corpses to grow, you fed them dirt. They came back as voices.

"Tell me what the voices say, Rose." That was what Ben used to ask. Say, be still. Be a deathless stone. She tried to tell him. Now, see: Ben was a plant today, it was Ben getting planted. It was ben-yen-hen-henny-benny-penny. . . .

"Hush, Rose!"

Well, she had tried to protect him. Rose protected the living by making them stones. It was heavy work. Heaviest Helena, always breaking through her skin with laughing. All of them today breaking through their skin with sadness. Rose used to have a skin, but now she was all bark. Rose, the Federal Man had called her, so she wouldn't have to be planted anymore. She never saw anyone feed a corpse anything but dirt.

When the Federal Man came—no, no, not rank-Hank, the other one! the father, the namer who called her Rose—he said to her, "Someday you will bear a sun." And she had to become like a stone with a hole (cave, that was a cave) to bear so hot a thing as that. She was cold dumb dead rock around an empty waiting space.

Meanwhile she had her tasks to do. Rose had her daily tasks. Sort these leaves, Helena-stone said. This leaf is life, this leaf is death, this leaf is life, this leaf is death. (Sort them? A task for the earth itself!) Fetch water, Pearl-stone said. The water comes from the womb of the earth, the water comes from the eye of the sky. (Dip into heaven, dip into hell?) The work was hard. The stones were heavy. Always breaking through their skins.

"Always dying," Jessica remarked to Rose. Pester, pester, fester-mind.

"No, no, no," shrieked Rose. "Stone-bone-groan—"

"Quiet, Rose!"

That man standing there with his feet in the earth and his face in a mask . . . (Was he standing there, or was he a memory? A remembered dream, a memory, or a man? Was he from this time or that time?) He looked like the man who came to them with the three globes, three tiny orange globes, toy suns. He gave them to be cut up. Cut up the miniature suns and offered them to eat. Hot! hot! hot! Ben said, "They're not hot. They're sour and juicy and delicious. Eat, Rose." Eat the sun, Rose!

Sunrise, sunset, I'll eat you, sun; I'll eat you yet.

What was that man glowing with? Skin. Look at him glow! What was he glowing with? Grief. "You are the sun," she called to him. "You have stolen the sun."

"Hush, Rose," said a stone. "That's Jermicho."

Ah, yes, something else of that man she remembered. He had died and come back with another name. She too had died and come back with another name. He came from another time, and so did she. They were enemies, and twins. Even his name remembered her. Jessico/Jermicho. She remembered that man. He was the man Rose was meant to be. She knew the crime he had committed, long ago. When Jessico was the sun, she destroyed the world. She had been the sun once, time ago, before her mother was even born. In that time ago, Jessico rose iron winged on the hot flames, her hair sparking on clouds of rage, hands of ash molding the fire into a globe, hurled howling against a night of nothing. That was the power. She once had the power of life and death.

See how all the bones melt to stone? The hair becomes grass, the blood water? But the eyes are everywhere, looking at her, at Jessico. "Look at what you've done," the eyes say. It was an accident, all that burning. She never meant burning. She was meant to be the sun, but she had to become a girl, a plant, a pond, a cave. See the stones? She could be those stones. See the river? She could be that river. She could be everything she saw, but not the sun. Not Jessico. And he? What would he become, to avoid the eyes, the burning?

Rose was her real name now. Rose, the Federal Man had called her, so she wouldn't have to be planted anymore. Unless Jessica came and confused her, Rose could tell the time in Idamore. Night followed day; day, night. Corpses were buried and people fed. They wanted the power but didn't burn for it. No one burned here. Sparks, sometimes: from Helena, from Pearl, but no burning.

Not like in Oakton in the mother-time, when there was a little girl Jessie. Hungry-sick-angry-hot men from the mines had come up out of the ground like corpses and walked the earth, saying everyone else shall die with us, everyone else. But death was not enough. They had to mutilate and foul, give the dirty finger to death, and their anger blasted and withered everything. Little Jessie lived among the corpses. The Federal Man, the namer, the father, called her and called her. "You can come out now. Come on out. They're gone. . . ." Never, never out. She gave him an empty girl. "What is your name, girl?" —Hunger. "I'll call you Rose. Do you like that?" Yes, she could be planted in Idamore; the men of the mines did not come here.

After the planting Jeremy took off his funny mask. He took off his gloves. He took off his clothes. He washed himself very hotly, and no one could go near him until those clothes were burned and that skin was washed. That was Jeremy. She could see that it was Jeremy. Jermicho. Jericho. Jessico.

When he turned, Rose could see what no one else saw. Oh, she often saw what no one else could see. On that first day he came to them, lengthwise by water, by design, she had seen that he was dead. Now he carried death with him. There were two sides to him. The part in the light was warm and beautiful. The part in the light was whole, the dark hair full of blue light, the blue eyes full of bright water. The other half was death itself. Jericho, the first great city of light, the place of water and health, the sun: Look, he left a foul trail from his dark side, clumps of waste, a dark prairie of bones. Bones fell from that backward-dispensing hand, death fell off him as he walked. He was bent double with death. He was defeated, he was fallen. Two-faced first sun, whole and hole, she loathed and loved him. Jericho! the first great city of the light! Jericho! the man with the green breath!

"Rose! Stop that!" said Helena-hands pinching. "Leave him alone, he's upset. We're all upset. Can't you see that?"

See? Oh, Rose could see everything. See the stones? She could be those stones. See the river? She could be that river. But if someone fed Jessica, she'd become a woman. She'd grow up to bear the sun.

Labor and deliver him there on the dark plain, the cave breaking open with light, the light vanquishing forever the man with the green breath. She was the one, and Jeremy was the sun. He was also the man with the green breath.

◦ NINETEEN ◦

Helena thought Jeremy was overworked, and protected him from the more difficult chores that everyone had come to ask him to do. She thought he was underfed, and set before him plates heaped with carefully cleaned vegetables and choice morsels of boned bluegills. She stalked crayfish in the twilight and stole from the winter stores to prepare extra vegetables for him. Several times she asked if he was feeling sick, but no thank you, he was feeling quite well. He didn't even seem particularly unhappy; just lethargic and indifferent. She was gentle with him; she was sharp with him: Nothing seemed to affect him.

"What's the matter with you?" Helena asked combatively, hoping to instigate an argument. He just shrugged: nothing. Everything.

"You get like this when people die, don't you? But it's time to come back now, Jeremy."

Jeremy failed to see the point of anything: Persisting was no more futile than giving up. He was going to die, or he was going to go on living in this plague world of sex without love, burials without mourning. His children would not survive, or they would survive to live an animal life where heroism meant only doing what was necessary to survive and reproduce.

If he used to throw his wrench at the recalcitrant windmill made out of oil drums, now he just stared at it. He couldn't think why he had imagined he could hook it up to a pump. "No way," he said to May and Laurel, who had come to stare at it with him. When

Mick insisted that Jeremy at least climb into the helicopter, he sat there, stunned by the complexity of the control panel. "Even supposing I *could* get it off the ground, I'd never be able to hold it steady enough to mount the generator. No way. Forget it." He left Mick rigging pulleys.

He shrugged when Rachel asked him why the gas from the full inner tubes wouldn't light at the burner he'd connected. "Forget it. It's too dangerous anyway. I can't do it."

When the calendar indicated that it might be Rose's fertile time, Jeremy listened dully while Helena explained the problem that Rose presented: She would dance, but she'd lie with no man unless forced or fooled. "So you want me to tie her up and rape her?" Jeremy said blandly. "Okay."

"We used to—with Hank—to do it together. Rachel and I would make love with her, and then Hank would kind of slide in to make a baby. . . ."

Jeremy shrugged. Group sex with a schizophrenic? Fine. The three women together, and Jeremy darting in from the sidelines to score a quick touchdown? Fine, okay.

But it wasn't fine, it wasn't okay. "You know what's the matter?" he growled the next morning. "I can't live like a fucking fig wasp."

"What's a fucking fig wasp?" May asked, and Jeremy thrust his fingers into his hair with an anguished groan.

He had fixed on the life cycle of the fig wasp as a perfect metaphor for his responsibilities—now unmet—in Idamore. To him it expressed everything, including the wasplike anger that frequently took hold of him, as now when he explained icily to May what a fig wasp was. Upon emerging from the egg in the innards of the ripening fig, the male fertilized a still unhatched female, then died. Then the female hatched, already fertilized, and bored her way out of the fig, in the process gooping her sides with fig seeds. She then flew to another fig, bored her way in, and laid her eggs, thereby procreating both figs and fig wasps. And the male, upon emerging from the egg, fertilized a female, then died . . . and so on.

"Is that a story, or true?" Laurel asked when he was finished.

Jeremy sighed impatiently. "It is true about fig wasps. The story is that I feel like one." He stomped away.

"That's a beautiful story," breathed Laurel. She didn't understand that Jeremy had meant to describe his painful sense of mortality, of an ephemeral animal life with procreation as its only purpose. What she heard was that the fig was Idamore; they were the wasps, and participated in an ongoing cycle of life which, though they might never live to see it, depended on them.

Jeremy's shrugging rebuffs—"nope, no way, can't do it"—became a refrain, in the bedroom and out. Though he could be bitingly polite or icily angry, he was by and large just indifferent. Even Helena finally let up on him. She continued to count the days and keep her finger on the communal pulse. When Rachel fainted in the cornfield, Jeremy was spared the others' anxiety: Had Rachel worked too long in the sun, or was she getting Hank's disease? Or was she pregnant?

It was Edgar, not Jeremy, whose sleeve Mick pulled to lead him over to the river. Mick squatted beside the pump and grinned up at Edgar. He'd attached it to the shaft of the welded oil drums by means of fan belts and gears and casings taken from bikes, cars, and odds and ends of machinery. When the oil drums were mounted properly, the contraption would pump water—slowly, and if the wind blew.

Nor was Jeremy included in the conference about the gas stove. "Well, if it lights here," said Pearl, "and it won't light at the burner, then maybe the burner holes are too small."

"Okay," said Rachel. "I'll try that."

"And don't *you* light it, Rachel. Let Edgar or Mickey do it."

"Yes, Pearl, I *know*."

They did consult him about May's discovered animal, but only as an afterthought. May came shouting, "A huge mouse! In the cabbage!"

"Rats!" said Rachel.

"Not so dirty-looking as rats. Nicer-looking than that. And it had no tail."

"What did it look like?" asked Pearl.

"Like a monster mouse . . . big, big ears, and big, big hind legs—"

"Must have been a rat—" said Rachel.

"And a little puffy tail," May added. "Eating cabbage."

"Uh-oh."

That evening they set out wire traps baited with cabbage, and the next morning conferred about the small brown creatures they'd caught. "Go read about rabbits, Laurel," commanded Pearl. "I think these are rabbits."

"I believe they're okay to eat," said Rachel. "And don't they breed well? Oh," she exclaimed, clapping her hands. "They breed like rabbits! They breed like rabbits!"

Helena giggled. "Let's show Jeremy. He'll know if they're rabbits."

"Augie. Jules . . ." called Laurel. "Sit down and I'll tell you a story before I go for mushrooms. Listen. Once upon a time, there was a beautiful, round piece of fruit, called a fig. And inside this fig, O Best Beloved, was a family of wasps. . . ."

Helena was close by, harvesting beans, and she listened with a faraway smile. Then she raised her head to stare toward the eastern horizon. Straight east there was another fig, another tree: Freehold. Suddenly she wondered how they were faring. How many people were dying from Hank's last visit? Was there someone like Lily dead in Freehold? Did they have someone like Dave, or Ben . . . or Jeremy? Helena frowned and shook her head. "I wish we hadn't sent such very *old* sheep to Freehold," she muttered.

"Wad?" said Edgar.

She stared at him blankly. She didn't know how to communicate the way her world had just tilted. Because she had wondered about particular people in another place, they were there. Oh, she had always known that there were people out there. Of course there were people out there: They belonged to the Federal Man; they were his *job*. But now they existed for her, changing the size of Idamore, and the space of her life.

All the people of Freehold could die, and Idamore would go on without missing them. Or she could die, and all of Idamore could die, and the world wouldn't end. As the imagined world expanded, the space of her life contracted, and Helena had an inkling of Jeremy's problem. She could almost see, like peripheral vision, the mind at the edge of an idea, that the continued existence of Idamore was somewhat meaningless. There were no words for this. "Nothing," Helena said to Edgar. She shook her head. "Nothing."

She looked along the row of beans. The long, lean pods grew among the dark leaves bushing out from the sturdy stem. A good harvest for so long a dry spell. . . . What was it she had been thinking? What had she meant? Idamore was the world; there was no life but theirs.

Later Helena sat with Jeremy in the dim living room, waiting for the water to boil for a cup of tea. From where she sat, Helena could see into the kitchen, where the circle of blue-based flames danced beneath the pot of water. She smiled, because she had un- consciously taken her seat next to the fireplace, where she was ac- customed to wait for a pot to boil.

It was just the same, in an opposite sort of a way, as Jeremy walking into the upstairs bathroom or reaching out to flick on a wall switch. Now it was her turn to be caught by custom. She wondered what other habits she'd have to correct. By dint of an extraordinary communal effort, they had raised the windmill gen- erator to the top of the tower. It didn't work. But probably it would, eventually. And then what? What other small details of ordinary life would be changed?

"Oh my," she sighed. She was tired, and glad to be sitting; and glad for a quiet moment alone with Jeremy. She wanted to tell him how funny it was that she was sitting by the empty fireplace, how wonderful the stove was, with its circle of tear-shaped flames. She often hesitated now before she spoke to him, rehearsing her com- ments to see if they would upset or irk him. These considerate pauses made her introspective, and she spent long stretches of time lost in thought, her original comment elaborated and complicated and still unspoken.

"Did you find a map?" she finally asked.

"Oh, no. I forgot." He got up with a look of taxed patience.

"Never mind, Jermicho. . . ."

"No, it's all right. I know where there's an atlas."

By the time he returned, she had made the tea and set up candles on the table. He opened the map and found Idamore for her. "Here. And there's Riverwoods."

"They're never so close together!"

"And this is the lake—"

"But we're not that close to the lake. I've never even seen the lake," she protested.

"And *this* is Freehold."

"It doesn't look so far." She took a piece of candle wax and sized it to the distance between Idamore and Riverwoods. "A morning's walk, would you say, to Riverwoods? So . . ." She counted the turns of the candle wax across the lake to Freehold. "Say five or six days—"

"You're planning to walk across the water, hmmm?" he said with that cutting politeness that baffled her with its falsity.

"Oh, no. How silly." She bit her lip and measured again. Then she sat back and looked at the map, with its red and green and blue roads, its yellow blocks of dense population, its pink- and canary- and mauve-colored boundary states. The section she had measured was a tiny portion, barely a hand's breadth. "It would be quite a long walk," she said neutrally.

"You're manipulating me, aren't you, Helena? You're just trying to get me into that helicopter, aren't you? Terrific thing to learn by trial and error, flying a helicopter. I wonder how many errors you're allowed—"

"You've been over these roads, haven't you, Jeremy?" she interrupted, tapping her finger against the map. "In a whatchit—a car? You know better than we do how big big is. So why would you think that everything anybody does in little Idamore concerns only you? The fact is, nothing concerns you anymore. You understand? You're about as useful as . . . as Jules! You won't even help me read a damn map!"

She stood and brusquely put out the candles with the palm of her hand. "I want to go to Freehold with some sheep. I want to trade some sheep for some salt. It has nothing to do with you. Nothing. Do you understand?"

"What a dumb idea! You can't *walk* to Freehold. For salt?!"

"I've got feet. I'm not helpless—"

"But I am. Is that it?"

No one else had ever been capable of making her so angry. She was amazed that she could continue to stand there and speak to him when he filled her with such a hot, trembling rage. "You have chosen to be helpless."

"Well, it's a choice, anyhow. I haven't got many, have I?"

There was that tone again, that charged nasty politeness. It prevented her from comprehending what he had just said. "*And* you're choosing to be alone. Who would want to be with you? I certainly don't." She paused in the kitchen doorway and glared at him. "Oh, I miss you, I miss you," she said, then slammed out the back door.

Dogged, mute, oblivious, Jeremy shut himself off, cocooned in his depression. He worked at one task: raising enough food to eat. He didn't see how they got on without him. He didn't hear the things they were talking about. No one pierced his isolation except Rose, who trailed after Jeremy everywhere he went. She flinched when he looked at her, darted away when he approached. He'd see her flitting off when he came out of the latrine; when he turned down the next row of corn or beans, he'd spy her lurking on her hands and knees. Jeremy tried to ignore her. Then he pleaded with her to leave him alone. He ignored her, he threatened her, he pleaded . . . she was always there, just behind him.

She began to approach him with her hand extended, offering him food—limp shreds of clover, raw green beans, smashed mushrooms. When he tried to accept it, she snatched her hand away and ran, twittering nonsense syllables. At first she had interfered with Jeremy's self-imposed isolation; now she was trying his sanity.

One morning Jeremy placed a dusky, loose-petaled rose on Rose's breakfast plate. Still standing, he tilted his plate to his chin and scraped the fried egg into his mouth with his fingers. He wiped his hands over his pants and then, still chewing, grasped the back of his chair. "That rose is a present for you, Rose. I have nothing else to give you. I have nowhere to go to get away from you. I'm begging you, Rose. . . ." He spoke quietly, in a rough quaking voice; his hold on the chair had tightened until his arms were trembling.

Rose frowned at the overblown flower next to the egg on her plate. Everyone else stared at Jeremy's white contorted face. Jeremy stood there shaking, his mouth working speechlessly. Then he raised the chair over his head and with a loud sobbing bellow smashed it against the floor. Kicking aside the broken chair, he stumbled from the room.

The three other women stared out the door after him. Rachel was the first to break their troubled silence. "I think Jermicho should go home."

"Ha!" said Pearl. "If he *could,* don't you think he'd be long gone?"

Pearl's voice, often like fingernails on glass to Helena's ears, was today intolerable to her. Helena flung her fork at her plate and scraped her chair backward on the bare floor. "No, he wouldn't! He would not leave."

"She only meant that Jeremy's in trouble here," suggested Rachel, mediating, as she was apt to do now that Lily was gone.

Rose dabbled the flower in her fried egg. "The sun . . . breaks," she said, dragging the flower through the yolk. "Eat, Rose. The sun, Rose. Eat the sun-rose, tee-hee."

"Oh-oh-oh," Helena stammered with rage. "You just do that! Just eat it!" With that, she put her hand on the back of Rose's head and pushed Rose's face into the plate.

"Laney," yelled Pearl. "What's the matter with you?"

Rose raised her head. Stuck here and there, like tusks or scales in the smeared yellow yolk, were dusky rose petals. The heart of the flower, with its tiny filaments of pollen, was glued to the tip of her nose. She smiled, blinking egg yolk off her eyelashes.

Then Pearl went to work on Rose's face with a spoon. She

shaved up the egg yolk, picked out the petals, and popped the spoon into Rose's mouth. All three women there had spoon-fed one baby or another, catching the runoff and spooning it back into a wide eager infant mouth. They watched now, in stunned silence, as Rose lifted her chin and held her mouth open for the spoon. "I'm sorry, Rose," Helena whispered.

"My name is Jessica," Rose announced. "I'm hungry. I'm hungry."

"Laney," said Rachel quietly, staring out the window, "I think you'd better go to Jeremy." Pearl and Helena turned to look. Jeremy had stripped himself naked to work among the abrasive leaves of the tall corn.

Moments later Helena vaulted off the porch. She had a towel and some clean clothes wadded under her arm, and a hunk of gray soap in her hand. "Laney," Pearl called, and Helena turned reluctantly. "Here." Pearl offered her the carefully guarded bottle of mild green soap, half-full now.

"Oh, Pearl!" With a grateful hug, Helena shook her head. "Keep it for Phoebe, old dear. Jermicho doesn't need *soap*. . . ." Helena turned and ran toward the naked Jeremy Echo, her husband, her lover, the Federal Man, a troubled boy.

She took the hoe from him and led him by the hand toward the river. "Let's go splash in the river."

"I'm afraid I'm going to hurt her," he mumbled. "I think I'm going to hurt her."

She went slowly and by way of paved streets, for he was barefooted, and where the land was unirrigated, the grasses were harsh with dryness and rampant with thistle and burdock. She could hear Mick already at the irrigating duct, turning a crank handle he'd attached to the pump. She avoided him, guiding Jeremy farther south and around a bend in the river. She led him down the bank and over a tiny spit of land, where she kicked off her shoes and waded into the water. She wet her hands and placed them on his sunburned, dust-gritty shoulders. "Wouldn't you like to bathe?"

"Bathe?"

Her eyes stung with the memory of their first meeting. Jeremy

Echo, she had dubbed him, thinking him stupid. She'd gone from thinking him stupid Jeremy Echo to regarding him as the magical man from the time of the light, ignorant of death and therefore exempt from it, and all weakness. He had given her so much— hope, eagerness, sexual joy she'd never imagined could occur with a man, feelings so vast that sometimes she thought her heart would burst its bounds. She had given him nothing in return. Now that he needed something, she didn't know how to help him at all.

She remembered that first day, when he had twice said his real name. The same way their old Federal Man used to say "Lewison-Clark," as if it were quite important to remember the second part. Lewison-Clark . . . Jeremy . . . she couldn't remember it. . . . Jeremy Falls. Jeremy Tall. . . . "Indeed he does," Ben had replied. . . . "Jeremy Towers!" exclaimed Helena.

Jeremy flinched away from her cool hands. "Oh, God, don't, don't." He bent down and scooped water over his shoulders and the back of his neck. "Let me be. Can't you see I'm transforming myself. They sent the wrong man. They sent no kind of a man at all." He walked gingerly over rocks into deeper water, and eased himself down.

Helena shucked off her jeans and waded after him. She squatted to wash his back, using the tail of her man-size shirt to rub his skin, all the while muttering indignantly, "The wrong man! You!" Her fingers browsed at his neck, picking off nits.

Jeremy slumped over his knees, letting her groom him. "Baboon heaven," he said with a shuddering sigh.

She came around and sat in the still water between his feet. The back of her shirt billowed airily behind her. She took off her hat and held it in her hands. "Let's say this hat means you're a Federal Man. And let's say you're a Federal Man, so you get the hat." She set it on Jeremy's head. "Too small," she said with mock sadness. It was comically too small, and perched on the crown of his head, an ineffectual bit of clothing for such long, broad nakedness. Her eyes lit up with her ready laughter, then darkened again when Jeremy looked away from her. Glumly, she removed the hat. "Shouldn't we change the hat, instead of the head, Jeremy?"

She watched his Adam's apple leap to the unnatural rhythm of his shallow breathing. "Wha-wha-what . . . ?" he said with an appalling stutter. "Ch-ch-change what?"

"What do you need to have changed?" she asked reasonably, though she knew she could change none of the things bothering him. Could she stop the spread of disease? give Mick or Edgar sperm in their loins? resurrect Ben? She looked down at their interlocked legs, where the river surged over their thighs. The slow water trapped between them dandled the tails of her shirt and the pale wattle of Jeremy's penis. It always looked that way now, and nothing they did to or for him would make it stand up. So they had taken everything from him: his name, his crazy optimistic energy, his manhood.

"I n-n-need . . ." Dumbly he shook his head.

"Once upon a time, there was a man named Jeremy Towers, O Best Beloved. . . ." She squinted downriver, not looking at him: It wouldn't do to cry. "And one day he came through a strange fog to a strange land where time had stopped. The stopped people said that he'd come from the land of light, but really he came out of time. And he brought time with him. 'Beat, hearts,' he commanded, and—"

"Ssssh," he said, swaying miserably back and forth. "Sssshh." The hissing moved farther and farther back in his throat, becoming guttural, and then he was crying. At first it was more like gagging, and Helena clasped and squeezed his hand, helpless before his grinning anguish. By degrees all the stopped places opened, and he broke into an easy rhythmic keening that she understood. He was mourning. He had needed to mourn all that he had lost, and oh, he had lost a great deal. She put her arms around him, stroking his back and letting her own tears dribble down his shoulder. The Ashago River, low from the long dry spell, flowed in a huge V around their hips.

When she saw Rose standing on the bank of the river, Helena narrowed her eyes at her, hoping that she'd go away. Rose hesitated on the bank, then walked into the water without taking off her shoes. There was something disturbing—and disturbed—about that, as if Rose were oblivious of the water. She waded toward them, the water lugging her loose khaki pants heavily around her ankles. She opened her hand, which was full of squashed berries.

"Oh, Rose, Rose, Rose," groaned Jeremy.

"If somebody fed Jessica, she'd bear a sun," said Rose.

"Rose is Jessica," explained Helena.

"What am I gonna do, Helena? What am I gonna do?"

"Feed her?" she said, climbing off his lap.

"Feed . . . ? Oh!" He swung his head around toward Rose. "I get it. You're *hungry.*" Berry by squashed berry, he fed Rose. She didn't take the food from his fingers with her lips pulled chastely back, but closed her mouth around his fingers, sucking lightly. Her long upper lip slid along his index finger, and she gazed raptly at him.

Helena hugged her knees, watching Jeremy react. His shrinking aversion relaxed to mystified sympathy. He glanced at Helena with an embarrassed smile, then held his head close to Rose's. "He's back! he's back!" Helena thought with a painful surge of love. She leaned on her elbows in the soft mud and gazed at him. His eyes were bloodshot, his nose was red and moist, and he had hiccups that made him start absurdly, but Helena had never thought him so handsome as he was now, feeding berries to Rose, engrossed, penetrated by Rose's impenetrable madness.

"Jeremy, see if she'll feed you a berry."

Jeremy wrinkled his nose, then put a berry between Rose's fingers. "I'm hungry, Rose," he said, leaning forward and pointing to his mouth. "This is silly, Helena."

"You are the sun," said Rose, shaking her head. "You are the man with the three suns in his hand." She extended her hand toward Helena, who took the proferred berry with her fingers. "We are hungry, and you are the one one who will not eat us."

"Oh boy," Jeremy and Helena said together.

Rose got to her feet and veered off, nodding her head with an oddly sly expression on her face. Her pants clung in tight wet pleats around her legs as she stumbled backward toward the bank, and she kept up that absurd nodding. "We are the hungry ones. Plants. You are the sun." She paused melodramatically, then pointed at him with a purple-stained finger. "You are the man with the green breath." Then she turned and clambered up the bank.

"Oh, geez, I'm not ready for this," he said. "The man with the green breath is—"

"Could be like the breath of spring, couldn't it?" Helena quickly interjected. "Greening breath, huh?"

"Oh, great. I am the resurrection and the life," he said with bitter sarcasm.

"Well—"

"No," he said sharply. "Please. Don't try to make me into—"

"Right," she said hastily. "Right. You're an ordinary man. That's all you *need* to be." Just an ordinary *healthy* man, she thought with a glance at his genitals shimmering in the water. That was it, of course: Not Jeremy, but his healthy genitals were the resurrection and the life. That was the mystery, and the problem.

She had never bothered to think about Lily's explanation, years before, of why they assisted the Federal Man with their rituals of feigned sexuality. Because a man could not passively make babies, as a woman could; he had to have an erection, which—Lily told her—some men couldn't get if their sense of self-worth depended only on their getting one. Was that why, Helena now wondered for the first time, was *that* why the Federal Men concocted all those other responsibilities? A huge fiction of government to enhance their self-esteem, and give them erections? She ducked her head to hide the smile that sprang to her lips.

Jeremy didn't even have the trappings of importance. No sector, no helicopter. And it was as if, in suppressing his penis, he suppressed himself entirely, perversely making it true that he was only as useful as his penis. True, it could never be as delightfully useless as her clitoris, which had absolutely no function except to give pleasure. But could it be like her breasts, say? Though they were useful in an absolute and crucial way, they didn't define her. Imagine measuring your identity or usefulness by your breasts! Still smiling thoughtfully, she ran her fingers along the inside of Jeremy's thigh.

"Don't, babe," he said, but there it was, rising above the current, making its own little V in the river, the phallus, straight as a stinkhorn mushroom. "Well, looks like I'm back in operation," he said. "Who's listed on the calendar?" Even as he spoke, his penis drooped.

Yes, she understood now. His impotence was a denial, a protest: He needed to feel that he was something more than an impersonal bearer of seed. He needed to feel that his pleasures were not solely for the benefit of some unseen future, but that they belonged to him. "No one's on the calendar," she lied, putting her hand between his legs. "Let's just . . ." What did you call what she wanted to do? If you did it with a woman, it was making love—to do it with a man was a forbidden thing. "Jeremy," she murmured, "Jeremy . . ." She looked at him with a deep blush spread over her face.

"Haven't you ever made love in a river?" he teased, misunderstanding her hesitation.

There was an event she had never seen—except once, halfglimpsed, an accident in a field, an outrage. And, oh! just once she wanted to *see* it. To watch, to feel with her hands the mystery of it, not to worry about wasted seed. "Let's just *touch*," she said at last, giving him a significant look.

"I'd say we're moving steadily backward here. Steadily backward," he remarked with a delighted chuckle. "Pretty soon we'll be climbing into the backseat of an abandoned Chevy. . . ." She didn't understood his words, but knew from his voice and his eyes that he was pleased, and not at all shocked. He was accustomed to pleasure for its own sake. Pleasure without function. Lord, think of it, Helena thought: The men in the time of the light were like women!

∘ TWENTY ∘

It was a season of plenty, and a season of preparation. They harvested beets, beans, and turnips; parsnips, carrots, onions, and early potatoes. Where they harvested, they sowed, hoping for another harvest before first freeze. Seeds were saved from the best of the crops, and moss collected for the storage cellars. The kitchen was a moist, green-smelling jungle of steaming vegetables, which were then dehydrated in Jeremy's solar ovens.

While they were scything the alfalfa and clover fields, Jeremy would have sold his soul for a horse-drawn mower. Afterward he was glad he had soul and sense left to enjoy the complex, wonderful beauty around him. The sky was dusted with fine cornmeal clouds. Curing on the sun-baked fields, the stacked stalks bleached gold and gave off the sweet smell of hay. Winter squash bulged like gleaming green rocks on the ground, and tawny tassels of silk hung over the deep-green stalks of the corn.

Standing by himself on the stubbly alfalfa field one late afternoon, he watched the sky change. The white dome was leaking teal blue up from the horizon, and the heaped clouds refracted the sun into striations of watery light. "Rain!" he exhorted the clouds. "Come on, rain!"

As he turned toward the house, he glimpsed Rose shrinking into some bushes at the edge of the field. Like a man with a favored dog, Jeremy had begun to carry morsels of food in his pockets. When Rose paused, quivering nearby, Jeremy would feed her, stroking her hair or touching her face. "Everything's fine, Rose, everything's fine," he'd murmur before resuming his work. Seeing her now, he pulled out slices of carrot, limp and gritty from the afternoon in his pocket. "Here, Jessica, my rose, my hungry bird, what's the matter? Why are you crying?"

"The sun's melting."

"No, it's just going to rain," he said. "The sun'll be back. It always comes back."

"Always?"

"Always," he said firmly. He daubed a piece of carrot in the tears on her cheek, and ate it. Rose patted her cheek in a startled way, then grabbed the carrots from Jeremy's hand. She wiped one, then another, over her wet cheeks, and held them out. "Let's say a toast," he said, holding the carrot up like a glass. "To life." Jeremy and Rose each solemnly ate a tear-salted carrot.

"Now we will make the sun," she said, pulling at his belt. "You. Put the sun. In the cave."

"Oh, I don't think so, Rose—"

"Quick. Before it melts. The man with the green breath must be coming. Quick, quick."

They coupled at the edge of the field under a watercolor sunset, which Rose anxiously gazed at the whole time. Afterward Jeremy pulled her to her feet and adjusted her clothes. "Come on, let's go ask Helena what day it is. Let's go check the calendar."

"It was not the sun," said Rose. "Not hot."

"Oh, Rose, poor baby, poor Froot Loop, you've got everything so mixed up." Jeremy held the indifferent woman as the first drops of rain fell on the dry field.

The rain was brief and hard. After it stopped, everyone felt heavy, as if the earth were exerting more gravity because of its rain-soaked density, and the air itself was drawn down over them, thick and denying.

"What a pig wallow!" Jeremy said as he came from the yard.

"Take off your boots," said Pearl.

"I wonder if they have pigs in Freehold," Helena mused.

"Helena, we have chickens and sheep and rabbits," said Rachel. "What do we need with pigs?"

"Pigs can be salted—"

"We've got no salt," said Jeremy, scraping his boots at the edge of the porch.

"Smoked then," Helena said. "Preserved all sorts of ways we can't preserve sheep."

"If Mick gets the wires working, can't we freeze anything?" said Pearl.

"Go, team!" cheered Jeremy, putting his arms around Rachel and Pearl. "You tell her." Jeremy was beginning to find Helena's obsession with Freehold not just inexplicable, but really annoying. Each time they talked about it, he considered the subject closed, and then it came up again. And again.

Just yesterday she had intercepted him in the field to say, "You're really the one who should go."

"Don't be ridiculous," he had said. "I have to be here for harvest." As soon as he spoke, he winced, for he'd somehow conceded that the trip was possible . . . as long as no one expected *him* to make it.

"Right after harvest, then," she had said imperturbably. "It would be too bad if *you* didn't go."

"Too bad" meant really bad, Jeremy knew, and he had found himself looking at the helicopter. Mick had removed its batteries, so Jeremy wasn't looking at it as a vehicle, but as a symbol. Then it was less the grueling trip than his role in the imagined place that bothered him. His arrival as a "Federal Man." He looked closely at Helena's face as he questioned her. "You'd have me go to Freehold, Laney?"

"Yes," she had said. Her voice and her glance were steady, almost defiant. Then her hands fluttered to the fragile cuplike place at the base of her throat. "Oh, I'm sure if I could see them, I would," she had cried.

"What is this thing you've got about Freehold?" he asked now, glaring at her.

"But don't you just wonder about them? Maybe they have *nothing*! No sheep or pigs or cows—"

"Why not wonder about Kendallville? Or Carbonville? Or any other place?"

"Too far away," Helena said, and pouted when everyone began to laugh.

They stayed up later than usual that night, sprawled around Rachel's screened-in porch and talking desultorily in the dark. The night sky pulsed with lightning. In the spasms of sudden light, everything briefly shuddered, then settled solidly again upon the dark earth. Rachel, lately given to catching catnaps wherever she happened to be, was curled up between Helena and Jeremy, who had one hand on Rose's back, quietly patting her. "Has Rose ever had a baby?" Jeremy asked.

"No," Helena said. "She's like me. Can't hold 'em."

Jeremy flinched.

"Well, this time will probably be different, Laney," remarked Rachel sleepily.

"This time . . . ?" Jeremy sat up. "Laney?" he said sharply.

"I think so. I wanted to wait a bit before telling you."

The news radiated through Jeremy like an electrical disturbance along his nerves. As if to confirm his own worst fears, Helena's face was briefly, hideously illuminated by a pulse of lightning, then blotted out by the darkness. He wanted to hold her fast—to himself, to the earth. He started awkwardly to his feet and squatted behind her, hunching himself loosely over her shoulders as if he were trying to protect her from rain.

His pleasure at Rachel's pregnancy hadn't been pleated with such dark feelings. He'd been almost as relieved as he was glad, for now he and Rachel could leave off the sexual activity that warped their friendship and Jeremy's very soul. The surge of vigilant protective love that he felt for Helena extended now to Rachel. To Pearl. And to Phoebe, noisily suckling. To Laurel. To all of them. He would serve and defend them all his days. "Oh, Helena. Oh, Helena," he said hoarsely.

When Jeremy woke the next morning, he could just hear, under the steady drum of the rain, the slick *pfft-pfft* of the turning windmill. He stretched happily and leaned on his elbow to gaze at Helena. She was not beautiful, this thin sallow woman, but he had come to cherish the scrawny robustness of her back, her long narrow nose, the dark hair inside her thighs, the down that ran along her hairline from her temple to her lower ear. As he smoothed back the hair that fell in a dark splash over her pillow, its fineness caught in his callused hand, and Helena opened her eyes. She blinked and nestled closer to him.

"Why don't you stay in bed, and I'll bring up your breakfast?" he said.

"Oh?" She put her hand over her forehead. "Am I sick?"

"Don't be ridiculous," he said, pulling on his pants. "It's still raining."

She raised her eyebrows, and when he'd padded down the stairs, she got up and stood at the bedroom door that faced onto the sunporch. Rain was caught in each tiny square of the screen, and her finger down the mesh released a dark trail of dripping.

She could see Edgar herding the sheep out into the rain from the side door of the Administration Building. When he raised his arm in greeting, Helena stood on tiptoe, trying to see below the obstructing sunporch. Jeremy trotted into view, barechested and carrying a basket. As his boots struck the ground, muddy water erupted around his ankles and splattered onto the backs of his pants. He sloshed his way across the yards toward the house where the chickens were kept.

He was in the chicken house quite a while, and when he came out, he set down the basket of eggs and stood in the rain like a man under a hot shower. This looked so pleasant that Helena pushed open the screen door and stepped outside to let the rain pelt onto her head. She stretched and turned in the downpour, rubbing the rain over her chest and under her arms.

Mick joined Jeremy in the yard and pointed to the windmill. Jeremy ran his fingers through his wet hair, then shook his head. Whatever he was saying must have involved her, for he gestured toward the second floor where she stood. As he pointed, he glanced up. Helena laughed out loud to watch his double take. He grabbed the eggs and galloped across the yard. "Get out of the rain," he yelled as he passed out of sight beneath the sunporch.

She was standing on one leg, struggling to pull denim pants over damp skin, when Jeremy's boots clomped quick and heavy on the stairs. He strode into the doorway, then hesitated, leaning against the doorjamb. Rain dripped from his hair onto his tanned muscular shoulders.

He combed his fingers through his wet beard. "Rachel says to tell you that we're almost out of soap, but we don't have enough ashes because we've been using the gas stove; and Edgar says that the second field of alfalfa is in half bloom, and he's worried about harvesting with all this rain. Also, the chickens haven't been fed, or the chicken house cleaned, so I'm gonna do that right now, while you cook breakfast. . . ."

With a groan, he knelt before her and buried his face in her stomach. "Oh, Laney, I wanted to treat you like a queen. I wanted to give you . . . But we can't. We can't."

"Pregnancy isn't a disease, Jermicho."

She sat on the bed and put her hands on his damp shoulders. "I've been listening to us and looking at us—"

"You and me?"

"Idamore. You've become one of us now, Jermicho, and I can't always protect you from the dying. Be strong now. I want to ask you something."

"Wait." He got up from the floor and sat stiff backed on the edge of the bureau. "Okay, go ahead."

"How small do you think a community can get, and still survive?"

His first impulse was to answer "Two," because he still believed that he and Helena could go away together and survive. But survive what? Even were they to survive for decades, what was it for? To leave what behind? Children with no commingling place? Helena meant community; no other survival mattered. Jeremy pursed his lips and gazed at the floor, where he noticed, with a fraction of his attention, his muddy track from the doorway to the bed to the bureau.

He put his hands on his knees, leaning with locked elbows. "We are still dying," Ben had said to him. Ben's terrible secret, which everyone knew and protected the others from knowing. It seemed a lifetime ago, that conversation with Ben. Well, it was, in a way— Ben's lifetime. They'd lost four working adults, and two of the women were pregnant. Maybe three, if Rose continued to watch sunsets. And the happiest, healthiest outcome of the pregnancies left them cruelly shorthanded next spring, with two (maybe three) postpartum women reliant on the labors of Laurel and May, Pearl, Edgar and Mick—and Jeremy. "I dunno, Laney," Jeremy said at last. "We're stretched a little thin here, aren't we?"

Helena gazed at him with a pleased smile.

"Is that good news?" he exclaimed. "What do you mean, 'Be strong?' What do you think I can possibly do—"

"Listen, listen a minute." She sat cross-legged on the bed, a scrawny Buddha with upturned palms. "I didn't mean strong enough to *do* something, but strong enough to accept something. I've been very happy since you came. Oh, not happy, really . . ." She flapped her hands impatiently. "Alive. Well, happy. We argue a lot, but we also laugh a lot, and I think you've been happy, too, lately—but I don't want . . . Oh, Jeremy, I don't want you to be too disappointed if we don't . . . if we don't . . ."

"I won't be," he said quietly. "I *am* part of Idamore, and if we don't make it, I won't be around to be disappointed. But, oh boy, I won't give up without a fight." He slapped a rapid staccato rhythm on his thighs. "All settled, then? I can't protect you, you can't protect me, and everybody stands together. Let's get going. Lots to do."

"No. Wait. I didn't say what I meant to say at all. Not at all." She knit her brows. "I was sure you'd understand, but you haven't. . . . Don't you see, now that the sector is closed, something has changed? We have—don't we have a choice now?"

"Hmmmmph?"

"Is Idamore the place or the people?"

"I'm sorry, Laney. I'm not following this. . . ."

"Would we continue to be ourselves if we weren't here?"

For one terrible moment he thought she was considering suicide. Then, when he understood the drift of her conversation, he was so relieved that he laughed and became playful.

"I mean," she said, "when we go to Freehold, we must consider—"

"What you mean *we*, white man?"

"Listen for a minute, can't you? We must consider more than exchange of good—"

"Goods," said Jeremy, grinning.

"Stop interrupting! I'm trying to say something awful—"

"I doubt it. But go on."

"When we go to Freehold, we should consider joining them." She put her hands over her cheeks, waiting for the enormity of this idea to register on Jeremy's face.

Once more Jeremy laughed. He drummed his thighs with delight at the simplicity, the clarity, the inevitable drift of Helena's persistent comments about Freehold. "When *I* go to Freehold," he said pointedly, "I'll ask them if they'd like to join forces with us. There if Freehold looks good, or here if Freehold's on a bum trip."

"Bum . . . ?"

Jeremy caught her head in the crook of his arm. "Never mind, genius."

"Then . . . we are not Idamore?"

"We are Idamore as long as we choose to stay here."

"Choosing . . ." She nodded happily. "That's it. We might choose to live in Freehold. Or we might choose to stay here. With or without the people of Freehold. But first we have to find out what's what."

The others were less easily convinced than Jeremy, who wondered if it was superstitious or sensible to feel such allegiance to a place. Idamore had so far permitted their survival, and it was, after all, the people and not the land which were unproductive. Using powers of persuasion worthy of Ben, Helena set to work convincing the others that this decision concerned only people, and not places. She pointed out that nothing was decided yet: Perhaps the people of Freehold would come to Idamore. As Mick had come to Idamore, she said, with a look for him that made him blush and fidget. As Rose had come. And Jeremy. They had never turned strangers away from Idamore. What was the difference if now the strangers were invited?

With all the talk of Jeremy's trip, and of people coming and going, Helena spoke more frequently than usual of Simon. Though Jeremy understood the emotional equation in her mind—he was about to leave on a long trip; Simon had left forever—it was hard for Jeremy to feel the compliment of her anxious love. He had come to be vaguely jealous of Simon, as a man might be of his wife's adored, deceased first husband. It was ridiculous, of course, because Simon was as much father figure as intended spouse, the focus of idealized adolescent longings thwarted by the discovery that Simon was sterile. And Jeremy knew he was ridiculous when, at the mention of Simon's name, he found himself mentally strutting about his own virility. But he did not share the others' admiration for Simon, who had gone to work at Carbonville.

The system was, apparently, that the able-bodied reproductive males took to the air, the able-bodied nonreproductive males to the mines, and the women were left to produce food and babies. Jeremy thought it was a lousy system, and couldn't for the life of him understand how it was enforced. The country—such as it was—seemed to depend on the patriotism of its citizens, their belief that they were working to re-create the cities of the light. To Jeremy it seemed a pitifully paltry reason for a man to walk away.

Sitting with Helena over the atlas, Jeremy traced the route to Freehold. He warned her not to expect him back for three or four weeks, and not to even begin to worry for at least five. "There are lots of things that could slow me down."

When her hair brushed his cheek, Jeremy decided that he couldn't leave. "Laney . . ."

"I know, Jeremy," she said. She bent over the atlas, apparently studying Michigan. "We must remember," she said, wiping her hand across the map, "that we have choices. No matter what happens, we still have choices." She scrubbed her hand across the page again, and Jeremy saw that she was wiping away tears.

° TWENTY-ONE °

Jeremy smelled the lake before he saw it: the brackish odor of fish and algae-covered rocks, of vegetable dross, of deep water. When he saw gulls wheeling on the horizon, he broke into a slow jog and ran, his pack thumping rhythmically against his back, until his feet slewed in sand.

He stood on a dune, marveling at how much the area had changed. The beach was huge, descending in soft ridges to the water, which was spiky with vegetation all along its margins. Tall dune grass grew along the ridges, and sand obscured the geometry of the littoral streets. To the north palatial beach houses foundered in water, while to the south . . . Jeremy turned his head carefully. He was prepared to see almost anything—a shadowy mountain of rubble, or nothing at all—and he shivered with pleasure when he saw several tall buildings. They looked like columns of dense smoke, hazy with distance, but they were there. To get to Free-hold, he'd have to walk around the southern shore of the lake; he'd have to walk through the destroyed city. Jeremy took a peculiar comfort from the substantial shape of those surviving buildings.

He wished that Helena were with him. How she would love the vast metallic sheen of the lake glinting darkly in the late afternoon sun. And the birds! The hundreds of birds! There were ducks and terns, cormorants and sandpipers and herons. Overhead, the rau-cous gulls soared and swooped, their white wings gleaming against the light.

He walked the dunes looking for second brood eggs and manag ing only to flush dozens of birds into the air. He gave up and stood still, up to his thighs in dune grass, savoring the ripe smell of the air. Vegetable rot, bird droppings, fish; the smell of conversion, of life washing over this little corner of the green planet. Smiling almost reverently, he watched the ducks paddling among the spikes of the water weeds. They popped over and waggled their pointed tails at the sky. The sandpipers skittered up and down the beach. The gulls swooped to pluck the surface of the water. Everything was becoming food, or getting it.

He assembled his fishing lines and baited one with corn, another with crayfish. As he sloppily cast his lines, the ducks and gulls all laughed—*rawk-auk-auk-aaah!* And Jeremy Towers, Jeremy Echo, the only self-conscious thing in the world around him, stood beside the huge lake, listening to himself laugh back.

In the northern section of Idamore one house glowed softly with its own light. Inside, it looked and sounded like a party, for music blared and candles flickered in the drafts of people's laughter. Idamore was celebrating the invention of electricity and the creation of music.

In quick succession they had experimented with a dozen machines. One machine at a time, as Mick kept insisting, gesturing fiercely toward the windmill, the basement, the wires. Each machine was more useless than the last, but some of them were wonderfully fun. The fan pushed air out at them, and the vacuum sucked air into itself, and the machine with the alphabet on it put the letters up in white on a dark-green screen. "I could write a story," said Laurel. "I could write a story for Jermicho!"

"Not just now," said Pearl. "It's my turn to try a machine."

"Oh, look, look!" yelled May, who had discovered an electric clock.

It was Rachel who chose the record player, fiddling with dials and buttons, then gasping when the machine suddenly sprang to life, its arm lifting and moving. The machine spun the thin black disc and out came such a sound! *Ba-ba-ROOM-dao-dao, ba-ba-ROOM-dao-dao.* The room filled with the regular whomp of drums and the thrum of electric guitars.

Mick slapped his leg and grunted his laughing grunt. He pointed at the record player and slapped his leg again. "You didn't know about this?" Helena asked. Mick shook his head and patted the lamp. Helena understood: They couldn't have electric lights unless someone mastered the manufacture of light bulbs; Mick was saying that it didn't matter. Music was better.

There were hundreds more discs in the cabinet. Like starved children rushing around a smorgasbord table, Laurel and May sampled a few measures of each record, then, squealing and shrieking, put on another. "Try this one. Oh, let's try a different one!" Bach, Bartók, and Brubeck. The Police and Vivaldi. "Another one! Another one!" The Beatles, the Bee Gees.

Suddenly the high nasal voice on the record player yawned and slid, blurring deeper and deeper until, with a last grotesque moo, the record stopped.

"Put on the other record, Laurel," said Rachel. "The second one. I like that best."

"Electricity's off," said Helena, interpreting Mick's slicing gesture.

Laurel stood in the doorway staring out at the night. "Fig wasps, O Best Beloved . . ." she said solemnly, and Helena smiled to herself. Laurel was in love—with Jeremy, with the future, with her own blossoming imagination. Laurel had wanted to go with Jeremy. "How will he forage?" she had demanded. But he wouldn't hear of it. He wouldn't hear of any of them going until he determined that the trip was safe, and the place worth traveling to.

"Fig wasps with time," Helena said, getting up from the couch to stand beside Laurel in the dark doorway.

"Fig wasps with windmills . . ." said Rachel.

Laurel turned into the room, smiling at all of them. "Fig wasps with books."

"And music," Pearl said. "Well, sometimes, anyhow," she added.

"Thank you, Mick," said May.

There was a startled rustle among the women as they exchanged glances. They had all been thinking of Jeremy, but it was Mick who had provided the electricity.

"Jules," Pearl yelled toward the kitchen. "Get out of the refrigerator! It won't stay cold, will it, if it's open?" She was on her way to the kitchen when she stopped. "We are . . ." She paused, searching for words. "Jeremy has planted seeds of want that we grow and harvest. Is it dangerous to want *too* much?"

A sudden gust of wind rattled the corn and clacked loose wires against the house. It blew through the open doors and windows on the east side of the house, bending the candle flames sideways and dimming the room. The record player came to life, startling them all with its raucous inappropriate song. Rachel turned it off.

"The only danger is disappointment," she said, with a quick sad glance at Laurel.

"More, more, more," said Helena thoughtfully. She twirled a lock of hair around her finger, filled suddenly with a great vague yearning. "Why, no matter what we do, we'll always want more!" she exclaimed. "More music! More food! More children! More light! Oh, Rachel, what's the harm? It's wonderful. Oh, Mick, isn't it wonderful?" And he sat there glistening with love, nodding his head, yes, yes, it was wonderful.

Jeremy trudged south along the shore of the lake, taking little note of what he passed: a yacht club; condominiums and elegant shopping centers with names like Edgewater and Plaza del Lago. One night he slept in the grandiose lobby of a condominium, another in the devastated living room of a nineteenth-century lakefront mansion. The farther south he got, the more restful the landscape seemed to him—as if the earth were trying harder to resurrect itself, reaching up to blanket what was settling into it. Cars, houses, overpasses, trestles, highways. Only when he faced north to survey his day's progress did he see that the southern exposure of everything still standing was blackened and scorched.

Soon grass was growing around weirdly cantilevered roofs, as if the world had taken its housing underground. The rubble became more and more dense, slowing his pace until at last he was like an ant in a giant's rudely dismantled playground. The vast jumble extended far into the lake, a crazy patchwork of metals and rocks that ascended like a mountain before him. He had reached the outskirts of the city.

He was only miles from a standing skyscraper, which gave him the notion that he had only to climb over the palisade of rubble to find himself standing on the clean windswept boulevard of a city street. He picked his way along steel beams piled like matchsticks, and levered himself over projecting hunks of pocked granite. He paused occasionally to peer down into the abyss of rubble beneath him or up at the heights he still had to scale, and his enthusiasm waned.

"We'll never get the sheep across this," he began to mutter. "No way. . . ." Behind him, the long beam from which he had just jumped began a slow, grinding slide, and Jeremy heard the mountain shift beneath him.

He sprang off his rock onto a section of wall to his left, and felt it give way beneath his feet as he vaulted again. He stood windmilling to keep his balance on the curved surface of a huge cement cylinder. There was a loud squeal of frictive metal, and Jeremy lunged off the cylinder to a length of steel duct. Everything he touched shifted under him. The mound was collapsing beneath him, sucking him into its center like a maelstrom that he himself had set in motion.

He was hanging from a piece of cable, scrabbling wildly up a nearly vertical block of smooth metal, when the metal abruptly settled, slamming him into a wall of jagged granite. He fell and curled up, waiting for the mountain to close in after him.

∘ TWENTY-TWO ∘

Of the many things that might kill him in this strange land, Jeremy thought the most fitting was this precarious rubble left by a nuclear explosion. Perhaps he had already died in the explosion. The primal blast had thrust his limbic soul floating through time, out of time. Yes, he must have died here. He had been present at the end, and was now just a wandering lost soul in search of the beginning. . . .

What blather! Jeremy thought, cautiously raising his head. The mountain had stopped squealing and belching around him, and he sat up, feeling not the least bit like a disembodied soul. His body! His body! How many times had he tried to shuck it off, too swollen with horror or grief to cart himself around anymore? He pictured himself stretched out beside his house in Cottage Grove, scooping dirt over his body. Or standing naked in the cornfield, hoping the sun would melt him out of his grinding impotent misery. And always what he was when he stood up again was a man: a collection of complex cells in charge of a mind, a mind that was the sum of its experiences within that body.

Jeremy picked his way up and out of the rubble, moving like a man through a minefield, breathless with caution. It was almost dark by the time he was back where he'd started. As his adrenaline subsided, his legs began to tremble, and he sank gratefully into the tall grass.

In the direction of Idamore, he saw a flock of martins describing spirals in the darkening insect-rich air. "Well, Laney, that's that. The city's impassable."

"Swim," came her determined amber voice inside his head. "Fly. Jump. Crawl." The southern shore of the lake was dead silent. Here there weren't even birds to laugh.

The next morning he began the trek back to the yacht club. Once there, he selected a tiny battered Laser as the soundest and most sailable of the boats he saw, and launched himself due east into the lake. Straight out onto the huge and unpredictable lake of which all sailors spoke respectfully. And Jeremy was no sailor. When the mainsheet broke, he looked east and saw nothing but water; south, and saw nothing but rubble; west, and saw the yacht club diminished to the size of a dollhouse. He repaired the rope with a clumsy knot that impaired the management of the sail, and limped back to the yacht club. There he did a proper repair, collected more rope, and started off yet one more time, proceeding now by a series of short shore-hugging tacks.

It was harrowing, that first day of sailing: afraid to go too far out, he was also unable to land. The mountain of rubble girdling the southern shore seemed to stretch endlessly. Vast loosely piled rubble ashore, the light failing above him, and beneath him the alien boat alternately wallowing in the water or heeling so far over that it threatened to capsize, taking all his gear and fishing tackle into the dark lake.

He spent that night hunched in the well of the boat, which he moored to one of the outsize bolts projecting from an enormous I-beam. The beam had melted into a grotesque but graceful curve, like the line of a willow growing over a steep bank. All through the night Jeremy kept checking the rope to make sure he was still moored, then leaning back against his life jacket to gaze bitterly at the silhouette of the skyscraper discernible as a kind of black hole in the starlit sky. He felt quite vexed and put out: no dinner, no bed, no harbor, no home. The people of Freehold had better make this trip worth his while, or he'd punch them all in the nose. . . .

In the days that followed, his sense of resentment and haste diminished. He stopped fretting at everything that slowed his pace, and resigned himself to the discomforts of life in a fifteen-foot sailboat. He caught fish, and ate them raw because even when he managed to land, he could find nothing to burn. Nothing that wasn't burned. He slept sitting upright in the boat, and swam every morning to restore the circulation in his legs, as well as for the sheer pleasure of stretching out horizontally.

He went naked and frequently masturbated, sometimes out of boredom, like a solitary caged primate, and sometimes out of loneliness, when he populated his solitude with the women of Idamore. All of them. At once. In fantastic positions. It was the tender orgy which he had forbidden himself and Rachel out of some unexamined but strongly felt scruple; in his fantasies, it was Rachel—or *he* was Rachel—who had the profound pleasure of a beautiful phallic hip-thrusting Helena.

When the mainsheet snapped again, he calmly and doggedly fixed it, and when the fish were slow to bite, he lounged patiently in the oblique beams of the setting sun, his long legs crooked over the gunwales. He talked out loud to himself, to the gulls, to Helena, and to old Allison Pachek, asking them to remark on his equilibrium, his steadiness of purpose, his imperturbable sanity.

Because—grim as it was, boring as it was—there were moments of pure exaltation. He was learning to sail. He learned to tack without losing momentum, and he developed a light, sensitive hand on the tiller so he could keep the boat headed steadily into the wind, the tattered sail taut. When the wind came up, the boat roused gaily out of the water, plowing forward, skimming past the sizzled shore faster than a man could ever walk. Then Jeremy would throw his head back and laugh. Look, Helena, look how I'm getting to Freehold. I'm flying! I'm swimming!

Jeremy had been gone almost two weeks on the night that Mick careened into the living room, snapping everyone to attention with his wild gestures. They all rushed behind him, clamoring and questioning as he led them up the stairs. At the two west windows of the big bedroom they divided into huddles, standing on tiptoe or crouching to see around each other. They fell silent as they peered out. A thin dotted line of fire danced in the southwest.

"I've never seen anything like that," said Edgar, grim with memories of fire.

"Probably just lightning on dry grass . . ." said Helena.

But the fires continued, visible each night as gauzy sulfurous halos that moved along the horizon in a gradual arc from the southwest to the west. Those are people, Helena thought. Then she stared skeptically, pressing her forehead against the screen. She couldn't think what else it could be but a line of people carrying torches. But there was something so improbable about it—about their existence, about their carrying torches or setting fires—that she said nothing.

The next night Rachel said, "Are they heading our way?"

"I hope so," Helena replied, in spite of the quiver of panic.

"But, Helena," said Laurel mildly, "they're burning everything behind them."

"They never are," she declared.

Mick tugged Helena's sleeve to get her attention, then drew his finger in a slicing gesture along his throat. "Don't be ridiculous, Mick," she snapped. "We don't turn people away from Idamore unless they have disease, and we sure could use some more people."

The progress of the fires was measured each night from a western window of Idamore. Again and again the line of torches disappeared, obstructed by buildings, and whoever stood guard in Idamore held her breath, hoping that the fire had gone out. But the distant town always erupted in a cheerful blaze, and the line of torches reappeared just east of the smoldering sky. East, and moving toward Idamore.

When the torches formed a circle and stopped moving for the night, the night watch sat back in the rocking chair, cuddling August or Phoebe, and stared at the distant lights, trying to imagine them, those arsonists peacefully encamped beneath the starless, smoky sky. She stared until the circle of lights, motionless and hypnotic, put her to sleep.

Mick went about quietly collecting and repairing hoses. He wired two electric pumps to the big mill, his jaw clamped with frustration: He hadn't yet mastered the batteries he'd been trying to hook up to the mill in order to store electricity. Idamore had to depend on the unpredictable wind until he understood the batteries, which he tinkered with in every spare daylit moment.

He stole away one night, walking west toward the fire. Traversing the adjacent town, which was laid out on a southwesterly grid, he lost his bearings, and when he broke into a house to take a sighting from a second-floor window, he found that he'd gone south of the torch lights. From the other side of the house he tried to see Idamore, and couldn't. He stood very still for a moment, fighting panic: How could he defend them if he couldn't find his way back again?

He walked on, later breaking into another house to get a fix on his direction, and finally approaching the perimeter of the earth burners' camp. He crouched in the grass and held his breath in order to listen more carefully to a man's deep voice. He shook his

head and rubbed gooseflesh on his arms, then crept closer to listen
again. Was it an army of ghosts they'd have to confront? For it was
Ben's voice he heard. Ben's special word-of-the-Bible voice.

". . . We eat the bread of adversity and we drink the waters of
affliction, my brothers, but we are the messengers of the Lord, the
angels of the bottomless pit, the voices of the seven thunders. We
carry the sacred vials of wrath to pour out upon the earth, to empty
out upon the earth, and behold, we make all things new. . . ."

It was not Ben. Those were not ghosts. They were real, and
would have been pitiful to anyone but Mick, who regarded them
without a flicker of sympathy. They were singed, blistered, gray
skinned with smoke and malnutrition, loose lipped from lost teeth,
gaunt, sunken eyed. There were nine of them, and their leader was
a man with a wonderful, familiar voice. It was Ben's voice. It was
Ben's brother. It was Simon himself, returned from the underground. And Mick knew, listening to him, that he had gone mad.

On and on he talked, a sonorous biblical garble, while the listless
living corpses sat around him staring blankly into space. Several
sank down upon the ground, cradling their heads on blackened,
bony arms, and still he talked on, not to them or even for them—
he was not exhorting or trying to convince—but for himself, perhaps to exist as a disembodied stream of words.

". . . The time is at hand, and we are the time, oh my companions in tribulation. Freed at last from the bottomless pit, we have
seen the mystery of hell and we hold the keys to the kingdom. Out
of this great burning shall come the kingdom, and from the
ashes—yea, of our very bones, brothers—shall come the tree of
life. No other way is given us to beget, for we are the sterile slaves
of the bottomless pit, and we have seen that the holy cities of the
light are a wilderness, the holy cities of the light are a desolation.
We are the messengers of the Lord, we carry the refiner's fire
across this polluted, sterile land, and lo, we make it new. In the
bottomless pit I saw a new heaven and a new earth, for the first
earth and the first heaven are passing away behind us, yea, even as
we walk forward through the fires of the vials of wrath."

Mick lay in the deep dark grass, gnashing his teeth with contempt and rage. Seed scorchers! Life burners! he wanted to yell. If he had had a weapon, he would have used it. On Simon's mouth. To still the filthy stream of words. Then turned to bludgeon the others out of their misery. But he was unarmed, and had come to value his life too much to risk it casually.

What he had seen was beyond Mick's resources to convey to the others, though he tried his best. All he managed to do was further agitate Edgar, who gabbled wildly about the sheep being trapped in a burning field. The more frightened Edgar became, the calmer was Helena. Mick watched her amble along the last unharvested section of the alfalfa field, once or twice running her hand lightly over the surface of the grasses. The evening was clear and cool, a muzzy blue, and smelled almost like autumn, with the pungent odor of distant smoke. "They will not burn Idamore, Mick," she said to him later. "Once they see what we have, they will join us here and work. . . ."

Mick was not so certain, and did an inventory of their defenses. One unreliable acetylene torch, to fight fire with fire. Shovels, to batter with. Knives, to pierce with. He held a hatchet, testing the edge of the blade gingerly against his finger, then wielding it to test its weight. He swung it in a high arc and brought it down against the porch step. The blade buried itself in the soft wood, and he looked quickly away.

He hoped he wouldn't have to do that to human flesh. More fervently, he hoped he'd know if and when he should. Because he didn't think that the others would use weapons, even to protect themselves. Spilled blood polluted the land. It was one of the things Ben always said. "For blood defileth the land." Perhaps it was true. It would explain why Cottage Grove had not prospered, defiled as it was by the murderous greed for life-yielding goods. Perhaps it was not true, and survival was a matter of random luck. It didn't matter to Mick either way. He was prepared to defend Idamore— with water or blood.

° TWENTY-THREE °

First there was grass, and then there were sumac bushes. The curve of the shore swung north. Michigan! At the first sign of a standing roof, Jeremy sailed ashore. He levered some lumber from the house, built a fire, suspended a big pot of lake water over the flames, then went in search of things to put in it. A hot meal. Fish chowder, seasoned with crayfish and thickened with strands of some kind of kelp. He walked around bent over to examine the various weeds. He found some nut grass, which he rooted up for the tiny nodules along its long running stock, and he ripped up some clover, flowers and all. He hunkered a long time over some mushrooms. Milk mushrooms, he thought, but which ones? He nicked the cap and observed the milky latex turn a greenish hue in the air. Was it green or purple stains to avoid in the milk mushrooms? He sucked his teeth, then stood up. Too chancy.

Later he sat cross-legged beside his fire, eating his soup right from the pot, sucking and spitting, crunching and grinding with rude gusto. The sailboat clanked at its moorings, the lake sloshed against the steep rocky bank, and the evening air was loud with the pulsing buzz and whine of insects. Jeremy added another board to the fire, whose bright snapping warmth made him feel his solitude more acutely than he'd felt it for days. He took the empty pot and held its diminishing warmth against his stomach, rocking back and forth. He couldn't think why he was suddenly crying, but it didn't matter. There was no one to see, no one asking for explanations or offering sympathy. He wept quietly over the empty pot, keening. He became convinced that there would be no one in Freehold when he got there, and that Idamore would be empty when he returned.

Still he sailed north—because that was his mission, to find Free-hold, then go back to Idamore. He checked the names of the towns, the once sleepy, slightly depressed resort towns of western Michigan, now undefended from the steady erosion of wind and water, the contraction and heave of ice and thaw, the stubborn seeds that took root in dusty crevices and created soil for them-selves by splitting cement and overcoming rock. "Nothing's perma-nent," he remarked to a brick house that was withstanding these ravages somewhat better than other houses he passed. "Nothing's permanent," he reminded himself. But surely—though even the lake he was sailing might change, atrophy, dry up—surely the sky would always be there. Surely something abides.

He wondered why that should matter so much, and understood suddenly that it didn't matter at all—except to a being capable of imagining the future. You need a little something to go on for that sort of job—a mental port for launching into the oceans of tomor-row. Above him, shapeless and flexible clouds were changing be-fore his eyes and in ceaseless motion. He gave another hitch to the mainsheet, glancing sternly at the mast. "Hold, you," he com-manded the frayed rope. The tiny boat heeled over, leaning into the wind.

Because he was alone and mostly idle, he thought a lot, defining and then dismissing his definitions of what was permanent, what was real, what was good. He talked to Allison Pachek—often out loud—for she too had tried to think about the difference between what the human mind sought and found, and what was real, that separate world which might soon be without the benefit or curse of human consciousness. Man, the mammal that laughs. The mourner, the lover of abstractions and music, paddler of strange rivers, dreamer of cities, nightmare maker, inventor of truths so imperative that he killed for them. A miracle, or an evolutionary mistake?

If they got a second shot at it, what did they need to change in themselves? Was it possible to change what was worst without also sacrificing what was best? "You tried, old bones, old scribbler," he said, then took the old woman to task for sifting the entire Bible

through that one sieve. To make personal violence a taboo as invio-
lable as incest or cannibalism seemed like a valiant program, but
not by closing everything out. Better to open minds than to close
them. Why, look at Helena blooming like a desert flower now that
she'd discovered "choices." Not that the choices would be easy or
painless. Just to have them, to know that you had them. To take
over your own life a little, saying I chose this, rejected that . . . But
what truths do you teach if you're pressed for time . . . or not
pressed *for* time, but pressed *by* it. What words do you utter when
you smell the dark reek of personal death and species extinction?
"Well, I don't know," he said. "I'm doing the best I can."

At that, something shivered inside his head. A ripple of scorn for
his own egotism. *He* didn't matter. No one of them mattered. Even
Idamore didn't matter. Representatives of the whole, that's all. It
was like stepping inside Helena's head and understanding what she
had meant on the day they'd had a discussion about death. Not a
discussion, really. A breakdown. A moment when they looked at
each other and knew that though they were speaking the same
language, using the same words, neither knew what the other's
words referred to. She had been trying to understand the dimen-
sions of Jeremy's grief and remarked that it wasn't the end of the
world if three people died. In his reply, Jeremy had quoted something. "One person dead is a tragedy; twelve million dead is a
statistic."

"That's disgusting, that's the most disgusting and stupidest thing
I've ever heard you say."

Impasse.

Now, alone on the huge lake, he saw both his own meaning and
Helena's. Every one of those twelve million lives was important,
individually; yes, but no single one mattered as long as the collective whole survived. People were like cells in a single complex
organic community, each cell thinking itself the center of the
world, and capable of mourning only the loss of other, specific cells.
It was a terrible failure of the mind, this mental ladder that it
climbed from the specific, where emotion was possible, to the ab-
stract, where one sat indifferent on the edge of the uni-

verse. . . . You cannot grieve for an abstraction; you must not grieve for a cell. . . .

North and north and north, the vegetation thickening, shrubs hauling up on spindly trunks to become small trees, the low canopy fretted with vines. Grapes, he thought, but wasn't certain enough to eat them. One afternoon, when he was examining yet another unfamiliar species of berry, a squirrel bounded out of the underbrush, twittered irritably at the startled man, then sprang away. "Hello," said Jeremy. "Come back and be a stew." He set up an unlikely sort of trap: a scavenged box propped up on a stick to which he attached a string improvised from vines. If the squirrel was lured inside the box—which Jeremy doubted; the squirrel could gather the abundant rooty nuts more easily than he had— Jeremy could yank the string and the box would fall over on the unwitting animal. Jeremy sat very quietly, enjoying the suspense. The underbrush rustled and snapped all around him. Battalions of squirrels! Or rabbits! Or—hmmmm—mice. Chipmunks. Ragout of mouse. Chipped chipmunk on rye grass . . .

Fish, of course. Broiled over an open fire. Tomorrow he would wrap it in those broad kelpy leaves and bake it. On the water he had wanted his fish cooked, and now he wanted something other than fish. There was, after all, always something to look forward to. Some unfulfilled dream to work on. Squirrel stew, and healthy people in Freehold . . .

It must have been an extraordinary sight, Helena later thought: to come upon a group of people farming the land in an abandoned town in the middle of a closed, unpopulated and vast sector of the Midwest. No wonder the first man who came upon them turned tail and ran. She caught a glimpse of yellowed eyeballs glaring in the smudged, terrified face. Vaulting onto a table, she called after him. "Bring the others here to meet us."

She looked down at her companions, who were staring after the apparition. "My God, did you see him? His legs are like sticks."

"I think everything's going to be okay," said Rachel. "Pearl, they're coming. Bring out the soup!"

"Oh, boy." Helena sighed. "Wouldn't it be nice to feed them up and have some more good workers in Idamore?"

Rachel nodded, her face flushed with excitement. She got up on the table with Helena and craned her neck. "They're coming," she said, grabbing Helena's arm. They both leaned forward, squinting at the group of men fording the river. The man in the lead was taller than the others and walked with a pronounced limp. He came up the bank, his men fanned out behind him like a wake behind a ship.

When Mick heard Helena's gasp of recognition, he put his hands to his face and groaned sadly. He stayed on the periphery of the group now crowding around Simon, who touched each one of them as if he could hardly believe that they were there. "Helena! My little robin, you're grown up. And this is Laurel?" he said. "The baby Laurel . . . ?" His eyes glittered in his blackened face as he turned from one to the other. "Somehow I thought you were all dead—dead long ago. . . ."

Helena dispensed soup as she chattered at him. There was so much to tell him, and though little of it was good news, Helena hopped and wriggled, interrupting herself to exclaim over him.

Mick felt a persistent tic of uneasiness as he watched Simon's men at the soup. They seemed unaccustomed to food, rolling it around in their mouths or tonguing it in the cups. Two didn't even approach, sitting blank faced on the ground. Furthermore, Mick counted only five men. He was sure that there had been nine of them last night.

Mick wondered how long it would take the others to see that this man was mad. He was burning with a mad purpose that made his eyes glitter and set his mouth in a strange, confident smile. When Helena announced that both she and Rachel were pregnant, Simon turned those glittering eyes first on Mick, then on Edgar, then in a scanning gaze around Idamore. When he saw the helicopter, he gave an odd little jump. "But this sector is closed," Simon commented.

"Ah, you heard," said Helena. Hugging and patting him, she related the details of Hank's last visit, of the disease that Hank had brought, and of those who had died of it.

"Ben?" Simon interrupted. "My brother Ben? But he's been dead for years . . . you were all long dead. . . ."

"Simon," said Edgar, stepping forward. "We have sheep with lambs," he said in his distorted, oracular voice. "We have two pregnant women. We have a healthy infant and good crops. There is plenty of life in Idamore."

"This sector is closed," Simon said, frowning so that the thin furrows of white flesh disappeared in ridges of blackened skin. Rachel and Pearl exchanged a troubled look.

"But Idamore isn't," said Helena. "Not Idamore. Come see." She took his arm with an adoring smile, and Mick trailed miserably behind her. As her questions were answered with one non sequitur after another, her bubbling enthusiasm slackened, and then her pace. When Simon spoke of the bottomless pit from which he was risen to carry the refiner's fire, Helena stopped in her tracks. "You're mistaken, Simon. There is no need for burning."

"Ah, my little robin, my little nestling, there is no more flock. The sector is closed. . . ."

"You will not burn Idamore, Simon?"

"I've been instructed to make all things new, Helena. The place I best love will be most new, passed over by the wand of the vials of wrath—"

"Simon! We have food, we have a future, we have—"

"—for my angels are weary from their time as slaves to life. Oh, we are weary, my brothers, and sick of the bread of affliction. . . ." Whatever restraint had been exerted on Simon by the sight of familiar faces from his past was now gone, and he ranted magisterially of the great burning, of how they would burn their way to the east, to the place where the sun rose, how they would burn as the sun itself burned.

"You will not burn Idamore," said Helena.

Simon gave her a scornful glance. When he raised his arms, Mick thought it was a signal and tensed for an assault. But Simon's battalion of cadaverous torch bearers had scattered. Simon boomed up at the sky: "From these ashes, a tree of life." Helena hesitated in front of him, hypnotized by his glittering eyes.

It was as if they were all paralyzed, caught up in the moment of

Helena's heartbreaking apprehension that this was not the Simon she remembered, this was not the man she had loved as a father and future husband. Though they saw the smoke rising from the cornfield, they stood with Helena, waiting for her to act, to release them all from Simon's terrible hold. Then Simon said in a husky seductive voice: "You will become part of the fire. It's what you were waiting for."

"Bullshid!" howled Edgar, breaking from the group and running first toward the fire, then away from it. "Bullshid! Thiz is bullshid!" It was Jeremy's word he was screaming in his furious terror, and Mick saw the shock of it register on Helena's face.

She snapped around, and put her hand over her mouth when she saw Simon's men setting fires to brush and field. "No!" she screamed through her fingers. "No!"

Then everyone broke and ran, shouting directions to each other. "Put out their torches," Rachel called to Pearl, who was hauling on a hose. "Get buckets," Pearl yelled to the children. Mick looked up at the windmill, which was motionless in the calm air.

Mick grabbed Edgar by the elbow and gestured with his chin toward one of Simon's men. "Wad?" yelled Edgar, as if he were deaf rather than Mick mute. Mick could hear the sharp edge of hysteria in Edgar's voice. Mick snapped the rope in his hands, pointing again with his chin toward the scrawny man wielding a torch, but Edgar was running purposelessly to and fro. Mick set off alone.

He grabbed one of the men by the shoulder, twirled him around, and slammed his fist into the man's face. He felt the bones give under his fist at the same time he felt the pain in his knuckles. As he put his hands around the man's scrawny throat, Mick felt a surge of almost sexual pleasure that frightened him. He was ready to push the bony frame deep into the ground with the force of his rage. He took a deep breath to control himself, and tried to steady his hands enough to tie the man's bony wrists together behind his back, but he couldn't do it. He stood up, delivered a savage kick to the man's ribcage, then stomped out the fallen torch. He left him writhing on the ground and shambled off toward the alfalfa field.

Mick was stalking the boundary of the field when he saw Rose prancing with a handful of flaming sticks along a row of corn. "Jessico!" she shouted gleefully, tossing sticks into the air. Her straight auburn hair was crinkled and dark from scorching, but she did nothing to avoid the descending flames. "I am Jessico. With hands of ash. Jessico, with hair of flame." Mick gaped at her for a moment before giving her a series of little pushes toward the house.

"Look, we have unraveled time," she argued mildly. "See, this is our chance to do it over."

"Uuuunnnnnhhh," he snarled in his most savage grunt, shoving her toward the porch.

Suddenly Edgar was there, scolding Rose as he snatched the burning sticks from her hand and plunged them into his bucket. "Go sit on the porch, Rose, or we'll tie you up like an enemy," he said. Then he turned toward Mick and with a brave nod indicated his readiness to do battle. "There must be no blood," he wheezed as they dragged Mick's first victim to the porch and tied him to the railing.

As Mick and Edgar approached, the man in the field threw back his head to glare at them. "You will be punished," he shrieked. "This is sacred fire, this is refiner's fire." He tried to hold them at bay with the torch, turning and wheeling in the field until he stood in a circle of green smoke. The crops were succulent with recent rain, and the fire, when it caught at all, didn't spread. But Mick could hear from Edgar's breathing the terror he felt of the fire. It was to spare Edgar that Mick threw himself at the man. They fell, and there was the vile odor of burning hair. Before Mick could pin his arm, the man flung the torch into the middle of the field.

"Buckets! Buckets here!" yelled Edgar, helping Mick wrestle the man out of the field. They tied the wraith to Rachel's steps, and turned to see where they should go next. Houses were burning, but the houses didn't matter unless they contained chickens or winter stores. Edgar was sobbing as he ran with Mick toward the cornfield, where smoke rose in green billows around Pearl and Rachel, who were stomping and shrilly calling for more water.

Behind him, Mick heard Rose laugh. A strange triumphant whinny that made him shiver.

Neither Helena nor Simon was anywhere to be seen, but Si-

mon's men seemed to become only more wily and determined
without him, for they had spread out and were encircling Idamore
from five or six fiery directions. These men had given their lives
over to Simon's mad mission; it kept them alive and made them
seem fearless. But Mick was sure that Simon's men were much too
weak to overcome the vigor of Idamore, if only Idamore would
decide to defend itself.

Mick spotted a man lurking in the far end of a corn row. He
crouched to circle behind him while Edgar tried to reason with
him. "This is corn. Delicious, sweet corn," said Edgar, stroking the
stalks, which were actually corn for fodder, and tough. "If you let
it grow, you can live here with plenty to eat." The man flapped his
lips at Edgar with an absurd expression. Like a toothless, black-
lipped sheep, Mick thought, watching him set his torch upon the
corn. Catching sight of yet another torch at the other end of the
cornfield, Mick shook his head.

"No blood," he reminded himself, because his own was pounding in his ears and beating at the back of his throat. He gave his
rope a warning snap and crouched to spring. "No blood."

Then he heard a scream—Rachel's voice?—and a strange strangled sound. Mick straightened and saw everyone frozen, a tableau
of horrified witnesses. In that moment he heard the high-pitched
chatter of birds worrying about the fire in the underbrush, the *glug*
of slow water from a hose, the creak of the great propellors beginning to turn in the wind, which was also wafting smoke across the
streets of Idamore. He heard too the splintering crack of metal
against bone. With a hatchet honed to a razor's edge by Mick himself, Rose was dismembering the two men tied to the porch. "Ya-
hoo, Jessico!" she shouted, waving the bloody hatchet over her
head.

° TWENTY-FOUR °

Just as he had feared, there was no one in Freehold. He clomped up and down the streets, hollering greetings and looking for signs of recent habitation. It didn't look as if anyone had lived here for years—no evidence of farming or herding or wood gathering. Just another moldering town. But Hank had been here for two days before he returned to infect Idamore. He had been here . . . where? Jeremy thought of the small group of people who lived in "Idamore"—at Idamore's very edge, in a place that had nothing to do with historic Idamore, but only with the local configuration of land and water. He wasn't looking correctly: He had to think of the accidents of geography that would yield survival to a small community of people.

He walked up a steep road to the highest point in the town, found a church, and climbed the rotting stairs to the belfry. The land was hilly, bolting down to hollows and tiny lakes, gouged out by a river. Beautiful, but even to his unpracticed eye not particularly good for farming. Perhaps they fished. He scanned the lake, huge and blue as a postcard framed by the spreading shoulders of land. He had come ashore just south of the high bluff that now obstructed his view in that direction. He looked farther north. Where was Freehold's famous salt? Where was Freehold?

Jeremy walked back down to his sailboat, which he sailed past the bluff and around the point of land. He swung the tiller when he saw the natural harbor, and sat there grinning at the two rowboats bobbing in the water. Resting on a trailer at the water's edge was a beautiful thirty-foot sailboat.

"Oh-boy-oh-boy," he said excitedly, talking inside his head to Helena: Look at this, Laney. Look at this fantastic place, my love.

See the houses? *That's* what I was trying to do. Just like that—earth houses like these, cool in summer and warm in winter. Perfectly insulated by the earth itself. A little damp, maybe, but better than an unheated wooden house standing out in the winter wind. "Hallooo?" he called, hauling his boat up onto the rocks. Oh, look: lots of small windmills up on the high ground, and the houses down in the hollow, protected from the wind. "Anyone here?" he hollered. And look, Laney, look at the trees up there! And what's this newly dug . . . ? Graves.

Jeremy walked through the silent, perfectly engineered village, his calls dying in his throat as if he were trying to shout obscenities in a church. He saw the nets hung out, the traps and lines and folded sails of a tidy fishing village. He followed a well-worn path up the sloping shoulder of land and saw in the next hollow the cultivated fields and an empty fenced enclosure for animals. Idamore's aged sheep, by the evidence of the droppings. The trees were not as big as he'd thought when he was standing below them, but several were taller than he was. He thought he smelled pines, and kept walking the slow northerly rise until he stood on another bluff overlooking a small inland lake. What was it that made it so perfect—the hills, the lakes, the forest rising before him, ever taller and sturdier? . . . They had taken down all the houses, that was it. They were methodically returning the entire area to a wilderness in which they lived almost invisibly. Like Indians. "Hank, you blithering idiot, did you kill them all?"

He avoided the sepulchral village, haunted by the recent failure, the recent dead. He was jumpy, starting at the sounds of small animals in the underbrush and hearing the wind in the trees as whispering voices. He fished from the other side of the bluff, and returned to the undismantled section of Freehold to find wood for a fire, and pots and utensils for cooking the corn and squash he'd picked on his way through the field. He went to a lot of trouble to set up camp in a shopping center, carrying utensils and pried pieces of lumber from the adjacent residential street onto the long walkway that fronted the stores. He didn't wonder why he was behaving so oddly; he was just setting up a camp in a shopping center.

Sitting with his back to the long glass wall of the drugstore, he faced the dozens of parked cars, some of them neatly parked between the diagonal lines. He set his fish and vegetables over the fire, then sat back with his arms crossed. He pretended that at any moment he'd become a freak. The electronic doors would hiss, automatically opening for shoppers with their arms full of bulging brown bags. People would rush toward their cars, pausing to comment over the weirdo barbecuing his fish on the sidewalk.

Jeremy got up and walked among the cars, opening all their doors. It gave them a festive look—a big community tailgate picnic, all of them stopped here to be with Jeremy. He returned to his simmering pot, gave it a stir, and bowed to the headlights eyeing him. He held his fist up to his mouth, a pretend microphone through which he murmured, "Good afternoon, friends. This conference has been called for the purpose of ending the nuclear arms race. . . . It has come to my attention that this matter is too urgent to leave entirely to the efforts of women and students. We have to get everybody involved in preventing this disaster." He scowled at the cars. "You old biddy, you Bircher," he said to the blue Buick. Then he dismissed his audience with a wave of his hands.

"Ahh, Laney, I'm too old for make-believe friends. I'm sorry I wouldn't let you come with me." He wished he could send her a telegram. A pigeon with a note: "Freehold closed, but you still can choose it: nice place. Sailing home tomorrow. When I get there, we will dance together. Now that you're pregnant, we can do anything, can't we?" Grinning mischievously, he slowly stripped to the music of his hummed bump-and-grind tune, and then, before the startled eyes of a hundred headlights, he danced Helena's dance.

The woman who had been following Jeremy since his first landing south of Point Sable Bluff had never seen a grown man naked in the daylight, and she wasn't entirely sure what he was doing. She gaped at him as he clambered onto the hood of a car, then up to the roof, where he sang and gyrated, that enormous swollen thing stuck out in front of him, the metal roof clonking as he moved.

All day she had tracked him on cat feet, so even when he had turned to listen, it wasn't any noise she made that caused him to jump and turn and mutter. A dozen times she might have killed him, and yet she hesitated: He was a stranger, but now that her own people were dead, she wasn't sure whether she should kill him or ask him for help. Trap him to kill him or to keep him. And then, Lord, he was so odd, coming and going, muttering to himself, traipsing all the way down here with his food, then taking off his clothes. . . .

By inches, she crept forward, curiosity overcoming caution. The FEMA man always took her in the dark, his bony hips sharp and heavy against hers. Always in the dark, the poor struggling man, so he couldn't know in the daylight which of Freehold's daughters he had had. And she had seen nothing on that long-ago afternoon she was raped by the stranger who had lived to walk away. She had clc ;ed her eyes—as if she could render the day night and herself unseen by closing her own eyes. She had never again left the village without a knife.

She held one tightly now as she crept forward. What had looked like joy suddenly turned to pain on this man's face: He was contorted, hunched over but with his head thrown back, and then . . . She gasped, suddenly connecting what she had dimly felt in the dark with what she was seeing in the full light, and the knife fell from her hands with a clatter.

For a split second he stared at her, then he belly flopped onto the roof and slithered over the far side of the car. Through the car windows she saw him put both hands over his face, shaking his head. Then he slowly stood up, standing behind the open car door. He had turned a quite remarkable red. He looked at her, his mouth working, then slowly sank down behind the car again. He repeated the whole procedure, except now he remained standing, and gestured with a limp hand, flicking his fingers first toward his chest, then toward her, and then, with a shrug, toward his dinner cooking over a fire. Puzzled, she glanced toward the fire. "My— ah—my clothes!" He hesitated, then scuttled across the parking lot, bent double, his hands crossed in front of his legs. She watched him try to get into his pants without standing up or moving his hands off his groin. A most peculiar man, a purple stranger who did private nighttime things in broad daylight.

Jeremy had never been so embarrassed in his life, and would gratefully have disappeared. Instead, rush after rush of blood suffused his face so he felt that he was pulsing like a neon sign. He could think of absolutely nothing appropriate to say to this apparition, who was certainly the tallest and possibly the most beautiful woman he had ever seen. He kept ducking his flushed face away from her staring eyes, wishing for instant walls, layers of loose clothing, amnesia. He fastened his jeans, rehearsing an apologetic explanation: that he'd been alone a long time, that he thought he *was* alone. . . . He looked up and saw her walking slowly away. He snatched up his shirt and struggled into it as he ran after her. "Hey, hello? Listen, miss, I'm harmless, I'm . . . Oh, please wait!" he called, then wondered if she was deaf, for her walk registered no hesitation or acknowledgment.

He loped after her, increasing his pace until he touched her on the shoulder. "Hey!" he began with a smile, then sprang away from her as he might have recoiled from a snake. He stared dumbfounded at the knife that flashed in her hand. "Oh, hey, wait a minute. I'm not going to hurt you," he said, slowly scissoring his hands in front of his stomach as he backed away from her. "Listen, I'm really sorry about . . ." He shrugged awkwardly, blushing again. "My name is Jeremy. What's yours? Would you like some of my fish?" He paused, peering cautiously at her. "Can you understand me?"

She opened her mouth, revealing large, white teeth with an appealing gap through which she spat at him. He wiped his face on the sleeve of his shirt. "I know it seems to you that I did something awful back there, but see, I really didn't think anybody was here. I called and called, and nobody . . . Oh, do you think I'm a Federal Man? Is that why you're so angry? Because Hank brought disease with him on his last trip . . . ?" Nothing. A deaf-mute.

He couldn't think what made her so astoundingly beautiful, since her features, taken individually, weren't good. Her nose was flat, the nostrils pinched too high behind the bulb. Though her lips were exquisite crescents, her mouth was too big for her face and huge above her tiny firm chin. High cheekbones, thin eyebrows, and dark-blond hair plaited in a dozen tiny braids that circled her head like a bowl. She might have been twenty or forty—ageless, proud. She stared back at him, her eyes—almost golden they were! hazel, he supposed—wary and defiant. The most beautiful woman he'd ever seen, standing eye to eye with him: six feet tall.

She slashed the air with her knife, then turned and walked away. He followed at an erratic pace, approaching to reason with her, then falling back when she turned on him. "Listen, I'm not anybody you think. I came a long distance across the water just to see the people of Freehold. . . ." He came too close, and sprang away when the knife flashed. "Jesus, will you quit threatening me, and let me talk? Couldn't we please just sit down for a minute and—Oooff!"

The moment that the rope tightened around his ankle, he realized that he was not dealing with a cranky version of Helena: This woman was carrying a knife she knew how to use, and setting traps she knew how to bait. The next instant he was on his back, his feet yanked out from under him, and before he could struggle, she had his hands tied behind his back and his feet bound.

She loomed over him, tall and angry. "My name is Amanda Barston-Clark. I do not want any of your fish. I can understand you perfectly. And I don't care who you are or where you came from." She hesitated, about to add something, then pinched her wide mouth and turned away. He watched her snap kindling and gather wood—a big competent woman with strong arms and a brusque manner.

Jeremy waited for her to talk, thinking she'd feel safe now that she'd manacled him. But she didn't even deign to glance at him. "Is there anything you'd like to ask me?" Apparently not. "Aren't you curious about me?" Nothing.

He watched her clean and spit a squirrel over the fire. "Out on the water I was eating raw fish. Actually, I minded that less than the loneliness. Do you get lonely here, Amanda?" Not lonely enough to talk to *him*.

"Barston-Clark. Amanda Barston-Clark. How nice. My last name is Towers, but in Idamore they call me Jeremy Echo because . . . well, that's a long story. . . ." Here, too, his name was appropriate: He was the only one talking, his voice oddly loud in this glade above the village. Conversational gambits kept bubbling irrepressibly out of his mouth, each one greeted by another speechless glance.

He felt increasingly humiliated, rejected, and uneasy. He thought that anything was possible: He didn't know the rules here, and it was clear that they were very different from Idamore's. Either that, or he was dealing with a person distraught and beyond reason. Perhaps she had watched everyone die in that lovely village over there, leaving her alone. Perhaps his performance in the parking lot had so offended her that she was refusing to talk to him. Perhaps . . . perhaps anything, Jeremy thought hopelessly. If she wouldn't talk to him, he'd have to watch her act out her intentions.

He lay back against his numb left arm and stared at the canopy of bushes over his head. "Well, okay. That's it. Not another word. You want to be silent, fine. I know about silence. Silence, exile, and cunning. What's that from?" Oh yeah. . . . Hey, you ever hear of Charles Darwin? I bet Darwin's finches are like Idamore and Freehold. Same species originally, but isolated so they evolve into totally different birds. Or is this a cultural difference here? Hmmmm. . . ." The silence during his reflective pause made him aware of his own maundering, and he giggled. "I've been talking to myself for days now."

She checked the ropes on his wrists, removed the squirrel from the fire, and walked away with it. "Amanda? Amanda!" She was gone only minutes, but Jeremy was sure that he'd been abandoned for the night, left hog-tied on the ground. He stopped struggling when he heard her returning through the underbrush. She squatted to clean and spit another squirrel. "What did you do with the other one?" Jeremy asked suspiciously. "Is there someone else here?" Gotcha! he wanted to yell when her head snapped up.

He waited a moment, then said sympathetically, "Well, I'm really glad you're not alone here. Loneliness can be really—" Suddenly exhausted, he lay back. "In Idamore I was never alone.

Everybody kind of swarms around in Idamore," he said with an inward-looking smile. "Mick's good with machines, and Edgar with sheep. I'm good with women, and the women are good with the land. It all works out pretty well. . . ." He closed his eyes, then opened them again when she gave him a little kick on the leg.

"I'll untie your hands now so you can eat. One wrong move, and I'll cut your throat."

"'One wrong move!'" he exclaimed, feeling that he was on the set of a remarkably bad movie. "Listen, Amanda . . ."

"Be still, man." Apparently seized with distrust of him, she tethered his bound feet to the bushes and then bent over him to tie more rope around his chest, passing the rope under his arms, behind his back, and around, a kind of plaiting action that brought her close enough for Jeremy to smell her. She smelled like the lake. Fishy, sweaty, sweet. Jeremy considered seizing her handsome arm between his teeth and drawing blood. . . . She gave a yank to the rope and he was tied in three places. A sturdy triangle that permitted no movement forward, backward, or sideways.

She untied the rope on his wrists and sprang away from him. He chafed the raw skin, shaking his head at her. "I'm not going to hurt you. Please believe me." Mutely, she extended the roasted meat to him by holding out the long stick.

How bad could her intentions be if she was feeding him? He bit into the crisp roasted meat, keeping his mouth full so he wouldn't interrupt with his obsessive babbling anything she might eventually say. She said nothing, removing yet one more squirrel from the burlap bag at her feet. He wanted to ask her how she had caught so many. Little questions like that. Also big questions: How many people had died from Hank's visit? And had the village been biologically prosperous before Hank came and defeated his one and only purpose in life? Determined to remain quiet, Jeremy snapped the leg bones and sucked the sweet marrow.

Amanda put her squirrel over the fire, then flicked the knife out of her hands and sent it whistling into the trunk of a tree maybe two inches in diameter. She removed another knife from the burlap bag and sent it after its twin. A third. The three knives were in a straight line along the tiny tree trunk. She wiggled them out of the bark, then repeated her target practice from farther away. Two hits, one error. Jeremy grunted uneasily and looked away.

The sun was setting into the lake, turning the clouds on the horizon into a cathedral of filtered light. *Whiii-ick! Whiii-ick!* went the knives, while the sun melted into the water, spreading out long and red. Into this belt of light walked a boy. The silhouette of a boy, his features hidden by the light blazing behind him. Jeremy froze, the gnawed bone held up to his open mouth. The boy crept behind a bush, then appeared again on the other side, the light angling over his face. Maybe eleven, twelve years old, with the first sign of his manhood happening in his shoulders. Amanda let out a stifled shriek and rushed after him, shooing him angrily away. "I just wanted to see him, Ma," the boy protested as he was bundled off.

Alone in the dusky glade, his thoughts as dark as the shadows creeping over him, Jeremy struggled to free himself. He flung himself back and forth against his harness until the bark split in the tiny tree trunk behind him. He reached back and yanked at the rope. Another split, and the tree bent. He rocked wildly back and forth, but the tree wouldn't break. He had maneuvered enough room to reach his ankles, though, and fumbled frantically over Amanda's expert knots.

He was shucking the rope off his chest when he heard her footsteps in the underbrush. As she entered the glade, he stepped up to the target tree and removed the three knives she'd embedded in it. He held one knife in his right hand the way she had, and it must have looked expert enough, for she was as tense and still as a trapped animal. He stepped a little closer so she wouldn't think she had time to run from a flung knife. "Okay, one question, and then I'll climb back into my little boat and leave you alone. One question, but you must answer it. I must know. Is that boy the son of the Federal Man called Hank? The one who was just here, and made everybody sick?"

She frowned, and stared at the ground.

"Listen to me, you fucking witch," he yelled. "I never planned

on hurting you, but I will if I have to. I don't know what's going
on here, and if you don't want to tell me, that's fine. But I must
know about that boy. Across the water is a town called Idamore,
full of women who laugh and talk while they work in the fields.
But the women of Idamore do not bear sons. I thought it was
Hank, I thought—" Jeremy's voice broke, and he was standing
there, sobbing and yelling at this mute gigantic female, threatening
to kill her if she didn't tell him whether Hank had fathered that
boy, he had to know, he had to know. . . .

Almost imperceptibly, she shook her head, her braids wagging
on her high forehead.

Jeremy walked a few steps closer in order to study her face in
the growing darkness. "No?" he said. "No, Hank is not the father
of that boy? Come on, Amanda, talk to me, talk to me! I'm begging you."

"He's all I got," she mumbled, staring at the ground. "Bought
him with pain and blood."

"I'm not going to touch him!" Jeremy snapped. "I'm not going
to take him away. I'm not going to hurt you. I'm not going to do
anything you don't want. Just, for God's sake, tell me straight, is
the man with the helicoptor that boy's father?"

She glared up at him, her teeth bared in the half-light. He gestured with the knife. "Say it."

"No."

Rubbery legged, Jeremy sat down. He was bone weary and emo-
tionally exhausted, but he couldn't rest until he was reasonably certain that she wouldn't cut his throat while he slept. "Listen, you
don't need to be alone here, you and that boy. If you'd like, you
and the boy could come with me to Idamore. What do you say,
Amanda?"

Amanda, she don't say nothin'.

"Repeat after me. 'The boy and I could go to Idamore.' Say that,
Amanda," said Jeremy, rearing up and gesturing again with the
knife.

"The boy and I could go with you to Idamore."

"Good. Or Idamore could come here." He paused hopefully,
then again commanded her to repeat his words.

"Or Idamore could come here."

"Would you like to meet the women of Idamore? Yes or no?" He saw from her clenched and trembling fists that he was pushing her too hard. In another moment, she would either break or attack him in spite of the knife, and Jeremy wasn't sure he was as skilled or as fast as she was. "Never mind, Amanda. You can think about that and tell me tomorrow before I leave."

He felt stymied. Exhausted, unsteady, he wanted only to lie down. "Do you know how to make tea? Maybe we could boil some water and put some of this ground ivy in it. Makes a nice tea, ground ivy. Little bitter, though. And maybe we could just sit with a nice cup of tea and, I don't know, just sit. . . . I'm sorry you don't like to talk, Amanda, 'cause I sure would like to know about that boy. . . . That boy is going to be something to see. Tall and straight as a tree. Couple of years, he'll be bigger than you. A big handsome strapping man . . ."

He watched her tall figure sink slowly to the ground, and he knew that he had won, though he didn't know yet over what.

∘ TWENTY-FIVE ∘

"Mandabar" was the name Jeremy imagined for her: Idamore's lazy softening and contracting of "Amanda Barston-Clark." Perhaps Amanda herself would soften in the society of Idamore's women, and complete her clipped-off sentences. She had a habit of ending her sentences with a little inflected "but," as if calling into question the little she had just said, or suggesting that there were volumes more she might say if she chose to.

If he had trouble picturing Amanda in Idamore, he had few doubts about her boy. Michael Clark (what would *his* name become?) would do just fine. As soon as the boy understood that Jeremy had no connection with the federal government from which his mother had been hiding him for twelve years, he was easy and open with Jeremy. It was not shyness but respect for his fierce, taciturn mother that made him whisper his many questions to Jeremy, who would answer in a booming voice—trying to prepare both Michael and his mother for the strange society they'd be joining.

Because Idamore would be strange indeed. Jeremy learned enough from Michael's questions and from Amanda's tortured conversation to decide that Darwin's finches had nothing on the people of these two towns. As an aboriginal citizen of the civilization now fragmented between them, he thought he could understand both of them, but he wasn't sure that they'd understand each other. The differences were stunning, yet each struck Jeremy as somehow characteristically "American": Idamore's pacifism and Freehold's combativeness; Idamore's candid sexuality and Freehold's sexual puritanism; Idamore's bond with the land to which they linked their communal identity, and Freehold's free-spirited roaming up and down the eastern shore of the lake; Idamore's obsession with a virtually mythic power, and Freehold's repudiation of it. The violence that was so taboo as to be unmentionable in Idamore was routinely taught in Freehold, where they practiced infanticide on children like retarded Jules, and they were murderously wary of strangers.

The transmission of two surnames was not a last vestige of feminism, but apparently a mechanism for controlling incest, though about this last topic Amanda was so rigid with embarrassment that Jeremy couldn't persist in his questions. He found out that Michael had only one last name because Amanda never learned the name of the man who had fathered him twelve years ago, when she was off foraging by herself. And he gleaned enough to suspect that he owed his life to Freehold's horror of incest: If Amanda hadn't imagined the consequences of life alone with her rapidly growing son, she would never have considered sailing with Jeremy to Idamore.

They were expert sailors, and worked effortlessly together. Sometimes Michael responded to commands from Amanda that

Jeremy could barely perceive, much less act on: a flick of her finger or a nod of her head had the boy leaping to adjust this or that line. Jeremy loved the choreographed sequence that followed Amanda's throaty calls, "Ready about" and "Lee-o." Jeremy spent a lot of time on the foredeck, watching Michael move among the web of wires, shrouds, and stays, quick and agile as a monkey, his hand always on one line before he let go with the other.

They set out from Freehold at a thrilling pace, the wind singing in the rigging and two wooly red telltales flying straight out from the wire shrouds. Amanda kept the sloop on a swift close-hauled reach, heading west southwest. Though Jeremy saw the telltales change direction, he rarely saw a luffing ripple in the sails, and he shook his head in admiration. At the tiller Amanda was constantly scanning—sky, sails, water, telltales. Her bright eyes and the swift bobbing motions of her small head reminded Jeremy of a bird—a beautiful, feminine, but predatory bird. Once, when the haphazard wind shifted, she let the sails out until Jeremy thought the boat had lifted itself off the water. "Wing it, Ma!" exclaimed Michael, and Jeremy laughed out loud.

They sighted the Wisconsin shore before sunset, and Michael threw himself down on the deck beside Jeremy. "Now we can let up a bit," he said. "Ma doesn't like to be out in the middle of the lake at night."

"Smart Ma," said Jeremy, smiling at the queenly figure in the stern. The full crescents of Amanda's mouth twitched. A nervous spasm, or the beginning of a smile? "Amanda," said Jeremy expansively, "Amanda, that was fantastic. What a sail! I'm not sure anybody in Idamore has even seen this lake, much less been on a sailboat. Maybe that's something you could give them. A trip on the water. A little travel . . ."

"They don't travel at all?" asked Michael.

"Well, with the sheep a little. But mostly they farm, which pretty much keeps you in one place."

"Do they have apples right there, then?"

"Apples?" said Jeremy, coming up off his elbows. "You have apples?"

"Well, we sail north and walk inland to pick apples in the autumn. Don't they *have* apples?"

Jeremy sadly shook his head, and wondered—not for the first time—if it might not be a good idea to move Idamore to Freehold. To his mental list of enticements—sailing, earth-insulated houses, working windmills, running water—he now added apples. He remembered Helena on that first day he'd met her, bloody gummed and hunkered with feigned indifference over the three oranges. He smiled and put apples at the top of the enticement list.

At some invisible signal from Amanda, Michael uncleated several lines and began to furl a sail. "Are we stopping?" Jeremy asked. "Couple of hours of daylight yet . . ."

"Can't land much south of here. It's all nuked out," Michael explained.

"Nuked! Nuked out!"

Michael shot an embarrassed glance at Amanda, then studied his feet. "I thought it was okay to talk about with everybody except the FEMA reps . . ." he murmured.

Jeremy hesitated, hoping that Amanda herself would tell the boy that he was free to speak. Amanda leaned slightly backward and pinched her mouth closed, as if she would dam up every word, all sound.

Jeremy spoke loudly enough for Amanda to hear. "Okay, kiddo, listen up. As far as I can tell, there will be no more FEMA reps. No more Federal Men. We're on our own here, and it's okay to talk about anything. Not just okay. Crucial. Important. You know how I'm always asking you what seem like silly questions?"

Michael ducked his head and giggled, acknowledging that some of Jeremy's questions—"How come your ma has two last names and you have only one?" "How'd you two get so handy with knives?" "Have you ever been far enough north to see the big trees?"—had been very silly indeed. "Okay," continued Jeremy. "But some of *your* questions sound silly to me. That's 'cause we've got things organized in really different ways. So sometimes we surprise each other. Sometimes you say things that shock me, or I say things that embarrass you. But that's all right, isn't it? Maybe what

I learn from you will change the way I think about things. And maybe"—Jeremy lightly tapped Michael's knee for emphasis— "maybe what you learn from me will change how you think. You know, like two people dropping pebbles into a pond, so all those circles meet and pass into each other . . ."

When Jeremy meshed his fingers to demonstrate, he felt a ripple of excitement, for he could imagine Michael standing between May and Laurel in Idamore's circle, chanting their reverence for the birds, the trees, the land. All their fingers meshed. A community. A biological confederacy. A band of cousins, lovers, friends . . .

Jeremy folded his hands and looked up at Amanda, who jumped and quickly looked away. But he had caught her. It *was* a smile.

"Never been south of here," Michael said the next day, pointing to a series of odd inlets where the lake had eroded the huge craters. "Southern lake's a sewer," he said with disgust. At Jeremy's prompting, Michael told him about his travels to the north. "Did you know there's another lake up there?" the boy said importantly. "Strip of land 'bout fifty miles, then another lake. Peerie's a clean, cold, cold lake. My grand—" Michael paused for an invisible communication with his mother, who must somehow have indicated her assent, for Michael went on: "My grandmother McGiverty-Winn lived up there, and we—"

"McGiverty?" exclaimed Jeremy.

"McGiverty-*Winn,*" said Michael. "And I stayed with her for a while. I was little, though, so I don't remember much about it, 'cept it was real cold. The water and the wind."

"Are there people scattered all over?" Jeremy asked, looking now at Amanda.

"Some, but."

"No, they wouldn't last long, would they?" Jeremy agreed. He looked down at Michael. Sturdy bright Michael Clark. Jeremy was so pleased with what he saw that he let go of the mast and lurched forward to hug him. Grinning, he looked over at Amanda, and caught the final stages of some incredibly complex emotional reaction. She was half off her seat, her expression going from alarm to dismay to perplexity so quickly that her arm—extended and held in midair—couldn't register the changes.

Jeremy ruffled Michael's hair, then made his way toward Amanda, holding on to the guardrails to keep himself steady on the plunging boat. He climbed down into the cockpit, sat cross-legged before her, and extended his right hand, palm up. "See this hand? This hand has done a lot of things—" Jeremy flushed, thinking of what Amanda had seen this same hand doing in the parking lot. Then, blushing and smiling, he fixed his eyes on her huge-featured face, which, like a mirror of Jeremy's, was slowly suffusing with color. "A *lot* of things." He grinned. "But it has never hurt anyone. Never drawn blood. Never even hit anyone, really, except my little brother once, when he broke my model plane. Hey, Amanda . . . I offer you this hand. In friendship. In trust."

She looked from his face to his hand and back. "You want me to . . . touch . . . your hand?" she asked.

"Well, yeah," Jeremy laughed, "but it's no big deal." He dropped his hand and stood up, turning toward the shoreline. With his knee on the seat and his hands on the guardrail, he leaned forward, studying the low long rolling hills of southern Wisconsin. The land was flattening out, stretching to meet the prairie. "Idamore's going to be very different. I hope . . . I don't know. God, Amanda, I hope this'll work out all right. . . ."

Amanda gave a little sniff, turned her face toward Michigan, and reached over to put her hand on Jeremy's. Her hand was so taut that her fingers were stiff and lifted, and only her palm touched his knuckles. He chuckled and turned his hand over, catching her fingers, then diplomatically released her with a light squeeze.

"It's *flat*," Michael called from the foredeck.

"You haven't seen flat till you've seen Idamore," Jeremy called back. "The only hills in Idamore are manmade."

"Manmade *hills?*"

"Little bumps and hillocks, like." He sat down, sprawling his legs out and hooking his elbows behind him. "'Bout a half day's walk inland to Idamore. If we get an early start tomorrow, we could be there by sunset tomorrow."

Amanda scanned the sky, squinting into the late-afternoon sun at the fat cumulus clouds on the horizon. "Yup."

"'Yup,'" Jeremy echoed.

Amanda averted her head and gave an audible giggle.

They started at sunrise, beating into a light wind. Sitting on the floor of the cockpit in order to be out of the wind, Jeremy pored over a navigational chart, trying to match the actual coast with the map. "What's that?" he'd mutter at some squiggle on the chart. Peering through the scratched binoculars at heaped rocks or dismembered harbors, he'd look down at the chart and mutter, "Where's *that*?" He was beginning to wonder how he'd find his bearings once he was on land, and imagined marching Amanda and Michael aimlessly up and down the coast while he figured out where they were.

Amanda gave Jeremy a light kick on the ankle. "What?" he said. She pointed with her chin at the shore. "You know who you're gonna get along with great, Amanda?" he complained. "Mick! You and Mick are gonna have some great conversa—"

She interrupted him with another little kick and handed him the binoculars. "Look ashore. Those strangers your people?"

His first thought was that Helena and Laurel had come to meet him, and that he would scold them soundly—how easily they might have missed each other! He trained the binoculars on the tiny figures on the beach. It was like seeing them for the first time all over again. They were all there, and they looked like refugees.

° TWENTY-SIX °

Helena woke with a start from a dark dream to a streaked and dazzling world of sunlight. It was an infernal dream—shadowy figures darting about in the lurid flames of a night fire—in which each of the miners somehow became Jeremy.

She jerked awake, looking around. They had walked all night to get to this place, where they sank down beside the sound of the lake, too weary to wait for the light of dawn to see what it looked like. It looked like nothing she had ever seen. The dirt was white and fine as dust, and the sun-dazzled lake stretched farther than she could see. "I had no idea . . ." she murmured.

Rachel was asleep beside her, and farther down the beach the four children sat shoulder to shoulder, their heads turning and bobbing as they followed the activities of the white birds overhead. Pearl was sloshing awkwardly about in the water, chasing the ducks, which skittered away to swim in lazy circles just outside her grasp.

Mick switched himself through the sand until he was beside Helena, and began to pat her arm with a long growling coo. "Yes, old dear," she murmured, saying for him what he meant to say. "Yes, we'll be all right." She leaned lightly against his shoulder, squinting out at the immense glimmering body of water, where the broad-winged white birds swooped and rose again with tiny wriggling things in their beaks. Fish, she thought wearily; we must fish. But had they brought anything to fish with? She sighed, resting her head on Mick's shoulder. "It doesn't seem quite fair that we have to haul so much stuff around, does it? Other animals are born with everything they need."

Effortlessly, the birds rode the wind. And there, way out on the water, was an odd bird—a huge white-winged puff of a bird. Helena frowned, staring at it. What *was* that? That wasn't a bird. As the thing came closer, skimming over the slate-gray glittering surface of the water, she was seized with superstitious awe. There was an ancient story of the man-god who could walk on water. What was coming toward them was not walking, but flying, propelled by the sun itself. An angel, a winged god of judgment . . . She spread her hands over her flat belly. "Not the baby," she murmured, crawling in the sand until she was behind Mick. "Oh, please, not Jeremy's baby." In her mind she had already named him, and she would have groveled before any god or demon to spare her until she bore him. Martin Towers. A male child with a winged name for soaring, and a tall name for striding.

Mick got up, pulling at her hand, gesturing for her to look again. Still crouching beside Mick's legs, Helena watched as the white wing swung around. She heard the distant slide and thwack of a metal ring over a metal bar. Why, that's just a boat! she thought. She scrambled to her feet, her heart clamoring. That was not a god, an angel, a man with wings. That was Jeremy Echo, coming to take them to Freehold.

"Could that be . . . ?" asked Pearl, shading her eyes.

"Oh, yes, yes," breathed Helena, and began madly waving her hat.

"Oh, look, he's brought two more—another man!"

Laurel and May were racing up and down the beach, waving and shouting.

The commotion woke Rachel, who came to the water's edge rubbing her eyes. "Well . . . imagine!" She looked around with dazed uncertainty. Bending to wash, she shuddered as she scrubbed sand over her soot-blackened knuckles. She paused, staring at her hands, then abruptly straightened. "Helena," she whispered urgently. "Helena, what are we going to tell them?"

Helena's face bleached white under the grime.

"Pearl . . . Laurel, May . . ." Rachel summoned the others into a huddle. "Jeremy's bringing two strangers from Freehold. If they hear what's happened, they might not want us in Freehold. And if they don't want us there, where can we go?" Rachel bit her bottom lip, and looked for a moment desperate enough to cry.

Like a child playing a party game, Mick kept walking the outside of their circle, stopping behind now one, now another, shaking his head, cooing sadly. He'd been saying "No" since their decision to leave Idamore. No, no, no, he said to everything, fiercely at first, then with sad resignation. No, he wagged now, stroking Helena's arm, patting Rachel's shoulder. No, no, no.

Helena turned to pull him into the circle. "Just be quiet a minute, Mick, while we think," she said absentmindedly. She watched, pulling at her lower lip, as the sailboat was anchored and a dinghy let down. Jeremy climbed down and extended his arm to . . . a boy! That was a boy! He handed a box down to Jeremy, then climbed into the dinghy. And that other person, tall as Jeremy: a woman. A woman and a boy. Coming toward them. The people of Freehold becoming distinct. Becoming real. "I wonder what *they've* been through," Helena murmured. "We must think first of them. . . ."

She watched the broad familiar back rowing the dinghy closer and closer. When he reached his arms forward, his shirt was pulled taut against his shoulders. Then, on the backward stroke, it puckered into a long fold along his spine. Studying the shirt, Helena could feel Jeremy's back under her fingers, and she clenched her wayward hands.

Jeremy felt buffeted by all their contending needs. His moment of alienation—his disbelief that he had eaten and slept and laughed with that band of dirty scarecrows he saw on the beach—passed as soon as he was among them. He wanted to take Helena in his arms and press her tightly the length of his body, while he talked through her hair to the others, finding out what in the world had happened. For he could see catastrophe written on their dirty faces. Rachel's mouth was taut and almost blue, and Helena's face was bleached with strain. But they were there, alive and well, and the children were clutching at his legs and arms and demanding immediate attention, while Amanda and Michael stood stiff with shyness before this boiling shrill crowd of strangers.

Jeremy had to pick up August, who had taken hold of his leg, yelling, "Germ, Germ!" August had been sucking his thumb, and there was a ring of sand around his mouth. Jeremy wiped his thumb along the moist, gritty mouth, and kissed him on the nose. Balancing the wriggling mass of excitement on his left hip, Jeremy clapped Mick on the shoulder, patted Pearl, peered fondly at Phoebe, hugged Laurel, then May, all the while inching his way toward Helena.

"Hello, my love." He put his palm on her cheek, then slid his hand onto the back of her neck. Agitation flowed from her like waves of heat. "Bad?"

"Oh, Jeremy, terrible."

"Can you come meet Amanda first?" He gazed into her dark troubled eyes.

"Of course."

Then, as if he were turning a bag inside out, Jeremy walked with Helena and August through the crowd, drawing them back toward Amanda and Michael. Amanda held the box like a shield before her chest, and Michael took a small diagonal step backward—into the water and slightly behind his mother. "Amanda. I'm Helena." Helena held her hands out.

Amanda, in the first of a series of misunderstandings, put the box into Helena's extended hands. Helena looked down at the box thrust at her, then up at the tall, wary woman who had stepped backward so her heels were washed with water. "Why, thank you . . ." she said, tucking the box under her arm and stepping closer.

Jeremy might have intervened by taking Amanda's wrist and holding her hand out for Helena to grasp. Or he might have murmured to Helena that Amanda didn't know the conventions of social touching. But in the moment that he hesitated, setting August on the ground, Idamore's irrepressible collective good humor broke through the awkward moment. Laurel and May, giggling behind their hands, burst from behind the grown-ups and converged upon Michael; Pearl came forward and put the bundled, gurgling Phoebe into Amanda's empty arms; and Rachel and Helena each put a light hand under Amanda's elbows and propelled her up the beach. Like two tugs escorting an ocean liner, Jeremy thought, for their dark heads barely reached Amanda's shoulders.

"That's our youngest you've got," said Pearl, introducing her infant Phoebe. "And over there is Jules. And that's August. . . ." Above the buzz of their voices came the shrill whoops of the older children as Michael, suddenly understanding the spirit of the girls' stalking game, tried to lure them into the lake by wheeling and feinting.

Relieved and for the moment happily useless, Jeremy stood with his hands in his back pockets, smiling first at Michael, who was too busy to notice him, and then at the dazed Amanda, who caught his glance over the others' heads. Seeing the twitch of her lips, Jeremy grinned more and more broadly, coaxing her smile. Behind him he heard a splash and a comic shriek—Michael had gotten Laurel into the lake—and was just about to turn when he saw it: Amanda's wide mouth going wider, the face rounding and lifting, the charmingly gapped teeth flashing in the light. He gave her the thumbs-up sign that she used with Michael when he correctly adjusted the foresail. Smooth sailing ahead.

At the next series of cries and exclamations, Jeremy knew that they had opened the box: dried apples. The last of last autumn's rubbery, moist, sweet dried apples. The three older children sat apart, coated with sand and chewing happily on the fruit. As they talked, they pointed, Laurel and May at the various people they were identifying, and Michael at the boat and the lake. A few minutes later Michael stood up. "Hey, Ma, I'm taking the girls out to see the sloop. They ain't had breakfast, so I'll bring back the nets. . . ." He swaggered off before Amanda could open her mouth.

"Hey, hey, *hey*," Jeremy yelled.

Michael stopped and turned.

"Show the girls how to put on the life jackets in the dinghy," Jeremy called.

"Yes, sir."

"And Michael," Amanda called, "leave the sloop *anchored*."

"I will, Ma."

"Showin' off," Amanda said, ducking her head.

There was a hitch in the general hubbub as the others realized that they had just heard Amanda speak for the first time. Once again it was her son who occasioned her reluctant lapse into words. Pearl, as if sensing not only Amanda's difference but the one crucial thing they had in common, chirped, "What a fine boy! What a healthy-looking, handsome boy!"

"Oh, and how are the Hermans?" Jeremy asked in a jocular tone, though his face was creased with sudden concern as he spread one hand on Helena's belly, another on Rachel's.

"We're all fine," Rachel assured him, patting his familiar hand.

Noticing Amanda's flabbergasted blush, Jeremy made a mental note to have one of the women talk privately with her about comparative sexual mores and baby-making procedures. Triumphant over eliciting Amanda's smallest gestures and spontaneous glances, Jeremy hadn't dared risk offending her by asking such personal questions, and often wondered if he might also be offending her by neither asking nor acting. He was completely in the dark about what—if anything—she expected of him.

He was about to settle everyone in a circle and find out what crisis had driven them here, but he was forestalled by Amanda, who lifted the hem of her pants and removed a knife tucked into her sock. Misunderstanding the startled rustle around her, she grunted. "For hunting some ducks . . . for your breakfast, heh? Wasn't gonna hurt you. . . ."

"Hurt us!" exclaimed Rachel.

"Good grief!" said Pearl. "Of course not. It's just that we don't—"

"We don't carry knives—"

"We trap our animals, and keep them in houses. Sheep, chickens, rabbits . . ."

"Hunt! I've never been hunting. Let's—"

But they all fell silent at the water's edge when Amanda gave a sharp casual flick and the knife's sharp blade was embedded in a drab duck. The bird flipped over, one wing flapping frantically against the blood-tinged water, then fell quiet, jerking. Amanda slogged through the water, removed the knife, and lobbed the bird onto the beach. Then she turned to nail another of the squawking, agitated flock.

"Mick, let's collect firewood, and Pearl . . ." Jeremy looked at their rapt horrified faces. He had never seen them squeamish before. He was the squeamish one, watching Rachel matter-of-factly wring a chicken's neck, or Pearl up to her elbow in sheep's gore, or Helena disemboweling a rabbit. "What's the matter? What is it?" he asked, wishing that in the rush of events he had made time to ask sooner what they were all doing here, half a day's walk from Idamore. All of them but Rose and Edgar.

"Amanda," he called over his shoulder, "I need to talk to my friends for a minute. . . ." He put his hand on the small of Rachel's back and his arm around Helena's waist and pushed them up the beach, where he motioned them into a circle. He set Jules in Mick's lap and August in Rachel's; then he sat behind Helena, straddling her with his legs and drawing her close. "Okay, now. Okay. Let's hear." Helena was taut as a trip wire against him, and he smoothed her hair and rocked her slightly, trying to alchemize her distress with his calm. He propped his chin on her head and looked at Pearl. "What happened? Where is Edgar?"

"The sheep are slow," said Pearl.

"And Rose?"

"Oh, Rose is . . . she . . . we . . ."

"Start at the beginning, and tell me what happened."

Pearl's account—of the fires they had watched, of the fires approaching Idamore, and of the earth burners who arrived—was supplemented by frequent interjections from Rachel and dissenting grunts from Mick.

Helena said nothing, sitting unnaturally erect inside Jeremy's legs and quivering at the mention of Simon's name. Jeremy stroked her arms, listened, nodded, and glanced down the beach, taking in the various stages of Amanda's stalking, the progress of Michael toward the sloop. Just as he saw a bright-orange life jacket clamber onto the sloop, they all fell silent, leaving him suspended.

"Yes? And then what? They killed Rose? Is she dead?"

"No, Jermicho. She's in Idamore. She . . . we . . . Idamore's polluted."

"Poll— What?" Everyone found something to study in the sand except Mick, who looked at Jeremy with a sad tremor. At least Mick knows what I have to do, Jeremy thought, though Mick was helpless to share the burden of making the others understand. Jeremy had to go back and hunt Simon down. No place was safe while he was alive and burning down the world. Simon, at whose name Helena trembled. Simon, whom Helena loved. God, no wonder they looked so driven. So haunted and worn down. How could he tell them that Simon had to be executed? Or that that enormous woman hunting ducks was a suitable companion in a manhunt?

Rachel buried her face in August's shoulder and said, "Jeremy, *we* polluted Idamore. We are defiled."

Jeremy craned his neck, leaning over Helena. "What? I don't understand."

"Ach, you stupid man," exclaimed Helena. She scraped his hands off her arms and flung herself away from him. "We killed them. We killed them! Rachel did, and Pearl did. And I did. Rose started it, but we *all* did it. We are defiled and the land is polluted. . . ."

As she ranted at him, Jeremy tried to interrupt to ask if Idamore had been left standing. But she kept talking, jabbing and pushing at his chest until he grabbed her wrist. "Is Idamore still there?" he asked Mick over Helena's angry head, and Mick, his eyes glittering with unshed tears, nodded: Yes.

"Will they speak to murderers? Will they live with polluters? . . ." Helena was spitting at him, jerking and yanking her wrist in his tight grasp. "Will they touch bloody hands? You saw the way she acted. She knew. She could tell. We have blood on our hands, and she didn't want to touch us. . . ."

"Shut up!" Jeremy yelled. "Will you shut up and listen for a minute?"

Rachel dropped her chin and sobbed, but Helena, on her knees in the sand, glared defiantly at him. "Ask her yourself," said

Jeremy. "Go ask her how many men she's killed with that knife. Ask her whether she'd have cut my throat as casually as you spit. . . . Go on. Go ask her."

Here Pearl too broke down and cried, and Jules climbed out of Mick's lap and sat by her side, using his fist to pat her. "Buh-buh-buh," he slobbered.

"Oh, yes, bad, bad, bad," echoed Helena, hanging her head. "Bad, bad, bad . . ."

Jeremy crawled closer to her. "C'mere. Oh, my babe, c'mere. You're not . . . defiled. You're not polluted. What you did wasn't even murder. Oh, please," he begged, looking at Rachel, then Pearl. "That wasn't murder. That was self-defense. And that man, that wasn't even Simon, but someone changed by the times, the work, the land. Why, the whole land is polluted. . . ." He paused, struck by the ghastly truth of that: for it *was* violence that had polluted the entire land. A push-button mass murder. Radiation and rubble. "People have always defended their homes, and some people took by violence what belonged to others. And the violence has gone on. Practically everywhere except Idamore. . . ."

Even when Helena put her hands over her ears, Jeremy kept talking, first about old Allison's devious method for creating their horror of bloodshed, then about justifiable violence and self-defense. "Oh, give it a rest, will you, Jeremy?" Helena finally sneered. She got up and walked away, staggering a little in the sand.

Helena was too tired to listen and too tired not to hear. They all knew the law, and they had taken the law at its word: "Ye shall not pollute the land wherein ye are: for blood it defileth the land," the law said. "And the land cannot be cleansed of the blood that is shed therein, but by the blood of him that shed it." But they had all shed it; should they all die? They could not, absolutely not, all die. Not carrying babies.

Without conferring, they had performed a new ritual. Rachel had started it by walking like a dreaming woman across the yard with her bloodied hatchet. Across the yard toward Rose. When she had placed the hatchet at Rose's feet, somehow Helena, too, yes, and Pearl and Mick and Edgar, had all shuffled from their places to put their bloody weapons at Rose's feet. And then they had walked out of the polluted land. Going nowhere but away from Idamore.

But apparently they couldn't leave the crime with Rose in Idamore. Apparently they were going to carry it around with them. And apparently the law against violence was not written straight, but like a story told at a slant. Like "Escape to Wisconsin," or the elephant's nose, or Laurel's tale of the fig wasps. It was written to protect them from themselves. From discovering in themselves that terrible dark place, where any crime could be committed and, once begun, could not be controlled.

And that tall Amanda, who was all mouth and eyes and shyness, had she done what Helena had done, felt what Helena had felt? That seemed impossible. Never in the slaughter of food had Helena felt what she had felt yesterday—as if she had crossed some boundary into a place she didn't even know existed. A place so vast and smokily blood-red that she thought she would never gain control of herself again, never again step into sanity and sunlight. It was like some ghastly version of childbirth. Her body took possession of her, contracting her, pleating her steadily down into the dark place—not, this time, of pain, but of some terrible instinct for which she had no name, and which impelled her to plunge the knife into human flesh. Plunged once, and the boundary was crossed. She could not stop. She became like the blade itself, sharp and shrieking and insatiable of blood.

She walked away from Jeremy's earnest voice and knelt among the dead birds Amanda had thrown onto the beach. Time to collect firewood. Time to clean the birds. Time to eat, pumping goodness and health to her baby. "You won't remember," she said to Martin Towers. "I'm sure you won't remember."

"Amanda, have you ever killed people?" she called to the tall woman standing like a crane in the water and waiting for the agitated flock to calm again into targets.

Amanda turned her big eyes toward Helena. "Never *people*. Killed strangers. . . ."

"Umm." Helena nodded, though the answer made little sense. She took up a limp teal whose feathers glistened jade green in the light.

Jeremy came and hunkered in the sand beside her. "You don't believe me now, but you'll learn to believe me."

Helena looked down at the limp beautiful bird in her hands. "Idamore is not polluted. Jeremy Echo says. I am not polluted. Jeremy Echo says. But I don't think he really understands, do you, bird? Not with his hands. Because *he* has never killed anything. Not a sheep or a chicken or a rabbit—"

"Come on, Laney. I've never *had* to kill anything. What do you want me to do, sacrifice a sheep and smear blood on an altar?"

How could she make him understand the excess, the crazed savagery? "But I, I, *I*. Put a knife into his stomach. Yes. And I pushed it in up to the handle, and I looked into his eyes while I yanked it up and down, up and down. . . ." Gagging, she put her hand over her mouth, then continued, panting, hectic with defiance of Jeremy's calm acceptance. "I *liked* it. I wanted to do it again and again. I was like Rose. Oh, Jeremy, I was like Rose."

"Do you think it would have been better if you had killed him without feeling anything?" he asked.

"Oh, how . . . ?" Her face collapsed. "How could I kill Simon without feeling anything?"

"Simon? You . . . Oh, Laney, oh no, oh darling . . ." He went on his knees to her, murmuring.

Helena ran her fingers over his neck, then opened his shirt and traced the triangle of deeply tanned skin at his throat. She ran her palm over the slope of his smooth chest and down his belly. In her dream the man under her knife was Jeremy. And the men who fell to Pearl's raised ax and Rachel's hatchet and Mick's pitchfork: all Jeremy. Sundered. The arteries pulsing. Murdered. Though she had put her weapon at Rose's feet, Helena carried the crime inside her head, and it was Jeremy she murdered.

She dipped her fingers into the duck's wound, and as she smeared blood on his chest, she said, "I dream that it's you. I dream that I'm killing you. That it's your blood and your stomach." He didn't flinch, but knelt before her letting her smear him with blood.

"I love you, too," he said. "I love you very much. . . ." He pressed her head against his anointed chest, and then, as if he'd assimilated the pain there, he began to cry, hanging his chin over her shoulder. She felt the sturdy heart of him thumping beneath her cheek and she heard his broken voice: "We must teach Amanda that there are no strangers."

◦ TWENTY-SEVEN ◦

After the ducks were cleaned and the firewood collected; after a pit was dug for the fire, and the fire was crackling from the dripping fat of the roasting ducks; then Jeremy organized a community wash. "Look at you," he said, "just look at all of you. Everybody into the water. . . ."

Rachel bent to splash her hand in the lake. "Awful cold, Jermicho," she said.

He stripped and waded in. "Come on, it's no colder than the river." Jeremy walked through the root-clotted margin toward the open water and slogged around until he found a sandbar. "Here you go," he called.

Helena stepped daintily out of her clothes, and then Pearl, who cupped her big blue-veined breasts under her hands as she toed the water. She waded forward, holding her elbows up, then plunged with a squawk. "Is it too cold?" Rachel called to her, already unbuttoning her pants. May took Mick's hand and escorted him in. They all fanned out, then converged upon the sandbar, clucking and laughing.

Laurel stood naked and gangly, gesturing at Michael Clark to come into the water with her. Michael hit on some sort of private compromise by remaining in the reeds, neither with Idamore nor with his mother.

"Come on, Amanda," Jeremy called. He watched her turn away from them, a tall, lonely Amazon on a strange shore. "By the waters of Babylon we sat down and wept," Jeremy thought. Though the psalm came to him in the usual muddle of half-recollected phrases, it nevertheless sharpened his sympathy into a stab of pity. "How shall we sing the Lord's song in a strange land?"

"Oh, Jermicho," whispered Helena, "she's so strange. I don't think she's ever seen people naked before. But that's not possible, is it?"

"I got the impression from things that she and her boy said that they lived in a very . . . well, private way." He was washing Rachel's back. He lifted the hair off her shoulders to scrub at her neck, and added, "We have to be careful not to swarm all over her, or push too hard. She'll get used to us just by watching. . . ."

"Well, maybe," said Pearl with a dubious glance toward Amanda, who was sitting on the beach with her arms locked around her legs and her head pressed against her knees.

"Wash my back, Rach, and I'll go talk to her," said Helena, and put herself between Rachel and Jeremy, who was now scrubbing the crusted blood off his chest.

Sitting down beside Amanda, Helena unconsciously adopted an identical position, hugging her legs and digging in the sand with her toes. "It's funny, somehow the people who come to us don't talk," Helena mused out loud. "See Mick over there? He *can't* talk, and sometimes he disagrees with us so hard, but he can't say what. Maybe after you feel more comfortable with us, you'll be able to tell us about things. About . . . you know, strangers. And, oh! about apple trees. And sailing . . . Stuff you've seen, and the stuff that's inside your head. . . ."

As Helena prattled, she gestured and constantly touched Amanda—on the knee, the arm, the back of the hand. She felt the tiny vexed flinches, and took an almost perverse pleasure in trying the woman's limits. "I used to wonder about you once in a while.

Not you, you know, but the people in Freehold. What you'd be like. After Jeremy came to us, I started to wonder all sorts of funny things about people I'd never seen. . . . Did you ever wonder about *us?*" Helena asked seductively.

"Nuh." Amanda turned her head, resting her cheek against her arm for a brief look at Helena before she hid her face again.

Helena felt none of Jeremy's pity for Amanda. Sympathetic curiosity, perhaps, and a vaguely erotic attraction. Was it her size? Her high round haunches? Or was it that Amanda could step back and forth across the boundary between sanity and raging violence without a sign of it on that closed, commanding face?

Jeremy was coming toward the shore, and as Helena watched the slow revelation of Jeremy's body from the dark water—the hard planes and the long lean lines of him—she said, "Oh, look at that. Oh my. Do you have—did you have—men in Freehold? Men like Jermicho, I mean?"

"My son Michael Clark's gonna be a *man.*"

"Yes, I can see that. Just think, Amanda, what beautiful children we're going to have—Jeremy's children, and then Michael's children. Do you keep a calendar? Because you and Jeremy really should make a baby together. You'd have giants, I think. . . . What is it?" Helena watched with dismay as Amanda put her arms over her head. "Oh, boy, what did I say?"

Amanda was rocking back and forth, her arms clasped over her head as if she were protecting it from blows. "Oh, Amanda, can't you have any more babies? Is that it? Or what is it? Oh dear." She tried to comfort the big woman by stroking her back.

Helena looked up at Jeremy, who came and squatted before them, his knees popping. "I did it all wrong," she said. "All wrong."

"Hey, Amanda, everything's gonna be fine," Jeremy said, reaching to touch her, then putting his hand back on his knee. "Laney, I don't think Amanda's used to having people touch her, and you're kind of all over her."

"Oh!" said Helena, suddenly contracting and looking hurt. "But we can't make things right if she won't tell us what's wrong."

"I'll leave Michael Clark here with you and go on back to Free-hold," said Amanda without raising her face from her legs.

"Oh, you can't do that, how could you do that?" Helena ex-claimed, while at the same moment Jeremy remarked more gently, "We'd like you to stay with us, Amanda."

"Can't stay in a place where folks carry on all their private stuff in the open daylight."

"Could you tell us just what's bothering you?" Jeremy asked.

No, she said with her head—just like Mick, Jeremy thought, only Lord, how lovely she was, with that high polished forehead and those funny little braids bouncing all over her head. He clawed thoughtfully in his beard, then exchanged a troubled glance with Helena. "Maybe you could tell Helena?" he suggested.

No, she wagged again.

"Go put some clothes on, Jermicho," Helena said, waving him away. When he was out of earshot, she leaned toward Amanda's shoulder, close but not touching. "He's right, you know. You'll have to tell somebody. But I think I have an idea. Private stuff . . . is that like touching? Is that like what we do with Hank to make babies?"

When Amanda's braids jigged on the back of her neck, Helena said, "Well, we know about privacy. Jeremy taught us about pri-vacy. He also taught . . . hmmm." She could feel herself blunder-ing, and didn't know how to continue without some clue from Amanda. She longed to put her hand on the long vulnerable neck exposed by the bent back, to unbraid the tight knots of her hair, to loosen her, fluff her out like a pillow. "Private stuff," she muttered. "Private . . . Tell you what. I'm starving. I'm going to get some of that duck, then I wonder if you could take me out to the boat. I haven't seen it yet, and do you think we could talk out there? Just you and me?"

"Touchin' and talkin', talkin' and touchin'," said Amanda, shak-ing her head. "Go ahead, and I'll get the dinghy, but."

Mick and the children were exploring nearby houses for suitable overnight lodging, and Rachel was curled up in a scooped-out nest of sand, sleeping like a turtle in the fretted shade of the tall grass. Leaning on his elbows, Jeremy stared at the lightly bobbing sailboat, thinking about Amanda and Helena, about Freehold and Idamore.

He understood that he wouldn't cure Helena's sense of violation merely by telling her that other people did casually what she considered unthinkable. After all, he too had compunctions that imposed restraints on his behavior. He knew he couldn't be stripped of them at a suggestion or a command. Nor did he want to suggest to Helena that violence was acceptable. He just wanted to refashion an unexamined taboo into a moral injunction that she might think about, justify, discuss, and, if necessary, occasionally break.

And what of Amanda's—taboos? or moral injunctions?—getting a severe jostling in the updraft of Idamore's crisis. Her son Michael wasn't as taciturn, so perhaps Amanda's stubborn silence was not culturally imposed, but the result of confusion and shyness and shock. Maybe she was even now talking to Helena, in the dim recess of the cabin, with its blue canvas curtains over the portholes. Telling her about "private stuff."

Jeremy wished for the hundredth time that his first meeting with Amanda Barston-Clark hadn't been so grotesquely awkward. If ever there was private stuff, she had seen it then. But, of course, he could be projecting his own embarrassment. Idamore had no qualms about masturbation—it was only forbidden to him because of "spilled seed"—so he shouldn't assume that by "private stuff," Amanda meant specifically sexual matters. She might be upset by something quite different—by people going naked or openly crying or who knew what.

Helena and Amanda were still out on the boat when Laurel came to say that they had found a nice house and cleaned the bones out of it, so Rachel might sleep inside now, on a bed.

Jeremy carried Rachel into the house and examined the bed before he set her down. "You're feeling okay, Rach?"

"Oh, Jermicho, I feel wonderful! The sleepiness will go away by autumn. . . . The nights are getting colder—have you noticed?" she remarked drowsily.

And they were still out on the boat when Edgar arrived with the sheep. During the exchange of news, Jeremy helped him drive the herd into an enclosed backyard not far from the chosen house, then took him onto the beach for some of the crisp roasted duck. Edgar surveyed the beach with a shepherd's eye, looking south along the shore and shaking his head. "Hard trip for the sheep."

"Impossible trip," said Jeremy, helping himself to another piece of duck for dessert, and offering Edgar the last of the dried apples. "We saved these for you. Fantastic."

Jeremy settled down for a talk with Edgar and Pearl. Both sets of children would occasionally join them, then wander off again, with Pearl yelling to the older ones to watch after the younger ones. "Impossible trip," Jeremy repeated, then described the southern shore of the lake. He concluded that they had three choices: to abandon the sheep, to return to Idamore, or to ferry the sheep across to Freehold in several trips. "What do you think?" he asked, and then, of course, he had to tell them more about Freehold.

"Well, it's not for us to decide," said Pearl.

"We'll have to talk to the others," agreed Edgar. "How many sheep you figure we could get on the boat?" he added.

Pearl was gazing dreamily east. "I've always wanted to see the big trees."

Jeremy adjusted her chin to the northeast. "That way, old girl. It's a long way. . . ." He was thoughtful, knowing the consensus that the group was going to drift toward, and wondering about Rose. "I think I'll walk back to Idamore tomorrow, and fetch Rose."

Edgar grunted, and Pearl slowly raised her head.

"Well, we can't just leave her there, can we?" Jeremy asked sharply. "Is that what you were planning to do?"

Pearl nodded. In that strangled oracular voice that Jeremy found so weirdly compelling, Edgar told Jeremy of the spontaneous ritual they had performed. "We put all our weapons at her feet, Jeremy. So we wouldn't have to die, we gave our crimes to Rose."

"But it didn't work, did it? Did you leave your crime with Rose?"

Pearl shook her head.

"And you, Edgar?"

"Yes," he said stubbornly.

"Well, I'm going back for her. Poor scapegoat . . ."

Pearl shivered and edged closer to the heaped warm ashes of the fire. She stared out across the water, then focused on the boat, which had swung around on its anchor in the changed wind. "That's a long *talk*," she remarked with a suggestive smile.

Jeremy scrambled to his feet, suddenly fearful. "Jesus," he whispered. The shapeless anxiety exploded into a vivid crowd of possibilities, and he galloped down the beach, ripping off his clothes as he went.

As he swam toward the boat, he pictured Helena manacled as he had been manacled at Freehold, and then he imagined her impaled with a knife like the duck in the water. In quick succession, he saw all the different ways that Amanda had killed her, and he couldn't raise his arms through the unyielding water fast enough to save her. . . .

As the two women sat together on the narrow bunk, the boat quietly rocking them, lulling them, Helena's mind was already ashore, arranging the necessary and peculiar details of the coming night. Necessary because Amanda was now fertile, and peculiar because—if Amanda was to do what Helena deemed necessary— she required total darkness and anonymity. A quick reproductive rut with a faceless stranger in the dark. Most peculiar, Helena thought, was that Amanda really imagined that Jeremy wouldn't know which woman he was with. As if Amanda was built anything like her or Rachel! Well, the whole thing was beyond belief. Absolutely beyond belief, and utterly sad.

She wasn't even sure she had gotten everything straight, what with Amanda's sentences being all chopped off and crippled by embarrassment. Amanda had turned her back to Helena, and even then covered her face in order to say her shameful things. About a feem-a-rap in the dark, how it must always be dark so that no one would know who it was. Then about her son. About breast-feeding her son. The only living thing she'd ever held against her body, she said, and how—here whole clumps of syntax disappeared—"a feeling, but. Deep. A pull. Let it out ma fingers onto his back, his belly. Wrong?"

Was that a question to her? Helena had wondered, and she murmured ambiguously, then once again asked Amanda if she kept a calendar. She didn't keep a calendar. She kept time by the seasons, the stars, the moon, and her menses.

"Your what?"

"Private blood."

"Ah yes. There we go."

But they were going nowhere. Amanda's voice sank down again, and grammar disappeared. "Then *he*. Doing a thing. Seen him?"

"Who? Michael?"

Amanda put her hands over her eyes. "Jeremy Towers. Pulling himself. Ever seen?"

Helena took Amanda's wrists and gently shook them. "This is absolutely ridiculous. Do you know I have no idea what you're talking about? Will you please use more words?"

Amanda did the best she could, which was more pantomime than words. Helena clapped her hand over her mouth, as amused as she was shocked. "He didn't! In front of you?! Oh, how bad he is sometimes, how thoughtless. . . ." It was the same sort of incident that had led to their making love for the first time, and she remembered her spitting helpless rage at him for wasting his seed, for so long denying them the future. "And that made you feel—how?"

"Nothing. Nothing then. But later . . ." Amanda tapped her temple. "Going   over   it.   All   the   time.   And   that same . . . tug . . . like nursing, heh? Only I . . . only I . . ." It was as if once she started to cry, the words were also unlocked, becoming a wild rush of toppling phrases. Helena listened openmouthed: to a woman who had never seen a man naked, who had never made love to anyone, and who was writhing with a need she couldn't identify.

She said she didn't know where to fix her eyes anymore, for

when she looked at Jeremy—or worse—just think of it!—even
when she looked at her son—she imagined them doing that thing,
and look how small the cabin was, look, too small for that live stick
always there under his pants, wanting to be touched by her hands,
so she kept her hands like claws, and she didn't know where to
look, so she kept her eyes jumping, and oh! she wanted to be a
man, she said; she wanted to do that thing, she had even wet herself one night, trying to do that thing. . . .

"You don't need to be. . . . Haven't you ever . . . ?" Helena
tilted her head. Surely she had misunderstood. It was impossible
that Amanda not only had never been touched, but had never even
touched herself. Helena thought of all the ways she had discovered
the pleasures of her body: facing upstream in the river and spreading her legs to the rush of water; riding horseback on Edgar in a
playful mood; sitting behind Lily in the warm tub and pressing
herself up against the hollow base between Lily's spreading buttocks. How could you bathe or pee or play without finding out
what was between your legs? "Just . . . just . . ." Helena couldn't
think how to teach so elementary a lesson. "You just put your
hands on the hunger. You don't have to be a man."

She had crossed the narrow space between the two bunks to sit
beside Amanda. "But best of all is somebody else putting hands on
the hunger. Best of all," she said, putting her open palm on
Amanda's knee, "is somebody creating the hunger, and then satis-
fying it. Want to see how simple it is?"

The undisguised moral revulsion on Amanda's face made
Helena recoil. This was the horrified response Helena had expected
to pollution and murder, to violence, to unnatural acts. But to making love? "Is it because . . . because I've got blood on my hands?"

"Don't see blood."

"I killed a man. I *knew* him. With a knife."

"'Cause it's bad stuff, all this body wanting."

"You *do* think it's bad, then. Murder. Oh, evil . . ."

"Unnnh. We're sailing two boats here," Amanda said. "Myself,
see nothing wrong with keeping people out of your space. Letting
people in too close—so they're inside your head, inside your"—she

described a vague circle in the air, then shrugged—"your *space* . . . well, that's what mothers do, and you got body for bearing, mind for mothering, but only so much. No place for strangers in that. . . ."

Helena was shocked by Amanda's comparison of intimacy to childbearing, for she herself had felt that her descent into that bloodthirsty nightmare of violence was like the experience of childbirth. Helena did not yet understand that the sexual drives rattling Amanda were as strange and terrifying to Amanda as murderous rage was to Helena: a violation, an abduction, a physical possession of her body by her body.

"No, but, no, listen . . ." Once again Helena was recounting her crime, obsessively dwelling on the horrifying details. This time, for the first time, she cried. Amanda gave her no lectures on self-defense or necessary violence; she only listened. Helena talked and cried, and when she ran out of words, she pushed past Amanda's stiff arm to crawl into her lap.

With wooden fingers, Amanda patted the quaking shoulders, then let the weight of her arm fall onto Helena's back. With a sigh she stroked Helena's head, smoothing the tear-drenched straggle of hair back from her temples. Then she put both arms around the sobbing woman and held her tight. "'S okay, baby. 'S okay."

When Helena had cried herself out, they held each other, talking in the murmuring voices of people half asleep. Mystified by their differences, respectful, each a little maternal toward the other's pain, they held each other, and finally fell silent, rocking slightly to the motion of the boat. And then—was it because she was thinking of Jeremy? Helena wondered; because she was thinking of Jeremy in the dark with Amanda?—there was somehow a hitch, a pause, a sigh, and they were moving ever so slightly in countermeasure. One of them must have reared back some, for where they had been pressed together, now they were separate, only their nipples brushing.

The friction set off a tumbling reaction in Helena's womb that she knew Amanda was also feeling, for Amanda had arched her back. When Amanda began to strain forward, tilting rhythmically from her pelvis, Helena obligingly pressed her knee against the inner seam of Amanda's trousers. "Please, please," Amanda whispered. "What I've gotta do to make it stop?"

"Well, we were kind of doing it," said Helena wryly, "but . . . hmm . . ." She unfastened Amanda's trousers, and with deft delicate fingers touched the moist swollen labia. "Oh, this is going to be—"

"Don't, don't. Something awful's—"

"No, you'll love it, and laugh to see how simple it is. Don't think about me, just think about Jeremy. Keep thinking about—"

And then, as if she had summoned him, there he was, standing in the doorway, his teeth bared and gleaming in the dimness, water streaming off his legs and puddling at his feet. His sudden presence gave Amanda such a start that she cracked her head on the beam of the upper bunk.

Helena thought it was perfect, perfect! but Amanda grabbed a pillow and put it over her face, while Jeremy, letting his breath out with a gasp, stood appalled in the doorway.

"Shee-it," he drawled at last, turning to go back up the stairs. He grasped the railing and flexed his arms—in and out, stretching and pulling, as if he were trying to leave but couldn't. When he once again turned into the room, his face was ugly. "You fucking whore, Helena," he said. Quietly the first time, but louder and louder, as if each repeated phrase were a stick he fed into a fire that now blazed hotly before her uncomprehending eyes.

His face was twisted, his words incomprehensible, and his dingy soppy shorts distorted by an enormous erection. She looked from his face to his underwear to his face again, looking for a clue to these contradictory signals, and her puzzled anxious glance seemed to further enrage him. "You make me feel like dirt . . . like shit," he growled. He began to punctuate the ugly words with a series of shoves, pushing her against the galley table, then against the cabinets. Helena offered no resistance. She was afraid of him, and horrified that she was afraid.

"Not to hurt her," said Amanda.

Jeremy whirled with a gasp, and Helena saw the clean incision in his shoulder, watched its channel thicken with blood that ran down his back as he grappled with Amanda for possession of the knife. Teeth clenched, shoulders braced, they wrestled, bumping against the fixed furniture in the tiny quarters, their right arms extended in a grotesque muscle-trembling dance. When the knife clattered to the floor, Helena sprang to retrieve it. "Okay, let's stop now," she suggested, and backed against the wall when they didn't stop. "This is not necessary," she announced, for she thought they were fighting over her. But as she watched the transformation of this primal match, she sensed that it *was* necessary—necessary and awful.

She knew that she would never really understand either of them. Only Jeremy could have said they must teach Amanda that there were no strangers, for only he understood what a "stranger" was. The rest of Idamore lived in a world of "we," with no boundaries or protective fences between "I" and "I." Their quarrels were different from this grappling. What were they doing, these two strangers, but savaging each other's boundaries, angrily ripping down the other's protective fences? And as she watched, fascinated and repelled by the angry racking urgency of it, Helena wondered if she would ever know—or ever want to know—the profound pleasure of that battle, or the profounder pleasure of its loss.

They were grotesque: scratched and welted; Amanda's trousers ripped from the waistband, which remained like an umbilical wrap; Jeremy's back caked in blood, and his legs awkwardly bent as he jerked upward, trying to enter her while she writhed and twisted in his arms. Each jerk and twist was a terrible intimacy, her erect nipples grazing his sweat-slicked chest, his swollen penis sliding between her legs. Amanda was making a high nasal sound—"nnnh, nnnnnhhh"—that wound tighter and tighter. When the spring broke, Amanda gave a frightened shriek, and shoved Jeremy sprawling backward.

For a moment, Helena thought Amanda was going to urinate on the floor, for she spread her feet and went straddle legged. She was rigid but for a tremor shaking her right leg. Then, with a desolate tearless sobbing—"hah-a-hah-a-hah-a-hah"—she began to masturbate, a desperate and savage clawing that made Helena wince. Jeremy butted his shoulder into her stomach, knocking her down. He knelt over her, pinning her arms to the floor and digging his knees into her thighs. He hovered motionless, smiling cruelly. From the tip of his penis, which was distended, almost purple with swollen veins, hung a glimmering drop of clear liquid, which fell, stretching like a bright filament from his genitals to her navel.

Still pinning her limbs, Jeremy levered himself down, stroking her with his penis. Amanda lay rigidly still, as if every muscle, every cell in her body had opened wide to listen to the cry of her blood. Helena unconsciously pressed her hand against her own crotch, as if she could restrain Jeremy's orgasm—or help accomplish Amanda's. She pressed and pressed until Amanda, without a sound, had a fit. It was Helena who cried out for her, while Jeremy, his arms trembling with effort, rode out the thrash of the long orgasm. Then he rocked back on his haunches, gave a low whimper as he entered Amanda, shuddered, and fell still.

No one moved and no one spoke until Jeremy, with a dazed glance around, leaned over to haul the blanket from the bunk. He shook it open over Amanda, who lay motionless, her eyes staring at the ceiling. Though he was the one who seemed to need a blanket, shivering and quaking, he spread it very carefully, covering her from neck to toe. Then he pulled another blanket from the top bunk and put it around his shoulders. He sat down on the bunk and put his face into his hands.

Helena felt sorry for them: Now they had stripped each other naked, and they wouldn't know how to look at each other. She slid off the bench and crossed the room, stopping first by Amanda, then joining Jeremy on the bunk. She pressed lightly against him, and when he winced, she asked, "Does your shoulder hurt?"

"My shoulder? No. Oh. Yes, it does. Oh, Jesus, my *soul* hurts."

"The sole of your foot?" She slid to the floor, touching his ankles.

"Oh, Laney, for heaven . . . Stop bustling! I need a minute to think. I don't even know what happened here. Something terrible has happened here."

Grunting, Amanda sat up and exchanged a look with Helena. Helena reassured her with a smile, then stood, pressing Jeremy's head against her stomach. "I think, Jeremy, that we all set up rules, like tall, brick walls to protect us. Then, when we want—or need—to do something against our rules, we have to smash or batter our way out."

Again Amanda grunted. Helena glanced at her, then ruffled Jeremy's head. "Which maybe you'd never think of doing, would you, unless you saw somebody walking around, like with no fence or wall, and doing something you thought was wrong and whore. That made you feel wrong and whore yourself, didn't it, because you wanted to do that too, but you had your big, high wall. So I think, you know, that what happened here wasn't so terrible. We all made love, but you and Amanda first had to smash each other's walls."

"Helena." Jeremy nuzzled against her belly. "Helena."

Clutching the blanket around her, Amanda stood up and began to root around in a cabinet. She threw a shirt behind her, then another. Two sweaters. Pants. While Jeremy pressed his face against Helena's stomach, murmuring her name, clothes rained around their ankles.

"Going back naked," Amanda asked, "or wearing walls?"

Helena giggled, and gave a signal tap on Jeremy's arms. He sat back, sniffing and wiping his eyes. "Yeah, time to get back. Hey, I hurt you, Amanda?"

She was trying to get into some pants while she held on to the blanket, and paused in this difficult maneuver to look at him. "I hurt *you?*" she parried.

He hesitated, glancing at Helena as if she could give him a hint at the right answer. "Yeah, you did." He picked up one of Amanda's shirts and held it up to his shoulders. "Jesus, an Amazon," he muttered. The blanket slid from his shoulders as he stood up.

Amanda stared at him. "Isn't that amazing?" she whispered.

Helena stepped into her line of vision and grabbed Amanda's blanket. "I'll hold it now. Get dressed," she said.

"But isn't it amazing?" insisted Amanda, craning her neck.

"Like a live stick," said Helena, biting back her smile. "Get dressed now."

Amanda pulled on her clothes, peeking around the blanket at Jeremy, who couldn't find a pair of pants that would close around his waist. "You said it was simple," Amanda accused. "That wasn't simple. Crawled my way up a mountain, mountain getting steeper and steeper, then I fell—brip—over the other side. Falling wasn't bad, but that mountain! . . . You call that simple, that mountain? Never do *that* again."

"Tssshh," said Helena. "All you need is practice climbing."

At that, Amanda slowly straightened, her height taking her head way above the place Helena held the blanket. She fixed her eyes on Jeremy. Helena turned just in time to catch Jeremy's double take. He was bent slightly, trying to fasten the pants, which gaped open. So did his mouth, now. "Practice?" he said, blanching. "With . . . ? Oh no."

Helena clapped the blanket against her mouth, choking and snorting. "You should see your face," she said, flapping the blanket like an unwieldy fan. "Oh, two whore," she shrieked, "we've got two whore and a feem of rap, what's next?"

"A feem of what?" said Jeremy, with a shocked look.

"A FEMA rep," said Amanda, her mouth twitching.

"Yes, that's it," gasped Helena. "Doesn't it come in the dark, like a man?"

"Ooooo," said Amanda, her face crumpling. She leaned her head against the cabinet, giggling helplessly. "He don't"—she jabbed her hand behind her back, pointing at Jeremy—"he don't come in the dark." Helena collapsed on the floor, shrieking and rolling around in the blanket.

They whooped and cawed, spurring each other on with half phrases. ". . . Brip—over the top!"

"I thought you were going to pee all over the floor!"

"Oh, almost did!"

"Wouldn't have helped."

They lay gasping and stomping their feet as if the idea of

Amanda peeing on the floor were the funniest thing they'd ever heard of. Their hilarity filled the cabin like light, making Jeremy's blue eyes flash with laughter.

° TWENTY-EIGHT °

Driven inside by the mosquitoes and gnats, they ate dinner in the dim, musty living room, which was dark long before the outdoors, where the sheep bawled placidly in the twilight. "I can't think how we'll wash up," said Rachel distractedly.

"Don't need to," said Edgar.

"Ah. Of course not."

"Not bad," said Pearl. "Just go from place to place, use the dishes and the beds, then move on. Not bad."

"Bunch of nomads, that's what you want to be," said Jeremy.

The Idamore children were overtired, their internal clocks upset by the previous night's long walk, and their sense of security and routine disrupted. August went from lap to lap, whining and demanding attention, while Jules planted himself in the middle of the room and rocked back and forth, humming tunelessly as he stared at the ceiling. Amanda visibly shrank from the child, whom Jeremy had come to see as eerily beautiful: He always wore an expression of such idiotic sweetness, and his pale-blue eyes gazed with such surprised love.

Even the older children had become shy and awkward with each other. After dinner they separated, placing themselves beside appropriate adults, who made no effort to talk about anything serious in the perturbed atmosphere, but sat companionable and patient, reassuring the children with their own calm.

Pearl and Rachel left to bed down the younger children, and Laurel and May retreated to an upstairs bedroom before anyone suggested they go.

"We sleeping here, Ma, or on the boat?" Michael asked.

"These our *people* now, Michael Clark," said Amanda. "All your aunties dead, so we gotta adopt."

Jeremy said nothing, though he wanted to cheer or hug Amanda or celebrate the moment in some way. Edgar was ticking quietly to himself as he went over to the mattress where Michael had flung himself. "You adopt me?" he asked the boy.

"No," said Michael. "No. Your face is too scary."

"Dudn't scare the sheep, though. Tomorrow I'll show you the orphans, the babies without mothers. You can adopt them, too."

"What happened to your face? You was nuked?"

"What's nuked? Burned? I was burned. Want to hear about the fire?"

Rachel called from the doorway. "Did anyone find extra blankets? Now that the sun's down, the wind off the lake is cold." So everyone was up again, pawing cautiously through dark cabinets and closets in search of blankets.

Later Jeremy and Mick broke into the house next door and groped in the dark through the unfamiliar rooms in search of more blankets. "Jesus, Mick," whispered Jeremy, "gives me the heebie-jeebies thinking what might be on the beds." Mick patted Jeremy's arm. Each time they stumbled against a bed, they pulled the blanket up by the corners, lifting slowly to test it for any grisly cargo. They found six beds, four of them with retrievable blankets.

There was no fireplace in the chosen house, and they had no candles. While they talked, they kept moving closer and closer, until at last they were all huddled together, reaching out to touch each other in the darkness. "Well," said Helena, "well, now. Let's see. How's Freehold fixed for the winter, Amanda?"

Her first question about Freehold was one Jeremy had not thought to ask. He had remarked how beautiful the land was, how tidy the village, how handy the windmills and the water systems. . . . He shivered, and tucked Rachel's blanket snugly around her shoulders. "Warm enough, Rach?"

While the others talked, comparing winters in Idamore and Freehold, Jeremy let himself float away, conscious less of their words than of their voices. Helena's amber, Pearl's metal,

Amanda's tree bark, Edgar's echoing cave, Rachel's wind across August corn. Winter. Winter coming. How long had he been with them? Was it September now? Was he actually standing in line at the registrar's office, paying his fees? Had he gotten into Wexler's popular course on the modern poets?

". . . don't you think, Jeremy? Jeremy?"

"What? Sorry, I wasn't listening." He shook his head to clear away the images of blond veneered desks and humming fluorescent lights.

"I said I think you're right to fetch Rose," said Helena. "We've decided that we can't go back to live in Idamore, because of the . . . because of the . . . Well. But we were wrong to leave Rose. *I* think. Edgar and Pearl think she may be dangerous now."

"Dangerous?" said Jeremy.

"Jeremy, Rose has gone crazy," said Pearl.

"She was always crazy—"

"No, but I mean, Jeremy, really crazy." Pearl bent toward him and lowered her voice. "She thinks she comes from the time of the light."

Jeremy laughed out loud. "Well, so do I, Pearl! So do I!" And it came over Jeremy in a cold wave that froze the grin on his face that he was absolutely insane. That his crazed mind had either concocted this place and these people, or that he had hallucinated his knowledge of an earlier time. He edged closer to Helena, pressing his thigh against hers. "Ah God, poor Rose . . . I can't imagine her dangerous."

"That's 'cause you didn't see what she did," said Pearl.

"Wait. I'd say there's a question here," said Jeremy. "To kill what threatens you . . . is that crazy or rational—um—sane? Maybe you're the crazy ones, hmmm? Not defending Idamore is like not defending your own lives."

"Oh, Jeremy," said Rachel sadly. "Oh, that's cruel. We *did* defend Idamore, and it was horrible. Now we can't stand to be there, we'd always be eating the blood that's in the soil."

"You *are* crazy," remarked Amanda. "I don't want Michael Clark to be hearing his people say they won't defend his home. Or teaching him that he shouldn't defend himself."

"But the defending destroys the place, somehow . . ." said Pearl.

"Bosh," said Amanda, while Jeremy thrust his hands into his hair: The evening was like one long déjà-vu. Was he really sitting in his dorm room listening to a discussion of nuclear deterrence? Or was he here, torn between two attitudes, two sentiments? He remembered a phrase from *King Lear,* which he knew he had read not here, but there: "O fool! I shall go mad." "Dear Lord, let me not be mad," he thought. "Or let me remain mad, for I want to stay with them. Let me live out my life here, where I am needed and useful. . . ."

"So Jeremy goes back to Idamore for Rose, and Amanda takes some of us to Freehold. Right, Jeremy? Jeremy?"

"Right," he said.

"Who's going with Jeremy," asked Helena, "and who's going with—"

"I'm going to Idamore alone," he interrupted. "I'll make better time by myself."

No one argued with him except Michael Clark, who spoke up from his dark corner. "I wanted to see that place," he complained.

"Well, I was wondering about you," Jeremy called to him through the darkness. "There are a lot of boats just south of here a ways. I was wondering if we could go down there and fix up a second boat for sailing to Freehold." He turned toward the place where Amanda sat in the dark room. "What do you think, Amanda? Could he handle that? He'd be sailing with a crew that had never been on a boat before, so you'd have to stick pretty close together. But if you think he could do it, it would cut the trips in half."

Amanda was silent for a moment. Michael urged her: "O' course I could. You know I could, Ma. I sail as good as you or Belle Lewison."

"You do, boy. You sail good. But how you feel about sailing a pregnant woman across the lake? How you feel about taking a woman with milk in her breasts and a baby on her back? How you feel about sailing then, boy?"

Jeremy enjoyed her brusque manner with the boy, knowing the affection they felt for one another. But next to him Helena was

murmuring unhappily. The dark room was silent while Michael
Clark thought. "I'll take the burned man and some of his sheep,"
he said at last.

"Sounds good to me," said Jeremy. "Okay, Amanda? And Rose
and I will be here by the time you come back for the second load of
sheep. And, let's see, who stays behind with the leftover sheep?"
Mick grunted, and Jeremy said, "Fine. All settled, then?"

Jeremy's fit of—what was it? anxiety? lunacy? It felt more like
hyperconsciousness, a precariousness of his own physical presence.
Whatever it was, it troubled his sleep and was gone in the morning, when he woke feeling hungry, sane, full of purpose.

He trekked south with Amanda and Michael to the yacht club,
where they prowled among the dry-docked boats. With winches
and a big pulley they hauled a forty-foot two-masted boat onto a
trailer, then into the water. "It leaks," Jeremy called from be-
lowdecks.

"Maybe the joints tighten up in the water. Give it some time,"
Amanda said. Jeremy sat in the cockpit, watching her check the
rigging screws, the cables, the shrouds. "Think I send my boy out
on the water in a leaky boat?" she asked him as she stepped over
his legs.

When Amanda glanced across the water at Michael enwrapped
and struggling with the immense, cumbersome sails, there came
over her face such an odd, secretive, and pleased look that Jeremy
sensed what was coming next, though he was floored by the form it
took. She looked at him, blushing furiously but not ducking her
head. "Still wisht I was a man," she said. "That's nice, what you
got."

Jeremy didn't know what to say to that, and stood up to give her
a shy hug. "Boy's watching," she said, giving him a shove that
made him stagger.

"Jesus, that's about all you're missing," Jeremy complained.
"Never met a woman so strong or rough . . ."

"Check the seams below."

"Please."

"Please what?" she said over her shoulder.

"Say, 'Will you please check the seams below?'"

"I just said that."

"But you ordered me. I don't like to be ordered around like that."

She turned to face him, a smile spreading over her face. "You people always fluffing up talk with a lot of extra words. 'What do you think' and 'please' and 'would you mind.' Well, I *don't* mind. I think I might get to like it. . . ." She cocked her head to look over his shoulder at the shore, gave him a quick kiss on the mouth, then fluttered away, giggling.

Her behavior wouldn't have struck Jeremy as so ludicrous if she hadn't been as tall as he was, with shoulders and biceps to match. A female lumberjack acting like a coy and petite teenager. Jeremy quickly went below, working the bailer to cover the sound of his snorting. " 'That's nice, what you got.' Haw! Why, thank you, miss, I like yours, too."

By midday they were back at the beach. Amanda spent the trip in the cockpit with her arms crossed over her chest. She gave no advice to Michael, who kept repeating the same orders to Jeremy, ineptly crewing on the foredeck. "Goddammit," Jeremy yelled at him, "I don't know which one is the leeward sheet, so don't keep shouting it over and over. Point, or something, for God's sake!"

When they sighted the figures on the beach, they put Jeremy off to swim ashore and continued sailing, tacking now this way, now that. Amanda sat with her arms crossed, letting Michael sail alone. Then they anchored and rowed ashore to get Edgar, who was told to attach himself to two grab rails and follow Michael's instructions. Jeremy watched the sails fill, luff, and swing about. Then the boat shot through the water. Michael adjusted course and sailed smoothly until they came about, when the foresails again went limp. They stayed out there, sailing up and down, until they had tacked several times without stalling.

Edgar came ashore trembling with excitement. "Oh," he said, hugging everyone and jigging up and down. "Wait till you feel sailing. Oh, sailing is— Oh!"

Amanda put her hand on Michael's shoulder. "Good," she said.
"That was good."

The next morning during the flurry of last-minute instructions—
Edgar's to Mick about the sheep and Amanda's to Michael about
the worn rigging screws—Helena and Jeremy walked hand in
hand on the sandy road. She too had last-minute instructions.
"Don't eat these red berries. They look good, but they'll make you
sick. And these are sour, but safe. . . ." Jeremy dutifully looked and
nodded.

"There are three mesh cages in the chicken house," she went on.
"If you can find any of the chickens, you might bring back a
few. . . ."

"Mad Rose and the chickens. Sounds like a rock group," he said,
trying to tease the anxious note out of her voice.

She was staring hard at the tangled thicket of sour berries. "The
last time we said good-bye, *you* were going to Freehold. . . ."

"You scared about the boat?"

"No, no, not at all. It's . . . I don't know what it is. Too many
good-byes, I guess. Let's make this the last one."

"Lan-eee," came Pearl's voice. Then Pearl and Rachel together.
"Lay-neee."

"Not even good-bye," said Jeremy. "I'll see you in a few days."
He squeezed her hand and released it. "Off you go, sailing to Freehold."

Helena rushed down the road, then stopped, turning almost reluctantly. "Jeremy," she said, wringing her hands.

"Last good-bye. I promise."

"Remember about the berries." With a little shrug at her own
foolishness, she waved, then ran down the road.

◦ TWENTY-NINE ◦

As he approached Idamore, Jeremy caught the improbable gorgeous strains of a Brandenburg Concerto. The music got louder and louder until at last, as he stepped into the central yard, he stood in the midst of that paroxysm of soaring energy.

Enveloped in that familiar sound, Idamore seemed as beautiful as Jeremy had ever seen it. The houses stood in the same rows, the columned orderly geometry of a suburb going to wild grasses. Off on a manmade hillock of the Botanical Gardens, the windmill gleamed metallically, its rotors a soft blur in the breeze as the generator sought the wind. Here and there were scorched patches, or evidence of trampling, but the place was far from devastated.

With his heart tripping to the rushing, twirling game of tag played by the flutes and the violins, Jeremy discovered Rose's garden of death. In a precise circle, set like stones into the soil, were eight ghastly faces. The black gaping mouths swarmed with flies, iridescent and apparently pulsing to the rhythms of Bach's Fourth Brandenburg Concerto. Eight faces. Where was the ninth? Not a symmetrical number . . .

When the next concerto began—darker toned and more stately—Jeremy heard the amplified scrape of the needle as it was picked up from the record. There was a moment of silence, during which Jeremy tried to see the scene as it was—silent and horrifying, not washed over with ecstatic flutes—and then the Fourth Concerto began again. Apparently she was playing the same piece over and over again, as long as the wind held. Maybe she was trying to resurrect the dead. If so, she had certainly hit on the right music. Bach could do it, if anyone could. A cadenza reaching and falling, dancing higher . . . order! Order flirting with chaos . . .

Rose came flying out the door, yelling happily. "It's working, it's working!" Aghast, Jeremy stared for a moment, the gorge rising in his throat, then he had to look away from her. She had flayed the ninth miner, and wore the skin. Over her own face a graying mask. The skin skewered together over her chest. Her healthy brown arms stuck through the skin sleeves. She batted at the flies swarming around her and peered at him. "Is someone really there?"

"It's me, Rose. It's Jermicho. I've come to take you—"

She slumped with disappointment, then came nearer. "I used to be troubled with walking memories. Not lately. Though I'm not entirely sure. May I touch you? To make sure you're there?"

Jeremy backed away. "I'm here. Alive and real. I want you to step out of that skin and be yourself now."

"I've been trying, Jeremy." She spoke with great dignity, sounding sane and sorrowful inside the gaping riddled face. "Something's missing."

"What? Do you need help? Shall I pull you out?"

"Remember Maddy's baby? Remember, Jeremy? The times are deformed. If I come out, I want to be whole, as I was during the time of the light. You and I are twins. Jessico and Jericho. But I've lost my power. I'm just a woman now."

"Oh, it's fine to be a woman. Wonderful . . ." Jeremy stammered helplessly, holding his shirt up to his face and waving his hand to keep away the flies.

"That's too long ago. We have new business now."

Jeremy left her bending to and fro over her circle of dead faces, and went to prepare a bath for her. He couldn't begin to talk to her until he got her cleaned up, and as he carried buckets back and forth from the sun-warmed tank of water to the tub, he found himself humming happily to the music. *Da-dee-ee-da-ah-ah-dum* . . . "Ve haf here an instance of cognitive dissonance," he said in a German accent. "Ja." But he welcomed the tension between the two orders of reality: The hectic joyous energy of the music transformed everything. All through that gusty afternoon, Mick's generator ran the record player, and the automatic return set the needle down in precisely the same spot somewhere near the beginning of the fourth concerto.

Jeremy later realized that the music probably impaired his judgment. It was rather like mistaking the plot of a movie because it was played out against musical passages giving contradictory emotional cues. But the effect at the time was dreamlike. To the tweedle of flutes, Rose ambled toward him in a cloud of flies. While the violins rushed up to the flutes and stole the melody, Jeremy delivered her, naked and bloody, out of the skin of a dead man. He bathed her under a rainbow of sound. And because he talked with her to the strains of a music rapturous with its own sane complex order, he discovered in Rose—a talkative, almost coherent Rose!—the same music. For what was she overcoming but chaos?

"Remember when you first came to us?" she said, and he heard about himself arriving at Idamore with three magic oranges—miniature suns—that reminded her of her impossible divine task. She was to bear a sun.

Jeremy could only surmise the various stages of the confusion leading her to identify the sun and the son. Not, apparently, the everyday sun traveling over their heads, or even a merely healthy male infant, but the Sun and the Son. Power over time. Power over death. "Time is death. You know that, don't you, Jeremy? Death is time." She was so calm, the music so full of rapture: How could he have heard the rage she felt?

Her version of the divine birth was all garbled up with the other myth, the story of the exploding sun. The time of the light was the time of the exploding sun. That was Ben's "power," and Jeremy recognized it, too, as part of his own myth: of mortal men tinkering with the mystery of the universe until they released its power. The power of the sun itself bursting in orgasmic fiery splendor. Who could abstain from such spellbinding, terrifying, absolute power? And if it belonged only to the sun—son—then who would want to be a woman?

Though Rose made no distinctions between her real and her invented memories, Jeremy did, and he understood how the crucial bloody event of her childhood had sponsored the fiction of herself as Jessico. The massacre at Oakton, that was real. And a little girl's terror and helplessness and rage, too real to suffer. So she had invented Jessico. Oh, trailing clouds of glory, she was, this androgyne who rose on molten iron wings from the chaos. A sun burning with rage, raging with power. "I burned everything because I was so angry, you see. And then I had, much later, to come to Idamore, and I was quiet here, a timeless plant. Until you came. You also came out of time, but you brought time with you. Didn't you come glowing with all the time I had forgotten? It troubled me, Jeremy, to see you bringing time. Time is death. . . ."

It was circular and age-old: a dream of immortality. To gain the prize, she had made herself a dreaming plant, and the people around her busy stones. She had denied life in order to manage death, and Jeremy thought she was on her way to being cured. For hadn't he just witnessed and midwifed her rebirth, peeling off the dead man's skin and asking her what she would like to be called now?

Jessica.

Jessica.

"Tomorrow we will walk to the lake," he told her.

He put the rest of the Brandenburg Concertos on the record player, and to the music of the first movement of the first concerto, he shoveled dirt over the miners' faces. Rose watched, silent and unprotesting, as Jeremy carted wheelbarrows of soil from the adjacent field, making a burial mound.

Then he attended to the chickens, some of which were strutting, as if proud of their freedom, among the rows of late beans. Jeremy put a rooster and two hens into the mesh cages, and hesitated only a moment over the slaughter of a fourth bird.

He was prepared to do everything, from burying the dead to preparing the dinner, for he wanted to reassure Rose—Jessica— that she could be safely dependent, safely sane, safely alive in time. She stood now on the burial mound, her head lifted high to the music, bright-eyed, attentive, and silent until she saw the rubbery yellow egg inside the hen. "Well, well. Well, well, well. Tomorrow's egg."

Jeremy, who hated nothing quite as much as the grubby, painstaking business of plucking a chicken, looked up at her only briefly.

"There must be two ways to unravel time. If you put your hand inside the warm cave, you can reach toward the future. I have a . . . Jeremy."

"I'm listening, Ro— Jessica."

"I have a son in my cave. Like the hen has an egg."

"You mean you're pregnant? Oh, that's fine. That's really fine." Jeremy smiled moronically.

"Is it? But he will be your Joshua."

"Oh?" He raised one eyebrow, taken aback by her prophetic tone. "Joshua fit the battle of Jericho"—he couldn't get the right melody into his head because of the Bach concerto, but he knew the words, he knew her meaning—"and the walls came tumbling down." He threw the chicken into a pot of water and stood up, wiping his hands on the back of his pants. "I'll put the chicken on, then. . . . Will you walk with me while I gather some vegetables for the pot?"

Rose put the basket over her arm. "Will you walk with me while I gather some vegetables for the pot?"

Jeremy smiled, more and more pleased with her. That she was anxious to gather food for him struck him as the best sign of all. A reversal of her adamant hunger on that extraordinary morning in the river, when she wouldn't feed him any of her crushed berries. "You are the one who will not . . ." eat us? Is that what she had said?

He strolled beside her through the vegetable patch, where she twisted off a fat zucchini, plucked some overripened beans, and pulled up onions, potatoes, and carrots. The piano played—fifth concerto, with violas—more softly from here, but distinct, clear, lofty. "Oh, Mick, you genius," sighed Jeremy.

Rose straightened to look around, then glanced anxiously at Jeremy.

"Oh, no . . . I was just . . . you know, talking to him in my head. He's not there, I don't see him . . . you know."

"Mick is there," Rose said, pointing along the length of wire leading from the windmill to the house.

"In a way," Jeremy agreed.

"I put on this record because it was the one Rachel liked. I was playing for Rachel, but she didn't come back. You came instead."

As they walked out into the tall grass, parting it to look for spicy edible weeds, Rose spoke lucidly of their night of music, then of the fires on the horizon. Jeremy listened, interrupting only to point out the spring-edible weeds that he recognized. She kept shaking her head, smiling over their tough fiber or coarse stalks or fuzzy seeds.

"But what really confused me," she continued, "wasn't the fire, but Simon's voice. Everything that happened was happening like before, and I thought I had unraveled time. I thought I was getting a chance to do it over, changing the end of the story. But . . . Simon had Ben's voice." She hesitated, swinging her leg to part the grass, but not really looking. "Do you remember Ben?"

"Of course!"

"I miss Ben."

"Do you, love?" he said, stroking her hair. "I miss him, too. Ben was special."

"Well, Simon had Ben's voice. It was like Ben had come back, and that confused me, because it wasn't Ben I wanted to kill, but the men who came up from the Carbonville mines to kill Oakton. But Helena killed Ben, then gave me her knife. So I put on his skin. But not his voice."

Jeremy frowned. "That wasn't Ben. That was Simon. Helena killed Simon. . . ." Sighing, he glanced up at the sky. "It's getting late. Let's skip the herbs."

He left her ambling up and down in the grass and jogged off to wash and chop the vegetables. He spooned the scum off the bubbling chicken, and dropped in the vegetables, watching them sink and bound to the rhythms of the sixth concerto. The return mechanism on the player was definitely askew, for the last record on the pile was now playing for the third or fourth time.

"That's enough out of you, Johann," Jeremy muttered as he

walked into the living room. He'd be humming the score in his grave, he thought, then chuckled: Could be worse. Imagine trying to hum his mother's cosmic-traveler computer music. He straightened slowly in the suddenly silent room. He felt it again: the precariousness that he'd felt last night, the brief quiver pulsing not through him, but through the floor he stood on, the wall he leaned against to steady himself.

He put his hand on his forehead. "I'll bet I have some chemical deficiency," he said, and found that reassuring: If he was going nuts, it was because he needed salt, or potassium, or iodine. A blood-milkshake, a liver pâté . . . He hurried into the kitchen and speared the soft brown chicken liver, which he was nibbling with great distaste when Rose came in. She was carrying mushrooms and herbs in her shirt, and shook them out onto the table.

"Mmmm," he said appreciatively of the forage, then offered her a bite of liver. She wrinkled her nose. "Yeah, me too. But it's really good for you." She dutifully bit, and sat chewing slowly as she wiped the shapely white mushrooms with the sleeve of her shirt.

"God, where'd you find those? Helena's mushrooms always look like horned toads or pig snouts. Those are gorgeous."

"The first of the autumn mushrooms," she said.

"Ah."

Jeremy kept jumping up to stir and poke and sniff at the steaming pot. "Almost done. Hungry?" He sat down again, placing his hands over hers on the table. He felt oddly formal, almost shy, wanting to make conversation but finding nothing to say, and thinking it eerie to be alone with her in a house that was usually full of women and children. She sat in a profound stillness, relaxed, her eyes cast down at their hands on the table. "Jessica."

She looked up. "Nothing," he said with a shrug. "Jessica. It's a nice name."

"I will serve dinner," she announced. She got up to peer into the pot, the steam rising around her face. Though she served up two steaming bowls of chicken stew, she didn't eat, but held her hands and her face over the bowl as if she were warming herself.

"Mmmm, it's delicious, Rose. Come on, eat up."

"I would like to tell you about something," she said, resting her chin on her folded hands. He nodded, his head bent hungrily over his bowl. (Helena's mushrooms were, after all, superior. Ugly but sweeter.) "I would like to tell you about one of my babies. One of damn Hank's bad babies." Her voice was so placid that the words startled him. He nodded again, determined to listen this time for the precise point—was there one?—when the lucid voice began to say queer things.

"This one was a girl, and I carried it almost to the birthtime. So for the first time after losing a baby, I had milk. My first milk, and no baby."

"Ah, Rose. Aah, my poor Jessica . . ."

"Tssshhh! Ben wanted me to . . . well, I didn't want to share . . . Wait, I'm lost." She looked calmly down at her hands on either side of the untouched bowl. "Oh, yes. The thing was, I wanted that milk myself. I thought—I still think—that would be, well, perfect. Better even than being a sun." Sun? Son? Jeremy wondered, holding his jaw still for a moment to listen carefully, then swallowing hastily, for the mushrooms were bitter in the back of the throat.

"But even full of milk, my breasts were too small. I couldn't reach them to suck. Maybe Lily could have done it, but she'd never think of such a thing. I doubt. And I was so sad. So sad, the milk was slowly drying up and I couldn't feed myself. . . ."

"Good Lord," he said. It was an astounding idea—repulsive, somehow, but absolutely logical, and as he followed the logic of it, he saw what appealed to her: It was a closed system. A loop. As long as she suckled herself, she'd produce the milk that nourished her. Ah, like a plant in a terrarium, only a step up in sentience; a self-sustaining mammal. Jeremy shook his head, awed and shocked by an idea that contradicted everything that milky breasts meant to him—bounty, nurture, selfless motherhood, all that—and he wondered if other women with milk in their breasts had such thoughts. He'd have to ask Pearl and Helena.

He tipped his bowl up to his chin and swallowed the last of his broth. "That, my dear Rose, is why we feed each other. That's what it's all about. Needing each other." Platitudinous bastard, he scolded himself. He stood up and carried his chair around the table, arranging himself beside her. "You served me. Now shall I feed you? You'd like that, I think."

She looked down at her bowl, which Jeremy was stirring. "There was an egg inside the hen."

"Yes," he said, holding the spoon to her mouth. She took the morsel of chicken with her lips drawn back, scraping her teeth along the spoon with a look of disgust. "What did the egg mean to you?"

She chewed thoughtfully, then swallowed. "What did the egg mean to the hen? Isn't that the question?"

"I guess it is," said Jeremy with a laugh. He supposed he needed a license in order to practice this game properly, so he stopped, and talked instead about Freehold. As he popped spoonful after spoonful into her mouth, he told her about Amanda and Michael, about the houses and the windmills, about sailing across the big lake. . . . He piled the dishes into the sink, and was ready to fetch water to clean up, so he concluded: "You'll like it there. Tomorrow we'll walk to the lake and wait with Mick for the boat."

"I doubt it," she said.

He turned abruptly. "You doubt what? That you'll like it, or that you're coming? You can't stay here, you know. Especially now that you're pregnant. So I don't want to hear any arguments about it."

She smiled mysteriously, her pale-blue eyes narrow in her face. "No arguments. Not now or tomorrow. We have eaten tomorrow's egg."

"Jesus, Rose." He walked wearily out of the house to get water, then came back empty-handed. There was no need to wash the dishes. It was dark, he was tired, and there was no need to leave clean dishes in Idamore. He ignored them, like a small unscratched itch, a tiny item of disorder, and sat in the living room listening to records long after Rose had gone to bed.

o   o   o

He woke at dawn, feeling unrested and vaguely sick. He listened to the racket of rain on the roof, then turned over and closed his eyes. No need to hurry: even racing, the boat wouldn't be back until late tomorrow or the next day. They wouldn't leave without him.

He slept fitfully, dreaming that they were in a line, an impossibly long line, hand in hand from Idamore to Freehold. Helena was first and over there; he was last, and here; they were vastly separated, but close, linked together by the chain of hands between them. Then, as he reached back for the tiny isolated figure that was Rose, Helena at the same time reached forward toward Amanda. The line began to stretch; all their arms became elastic and attenuated, no longer human. "Hold on to me," he screamed as the chain broke.

Jeremy jerked awake, dripping with sweat and tense with nausea. In the bathroom, shivering and miserable, he hugged the dry toilet, not really caring where he was sick if only he could be sick. "Oh, shit. Goddammit. I don't believe this," he muttered, staggering down the stairs for a glass of water, which didn't help. He was doubled over with stomach cramps, and had to grasp the railing to get back up the stairs. "Was it the mushrooms or the herbs, Rose?" he called, then realized that whichever it was, she had eaten it too. "Rose, honey, are you sick?" he called.

He wanted desperately to find out that she was innocent. That he just had a flu, or that she hadn't known what food she was picking yesterday. Because otherwise . . . otherwise, he was a fool.

She had known.

"We have eaten tomorrow's egg," she had said last night, then come up here to quietly cut her wrists. Around her was the entire arsenal of Idamore's unique violence. Idamore had laid its bloodied weapons at her feet, and she had taken them into her bed.

Whatever he might next have felt or done was routed by the explosive turmoil of his bowels. He rushed down the stairs and out the door. Bent over, he scuttled through the rain toward the latrine. Between spasms, he rested his forehead against the damp spongy wood and rubbed the gooseflesh that rose on his distressed skin.

"Oh God, let me not die in a moldering old latrine," he said; by that time he was improved enough to care where he was.

He tottered out of the latrine and stood indecisively in the rain, starting now this way, now that. Go back to bed . . . get to the lake . . . bury Rose . . . go back to bed . . . Though he dragged himself up the stairs, he didn't lie down, for he was suddenly afraid to go to sleep, to be the only living thing in Idamore.

He changed his clothes, put on his yellow slicker, and wrapped Allison's Shakespeare in a waterproof bag, which he slung over his shoulder. Then he took all the hangers off the wooden bar and removed it: a shoulder pole on which to carry two mesh chicken cages. If he'd had a hat, he would have looked like a coolie setting off.

But he didn't set off. By the time he got down the stairs, his legs were trembling, and he sank heavily onto the porch steps. He let the intolerable weight of the book bag slip off his shoulders, and immediately felt better. He was having a little trouble focusing, and couldn't decide if it was his eyes or his mind. "Now let's see," he said, trying to think. He had to get the chickens to the lake. No, not the chickens. Himself. Helena would know what to do for him.

He set himself a series of small goals—from here to the water barrel, from the water barrel across the field to the street. . . . He imagined stepping over the boundary into Trampalow. He had only to get to Trampalow to take that one small step. As he drew his legs under him, he noticed that he'd been sitting half in the rain, and his shoes were heavy and waterlogged. He wondered how long he'd been sitting there, and felt a ripple of panic: It was almost night! He blinked rapidly, feeling the day change shades of gray. Not night. Too cloudy to tell what time it was, but certainly time to move.

He lurched down the steps, conscious first of his feet, and then of his legs. Apparently his feet were absorbing the rain, for they felt fat and spongy inside his water-heavy shoes. He resented the effort of lifting them with those long rippling willow twigs of legs, and saw himself become his own image in a fun-house mirror. At the water barrel he cupped his hands to drink—not because he was thirsty, but because he wanted to flush this poison out of his system. He was proud of himself for being so rational. Then he noticed his swollen fingers. He didn't need to bother about the water, he thought fuzzily; he was absorbing it through his skin.

He sat down beside the water barrel to think, then worried again about the time. "Got to get a move on, here. Got to . . . got to . . ." Now, what was it? Oh yes, the chickens. But he had left the chickens over at Lily's house, which was an impossible distance to walk. "Sorry, Laney. Forget the chickens. Too far."

When he hit on a plan of travel, he felt quite wily. From Idamore to that point east southeast on the lake could be seen as the hypotenuse of a triangle, and the shortest distance. But not necessarily the easiest distance, for one of the imaginary triangle's sides was the river. He could canoe down the river. Easy downstream travel to . . . wherever . . . and then walk due east. Or hitchhike! Or, for heaven's sake, just steal a car . . . Laney had stolen his canoe once, taken it up to Riverwoods. Had it been brought back? Yes, he thought it had.

He walked, careful as a drunk, terribly perturbed about the time—so dark!—and furious at his feet, which somehow were not where he thought they were, so he kept pitching forward onto his hands and knees. Finally he sat down on the rain-runneled street and slipped off his shoes. They *had* absorbed water, he thought, poking glumly at toes like tiny water balloons. He examined his edemic hands, then ran his hands over his face, feeling the watery mounds swelling under his eyes. "What *is* this? Kidney failure?"

He tried to goad himself into a panic that would help him travel, but he felt more peaceful than frightened. The sensation was not of pain, but of distortion. Something like the effects of nitrous oxide at a dentist's office—that same torpor and elongation of the limbs, the body blurred and remote. He crawled toward the river, feeling quite at one with the waterlogged mud, the rain, the shadowless day closing over his head.

He was going on only because of Helena. Because he wanted to get to the lake to tell Mick what to tell Helena. "Tell her it wasn't berries, Mick, but mushrooms. Tell her I'm not a sun, but a father. And tell her that she still has choices. . . ." Mushrooms? Jeremy thought with a shudder. Which mushrooms? The ones Rose gave him, or the ones he himself had picked and eaten on his way to Idamore? And Idamore—Rose, Rachel, Maddy—the whole thing?—Helena!—all of it one long drug-induced dream in which he got to save some part of the world before he died? God, was he dying—or waking up? Was he ever going to find out what was real?

There was the canoe. Its metal skin shivered, and the gunwales bobbed and shimmered below him. His treacherous feet skidded as he slid down the muddy embankment, *slid down the bank, arriving at the canoe feetfirst on his back* . . . "Wait, what's happening?" he whispered. He pushed off clumsily, and the canoe shot into the stream, *responding gaily to his hasty, shifting weight* . . .

Jeremy flailed, then fell, bruising his ribs against the thwart. He felt dilated with darkness, distended, a concourse of kinks, and he closed his eyes, exhausted with effort. He was lying down, but floating; heavy-limbed, but swaying. Floating downstream, swaying on the water, *riding the current south into the ordinary, into Cottage Grove, home* . . . Not, not, not home anymore.

He forced his eyes open for a moment and saw a swirl of gray fog, a spinning watery sky. Consciousness was nauseating vertigo, and he let go of it with a groan, sliding down into the darkness. Down, down into the darkness, hundreds of tiny electronic butterflies tittering and flashing at him as he floated past. Down, down that dark narrow corridor, down toward a blazing light, and breaking free into that light blazing with—ah, listen!—Helena's laugh.

∘ THIRTY ∘

Jeremy. Jeremy.

We found the book, we found the chickens, and we found Rose. We looked and looked for you, but it wasn't until we headed back toward Freehold that I felt we were going the right way. Can you understand that?

You once told me something you'd read or heard—about the future not being a place we're going to, but one we're creating. Do you remember telling me that? That was really important to me, then. Partly, I suppose, because the only path that Ben saw went backward, and the only one going forward was all laid out for me. I guess it's true that the path to the future has to be made, but I think it's also important to know that we're probably not going where we plan to. Because of accidents, fires, diseases, and crazy people, for one thing. And for another, because the choices we make run right into other people's choices, so what you get is two paths meeting and going off in a third direction. Not to the place that either person was trying to go to, but some other place. Call it Freehold, but it could also be Carbonville, couldn't it?

I guess I'm trying to tell you that if we had it to do all over again, I'd still have you choose to go back for Rose. It was the right thing to do. As long as we can't see into the future and know the results of our choices, that's the best we can do—choose right. If we *could* see into the future, I suppose our choices would be so easy and obvious, they wouldn't feel like choices anymore. I know that now, so I'm not mad at you anymore for going away. And I don't feel guilty anymore for letting you go. How could we know the price of our choice? And if we couldn't know, what was right *then* still is. Mostly I do think so.

Laurel and I talk about this stuff. Amanda says it's dumb, but. I didn't think I'd ever laugh again, not ever, but Amanda makes me laugh. And look, Jeremy, don't they just make you laugh? Martin Towers toddling about on his fat little legs? And Jerell, who is funny because she's so serious. She has your dark-blue eyes and Rachel's fine curly hair. And Amanda's (imagine, just that one time, Jermicho! I forget your funny word for hitting the target— *bing!?*)—her son is named Paul, but not after Idamore's old Paul. After a big man in a story Laurel read us. About a big man with a funny huge ox named Babe. Rachel says she wonders if we shouldn't have named him after the ox.

We've been reading Allison's scribbledy scrawl (Laurel has, out loud), and kind of tracking things down. The stuff in the Bible, and some of the other stuff, like the Black Plague. Allison makes me so mad, always complaining that she's going to die before she knows if the human race will survive. Well, so will I. And so will Laurel. And so will Phoebe. Because that's not a thing any person can ever know, is it?

When we read about the Black Plague, it seemed to me that a person who died back then might have died wondering if the human race would survive that last terrible illness. And I remember you bellowing—remember the day you came up to Riverwoods to bring me home?—bellowing at me about the Future Death that everyone in your time worried about. So people in the best time of all worried about the same things that people in the Middle Ages worried about, and that we worry about. Will the human race survive? We'll never know. We never have, and we never will. I don't know why I should find that so comforting, but I do.

Michael Clark used to look for you every autumn. Every autumn, he'd sail back across the lake and walk to Idamore. But last year he found four people from Kendallville there. Three more women and a little girl. They'd like to stay in Idamore, and they've changed his reason for going there. He's a man now, and though he still misses you, he's stopped looking.

I still look for you. In the spring. That's when you came to us, so that's when I think you might come back. But spring is such a busy time, Jeremy. I can't be standing here all day, talking like a fruit-loop, and watching and waiting for you to come over the water.

Sometimes when I stand on the big bluff, looking for a sail, a gull will rise up off the water, and I think you're looking us over. I know it looks as if we don't miss you, but oh, my love, we really do. And when you fly over, going *yawk, yawk, yawk,* are you scolding me for laughing, or are you laughing too?